# KINGS
# FALLING

Center Point
Large Print

Also by Ronie Kendig and available from
Center Point Large Print:

*A Conspiracy of Silence*
*Crown of Souls*
*Thirst of Steel*
*Storm Rising*

**This Large Print Book carries the
Seal of Approval of N.A.V.H.**

THE BOOK OF THE WARS • 2

# KINGS FALLING

## RONIE KENDIG

CENTER POINT LARGE PRINT
THORNDIKE, MAINE

This Center Point Large Print edition
is published in the year 2020 by arrangement with
Bethany House Publishers,
a division of Baker Publishing Group.

This is a work of fiction.
Names, characters, incidents, and dialogues are products
of the author's imagination and are not to be construed as
real. Any resemblance to actual events or persons,
living or dead, is entirely coincidental.

The text of this Large Print edition is unabridged.
In other aspects, this book may vary
from the original edition.
Printed in the United States of America
on permanent paper.
Set in 16-point Times New Roman type.

ISBN: 978-1-64358-599-4

The Library of Congress has cataloged this record
under Library of Congress Control Number: 2020930829

# KINGS
# FALLING

# PROLOGUE

## STUTTGART, GERMANY

Being hunted by the monsters she had created was a horrifying, well-deserved death. God forgive her for the terrible things she'd done, but it had been for good. For the good of all humankind.

Only it hadn't turned out . . . good.

Cobbled streets threatened to catch her heel and wrench her ankle as she hurried behind Dieter, his large frame casting deepening shadows. Katrin stumbled down the wet, darkened road, gulping air and adrenaline. A whimper begged for freedom just as she begged for life. But neither would come. Gods and demons had nothing on the men chasing them through dark alleys. In their attempt to prevent the unimaginable, to thwart a focused, shrewd enemy from succeeding, she had helped breed a pure form of violence. And now that violence demanded blood. Their blood.

"Wait, wait," Dieter said, shoving her back into a doorway of shadows. "Here. Quiet."

Was he crazy? They would be found! But his bulk pressed her into the corner next to some rubbish bins. The former warehouses now held low-wage factories and small flats crammed with numerous families. Flattened against the damp

7

stone of a factory building, the chill seeping through her thin blouse, Katrin tried to steady her racing pulse. With aches and exhaustion squeezing her muscles and lungs, she found it impossible to breathe normally. Her heart thundered after running for blocks.

In novels and movies, people in their position would hear the slapping feet of the approaching killers. Grunted threats. But not in real life. Not with those who hunted them. They were fast, stealthy.

She rested her head against Dieter's back. It was no use to calm herself—she would never again be calm. *We were wrong. We were so wrong.* Her fingers trembled as she wiped her tears. Was there no way to fix this?

Black shapes slithered through the night, streetlamps caressing lithe forms that moved as if they did not need light to see. The air swirled and stirred a reek of the refuse around Katrin. The stench of death.

*It's your imagination.*

A tremor spirited down her spine as she watched the four figures fade from sight. It should be no surprise that, of the lot, he'd sent the most violent. Which warned Katrin she would not survive the night.

But she must. They must.

When they reached her brother's home, he would chastise her, say she should have listened to him. He always said that, even as a child. He was six years her senior, and though she had multiple degrees, he had power and prestige. His name carried weight and influence.

She was the weight. He'd supported her, since the career she had fought so hard for provided little income.

The fabric of Dieter's wool jacket pulled away, pushing her breath into the back of her throat. *No, no. Wait awhile longer.* Fear's voice held her hostage in the cold, damp evening.

She watched as he slipped to the edge of the building, her nerves jammed yet buzzing. He would be detected. And their escape would be for naught.

To her surprise, he motioned her from the hiding spot.

But Katrin could not move. Dared not twitch a muscle for fear of discovery. When his motioning grew frantic, she peeled from the cocoon of darkness and stench. She drifted toward him, expecting with each step to be set upon.

He caught her hand and pulled out onto the open road. "They are g—"

"No," she breathed. "It's not safe." It would never be safe again.

Dieter cupped her face. "My Katrin, trust me. We are halfway there."

Halfway. Her heart crumbled both in relief and agony. Halfway meant they'd managed to get this far, which she hadn't thought possible. But halfway also meant they had a lot of distance yet to cover. A lot of risk and opportunity to get caught. To be killed.

"What if we don't make it?" It was a stupid question, but desperation forced the words from her mouth.

"We will," he said ardently. "Remember, plans are in place, and we have the documents to end this." He patted his satchel and nodded to hers, tucked beneath her coat.

They both had a set of files for when—not if—trouble came. That way, if one went down, the responsibility rested on the shoulders of the other to survive and succeed.

It was insane to think they could.

But the thought of this information never getting out made her heart writhe. What that could mean. What the world would look like in a few years.

"Come." Dieter stuck close to shops and stoops as they darted through the warehouse district.

They rounded a bend onto a long, narrow road. Scurried across it. Each step made it easier to breathe, fanned the dangerous flame of hope. When they stepped around a manhole to avoid making noise, a shape dropped in front of them from a rooftop.

With a gasp, Katrin leapt back and grabbed Dieter's coat. She saw another shape appear on her right. Heard a thump behind her.

"Game's up, old man," the leader said.

Unwilling to fail, unwilling to die here and let all hope be lost, Katrin looked for a way out. Willed a car to come down the empty road. Searched for someone to help. But they were surrounded only by dark shadows, flanking alleys, and a vicious enemy. She shifted behind Dieter, easing to his left. Closer to the alley. Could she make it? A lazy fog snaked around them, adding to the ominous threat these men posed. No, not merely a threat. A foretelling.

Dieter reached back with both hands.

She touched him—only to feel that he held something cold and hard. A gun? She glanced down, strangled at the thought. But the shape—not a gun. It was cylindrical. With a tab and pin at the top.

Pulse slowing at the sight of the grenade, she wondered if he meant to blow all of them up instead of surrendering. "Dieter," she whispered.

He tugged her close and pressed his lips to the spot in front of her ear. "When I say *go,* run!" He spoke so quietly, the fog nearly captured his words.

Terror gripped her. "No."

"What'll it be?" the leader demanded. "Now or never, Dr. Wagner. We are out of time and patience."

Dieter shoved her aside. "Go!" He lifted his hand. Even as Katrin threw herself toward safety, she

11

heard the pin hit the cobbled road. Felt the tension thicken. Rustling fabric—the men shifting and taking aim. Shouts of "grenade" erupted. She raced to the alley, hunching low to use the fog for cover, and flattened herself against the wall.

The explosion punched the night, loud and painful in the confined space. It popped her ears. Heat gusted her hair, but the wall protected her.

Seizing the chaos, she rushed on. Wouldn't stop. Wouldn't look back. Though she didn't hear the *thwap* of feet, she knew they were coming. She had the vain hope that Dieter had survived the detonation, but it could not be. He was dead. It was up to her now. She must get out alive.

*It is impossible!* She had no training for this! Katrin was not a soldier. She was a scientist, a doctor.

Which meant she had brains. A brain to use. But she was slow, and they were not. She was tiring, and they were not. Still, she ran, not heeding the aches and blisters that throbbed. In one alley, out onto a street. Through a market with stands that allowed her to dart in and out of view.

Shots cracked behind her.

Tapestries hanging overhead swayed violently— no doubt struck by bullets—and moonlight betrayed her location. Katrin ducked and hurried on, scurrying from stand to stand. From one shop to another. Then many alleys.

Another gunshot. Fire burned.

She tripped, pushed herself back up, and shoved onward. Dieter had made her vow not to use phones because they were too easily tracked. And whoever they called could be drawn into this nightmare, which she would not wish on anyone.

But they had hoped to do this together. Now she had to find a way to reach her brother.

At the end of another alley, she hesitated a few feet from the corner. Listening around the wild thunder of her pulse, she breathed deeply through her nose to slow her breathing. Her legs buckled. She frowned, catching herself against the wall, her shoulder scraping the brick. A strange ache pinched her side. She touched it, and her hand came away sticky.

She glanced down, stricken at the dark stain there. Oh no. They'd shot her. Mentally, she assessed her body and aches. There was too much blood loss, weakening her. Very quickly.

*I'm going to die.*

*Not before I get this to my brother.*

Death creeping nearer, Katrin slipped around the corner, using the wall for support. She had no time to waste. No time to pity herself. She must do this. For Dieter. For all those soldiers.

Light flickered ahead.

No, not light. A light-haired man. Bobbing in and out of view, scouring the market.

"She's here," another said. "I saw her."

Katrin tucked herself into a shop alcove and up

13

against the wall, protected—for the moment—from view. Tears burned as failure plagued her thoughts. The plaster dug into her spine. She struck the wall. Why? Why could she not make it? This had to happen.

*Please, God!* She blinked and saw her reflection in the shop's glass door. With a start, she realized the men probably could, too. She sank deeper into the corner and noticed the counter inside had a cash register. And a phone.

Hope dangling, her heart quickened. She reached for the knob, but her palm was slick with blood and slipped. She tried it again. Locked. If she broke the glass, it would alert the men. But how else would she get inside? Jiggling the knob, she felt it give. Shielding the noise with her body, she jiggled harder. Shouldered into it. Ignored the pinch of pain.

Shouts in the market tore into her awareness.

"What's that noise?"

"Came from over there."

"Find her!" The barks came all at once, it seemed.

Panicked, Katrin glanced over her shoulder and saw them searching the far side of the market. Somehow the door gave. She stumbled inside and fell to her knees. Gritting her teeth, she refused to cry out and ignored the blood that coated her blouse and slacks. They would notice the open door. Carefully, she toed it shut. Dragged herself over and turned the lock. On all fours, she crawled to the counter, grunting at the pain slicing through her side. Behind it, she peered out the glass storefront.

A man stalked closer.

Fear nearly paralyzed her, but she snatched the phone. Dropped back out of sight. Dialed. Hand trembling, breathing hard, she put the phone to her ear. It rang . . . and rang. . . .

"There's blood in the alley. I tagged her!"

"Then she's around here somewhere."

*Ring . . . ring . . .*

"Please," she whimpered around tears that blurred her vision. She tried to blink them away, but realized she wasn't crying. Her vision was blurring, fading.

"Hello?"

"He—" Her voice cracked. "Hello."

"Is someone there?" came her brother's annoyed voice.

"Yes. I know it's late."

"Ka—"

"I am calling"—she hurried to protect him from saying her name and drawing the attention of those who might listen in—"from Goldmeier's Watches to let you know . . . watch . . . ready." She wouldn't make it. "You . . . you were right. . . ."

"*Mein Go*—I knew it. I'll be right over. Just don't—"

Katrin's world vanished.

# CHAPTER 1

## RIYADH, SAUDI ARABIA

"Let them try. *Qui audet adipiscitur.*" Special Air Service Corporal Wafiyy Ibn Sarsour spoke into his comms piece, gaze roving the lush grounds and hundreds of workers hurrying about.

*Who dares, wins.* And it sure wouldn't be some rogue element attempting to thwart the shocking marriage of a British royal to a Saudi prince. For the first time in decades, the world didn't have their noses stuck in a rugby match or on social media. They had tuned in to watch the lavish wedding of Britain's Lady Selene Northcott-Hale, daughter of the Duke and Duchess of Kelton.

With practiced calm, Wafiyy positioned himself a few feet from the happy couple, who had returned from the mosque where the *nikah*, the official Muslim ceremony, had taken place. When the king and crown prince entered the room, Wafiyy assessed their escort, noting that both men were regular detail.

"They're ready," said Richard Northcott-Hale, the bride's cousin. He clapped Wafiyy's elbow. "So glad you could do this for us."

"It's an honor, my friend," Wafiyy replied before keying his comms. "Royals ready to take the lawn."

"Copy that, Six. Blades report your situation," came the voice of Captain Shanks. The British SAS had joined forces with the Royal Saudi Land Forces, also known as the Saudi Arabian Army, for this auspicious occasion after a credible threat targeting the event had been detected and confirmed by both governments.

"Two all clear."

"Four as well."

As the reports trickled in, Wafiyy monitored the couple. Wondered at the ability to blend two entirely different cultures. Many spoke of it. Many tried it. Few succeeded. Even though he'd been born in Sussex and raised in London, had a proper British accent and education, most people could not get past the color of his skin or his Arabic heritage. Jess was the girl who'd persuaded him to try, and the royals convinced him such a relationship could be successful. Then again, they had only been married an hour.

His ethnicity had been a bonus for this mission, though the House of Saud had been reluctant to accept a "Westernized Muslim" on the detail. However, his high marks from Oxford and his SAS record won their approval.

"How is Jessamine?" Richard asked.

Wafiyy smirked, still listening to the team updating statuses. "Jealous she turned you down?"

"It's not every day a man in line to the throne gets rejected," Richard said with a wink.

"She's good." Wafiyy smiled. "In Switzerland skiing with friends."

"Six, we're all clear," Captain Shanks reported. "And we have one hundred percent agreement from their team as well."

Wafiyy nodded to Richard. "They're ready." Then he eyed the royal security detail and inclined his head, indicating his readiness.

A colonel whispered to the crown prince, who in turn nudged his father. And with that, the entourage headed to the lawn amid applause and cheers from the hundreds waiting for the celebration to begin.

"Eyes out," warned Captain Shanks. "They had trouble at the gate."

Wafiyy felt the hairs on the back of his neck prickle as he trailed the wedding party out into the evening. With no expense spared, the lawn had been transformed into an affair that glittered with lights, flowers, and sheer curtains billowing from columns. Guests were adorned in bejeweled gowns and tuxes that cost thousands. Live TV crews filmed from the side, because tonight not only did King Ahmad bring a Briton into his family, but he would also push a peace initiative between the West and the Muslim world unlike anything attempted before. At last, the millions funneled into Saudi Arabia by America, Britain, and France would pay off.

An hour into the festivities, Wafiyy battled

a tension headache and began to question the credibility of the threat against the royal families. His phone buzzed, and he glanced at the caller ID. With a smile, he made sure his comms mic was off as he put the phone to his other ear and answered. "How is Switzerland?"

"Cold," Jessamine said. "And I'm jealous you're there at that magnificent party. I can see you on TV."

He arched an eyebrow, glancing to the bank of cameras. "You can?"

"Yeah. You're in the background, but I know my man when I see him."

"Why are you not partying instead of watching TV?"

"We're heading out now. But I had to call. Let you know I'm officially jealous that you're there with a king and a proper duke." Her smile bled through the phone. "Think they'd miss it if you nicked a ring for me?"

"Are you proposing again?"

"You have to say yes sometime."

He grinned like an idiot. "I must go."

She gave an exasperated sigh. "A ring—at least try."

"I love you," he said, still smiling. Thinking of the ring waiting for her back in London. He'd propose at Christmas. He'd already asked her father for his permission. Old-fashioned, yes, but it was a good show of respect.

His comms crackled as he pocketed his phone and wandered closer to the tent, adjusting his earpiece.

"Six, you're needed near the king."

Stiffening, Wafiyy didn't hesitate. "Roger that. Moving in."

When there were only two meters between him and the king, one of the Saudi soldiers trudged toward him. "Sorry, brother. Not feeling well."

Again Wafiyy's comms crackled. "Harbah. Two. One. Five. Initiate rise. Rise. Rise."

Warmth sped up his spine and neck, then arched over his crown and ears. A pain much like drinking a milkshake too fast on a hot day. Heel of his hand to his temple, he grunted.

"Who is this? Clear the line!" Captain Shanks ordered.

"What was that?" one of the team asked.

"Strange. Sounded mechanized," another said.

Wafiyy swept his gaze across the festivities. Noted the Saudi soldiers, the British Blades—as they called themselves—and then the royals laughing and chatting beneath the white tent's dangling net lights.

Spine straight, blood cold, he intercepted the king's server and lifted the glass from the tray. Using a test strip, he dipped it in the sherbet drink, a favorite among wedding guests and the king himself . . . and let the pill slip from his cuff.

Sudden awareness spiked through his mind as

21

the tiny white tablet plunked into the liquid and melted.

The pill. He didn't recall concealing it there yet knew he had. Must have. Why was he not alarmed?

He was alarmed.

Yet he delivered the glass back to the official server, who glanced at the test strip, which did not discolor, indicating the sherbet was safe—or had been a moment ago. Wafiyy watched with satisfaction as the crystal goblet was set before the king.

Deep in conversation with the Duke of Kelton, the king reached for the glass and sipped it. Nodding, he returned to his discussion.

But only for a second.

His throat would tighten. His blood would thin. Run down his nose.

The crown prince quickly handed his father a napkin, thereby coming in contact with the blood. With the chemical. Father and son would die within minutes, despite the medical staff rushing to their aid. The bride's dress was now stained crimson. Another casualty. That couldn't be helped. It was symbolic, yes? The blood by which her husband—being dragged from the king and his brother—would take the throne. The blood by which . . .

*I will rise.*

# CHAPTER 2

## JABAL SHAIB AL-BANAT, EGYPT

It had all started here five years ago, and if Leif Metcalfe had any say, it would end here, too.

Crouched atop the mountain peak, he stared out over the rugged terrain. And that was putting it mildly. The ridges in this section of the Sahara Desert were serrated and forbidding. If you fell, you fell to your death. To his three were the glittering waters of the Red Sea. He shook his head. If he and his team had headed east, they'd have found water. Civilization. But they'd chosen the mountains for protection from the sun, heading south, then west.

Leif roughed a hand over his face. That whole mission had been screwed up. It didn't make sense. How could he recall the mission with perfect clarity, but not the chopper crash or the faces of the team, half of them left dead on the mountain? And what about the months preceding it?

*"You don't expect us to buy that, do you?"*

*"It's the truth,"* Leif growled. *Yeah, it looked bad. Smelled bad. But that was the truth.*

*"Guerrero is dead,"* Reimer bellowed. *"Died on the table."*

*Stricken, Leif leaned forward and grabbed the*

23

*back of his head, hiding his face in his arms. They
were dead. All of them. Nine soldiers crashed on
a mountain, only one came out. It was like some
sick, twisted joke.*

*"Your whole freakin' team is dead—except
you!" Reimer's dark eyes condemned. "Mighty
convenient. What'd you do, run? Leave them to
burn and die?"*

*Leif came out of his chair. Launched over the
table. Struck Reimer in the nose. A strike so hard
and fast, Leif didn't know he'd done it until four
Marines were stacked on him, pinning him to the
scuffed vinyl floor.*

Now he stared out across the land, trying to
extract any little nugget from the debris field of
that disaster. Trying to reassemble the puzzle
with most of the pieces missing. Recall those
faces, men he had fought with.

They'd crashed here—well, not on this peak,
but lower. The al-Banat range comprised four
mountains. Impact had happened southeast of
Leif's current location. He'd come to amid the
mangled chopper. Chunks on fire, billowing
smoke and fumes into the air. The black plume
had drawn the attention of local ISIS fighters.
He and those of the team still alive regrouped,
inventoried their wounds and weapons. Fought
their way out of the hills. Even though several
of his guys were badly injured, they managed
to give the fighters the slip. Leaving their dead

behind hadn't been by choice. Survival forced them to mark the location and return.

*"There weren't any bodies, Metcalfe! There was nothing but charred wreckage!"*

Leif's attention skipped to the hillside in the distance. After five years, most of the evidence had been scavenged, but he'd come all the same. Allowed himself to climb Jabal. Yet he could still see the darkened area of the explosion.

How? How had they gone from a mission to quietly interdict on behalf of a village to waking up on a mountainside, burning?

*Smoke from the crash stung his corneas and tickled his throat. He heard Guerrero cough again. "You need help, G?"*

*"I'll live. Check Krieger and Zhanshi. They don't look so good."*

*Leif spotted two of their team a yard from his boots. They were piled over each other on a dark patch of the sand and gravel. Coming to his feet, he got a better angle—and cursed. That wasn't a dark patch. It was a* bloody *patch.*

*He lurched forward, jagged pain clawing his leg. With a growl, he grabbed the wound and negotiated the rocky terrain. His boots slipped and twisted as rocks gave way.*

*He dropped to a knee beside Zhanshi. Head and shoulders were at wrong angles, lips blue against chalky skin. Beneath him, Krieger groaned.*

*Protecting his injured leg, Leif guided Zhanshi*

*to the ground so Krieger could extract himself. He didn't look wounded, but internal injuries were deceptive. "Hurting anywhere?"*

*Krieger shuffled back to the wall of dirt. Slumped against it, a distance in his gaze. A shake to his limbs.*

*Leif gripped the man's shoulder. "Hey. You with us?" He cringed at the fresh pulse of warm blood sliding down his own calf.*

*Confused eyes wandered to his. Then Krieger shook his head. "Yeah . . . no." He ran a hand over his face. Glanced up. Cursed as he threw himself away, toward a ledge.*

*"Easy, easy!" Leif warned, motioning to the gaping drop-off behind the big guy, then pointing at the chopper wreckage looming above. "It's lodged. Not coming down." He nodded behind him. "You're on a precipice."*

*Krieger's knees and panic buckled, sending him to the rocky path. He let out a string of curses and cradled his head. "Why do I feel so screwed up?"*

That was the one thing they'd had in common—for some reason, they had all felt off. Shock from the crash, he'd guessed.

A chill settled into Leif's bones, and he blinked back to the present. Night had fallen. He retrieved his gear and set up camp. Beneath the twinkling black, he tugged out his phone and stared at the blank screen. Imagined there were messages from Iskra. He sighed, roughing a hand over his face. He'd never met a woman like her. She'd altered his world, and making sure his team eliminated the man who'd wrecked hers had opened something in Leif he didn't think possible—love.

Yet she had also upended his strategically placed walls. Ones that kept nosy people out and shielded him from whatever those missing six months hid. Then there was the mission, the Book of the Wars and its warning about some super-army, which was important to Iskra. To finding her brother.

Somehow, through two separate situations, that book made Leif want to find himself. She wanted to help him, but . . . something in those dark corridors of his past said to do it on his own. That she wouldn't like what she found. He probably wouldn't either.

He powered up the phone. It came to life with a short vibration. A few seconds later, a dozen messages populated the screen. Four from Iskra, six from Iliescu, and two from Canyon.

With a groan, Leif shut it off and dropped back against his sleeping bag. He hooked an arm over his eyes. Not yet. He couldn't face them yet.

## OUTSIDE BETHESDA, MARYLAND

She had killed people for a living, left others devastated, and now she had a personal vendetta against the car in front of her. An RPG would be overkill. Maybe a few well-placed shots through the back window.

No, too messy. And someone would see.

Walk up, knock on the window. When the guy rolled it down, she could pitch in a canister of sarin gas.

No, it could leak out and kill her objective, the person standing on the corner in a reflective jacket.

Options, options. What was left?

Ram his bumper, say it was an accident. And then Leif would be angry when he returned and she had to explain the damage to the SUV and the bill for repairs.

That was, if he ever returned. Iskra glanced at her phone. *Why* was everyone trying to teach her patience today? It was her one failing in life.

*"Mama, pochemu on tak dolgo?"* Taissia asked from her booster seat in the back seat.

"English, remember?"

With a huff, Taissia rolled her eyes. "Why is he taking so long?" she repeated in English, gray eyes flashing. "Better?"

It was hard not to smile. "Much." Her daughter had Iskra's impatience and her father's intelligence. It was nice to be free of Hristoff and start learning things like that and—finally— calling her daughter by the name she and Valery had chosen. "And he's taking so long because he's"—*a jerk . . . no, too mean*—"slow." She tapped her fingers on the steering wheel, resisting the urge to nail the horn.

"You do realize it's a crime to plan assassinations in the school drop-off line, right?" taunted Mercy Maddox from the passenger seat.

"It's not, actually," Iskra said, sliding a glower toward her friend, who shared this morning's ride to the belowground facility that housed the team's headquarters. "The real crime is that we have to wait behind people like this who are not ready and don't have the world to save before their first latte."

"Mobile-ordering that latte right now before you decide to take out a hit on a single father of twins." Mercy lifted her phone and opened a coffee shop app as boy-girl twins emerged from the luxury vehicle in front of them. "Ha. Called it."

"You only knew it was him because you have a crush on him," Iskra said as the sedan finally eased away, allowing her to pull forward in line.

"Can't have a crush on someone I don't know."

"Of course you can," Iskra argued. "Fans do it every day with music idols and actors." She rolled down her window and smiled at the monitor standing on the school sidewalk. That reflective jacket flicked early-morning light into her eyes. "Good morning." She reached back and released her daughter from the booster seat.

"Morning, Taissia." The monitor opened the car door. "How are you?"

"I'm good." Her daughter flipped her long brown braid over her shoulder as she hiked up her lavender backpack and retrieved her doll from the seat. "But my mom needs a latte before she kills someone."

Iskra sucked in a breath, faced front, and slid her finger to the window control. As it rose, she said to Mercy, "If you laugh, I will kill you."

"I like my body parts too much to risk it."

Breathing a chuckle, Iskra exited the parking lot and merged into traffic.

"I did order you a latte, though." Mercy shrugged. "Better to be safe than dead."

Iskra groaned. "You have to stop that. Look what you're teaching my daughter."

"Self-preservation is a vital lesson in survival. I thought you knew that."

A few months ago, Iskra wouldn't have guessed that Mercy Maddox would become a friend she could trust. "I will give you grace," she teased, "because you help me navigate the domestic bliss of motherhood."

"And a love life."

On that subject, they would have to agree to disagree. Especially since Leif had been gone for the last month. "Each afternoon, Taissia asks about him, when he's coming home."

The silence carried them for several miles,

letting Iskra wander the emptiness of his absence. They weren't married or living together, yet they had spent most of their time together after his team killed Hristoff.

"I check every day for proof of life," Mercy said quietly.

There had been no ping on his location because that was the way he wanted it. "Leif might not have been an operative, but he knows how to move without tripping protocols that will tell us his location."

"True, but there are . . . methods of finding him—without facial rec."

"But they *haven't* found him. You haven't."

Mercy sighed. "No." She grunted. "He's totally Rip Hunter."

"Who?"

With a wave, Mercy shook her head. "Nothing. Not worth mentioning, and I will kill Leif for making me come up with a DC hero who matches him." She shifted toward Iskra. "But it works, you know. Because Rip was able to navigate the time barrier and was also a skilled tactician and strategist. So it's really no surprise that Leif has been able to avoid detection and stay off my radar, even considering my mad HackerGirl skills."

They stopped by the coffee shop, where Mercy ran in and picked up their drinks.

"I told him I would go with him," Iskra said

as they sat in heavy traffic again. But that hadn't been realistic because she had a daughter, who was her priority.

Never had she felt this conflicted. The last three years of her existence had been all about securing freedom for Taissia from the stranglehold of Hristoff Peychinovich. But then she kissed a blue-eyed sailor and forgot her priorities. Now she was here, being a mother to Taissia. Trying to give her daughter a normal life. But Iskra Todorova never had a normal childhood. How could she give what she'd never experienced?

Maybe, if she just played the role long and hard enough, it would work.

"What about you and Baddar?" she asked.

After a guffaw, Mercy eyed her. "Wait. You were serious?"

Iskra shook her head as she drove into the belowground parking. "You can pretend if you want, but I am not fooled. He is smitten with you, and you—"

"—are not interested in dating anyone. Besides, I have that guy to find, Andrew." Mercy lifted an eyebrow. "He tipped his hand, and I'm going to hunt this dude down until he begs me to stop."

It was Iskra's turn to wing up an eyebrow. "If he is as skilled as you say, I would be much more careful about trying to find him. An operative who doesn't want to be found will deem you a threat."

"Baby, I *am* a threat!" Mercy snorted, retrieving her messenger bag from the floorboard as they parked. "But kidding aside—I hear you. I didn't get here by being stupid but by being smart and relentless."

Iskra smiled and reached for the door handle. "That is why we get along so well."

They entered the bunker but hesitated at the cacophony skittering up the concrete steps.

"Sounds exciting," Mercy said. "And loud."

"But not involving many." Lured by the voices, Iskra descended into the hub.

In his office, Deputy Director Dru Iliescu stood behind the desk, one hand on his belt, another holding a file, which he stabbed at a cowering Barclay "Cell" Purcell. "You get on this, and you get it sorted. I find out you're not doing everything in your power—"

"I *am* doing everything in my power."

"You've had it for three months!"

"Yes, and it's written in a two-thousand-year-old language and references code names that aren't used today, because, hello? None of us was alive then to record them," Cell said, his voice pitching.

"Don't get a mouth on you now." Iliescu glowered, his gaze sliding to Iskra and Mercy before again skewering the comms expert. "I need more than three names."

Cell rubbed the back of his neck. "If you want

more, you have to let me off the leash." He almost seemed repentant. "Just . . . a little."

"What part of 'heck no' don't you understand? We are not opening this up to foreign analysts."

"*I'm* foreign," Iskra said, inserting herself into the conversation.

"And you're *here*," Iliescu snapped, "where I can monitor what you do with intel you come into contact with."

"Sir," Cell said with a huff, "it'd only—"

"No!" Iliescu nailed Iskra with a look, then Mercy. "Briefing in twenty in the hub. Now, clear out. I have work to do."

Cell snatched the file and pivoted toward the door, brow knotted as he shoved between them.

"Barc," Mercy said, hurrying after him.

Iskra kept her distance yet remained close enough to hear.

"Who were you asking to talk to?" Mercy asked.

Cell skidded a look to the side but stopped. Quietly, he said, "Mei."

Mercy recoiled, her spine and neck swaying as if she were about to throw up. "*Dragon* Mei? Are you *insane?*"

"Already got the lecture from Iliescu. Don't need it from you." Cell swung around her.

Wide-eyed, Mercy turned and met Iskra's questioning gaze. "He's a loon to—"

"Who is this person?" Iskra asked, following him.

"A vicious analyst recruited out of China's intelligence service. She's the type of hacker I can only dream of being." Mercy shook her head. "But I wouldn't give her an inch of room, if that much."

"Yeah, well, don't," came the voice of Director Iliescu, bringing them both around. "If I get you cleared, will you work with Cell on that list?"

Mercy blinked. Snorted. "Is the Hulk fueled by gamma radiation?"

Iliescu scowled.

"That would be yes, he's fueled—"

"Yes or no, Maddox?"

"Of course, sir."

"Good." He whipped back toward his office.

"What about Leif?" Iskra asked.

"What about him?"

"You said there was a briefing in twenty minutes, but"—she checked the hub to be sure—"Leif's not here."

Something fidgeted in his expression before he shrugged and stepped into his office. "Just be there."

"By all that's holy, what is it with you people?"

"I won't apologize," Leif said. Not for doing the thing Dru had been promising to do for the last five years. Yet hadn't done. "I need answers—"

"I need *your* head in the game *now,*" Dru bellowed. "That going to be a problem?"

35

"Why do you think I'm here?" When the director frowned, Leif chose the path of least resistance. "No, not a problem. Tell me you have something to work with. How's Cell coming with the list?"

"Three flipping names," Dru growled, stabbing the air. "That's it. Three months and three names." He huffed. "How are we supposed to stop Armageddon with *three names?*"

Glad to have the attention deflected from his rogue intel-hunting, Leif scratched his jaw. "It's a starting point."

"Which is why I've called in the team." Dru nodded to the hub. "You're lucky you came back when you did."

"Not like you didn't have a way to track me down." Leif shook his head, knowing it wasn't worth the breath to argue or accuse. "Is Iskra here?"

"Yeah. That's two people ticked at you in this building." Dru glowered. "Tread carefully—she won't like that you returned and didn't tell her."

"You're assuming I didn't."

"I *know* you didn't because she was in here fifteen minutes ago asking where you were!"

Okay. Yeah, that was trouble. Leif shifted gears. "Why're you mad?" He nodded to Dru's desk. "I'm allowed personal time."

"*Personal* time would be spent with the woman you nearly killed to protect two months ago. *Personal* time would be a vacation in the Caribbean or a cabin in the mountains or, heck"—he flicked a hand at the door—"down with the big mouse in Florida, treating that little girl to a theme park."

That was a whole lot of anger being thrown around. Then it struck him. Leif snorted, disbelieving this whole act. "You did know." He smoothed a hand down the back of his neck. "You knew where I was."

Probably from the moment Leif had picked up his ruck to head out. But how? Other than his phone, which he kept off, Leif hadn't taken any technology with him other than very basic, nontraceable handhelds for GPS and emergency beacons. He stilled as a thought hit. "You're tracking me." He planted his hands on his belt. "Did you put a device in me?"

"You were told to leave it alone."

"Yeah." Leif felt anger rising. "Four *years* ago. *Four!*" The only thing that kept him in check was the fact that a year after the incident, Dru had thrown him a lifeline, pulled Leif out of a destructive path—in exchange for his agreement to let Dru handle things. "You said you'd get answers. Find out what happened to me. Who did it. Five years after the Banat, and I've got exactly *zero* answers."

"I told you," Dru said quietly, skating a glance to the door, "digging into this is tricky."

"*Dangerous* is the word you used."

Dru conceded the correction with a nod. "If we push too hard, whoever did this . . ." Torment churned through his gaze. "Leif, we don't know who's behind it. We go in guns blazing, we might find ourselves getting mowed down before we can do anything."

Leif moved to the desk and pressed his fingertips to its surface. "Just . . . tell me something—anything." The ache grew. "Please."

Dru considered him. "If I do that, then I *undo* everything I've worked to protect and unearth. I put you at risk, leave you exposed to threats we cannot thwart. The last time we did that—tell me you remember."

How could Leif forget? Coming to in a burning, upside-down car. He'd crawled to safety before it blew.

"Don't ask me to be the cause of that. Not again." Dru shifted around his desk. "I don't know who they are or how they know, but they always do. And they burn us. Every time."

Leif appreciated the director's candor, but he'd heard it for four years. He was done playing it safe. "I'm not asking *you* to do it, but I refuse to sit around while more years pass without answers." He tapped the desk. "I'm going to find what's missing. Even if it costs me everything."

"Including Iskra?" The challenge was unmistakable.

That hurt. But it just proved one more point. "You don't get it." Leif shook his head and huffed. "*She* is why I'm pushing. If I'm going to have a life with her, I have to get this void out of my head. And every day that goes by without knowing makes me feel like a target. I can't move forward with her until I know what's missing."

"Then you may just throw away the best chance you've had at love." Dru squinted at him. "What if they go after her? I can't hide that she's here now. What if they—"

"From what you've indicated, they know me. Which means they know going after her would be a mistake." The thought of losing Iskra and Taissia pained him. "But I will find out what was stolen from me. What happened." He set his jaw. "I've let it stay unresolved long enough."

Dru's shoulders sagged. "Leif . . . please." His phone buzzed, and he glanced at it. "Promise me you'll see the Book of the Wars through first. We—*I* need your eyes on this."

Leif curled his fingers into a fist. "I'm committed. I'm not going to walk away from something I haven't finished."

Dru nodded to the door. "Let's do that briefing—and I'd gear up."

"Why?"

"Have you responded to Iskra's texts or messages?"

Guilt left a funny taste in his mouth.

Dru offered a weak smile. "I expect it's going to be a war zone when you walk in there. Once she sets eyes on you, the blast radius—"

"You could've told her I was okay, since you were tracking me."

"I did. Every time she asked."

Leif drew up short. *Every* time?

"But she didn't want to hear it from *me*."

# CHAPTER 3

## TEAM HEADQUARTERS, MARYLAND

If by *blast radius* Dru meant arctic blasts, he was right. Leif could've worn extreme-weather gear and still come out with freezer burns from the cold shoulder from Iskra.

Culver Brown met him outside the director's office. "When'd you get back?"

"Now," Leif said, eyeing Iskra.

"That explains a few things," Adam Lawe mumbled, glancing across the hub. "Like that blistering look Viorica is shooting at you."

Viorica. He hated that nickname. "*Iskra* has every right to be mad."

"Then you'd better don some humility," Culver said with a chuckle. "Tuck your tail between your legs, scurry on over to her, and apologize."

Dai Saito joined them. "Apologize. And *beg*."

The guys high-fived and laughed.

Shaking his head, Leif started toward where she was talking quietly with Peyton Devine and Mercy. All three women turned away from him.

"Oh, ouch." Culver chuckled. "Looks like you'll need flowers."

"And a ring," Dai added.

"No way," Lawe called. "Too soon."

"Maybe that's why you lost Devine," Saito taunted Lawe.

Banter behind him, Leif joined his friend and former Afghan commando, Baddar Amir Nawabi, and tapped his arm. "You going to join the fun?"

"It is not for me to lecture." Baddar inclined his head. "You already know it was a mistake."

"I meant the briefing," Leif groused.

"Okay, folks," Dru called over their snickers as he entered and acknowledged Rear Admiral Alene Braun and Cell, who arrived at the same time. "Let's get down to business."

The team crowded around the obsidian conference table, and Leif lingered at the back, waiting to see where Iskra sat. Maybe he could—

Negative. Devine and Maddox provided protective cover, positioning themselves on either side of her.

Come on. Were they going to make it impossible? He considered insisting they make a hole for him. He'd always been one to cut it straight. But something in him had changed. Shifted. Altered course.

Dru stood at the head of the table with Cell. "Time is short and resources shorter," he said. "So, Cell, Harden—go ahead. Tell us what you've got."

Senior Intelligence Analyst Charlie Harden nodded. "As a recap for those who forgot—"

"You think we're so dumb, we'd forget in less

than three months after a near fight to the death?" Saito snorted.

"—*and* for the recording," Harden continued with an arched eyebrow, "the Book of the Wars is mentioned in the Hebrew Bible's book of Numbers, but it's only a brief reference. The text was lost to humanity until it was discovered in the salt mines of Israel. It has since been stolen by one organization or entity after another and is, at this time, believed to be in the hands of the formidable Armageddon Coalition, aka ArC."

"Which we plan to change," Culver asserted.

"For now, since we do not have the book, we are working only with the corrupted information provided by scans of the actual book. As far as we can tell, the book lists particular wars that have not yet occurred. We intercepted the devices ArC used to stir up storms, and now . . ." Harden indicated the screen. "This is what we talked about a few months ago, but I've been working on it, and Mr. Purcell has been sorting another aspect. Let's take a look."

Harden cleared his throat and began to read. " '. . . and those from below were come, the mighty and the vigilant like a plague. Garbed in authority, they lost their lives, breath snuffed like lamps doused. Rage in the right hand, vengeance in the left, there was naught but blood upon the lands. Kingdoms shifted. Countries collapsed. Chaos seized and reigned in answer to the summons of the enemies of kings. Upon those from below is marked the quest that tethers their soul in darkness . . .' "

"Hold up," Saito said. "I'm not really fond of that second line."

Culver nodded. "Isn't that a sign we *shouldn't* do this mission?"

"Hooah," Lawe agreed. "I'm not up for my breath being snuffed out like a lamp."

Ignoring the men, Devine narrowed her eyes at the scan and the translation below it. " 'Kingdoms shifted. Countries collapsed.' " She rubbed her lower lip. "A global war?"

"How do we intervene in something on that scale?" Iskra asked.

"That's a really good question," Harden said, "but I think, by considering the previous line about rage and vengeance, we might be able to interpret this war as a response to the storms."

"This is where Charlie and I disagree," Cell said. "He believes the retaliation line, but to me, those are unrelated. However, mention of 'those from below' happens throughout the text—well, what we have of it—so I don't think that is about retaliation. And honestly, I don't believe the two are connected."

Noting an eagerness in Cell's expression, Leif shifted. "You have an idea?"

"Yeah." Cell aimed a remote. Images splashed over the concrete wall. "I think we were wrong."

"We?" Culver asked with a snigger. "What, you got a mouse in your pocket?"

"Hey," Saito said, "wasn't it you who sent us to the Bahamas when we needed to be in—where was it again?"

"Greece," Lawe said, smiling.

"I wasn't *wrong*," Cell countered. "The intel and situation changed, so we adjusted the mission."

"Convenient," Saito teased.

"Anyway," Cell said, "in translating what was salvaged from the corrupted USB that Viorica—"

"Iskra," Leif corrected.

Glancing at him, Cell went on. "We have been translating it as 'those from below', but I believe it should simply be transliterated"—his gaze rested on Iskra—"as 'Neiothen.' "

She lifted her chin, fingers going to her mouth. "That is the super-army Vasily mentioned."

Leif's heart thudded. "You referenced the super-army before the book did."

"Vasily told me on the yacht while it was being scanned that it mentioned them."

"How'd you miss that?" Leif asked Harden.

"Not missed," the analyst said with a shake of his head. "When translating an ancient text, you take words or symbols in the text and extract a meaning. For example, in Hebrew, the word *phileo* means "love," so we say *love,* not *phileo.* There are also several meanings for *love,* but in

English, we use one word. In Hebrew there are multiple words."

"Right." Cell nodded. "And in reading the Book of the Wars of the Lord, we took *neiothen* down to its meaning, which was 'those from below,' rather than accepting the prophecy may have meant Neiothen as a name. That for the sake of the Book of the Wars, when directly transliterated as the whole word, it's a proper noun."

"And what makes you think this is legit?" Leif asked. "I mean, that Neiothen are real, and it's not referring to someone from below. Because we used that phrase to go to Burma, and it was right."

"And I recall," Lawe asserted, "telling y'all that this Neiothen thing was a hoax bred on the backs of veterans about some experimental program."

"I have no intel on that," Cell said. "I only know what this fragment and the transliteration tell us."

The words had a bitter taste to Leif. "So we're talking about 'and those from below were come, the mighty and the vigilant like a plague.' That's who you're talking about?"

Cell blinked, glanced down at a handheld. "You said that word for word."

"Yeah, we stopped being impressed with his near-perfect recall years ago," Lawe grumbled.

"So you're saying it should be read as 'and Neiothen were come, the mighty and the vigilant like a plague.'" Leif leaned forward. "Which means we're hunting *people* who are likened to a plague."

Expression heavy, Cell nodded. "Yeah. Soldiers, probably."

"When we first considered the text of the scroll," Harden spoke up, sounding older than his forty-something, semibalding self, "we read it as if those people were saviors. Avenging angels, if you will. But the more we look at the wording, the more we examine the context and references, we are convinced that *they* are what we need to stop."

"We all are," Dru pronounced with a sharp nod. "Which is why we've taken our time analyzing and dissecting what little we have. It's also why it is absolutely imperative we reacquire that book. I have Cell and Mercy looking for it, scouring channels and searching for trigger words."

"Think that'll work? It's not like someone will be on the radio, saying, 'Yo, Big D, I got the book that talks about the Neo-whatever.'" Though Culver taunted, he was concerned, as evidenced by his thinned lips and knotted brow.

"True, but we have specific intel and terms to aid us in that search," Mercy reassured them. "This isn't our first rodeo. And it has worked"— she eyed Cell—"to a degree."

"Right," Cell said. "So, using that terminology, I started following a hunch that maybe Neiothen—

whether an organization or whatever—was tied to a government project. It's a delicate process, digging into these channels without tipping our hand or drawing attention. However, it seems likely that the Saudi Arabian wedding murders are connected to the Neiothen, because I think the suspected killer, Wafiyy Ibn Sarsour, is on that list."

"Bull," Leif objected. "I saw the names you pulled, and he wasn't there." But what if . . . "Unless there are more you haven't shared with the team."

"Why would I hide vital intel from Reaper?"

Culver frowned. "Reaper?"

When the others shared the same confused look, Cell shrugged. "We needed a code name."

But Leif noticed Cell hadn't denied withholding information. "There was no Wafiyy Ibn Sarsour in that excerpt."

"True," Cell agreed, seeming a little too happy. "We aren't going to look in the Book of the Wars and find Culver Brown."

"Right," Culver asserted, "because I ain't one of them."

*"Because,"* Cell said, "the names in the book are more like code names or ancient call signs. And the three I was able to lift from the excerpt have been decrypted. Interesting thing to note: all of them mean *warrior* or *fighter*."

"If they're call signs," Lawe asked, "how were

you able to connect one of them to this Waffle person?"

"As I explained," Cell replied with a growl to his words, "we've been using keywords to track down the book, but I've also used those words to"—his gaze skidded to Dru then quickly away—"lurk on foreign servers."

"Lurk," Leif repeated.

Cell nodded. "I have a worm digging under the radars of certain military and government servers. It's looking for trigger words. When you walk through an airport, NSA, CIA, etc., can pick up words, filter out insignificant ones, and isolate key phrases connected to possible threats. Using a similar but not nearly as sophisticated program—due to lack of time—I've got my worm-bot searching keywords to identify these next two Neiothen. When it detects any of the trigger words, it'll shoot a code back to C&C. From there, I figure out how to get into the server and retrieve the data."

"C&C?"

"Command and control."

"Why not just have the worm send back the intel?" Lawe asked.

"Because," Mercy spoke up, meeting Cell's gaze, "most of the servers he's got his furry little friend digging around in are very sensitive."

"If the Neiothen really are a super-army, then intel about them—and the identities of those involved—is clearly TS-1 clearance or above," Cell said, "so there are most definitely measures in place to alert them any time that information is accessed or leaves their servers. Which means it's a freakin' flaming arrow straight into the heart of our bunker."

"Director!" The barked call rang through the bunker, pulling everyone's attention to a Marine. "You and Admiral Braun are needed immediately."

Iliescu stood, glancing at the team. "Stay close. We aren't finished."

# CHAPTER 4

## REAPER HEADQUARTERS, MARYLAND

Four hours later, the deputy director and admiral returned with grim expressions, and the team regrouped at the main hub table.

"MI6 relayed a video interview with Wafiyy Ibn Sarsour." He nodded to the wall, and Braun hit the lights as the video went live. "There is about an hour's worth of footage here, but for our purposes, we're focusing on this section."

The video looked to have been shot in a hospital and showed a screen split in three—the larger portion focusing on the killer, the upper right zoomed in on his eyes, and the lower right displaying a series of vitals, including heart rate.

*"Why did you kill the royals and the king?"*

*Eyes hooded, Wafiyy shook his head. "I didn't . . . I-I don't know."*

*"But you did, you put the poison in the drink."*

*"Yes." His eyes sharpened as if he remembered something. "It was an order."*

*"From who, Corporal?"*

*"I—" His gaze went distant again. "I don't know."*

*"You had the poison."*

"No, I didn't."

"It was in your sleeve."

He frowned. Sweat beaded his brow, and a busted lip added to the macabre scene. "I . . . know. But I don't know why."

"Was this your mission? Kill the royals and then kill yourself?"

"No! Why would I? I was getting married."

"What does Harbah mean, Wafiyy?"

Again that sharpened gaze, as if life came back into focus. "My code name. The initiation code—no, activation—" He squeezed his eyes and growled in pain. The vitals went crazy. "Stop them. You have to."

"The codes—"

"Yes," he said around clenched teeth, as if fighting something, "two codes—one for activation. One for initiation. They activate us. Then initiate our mission."

"What mission?"

"I . . . I don't"—another long growl—"I don't—" He screamed. "Make it stop."

Lights flared in the hub once more, and the screen died, but a buzzing over that name tremored at the back of Leif's mind.

"He goes on like that for a while," Braun said. "They didn't get much after that, but they're still trying. Some think he's just messing with the interviewers because half of what he says doesn't make sense."

Peyton shifted. "So . . . they're what, operators? Spies?"

"Assassins." Defiance spread across Iskra's olive complexion, indicating the strength of the woman who'd been a hired killer for years. "That is what you are suggesting, yes?"

The director nodded. "It is."

"However," Admiral Braun said, "do not think that we can simply go through our phone book of spies and find these operators. The names in the Book of the Wars are not directly tied to active operators or operative call signs to our knowledge. From what we can tell, the Neiothen are sleeper agents. That would explain a lot, since Ibn Sarsour wasn't a spy. He was British SAS with an impeccable record and was, at the time of the murders, assigned to security detail for a British royal family whose daughter was marrying a Saudi prince. Since the killings of his brother and father, that prince is now poised to become king."

Lawe grunted. "And nobody finds that suspicious?"

"Everyone finds it suspicious," Dru countered. "But the kid nearly wet his pants watching his father die. There's no sign he was aware of or a party to the murders."

"Maybe he was sympathetic but not active." Saito glanced around the room. "He wanted to rule but didn't have a way, so ArC stepped in and said—here, we'll kill them if you'll be our lapdog."

"We thought the same thing," Braun said, "but we have probed deeply into the prince's connections, banking, and business dealings. There is nothing linking him to Ciro Veratti or any other known ArC higher-ups."

"So what are you saying?" Leif asked, frowning.

After Braun nodded to her, Mercy sat up and worked her laptop. "Through witness testimony and videos from the wedding, we know a voice spoke over the secure communications used by the security personnel on-site." She hit a key.

*"Six, you're needed by the king."*

*"Copy. Moving in."*

*"Harbah. Two. One. Five. Initiate rise. Rise. Rise."*

*"Who is this? Clear the line!"*

Buzzing hit the back of Leif's head. "Harbah." Finally connecting the dots, he rammed his gaze into Cell's. "That was in the book."

Cell nodded. "Yeah, it is."

"So like Iskra said, we're hunting assassins," Leif thought out loud. "Assassins who, according to that prophecy, will turn the lands to blood and be a plague."

"Sounds a lot like the four horsemen of the Apocalypse," Culver noted, stroking his red beard, something he did while deep in thought or concerned. Or both. "Wasn't one of them Death?"

"The others were Conquest, War, and Famine." Leif roughed a hand over the back of his neck.

"But remember," Mercy said, angling in, pointing at them with a stylus, "the Neiothen are tied to the Armageddon Coalition—ArC—who want to beat Armageddon by taking over the world before the biblical prophecy can be fulfilled."

"Doesn't that just blow your mind, thinking they can outrace God?" Culver clicked his tongue.

"To them," Baddar said, "the Christian Bible is wrong. That is why they push to do this, to prove God does not exist."

"Well, that. And rule the world," Lawe said. "And turn the land bloody."

Leif was ready to get down to business. "You said you had more names—did you connect them?"

"We do, and I did," Cell said. "The next one listed in the Book of the Wars is Hami. Which, thanks to the Harbah recording, I identified."

"How did that help?"

"Took a shot in the dark," Cell admitted. "The numbers seemed significant, so I played with a series of numbers and code names. Hami came up pretty fast, so we're hoping that's a good omen. The worm is still searching for the others."

"Hami is the call sign for Qiang Kurofuji," Admiral Braun announced, seemingly annoyed with Cell's long-winded explanation.

"Japanese?" Saito said, sitting a little straighter.

"Actually," Cell said, "Kurofuji was born in Hoboken, New Jersey, to Chinese immigrant parents."

"Then why is his name Japanese?" Saito asked.

Cell shrugged. "Dude. I have no idea. Just is. Maybe his mom had an affair with some Japanese guy."

"Moving on." Braun splashed a photo of their target on the wall. It was a standard military photo of a Marine in front of the American flag. "Kurofuji was Marine Force Recon. Got out last year and went private contract. At this time, we only want to bring him in to talk."

The obvious prickled at the back of Leif's neck. "Contract company? Do they partner with U.S. forces?"

"They do."

"So have one of our guys bring him in."

"Already tried," Dru said with a huff. "He and his team were embedded in Africa. One night, he up and vanished. Nobody's seen him since. I want Reaper heading over there to find them. Find something that will prove or disprove this Neiothen theory."

"Find *them?*" Leif asked.

"Right." Cell eyeballed his tablet. "The second name we were able to pull from the USB scans was Arvi—"

"You got all that since the Saudi killing?" Leif wasn't buying it.

"Just needed the key to unlock the secrets." Cell didn't meet his gaze. "Um, so—Arvi. We tied that to a heavily redacted Navy file. In fact, when I snagged this off the system, something went wonky."

"Wonky?"

"Wonky," Cell confirmed with a nod. "And now we can't get the file to pull up again." He tossed the device onto the table. "We may have exposed ourselves."

Lawe muttered a curse.

Cell nodded toward the wall. "This is the only part we could get. They sent a scrambler through to blur everything, but we were able to save this. Last name, Gilliam. First name," Cell continued, "as you can see, got butchered before we could barricade the file from their scrambler. The middle letters are too blurred to be decipherable."

It was Leif's turn to curse, but he bit it back, waiting. Staring at the writing on the wall: CAR . . . N.

"Carsen Gilliam," he said, unwilling to believe what this meant. "I worked with him. Good guy."

Dru snapped his attention to Mercy, who had already lurched toward a keyboard. She quickly typed in the name and waited for the results.

Leif's mind refused to connect these dots. "No way. No way I accept Carsen is a part of the Neiothen."

"That's just it," Braun said. "All the intelligence

shared since this event speaks to the fact that everyone who knew Wafiyy Ibn Sarsour called him fiercely loyal and patriotic. Friends, battle buddies, and family said he loved his country and work. That he'd never do something like this."

"Yet," Lawe said, "we have proof that he did."

Mercy looked up from her keyboard. "As of 1700 hours yesterday, Carsen Gilliam is MIA from the FOB in Afghanistan from which his unit was operating."

"Should we be concerned," Lawe asked, glancing around, "that these two are both American?" He folded his arms.

"Yes"—Dru pitched his file on the table—"be concerned. But as to nationalities, we have no way of predicting that. However, a pattern does seem to be developing. What we know is that they have skills. Right now, the best thing we can do is bring them in."

"Rules of engagement, sir?" Saito asked.

"Bring them in—at all costs."

# CHAPTER 5

## REAPER HEADQUARTERS, MARYLAND

Trust was a rare commodity right now. And he had a gap to bridge, so Leif turned to Iskra. "Where would you start this hunt? Tell me, and that's where we'll go."

"Actually," she said, "I think . . . I must stay here. For Taissia."

He frowned, sensing this was about more than her daughter. "You're assigned to the team."

"I know. But she must come first until I get things sorted." Iskra sounded like she needed to convince herself. "Taissia needs me. I have no one to look after her when I am gone."

"I do," Leif said. "Canyon and Dani might let her sleep over. I bet my nieces and nephews would be good buddies for her."

Iskra hesitated, turning her head so that her long dark hair slid over her shoulder, as if that inky color was her grief spilling over. Killing him with the hurt and the anger roiling through her eyes.

But she hadn't rejected the idea. "I'll make a call," he offered, hoping to win back some of the brownie points he'd lost going incommunicado. "Okay?"

She still hesitated.

"I can see you want to go on the mission. Don't do this just because you're mad at me."

Indignation flared through her irises. "I am doing this because Taissia depends on me for her safety. I am all she has, and she is all I have." Her breath tremored as her meaning wedged between them like a concrete wall. "But I also do this because of *you.* If you cannot show me simple consideration and respect by letting me know you are alive—that you have returned from wherever you went—how can I trust you with my child?"

Catching her hand, he swallowed his pride. "I get it." But things were seriously whacked, and that void couldn't handle both of them. "I had to do this—"

"On your own." She flung off his grip. "I made fine progress finding my brother before this team. Clearly, I need to take care of this and my daughter. On my own."

"Iskra, pl—"

"Runt?" Peyton Devine came out of the hub with intention in her stride, but she slowed and glanced at them. "Sorry. When you have a minute."

But Iskra was halfway up the steps out of the bunker.

Leif deflated, sliding a hand down the back of his neck. He forced his gaze to Devine. "What d'you need?"

"First," she said, arching her brow toward the stairs, "you need to fix that."

"I was in the middle of trying to when you interrupted." He huffed and started back to the hub. "So. What's up?"

"I want to go with you to look for Gilliam."

"Why?"

"Because I think I know his sister."

At his station, he turned back to her. "Carsen?" He dug through his mental file on his Navy buddy. "He never said anything about a sibling."

Devine shifted on her feet. "I'm not certain it's the same Gilliam, but there was a Sienna Gilliam in my unit. She had a twin brother."

"Let's find out." Leif motioned her to follow. "So you two were friends?"

"Kind of," she said with a lazy shrug. "If you count enemies as friends."

"Seriously?" Surprise lit through what he knew of the winsome Peyton Devine, former NFL cheerleader-turned-Army-cultural-support-unit-member cum sniper. One of the best assets in the field. "I thought enemies were against your religion or something."

"Yeah, well, the ones I haven't put a round through are few and far between." She pursed her lips and shrugged. "It's a long story."

He angled into the door of an office just off the hub. "Cell?"

"Right here, Usurper."

"That's getting old."

"Just like you."

Leif smirked, abandoning the banter. "Can you confirm Carsen Gilliam had a sister?"

"I . . ." Cell frowned. "Uh, lemme check, see if any next of kin is listed." He scanned the files. "Not seeing anything, but like I said, they scrambled the file, so what I have is more than half redacted."

"What about her record?" Devine suggested. "Check Sienna Gilliam."

Cell's fingers flew over the keyboard. He grunted. Frowned. "Not seeing . . . She listed next of kin as Brandon Gilliam, father." He scanned the data. "Wait—here." He chuckled. "You'd be surprised what you can learn about people by looking at their life insurance beneficiary. Listed as Carsen Gilliam."

Devine seemed pained.

Dru stalked into the hub and spotted them. "Made some calls. Fort Lee is expecting you. Get over there and find out what you can about Gilliam. I'm working on getting you to Africa to hunt down Kurofuji."

"Understood," Leif said, noting the team huddling up. "Devine thinks she might know his sister, so I'm taking her with me."

"Director?" Mercy said. "I just found a condo in New York City under Kurofuji's name. We should send a team to look around."

"How'd he afford that on grunt pay?" Lawe asked.

"Good question. Find out," Dru said. "Mercy, go with Culver and Lawe to check that out."

"Man, isn't this what the DIA's for, investigating?" Culver asked.

"We need this intel retrieved before anyone's the wiser or it's redacted. Neither of these men has done anything wrong other than vanish."

"That vanishing thing is a problem, though," Cell said. "Why would they vanish if they were innocent?"

"Roger that." Leif thumbed toward the door. "Baddar, Cell, Devine, let's head out."

Iskra hadn't meant to lie to Leif, but he wouldn't like the methods she needed to use to get answers. But it was . . . tricky. After picking up Taissia from school, she returned to their apartment. Once Taissia had a snack and cartoons playing, Iskra retrieved her laptop. She might have shed the persona of Viorica, but she still had her contacts and skills. While Leif looked for the missing soldiers, she would find her brother.

Mitre was out there somewhere. And now she had three more names to work with. She pulled up the picture of the last time they were together before she was sent to Hristoff. A snapshot outside a church. He'd had his arm around her, their grins infectious and wild. Back then, she thought they would be together forever. That he would always be there to protect her. Instead, she never saw Mitre again.

Enhancing the image, she studied the oh-so-familiar scar on his right hand, between his thumb and index finger. A scratch of three lines, two parallel, one capping them off. *N* for Neiothen. Just as Bogdashka and Vasily had suggested. Just as she'd told Leif. Though they listened to her words, she had been dismissed.

But there was someone who would take her seriously. Someone who had the necessary resources. Iskra lifted her phone from the counter. Stared at it, knowing if she did this, if she made this call, Leif would never forgive her. It wasn't every day she climbed into bed—figuratively— with the enemy of the man she loved.

She bristled. Why was she worried about Leif? He had not cared about leaving her and Taissia while he hunted for answers. He thought she did not know where he went, but there was a reason Viorica had become known worldwide. Something happened to Leif a few years ago. He said he had lost six months of his life and was determined to find them.

Phone to her forehead, she struggled. She did not want to break his trust. He had given it so freely in one respect. Withheld it so violently in another.

*What is wrong with you? You are Viorica! The Wild Rose . . . of a dead man.*

Hristoff might be dead, but she was not.

She lowered the phone to dial.

Before she could, it rang. An unfamiliar number appeared on the screen. Drawing in a breath, she disregarded her better judgment and hit TALK. "Hello?"

"Hello. Is this Iskra?" a female voice asked.

"Who is this?" she asked. How had she been found? Was she in danger? Was Taissia? She eyed the living room where the little head rested against the sofa.

"I'm Danielle Metcalfe, Leif's sister-in-law."

# CHAPTER 6

## FORT LEE, VIRGINIA

"Just like the military," Cell muttered. "Hurry up and wait."

Metal back digging into his spine, Leif shifted on his chair. "Designed to make us sweat."

"But we're not in trouble," Cell noted.

"Then why are you in my office?" Major Acton barked as he stalked into the confined space.

The four of them came to their feet, and Leif met the officer's gaze. "Major, thank you for seeing us. It's our understanding you were notified by Deputy Director Iliescu that we were coming."

"I was," Acton said, setting a file on his desk, "but I want to hear it from you."

Baddar closed the door and gave one of his infectious smiles, which seemed to unnerve the major.

Leif inclined his head. "We're here to talk to one of the soldiers under your command."

"Why? What's he done?"

"Besides going AWOL?" Leif knew the major wasn't happy. "Look, I get it—not cool that a CIA-DIA-DOD unit comes looking for answers on your territory, but your uniform"—he motioned to the major's ACUs—"suggests your priority is the safekeeping of this country and its citizens."

"I don't need a lecture, Mr. Metcalfe."

"None intended, sir," Leif said, backing off a little. "However, our purpose here isn't one we're authorized to discuss. Now, we can waste time and jeopardize progress, or you can help us out." Noting the major's expression hadn't budged, he pressed on. "Or if you refuse, I will report back to Admiral Braun your unwillingness to cooperate."

"Braun." The major stiffened. "Alene Braun?" It seemed his brain was finally firing on all cylinders as a look overtook his face that asked, *One of the joint chiefs?*

Leif nodded.

Acton huffed and dropped into the chair behind his desk. "I know little about Gilliam. He was reassigned from Colorado last year. Exemplary record. Loyal patriot by all standards. Multiple commendations. The best." He nudged a manila folder. "It's all in there, including statements from his former CO."

Though Leif eyed the file, he didn't retrieve it. "When was he last seen?"

"His unit had been back about seven months. They redeployed two days ago. That's when I was made aware he hadn't reported in since the tenth."

Leif started. "A week."

Acton nodded.

Carsen had a week's head start.

"You said his team just deployed?" Devine asked and waited for a nod. "Is there anyone still stateside who knew him and would talk to us?"

"About what?"

"To see if anyone knows where he went, what he was thinking or saying before he went AWOL," Leif said.

Wariness parked at the corners of the major's gray eyes. "Not to my knowledge but like I said—he hasn't been here long, and my job is to make sure this base runs smoothly, not babysit personnel. There's no way I can be intimately knowledgeable about all three-thousand-plus on this base and their personal lives."

*A little defensive?*

"Where was he living?" Devine asked.

"Record says a townhome off base." Acton flipped open the file and fingered a line on the second page. "Missing Persons was filed by a Sienna Gilliam. Appears to be his sister."

Cell shifted. "Did she provide an address?"

"Just a phone number, and it's not local," Acton said. "But his residence is listed on his records. MPs went out there after his commander reported him AWOL. Nobody home. Not sure what good it will do you, but I suspect you're going to drive out there."

Leif smirked. "Good guess." He took the

file. Questioning Acton further would get them nowhere. "Thanks for your time, Major."

Back in their rented SUV, Leif stared out the windshield.

"You okay?" Devine asked from beside him in the front passenger seat.

"I'd really like to talk to some of his guys. Get a bead on what his state of mind was before he went AWOL." Leif pulled into traffic, allowing GPS to guide them to the residence, sorting through what they'd gleaned from the major. After a while, he eyed Cell in the back. "What was with asking him about an address? We had that."

"Dunno. Had this sense about the major. Felt . . . off." Cell looked out the side window. "Wanted to see if he withheld the address or something."

"Testing him?" Devine challenged. "Have we seriously gone that low with this?"

"No, *they* have," Cell countered. "Haven't you watched any spy movies?"

Devine sniffed, then focused on Leif. "So," she said quietly, "did you fix that thing we talked about?"

Leif kept his gaze on the road, irritated that she had the gall to push him on this. "Did you fix that thing with Lawe?"

She dropped her gaze, then pushed it out the window.

*Thought so.*

"What thing?" Cell asked. "Is this about Iskra?"

Leif again eyed him in the rearview mirror. "You like living?"

Cell bobbed his head. "It's about Iskra."

Thankfully the GPS interrupted and declared their destination was on the right. Leif eased to the curb and parked, staring at the townhome. Yard was kept up, but there were several papers lying around.

"Mailbox is full," Devine noted.

Leif climbed out and took in the quiet of the cookie-cutter neighborhood. Nearly all one-story homes. Probably the community's answer to housing for the ever-expanding base. A small step up from the barracks. Grunts didn't need more than a pillow and a flat surface to sleep on, but it was good for morale to get off base and decompress. Feel normal, or as close to normal as possible, for a few hours.

Gathering newspapers that littered the sidewalk as he made his way to the door, Leif stayed eyes out. The papers gave him an excuse to scout the side of the house, where he dumped the papers in a bin. Then he met the others on the small front porch and rang the bell. No answer, as expected.

"Cover me," Leif said, drawing out a pick set.

Cell sucked in a breath. "We are not seriously breaking in—"

"Iliescu said to do what we had to."

"Excuse me," a woman called from behind. "Can I help you?"

Pocketing the pick, Leif turned, the others already facing the woman.

"We're looking for Carsen Gilliam," Cell said. "Do you know him?"

But Devine's glower warned Leif that this was Sienna Gilliam. Either she wasn't still in the military, or she'd shed her ACUs for the day. Platinum blond, a little plastic injected around her eyes and lips, Sienna seemed to be trying to reclaim her good looks.

"And you are?" she asked.

"Leif Metcalfe," he said, stepping forward. "I worked with Carsen in A-stan."

She hesitated. "You don't look Army."

"Good." He smirked. "I'm Navy." Maybe he should try something. "Things . . . I needed a break." He shrugged. "Carsen told me to look him up if I was ever out this way. Just got reassigned."

"Norfolk?"

Leif didn't answer. Diversion was better. "Any idea when he might be back?" He motioned to the others. "We aren't here for long."

Sienna lifted her chin toward the porch. "If you'll let me get to the door, we can talk inside." She took a step forward. When her gaze hit Devine, she faltered. "Peyton."

Devine played it cool, angling her head. "Do I . . . ?"

"Sienna. Sienna Gilliam, we—"

71

Gasping, Peyton widened her eyes. "Oh my gosh!" She laughed. "I had—I didn't recognize you." She frowned. "It's the blond hair that threw me." That wasn't truth; it was a rub.

Sienna went crimson as she aimed a key at the door and unlocked it. "I'm trying something new."

"So you live here with Carsen?" Devine asked.

"No."

"You have a key," Devine pointed out.

"I helped him move in." Sienna shrugged. "I finally had a chance to come here since the base notified us he was missing."

Leif narrowed his eyes. The major had said Sienna filed the missing person's report. So which way was it?

She shuddered. "I can't believe he's MIA." Blowing out a breath, she entered the house. Hit the lights. Then moved down the hall.

"MIA?" Leif asked, recalling that they weren't supposed to know his status and nodding Cell ahead of him. They needed to look around, so he'd have to fudge his story somehow.

"Technically, I guess it's AWOL." Sienna tossed her keys on the counter and shrugged. "Failed to report in for duty one morning." She brushed her hair back, her gaze veering toward Devine but never quite making it. Then she flipped another switch, opened the fridge door, and retrieved a bottled water.

"That's weird for Carsen," Leif said, frowning

as he took in the small home. Not more than 1600 square feet, if that. Spartan furnishings. A sunken sofa, large-screen TV, and gaming console—the saving grace of anyone returning from deployment who didn't want to hit the bottle or pills—and a three-legged coffee table propped up with pizza boxes.

Sienna shook her head. "Mind where you step. Carsen never cared about housekeeping, just wanted his own space. It's a pigsty."

"Was he okay?" Leif ventured. "I mean, the guy I worked with in the field was all-in, sold-out to the mission. For him to do this . . ."

Hands in his pockets, Cell walked the perimeter of the living room, eyeing the bedroom and bathroom.

"Things changed for him about eight months ago," Sienna said, hugging herself. "He's my twin"—her gaze diverted to Devine and her lip curled—"and we were always close. Until then. That's when he became constantly angry and argumentative. Grew combative . . . aggressive." Wincing, she drew in a long breath and let it out. "I've never seen him like that."

"Crap happens," Leif said, knowing the agitated feeling that never really left your veins.

She skated him an annoyed glance. "I told him to get help, but Carsen insisted he was fine. Said he'd handle it." She frowned at Cell checking out the place. "You looking for something?"

Cell shrugged. "My lease is up in three months. Thinking about getting a new place."

While Sienna was distracted, Leif peeked into the bedroom, too, and spied a mattress thrown against the floor with a pillow and blanket. A box for a nightstand. Charging cable. The other bedroom was empty. It felt like he was missing something. It was here. But . . . what?

Baddar hovered close, his back to the others. His expression echoed the buzzing in Leif's mind. He shifted and eyed Leif. Something ominous flecked in the commando's eyes.

"Know how much he was paying?" Cell asked.

Sienna bunched her shoulders. "No idea."

"What?" Leif whispered to Baddar as he shifted around him, careful to keep his back to the women.

"It is like this home I go into with Muj. I—"

"Why are you even here?" Sienna hissed at Peyton, no doubt thinking nobody else could hear her. "Trying to destroy someone else's career?"

Leif glanced over his shoulder at the two women.

Devine's brow crashed into her green eyes as Sienna got in her face. "I never ruined anyone's career."

"Tell that to—"

"I'm sorry your brother is missing," Devine said firmly. Loudly. "I'm sure you're doing everything in your power to locate him and bring him home safely."

74

Sienna went crimson. "I do not need your *insinuations* or help!"

"Oh, sorry." Devine's soft features had hardened. Eyes dark, lips stretched tight, she was about to put some combat training to use. "I thought you might actually want to find Carsen. I didn't realize this was about *you*."

Time to interdict.

"Thanks for your time," Leif said, striding up to them. "Appreciate you talking to us. We should get going." He nudged Devine toward Baddar, who followed her to the front door with Cell poorly concealing a snigger as he ducked outside.

Leif started after them but felt a touch on his arm.

"Hey. Thanks for your help with that," Sienna said, her words snarled.

Somehow, he knew he hated this woman. "Sure."

"Do you think we could trade numbers in case I find something—or my brother?" It sounded legit, but her eyes told him it was more. And that *more* wasn't flirting.

"I already have your number," Devine called from the porch.

She'd been raised by a good Southern family. Mama grew up on sweet tea and sweet words. Taught Peyton to be loyal to God, family, and country. Taught her to give others the benefit of the doubt and turn the other cheek. But she'd turned so many cheeks with Sienna Gilliam during their year as CST members that she'd vowed never to do it again. She growled as she slapped herself into the seat and buckled up.

Leif smirked at her. "Never seen you get lit like that." He pulled the car away from the curb and headed back to the base.

"She is the one person on earth who can do it just by breathing the same air." Peyton gave a shrill growl this time. "I hate that woman. I hope we can find Carsen without ever having to deal with her again."

"There a history we need to know about?"

"Yeah, that was some serious venom you two were spewing at each other," Cell said. "What'd she do to you?"

Peyton scoffed. "What *didn't* she do? She was so jealous and resentful of me because of my NFL cheerleading career. More than once, she sabotaged my CST efforts with locals, which affected my job performance and promotion, not to mention putting our team at risk."

"What was she jealous of?" Leif asked.

Jaw dropped and eyebrows raised, Peyton gaped at him.

"What? I didn't—"

"Dude, you screwed up," Cell said with a laugh. "You just said there was nothing to be jealous about."

"No," Leif said slowly and carefully. "No, I didn't. I asked—"

"Even I know not to say such a thing." Baddar laughed from the back seat.

She had to appreciate the way even the big guy stood up for her.

"Not helping," Leif warned Baddar, but his blue eyes came back to her. "You're a killer sniper and a beautiful asset, but I meant what ate Gilliam's lunch?"

"Everything!" she snapped, hating the way even one encounter with Sienna had her defensive and reactive again. "She acted like my entire career and life were designed to compete with her. I was an NFL cheerleader, she was a college cheerleader. I made CST before her, got assigned to a spec ops unit before her, dated someone I shouldn't have—then found out she'd been crushing on him. It was like"—Devine touched her temples—"I couldn't walk into a room without somehow ticking her off."

"So, petty jealousy?" Leif scoffed. "Seriously?"

"When she affected my promotions, I started training to get out of CST and away from her."

"Sorry," Cell said, "but that was a whole lotta ugly back there for middle-school jealousies."

Peyton sighed and slumped against the seat. "I know." She squeezed her fists until her arms shook. "She brought out the worst in me. I wasn't at my best around her. Except with sniping."

She grinned. "She couldn't hit the fat side of an elephant at fifty yards."

Leif snorted a laugh.

"It's true!"

"But you seem happy about it."

That guilt Mama talked about was thick as country gravy. "I am—was. My skills behind the scope got me away from her." There was definitely more to it, but they didn't need to know what. They had a mission that had nothing to do with Sienna.

"Did you notice anything off about her, her story, or anything connected to her brother?" Leif asked. "Something bugged me in there, but I couldn't put my finger on it."

"That's because you are the wrong expert," Cell said, leaning forward in his seat. "Carsen didn't have much, but he did have some serious hardware and internet."

"For gaming?"

"Yeah, maybe, but where's his system?"

"Or his phone—charger in the bedroom but no phone." He met Cell's gaze again. "Did one come up when you were running his profile?"

"Not that I recall, but I'll get on that back at the bunker."

"One thing's bugging me," Peyton said, her thoughts and emotions whirling.

"Just one?"

She glowered at Leif. "Sienna was comfortable in that house. It wasn't her first time."

Easing forward, Baddar inclined his head. "She went into the house like it was her own. She knew where the lights were, that the fridge had water bottles."

"Yet she said she was just finally making it there." Peyton bristled.

"So . . ." Leif leaned on the center console, rubbing his jaw. "Sienna Gilliam is lying."

"But why?" Cell asked. "This is her brother—shouldn't she be worried?"

"The only thing that worries Sienna is position and power. If she wasn't stealing it, she was sleeping with it."

"Whoa, that's harsh," Leif said around a laugh.

"I warned you she brings out my ugly side. But really, is it harsh?" Peyton challenged. "Is it a coincidence she just so happened to show her pretty face at the same time we are there? The location we had just told Acton we'd be visiting?"

"Boom!" Cell said. "Told you that guy felt off."

# CHAPTER 7

## REAPER HEADQUARTERS, MARYLAND

"Can we talk?"

Leif stopped short, surprised to find Iskra in the bunker again. "Sure. Always." He guided her to the side, noting Iliescu and Braun talking near the hub. "What's up?"

"Your sister-in-law called me."

"Okay."

"No. It is not." Color flushed her cheeks. "I appreciate what you were trying to do—"

"I didn't have an ulterior motive," he said, feeling the need to lift his hands. "You said you had no friends or family here, so I reached out to mine." He wouldn't mention how much he hoped the kids would hit it off so Iskra would be more comfortable around his family. "It's important to be connected to people. And I figured it wouldn't hurt Taissia to have other children to play with."

She narrowed her eyes. "That's nice."

"I'm a nice guy."

"And a liar."

He blinked. "What?"

"You did not do that for my daughter."

"Then why did I do it?"

Iskra looked so conflicted with her shoulders

bunched and eyebrows drawn together. She darted her gaze to the hub, then back. "It was a nice gesture, Leif. But please—let me take care of these things."

Now it was his turn to frown. "I don't get it. I was trying to help—"

"I know." She seemed to struggle with something.

"You said you couldn't go on the mission because there was no one to take care of Taissia. Now that's resolved." He shook his head. "How did I screw up?"

"Because I don't need *you* to do these things for me."

"We are zero for two," Cell announced at the hub, severing their argument. "Yes, Carsen Gilliam has a cell phone. No, I cannot get a lock on it."

When iskra walked off, Leif sighed and joined the others around the conference table. "So it's either off or dead."

"Or he's somewhere signals don't reach."

"Pretty sure they don't reach hell," Lawe snarked.

"How can you know the condition of someone's soul?" Devine challenged. "I think you should look to your own, Adam."

"It was a *joke,*" he said.

"Lawe, Culver, and I found absolutely zero at the New York condo," Mercy reported. "It was more sanitized than an operating room before surgery. Not even sure I saw any fingerprints."

"So that's a bust," Leif said.

"Carsen's laptop is another story," Cell went on, ignoring the drama. "I can't trace it now, but two days ago it logged IP addresses in North Carolina, Georgia, then Miami."

"So he was on the move," Lawe said.

"Well, his system was," Leif countered. "Can't definitively prove that's where he was, but it's a starting point. Have you identified what was at the location of those IP addresses?"

Nodding, Cell clicked a few keys on his laptop. "A bookstore in North Carolina, an all-night pancake place in Georgia, and then a coffee shop in Miami. All free Wi-Fi spots."

"Are you able to see what he did on the computer at those spots?"

"Negative, not without the device itself or a direct link." Cell shrugged. "But Mercy could probably piggyback his system if we can catch him online next time."

"Of course I can," Mercy scoffed.

North Carolina, Georgia, Miami. "He was driving down the Eastern Seaboard, basically," Leif noted. "Why? Where was he going?"

"That's what I'd like to know," Dru said. "We're scouring SIGINT for him, but have yet to find anything. My guess is that he's looking for a quick, anonymous exit from the States."

"If he gets off U.S. soil, we are unlikely to find him again," Braun added.

"So we just sit and wait until he shows up?"

"Negative," Leif said. "We head to Africa to find Kurofuji."

## CAMP LEMONNIER, DJIBOUTI CITY, HORN OF AFRICA

"It's too hot here to be May," Lawe grumbled.

They'd landed and exited the plane and had to hoof it to the hangar in the African heat. After stacking their gear, they checked for updates from Iliescu and even had time to scout the mess hall.

"Thought we were meeting someone," Saito said as they settled back into their space in the hangar.

On the far side of the room, Culver and Lawe were going at it on the Xbox while Devine serviced her rifle and chatted up Maddox and Iskra.

"Okay," Cell said from the corner where he worked his laptop. "I've given y'all call signs to make it easier during sensitive missions. As I said before, the team is code-named Reaper."

"Reaper's cool," Saito said. "And our call signs?"

"Leif is still Runt, since it has no bearing on his true identity."

"And the rest of us?"

"Peyton keeps her field name, Coriolis—"

The former cheerleader looked up. "For the Coriolis effect. Any object moving horizontally on or near the earth's surface is deflected slightly off course due to the spinning of the planet." Nodding, she smiled. "It's legit."

Cell's expression seemed to waver between relief and pleasure. "So, Culver is Tabasco."

The southern guy snorted. "Because I'm just that hot."

"Uh, well, because of your red hair."

Lawe guffawed.

"Lawe is Badge."

"You mean badger?" Culver suggested.

"Dude." Lawe frowned. "Lame."

"It works—Lawe, law enforcement officer, thus badge," Cell countered. "Baddar is Smiley, Iskra—I'm stealing Mercy's nickname for her—Storm. And Mercy is Kitty."

Mercy pumped both hands in the air. "Yes! Katherine Pryde, folks, at her best."

"And me?" Saito asked.

"I hope you won't think this is racist, but I went with Samurai."

Saito's expression was implacable, but then he grinned. "An honor."

"So, now that we all have goofy names, let's get ready for RTB," Leif said.

RTB Concepts was the paramilitary contractor

that employed Qiang Kurofuji and the reason he'd been in Djibouti when he went MIA. While civilian contractors were paid well and often had approval to operate in-country, sometimes they didn't. Just as with any organization or entity, some were corrupt. Most weren't. Though it put him on edge to work with their kind, Leif set that aside. They were here to meet the men of RTB and find out what they knew.

Leif heard steps beyond the door before it opened and whistled to the team. Heads swiveled, games ended, and silence fell as a brawny, bearded guy in a ball cap entered, flanked by two equally beefy guys.

Slowly, Leif came to his feet. "Can we help you?"

"You Runt?"

He started toward the newcomers, sensing Reaper forming up. "Spill?"

The lead guy grabbed his hand. "That's me." He tossed his head to the left. "That's Dribbler, and the little guy"—which was like asking which mountain was smaller—"is Ghillie."

"Appreciate you coming out to help us," Leif said.

"No problem," Spill said as he tugged the brim of his hat, then folded his arms. "Glad to assist anyone looking into Fuji's disappearance. You ready?"

Noting Spill didn't care that he hadn't provided

Reaper's names, Leif grabbed his ruck, and the team did the same. Outside the hangar, they piled into two armored SUVs.

"So, what'd they tell you about Fuji?" Spill waved to the guards at the security checkpoint before they pulled onto the road.

"Well, I didn't know he was called that."

Spill grinned, navigating Djibouti City like a pro. "I hate long names, and so do the guys."

"Is that why you're called Spill?"

"Spiliotopoulou." He turned onto a congested four-lane road. "They used to cuss me out in Basic because they couldn't fit my last name on a tape or pronounce it. Everyone mangles it. And out here, you don't want people knowing your name anyway."

"Which is why you didn't care when I didn't introduce my team."

"All I care about is finding Fuji and making sure he's not in trouble or dead."

"I hear you." Leif tagged each street sign he saw, memorizing the route as they slipped deeper into the city, passing slums one second and a massive compound the next.

"Looks like Ghillie's hitting it off with one of your team," Spill said as he gunned it around a tangle of cars, the SUV barreling down a sidewalk.

Leif glanced back and saw the heavily tattooed guy deep in conversation with Devine. He snorted. *Ghillie.* "He a sniper?"

"We all are." Spill shrugged. "But he's obsessed with it."

"So's she." Leif scanned rooftops and alleys and kept eyes on the second SUV behind them. "What's the temperature like here?"

"Up and down," Spill said, knowing Leif wasn't talking about the weather. "Things have been tense, and now with the adviser's death . . ."

Right—he'd heard the American ambassador's adviser had been gunned down. "What's RTB's focus?"

"Mostly helping local military with training and security. When Lemonnier brings in VIPs, we assist."

"What was Fuji working on last?"

"We'd just signed a two-year contract with Global Initiative Alliance, who's looking to set up a company here."

"Haven't heard of them."

"Me either." Spill angled down a road flanked by cracking, peeling, abandoned warehouses. "But they paid well, so we took it."

"And Fuji signed on, too?"

"Happily. He'd been putting away money to get a place. Had a girl he wanted to bring over."

Maybe that was how Fuji paid for that NYC condo. "Foreign bride?" A klick down, the road seemed to end, and they were moving pretty fast toward it.

Spill shrugged. "Think it was an arranged thing.

He might've been born and bred in the good ol' US of A, but he was hard-core Chinese."

"And yet Kurofuji is a Japanese name."

"Yep. He said his dad was Japanese and died, then his mom remarried. His mom has some serious power over him. Know what I'm saying? Still has pretty big connections in China and was key in setting up the bride. Fuji was stoked—they'd Skyped and all that. He was hot for her."

"And yet he walked."

"Messed up, isn't it?" Spill shook his head as he lifted his phone, thumbed in a series of numbers, and flicked his gaze to the looming dead end. A series of concrete barriers set in a switchback pattern forced them to slow. A steel gate topped with barbed wire trundled out of the way, funneling them into a bottleneck between another gate that remained closed. Spill pulled in until the SUV's grill nearly touched the gate so the second SUV could squeeze in.

In his side mirror, Leif watched the first gate lumber back into position. When Spill entered another code, the second gate surrendered, allowing them into a parking lot. On his three there was a small garage-like structure. Straight ahead loomed what looked like an old apartment complex.

"Welcome to Fort Dodge," Spill said with a grin. "Where even the bullets dodge bullets."

"Sad," Ghillie said, throwing open the door and climbing out.

Leif scanned the whitewashed building as the second vehicle emptied out. "That's a lot of area to cover."

"Eight levels," Spill said, waving them in through the main doors. "All empty save the second"—he strode down the hall to the left and flicked open a door to a flight of stairs—"and what we call the penthouse, which gives us a bird's-eye view of the street and surrounding city."

They hiked up a flight, then in through a door to an elevator, which took them to the eighth floor and dumped them into . . . some serious luxury.

Dumbstruck, Leif hesitated at the main area.

Culver let out a long, low whistle at the space. High-tech and manned with a half dozen men, the center had a circular command area with five or six computers. Monitors hung from the ceiling at an angle. Around the perimeter were workstations and glass-walled rooms protecting tables and chairs. The far side had three doors, set equidistant apart. Offices, Leif guessed.

"Fuji's station is over there," Spill said, pointing to a cubicle in the hub. "His bunk's through here." He stepped back and flipped a door handle, moving into a hall lined with a dozen doors. "There are more bunks on the lower level, but we haven't used them in a while."

Cell shifted, messenger bag slung over his shoulder. "Mind if I check out his system?"

"Great minds think alike." Mercy slid up next to Cell and smiled at Spill. "I'm sure you have your security protocols in place so we don't bump into something we shouldn't see, right?"

Leif wanted to laugh—there wasn't a protocol in place that could block Mercy Maddox. And while he didn't condone her hacking one of their own, it could be exactly her skills that would find the unfindable on Qiang Kurofuji.

Lifting a hand, Spill looked past them back into the hub. "Jeeves!"

"Yeah, Boss?" A guy in a black T-shirt and jeans pushed to his feet from the far side of the circular setup, headphones around his neck.

"Show them Fuji's station and help them get logged in."

"Sure thing." Jeeves came around the hub and met Mercy and Cell.

"Doubt they'll find much." Spill turned back to the bunk rooms. "Besides video conferencing with his girl, Fuji wasn't a tech guy. Said he was old-fashioned. Didn't even like to read books on a device." After opening the door, he stepped aside and let them enter.

Grunting, Leif moved into the space, a place he couldn't call a bunk room. More like a four-star hotel with a bed, sofa, table, and kitchenette. A tapestry depicting Buddha hung on a wall.

"Son of a . . ." Lawe muttered. "I think I'm getting ripped off."

"We're always recruiting skilled operators," Spill offered.

"Back off," Leif said, forcing a smile he didn't feel. "He's mine."

"When am I getting that raise you promised?" Lawe asked as he walked the room, eyeing the packed bookshelves, nightstand, and coffee table.

"You got a bad memory," Leif said. "Gave you that raise when you left the Army for our team."

"Is that what that extra two dollars in my paycheck is?"

"Two? It was supposed to be one." Leif opened a door and found a closet with clothes on one side and on the other, shelves—ammo stacked neatly next to cans of chili. Nothing like priorities.

"Spill?" a voice called from outside the room.

RTB's chief moved back into the hall and glanced toward the main hub. "S'up?"

"HQ's on the line for you."

Concern flicked through Spill's face. "Coming." He looked at Leif.

"Yep." Glad for the opportunity to be alone, Leif waved him on. "We want to check around some more. We'll find you when we're done."

With a nod, Spill left them to their own devices.

"Seriously," Lawe grumbled, "we're getting ripped off with bunks and vinyl mattresses. I need to talk to Iliescu."

"Good luck," Saito muttered.

"It ain't all about money," Culver said, moving away from a bookcase to a small table.

"Arrogance, then?" Devine offered.

Leif scanned the spines on the bookcase. There were contemporary thrillers, historical accounts, a Bible, and a couple dozen paperbacks, but the majority were nonfiction about military operators who'd gotten out and needed a way to keep the cash flow strong. Lucky for those guys, their work could be shared—once it was declassified.

"Did you see this?" Culver asked. "This is some piece of work."

Leif glanced over his shoulder at Culver, who was studying the tapestry. Dark teal and orange were set off by cream-colored figures and a very prominent Buddha at the center. Surrounding him were several characters, each doing something different. "What is it?"

"Buddha," Saito said.

"I know that," Leif growled. A nebulous thought swelled at the back of his head but refused to take shape. "It has . . . meaning."

"Of course it does," Saito said. "In Chinese mythology, Mara is a demon. This is a painting called *The Assault of Mara*, in which Mara and his lusty daughters try to tempt Buddha away from the right path so he will not attain enlightenment."

There was something about this that went beyond its oddity. Mesmerized by the depictions within the tapestry, Leif focused on each figure to memorize them. He couldn't explain why, but it felt important. Significant.

Wait.

Leif shifted back. Buddha tapestry. He checked the bookshelves. Strode over and tugged the Bible from between two thrillers and flipped it open. Rifled through it, noticed some marks. A sticky note. Highlights. At the front, an inscription in Mandarin.

"Saito."

"Yeah?"

"Can you read this?"

Saito came over and eyed the Bible. " 'For Qiang and our future. Your most loyal Ru Shi'."

"And how do you read Mandarin so well, being American and all?" Culver challenged.

"Military wanted me to learn it for a mission. Quite extensive and intensive." Saito shrugged and glanced again at the inscription. "I took it as a challenge."

After a nod, Leif refocused on the inscription. Loyal. A Bible with notes scribbled in it. Read. Studied, it seemed. And yet . . .

"What're you thinking?" Saito asked.

"Dunno," Leif muttered, and glanced at the wall tapestry of blues and grays depicting the seated, round-bellied Buddha. "Why would Fuji study the Bible, then have a tapestry of Buddha?"

"Guess he likes religion," Lawe said. "All of them. Doesn't want to anger any of them."

"Or," Iskra said quietly, "he might have this for its artistic merit or cultural pride." She shrugged. "Maybe it was a gift or a souvenir."

Leif had to admit she could be right. Yet . . . "No. It's more."

"Runt." Spill had returned. "Got a call from HQ. Business owner on the other side of the city saw Fuji in his café a couple days back. Has footage we can check. Wanna head over and see what he's got?"

Leif hesitated. Glanced at his team.

"I'd like to stay." Devine came toward him. "I was hoping to talk more with Ghillie. He mentioned a nest on the roof."

"We'll hold it down while you're gone," Lawe said.

Leif hadn't been looking for permission, but that was exactly what they'd given him. Ironically, Lawe probably just wanted to stick around RTB to make sure Ghillie kept his nose in his own business, not in Devine's. Leif's hesitation was more about splitting up Reaper. Being away from his team. Which meant he couldn't protect them.

But they'd be safe with RTB.

There was nothing as annoying as a piggyback. That heat of irritation flashed through Mercy when she noted the new user surfing her cybertrail.

Laptop hooked up to Kurofuji's via a splitter, Mercy ran a dummy program over her real work to conceal her digging, but it seemed the so-called Jeeves wasn't your typical systems analyst. Since she and Cell had sat down at Fuji's system, the Brit had been too attentive. And chatty. But she started noting a pattern: when she went quiet, so did he. When her keys were clacking maniacally, so were his. Tracking her movement.

*Game on, Jeeves.*

"Heard you work for the CIA," he said.

In her periphery, Mercy noted that though Cell didn't lift his head, his gaze drifted to hers. He was either worried about or just as annoyed by the chatty contractor. Their affiliation with the CIA wasn't openly known. The Brit was guessing.

"So . . . Jeeves." She sat back, fingers on the keyboard, and squinted at him. "You really tolerate that nickname? Isn't it a bit . . . I don't know, degrading?" She kept working, noting her intent to incite worked.

"Around here, you don't get to choose your call sign."

"Shame," Mercy murmured. "I sure would." But then she recalled the new name Barc had assigned her. In a way, she *had* assigned her own name.

"I'm not ashamed of what I am," Jeeves said. "British isn't bad."

"Well, not all bad," Mercy allowed, but her

adrenaline spiraled. The coding she'd attached to his cyber movements was going wild.

Jeeves watched from his terminal. "What do they call you?"

" 'Master' is usually the first name," she said with a laugh. It came out hollow because something hiccupped in the system. A notable difference in the usual size of files compared to this one. *What is hiding behind door number five, Bob?*

"Smiley calls her beautiful," Barc injected, bobbing his head toward Baddar. "He was an Afghan commando known for his high kill record, so I'd be careful flirting with her when he's present."

No doubt buying into Cell's lies about that kill record, Jeeves slid a nervous glance at the commando, who sat to Mercy's right, smiling as usual. A good distraction as she logged a marker into the file so it'd be easier to find in the copied system when time allowed her to examine this more closely. It was all sleight of hand, made more ominous by the ever-attentive Jeeves.

"What are you looking for?" he asked for the fifteenth time. At least.

"Like we said," Barc ground out, "just going through his history to see if anything's out of the ordinary."

"Hey, y'all." Culver waved a half-eaten hoagie in the air. "Food's here." He motioned to the conference room that had been allocated to them during their visit.

"I'm ready for a break," Mercy said, unplugging her system. "How about you?"

Barc frowned at his screen, brown eyes flashing back and forth over what he was seeing. Poor lump wasn't as good at hiding what he found.

"Cell."

His brow tightened, his confusion apparently deepening.

*Why don't you just stand up and shout that you found something weird?*

"Cell!"

He blinked. Scowled at her. "What?"

She lifted her brows and cocked her head toward Culver. "Food. Let's refuel, then hit it again in a bit."

Several heartbeats boomed amid his hesitation. "Yeah," he breathed, but his attention again fell on the monitor. "Merc . . ."

"Merciful heavens, what?" she said, trying to play off his misstep in using her real name. "It's like you found some alien hiding in the computer."

His gaze hit hers, confused. Then understanding washed over him. "Ha. Ha." He skirted a glance to the side—in Jeeves's direction. Slapped his computer shut and unplugged it. "I'm famished." He grinned at Jeeves. "That's what proper Brits say, right?"

"Not unless they want to get killed," Jeeves replied.

Cell frowned.

Mercy turned—right into Baddar. She had to admit a lot of attraction toward the former commando, but the hovering thing . . . With a wavering smile, she navigated around him into the conference room. She grabbed a sandwich and chips before sitting at the farthest end of the table, facing the main hub, her back to the exterior wall. She didn't want people hovering over her shoulder and eyeballing her work.

Barc joined her. "Did you find—"

"Yep."

"Shouldn't we—"

"Nope." She pointed to the chair. "Sit. Eat."

He lowered himself into the seat. "But—"

"There are eyes on you, *Cell*."

He stiffened, hoagie gripped between his fingers. "I don't get it."

"Me either, but we play cool for now." She didn't know who or what Jeeves was, but she was starting to believe he was more like the Marvel Universe's supercomputer Jeeves, which took over Braddock Manor, than like some dimwitted special operator.

"I saw a suspicious group of males approaching, and I was given the clearance to fire. Lined up the shot—well over 900 yards. Took the shot."

Ghillie snorted as he smeared mayo on his hoagie. "One had a suicide vest, so I killed all five with one shot."

Peyton gaped. "That was *you?*" She laughed. "We were all talking about that."

His dark brown eyes sparked with pride and amusement. "It was luck."

"Every shot has a bit of luck to it, but that . . ." She shook her head as they moved down the food buffet together. "Sweet."

"So, are you the Coriolis who used that effect and managed to take out three Daesh holed up behind a wall?"

She grinned, thrilled someone knew. "I didn't realize that had been declassified."

He touched her shoulder in awe. "It *was* you?"

Peyton shrugged. "I'm a bit obsessed with the Coriolis effect. I mean, it all fits together for that perfect shot, right? The earth, the wind, the trajectory of the round."

"Exactly," Ghillie said, giving her a lazy smirk that had a whole lotta attraction attached to it. But it was a little too weird.

"Excuse me." Adam shouldered between them to reach something on the table. Jealousy roiled off him. Served him right, after what he'd done.

"In all," she said, deliberately pursuing more conversation with Ghillie, "no one will ever be like Hathcock."

"My hero. Well, him and Chris Kyle."

"Mm," she said, sipping a bottled water. "My brother had Chris Kyle posters on his wall and read his book. We all bawled when he died. Even joined the Chris Kyle Frog Foundation." When she glanced toward where Adam had been standing, he was gone. Her heart sank a bit. It was no fun taunting him when he wasn't around.

She and Ghillie ate their sandwiches while talking about their favorite long shots and shooters.

"You want to check out the nest?" he offered.

"Sure—yes."

She tossed her paper plate and water bottle in the nearby bin and trailed Ghillie out of the small conference room. Brushing off her hands, she scanned the bodies in the hub. Adam had vanished. Disappointment pushed her into the stairwell access to the roof.

It surprised her that she was looking for him. She shouldn't. He'd made his choice. Crushed the tar out of her. He'd have to live with that.


"What made you leave the service?"

The SUV jounced across the city, delivering them at seventy miles an hour to a residential area with buildings crammed up against one another, tarps and aluminum acting as walls. Women and children sat in an area that, if it'd had grass and seesaws, might be a park. A soccer game distracted the children from their impoverished conditions and rumbling bellies.

Their host knew a lot about him and the team. "I could ask the same," Leif said with a smirk, checking their six in the side-view mirror—and catching sight of Iskra in the back seat, squinting into the sun as the city whipped by.

Spill snorted. "I signed up with RTB for the money. Half mill on sign up, then the same each year. Hard to beat. Takes care of things, ya know?"

"No," Leif sniffed. "I don't know."

"If you're leading this team for what I guess to be the CIA or DIA, then you could sign on with RTB for at least as much as I did," Spill said. "Probably more, with inflation."

"You always proselytize this hard?"

"Any chance I get."

"Commission?"

"Twenty percent off the top." Spill had no shame.

Leif chuckled, glancing around as they continued. He wondered what Iskra thought of the contract lifestyle. She'd essentially been a contract operative most of her life, only she hadn't been paid. Well, not the way anyone wanted to be paid. "I'd like to talk to your men, especially anyone who knows Kurofuji well."

"That'd be Dribbler. They shared a bunk room for a while when we were at max." He glanced at Leif, his eyes shaded by ballistic sunglasses. "Anything you can tell me about Fuji and what's

101

happening? He was my guy. I mean—imagine if I came and started asking about one of yours. Or her." He glanced back at Iskra.

Though Leif smirked, he said nothing. Iskra held her own. If someone was looking for her, they faced a bigger problem than Leif's jealousies.

"Anything?" Spill pressed. "C'mon. I'm not an idiot. What's he mixed up in?"

"We're not sure," Leif said. "That he's now MIA"—he bobbed his head—"makes us more convinced and determined to find him."

"Well, y'all are some pretty serious slag," Spill said, glancing between him and Iskra, "so I know whatever you're looking into is messed-up bad."

"I would think," Iskra said from the back, "that having us searching for him would be indication enough."

"My point exactly."

"And you want me to go contract? Trade top-secret classification for money? No way. I like being in the know." Leif didn't really. Sometimes it just royally screwed things up. Yet it gave him an in for getting intel on those missing months.

"I don't know, man. Having that kind of knowledge sometimes isn't worth it. You have to sit on things you can't do spit about." Spill grunted. "Not sure I could handle that. I'm a man of action."

"I hear you."

Spill pulled to the side of the road and parked. "There's the shop." He gestured to a squat whitewashed building with a hundred different chocolate and soda posters plastering the façade.

Something glinted off the hood of the SUV.

Leif sucked in a breath and reached for his thigh-holstered weapon.

Spill laughed. Slapped Leif's chest. "That was Ghillie up in the nest, letting me know he's got a bead on us."

Adrenaline tanking, Leif struggled through a smile and climbed out, donning a brain bowl in the hope of keeping his gray matter where it belonged. It'd do little against a sniper's slug, though.

Iskra was behind him, taking in the road and buildings. "Something's off," she muttered.

"I feel it, too. Stay close."

They stepped into the shop, and Spill entered last, flipping the lock, smartly preventing anyone else from coming in and ambushing them. "*Salaam alaikum*, Dini."

"*Wa-alaikum salaam*, Mr. John." The man's smile was faker than the "authentic" iPods he had for sale behind the counter. "How are you?"

"Doing good. How is your family?" Spill said in near-perfect Arabic as he reached the counter and palmed it. He showed deference to the shopkeeper by asking after his family, but his gaze never stopped moving. He glanced at the window, then back to the short man with spriggy curls. "Got a call that you had seen Mr. Qiang."

"Yes, two days ago," the shopkeeper said.

Leif backed into a corner, keeping a line of sight on the front door, counter, and rear exit. Considering the sense of foreboding prickling his neck, he listened to the conversation but maintained vigilance and noted Iskra doing the same.

Across the street, shadows in the narrow space between two apartments skittered and shifted. A glint.

Iskra glanced at him, then back at the window.

"Yep." Cradling his weapon, Leif angled to peer down the street. Two vehicles—a beat-up Nissan and an old Toyota pickup—slid to a stop on the opposite corner. He backed up, keying his comms. "Coriolis, come in."

"Go ahead."

"You got eyes on our location?" He was hoping she was up in that nest with Spill's sniper.

"Roger that."

"Possible unfriendlies converging on this location." Had they been set up, lured here by the promise of intel on Fuji?

"What d'you see?" Spill asked, hustling closer, brow furrowed.

"Two vehicles just pulled up. Saw something in that alley across the street—possible spotter or gunmen."

Spill pivoted. "Dini, what—" He cursed at the now-empty counter area. "Out the back!" He started running down the aisle.

"Go!" Leif barked to Iskra, who was already in motion.

They trailed the owner to the rear, but before Leif reached the stockroom, he heard two things: shots in the rear alley and glass shattering out front.

"Ambush!"

# CHAPTER 8

## DJIBOUTI CITY, HORN OF AFRICA

Claxons rang through the RTB facility, yanking Adam to his feet. "What's going on?"

"They're under attack." Dribbler ran to a hub terminal.

"Who?"

"Spill and Runt." Dribbler hit the comms as he and another half dozen men jogged to a wall that slid aside, revealing tactical kits and weapons. They geared up, and he motioned for Reaper to do the same.

Adam didn't need to be told twice—but where was Peyton? Still on the roof with lover boy?

"Boss." Dribbler hustled toward the door, keying his comms. "We're heading down to the vehicles. ETA in ten. What's your sitrep?"

"Dini set us up," Spill barked, his voice carrying loud. Gunfire cracked over the connection. "We're holed up in the shop. Multiple shooters. Looking for an exf—"

"Grenade!" Leif's voice punctured the speakers.

Dribbler lifted a handheld. "Ghillie, you have eyes on the boss?"

"Eyes on the building, but not on him. Combatants have surrounded them." *Crack! Boom!* "Approximately fifteen, twenty closing in."

"Hold them off, Ghillie. We're heading down to the MRAP," Dribbler ordered as he darted into the hall and accessed a door to a freight elevator.

Adam joined him with Saito, Culver, and Baddar. The elevator dropped faster than his stomach could compensate, nearly tossing his hoagie back up his throat.

Dribbler grinned. "Sorry."

"Doubt it."

The guy laughed as he slid back the mesh and steel door. Three RTB guys were hoofing it up the rear hatch into the MRAP. A bay door climbed into the ceiling, spitting glaring afternoon sun into the open warehouse.

They sprinted into the rumbling mine-resistant personnel carrier, which heaved forward as Adam yanked the door shut and secured it. Lurching out of the garage, the MRAP seemed to fly out of the barricaded parking lot, knocking the main gate as it swung wide, and then they were barreling down the narrow road.

Ears ringing, Leif came to in a haze of smoke that made his eyes burn. A shape hovered over him. His arm flung out before his brain registered— Iskra.

She cuffed his wrist and nodded. She was speaking, but he couldn't make out her words.

He peeled himself off the ground and glanced around to get his bearings. The last thing he remembered was bolting toward the door and diving into the alley. An explosion had pitched him into a wall.

He cupped his ear and felt the sticky warmth of blood. But he had to unplug it or he'd be useless. Pressing his finger to his cartilage, he braced. Pushed in and released—and flinched at the painful pop. He stretched his jaw to ensure it was clear, and felt his adrenaline-drenched muscles resetting. "Where's Spill?"

Iskra gestured to his three, and when he looked, he tensed. Spill was laid out in the street. Bloodied. Not moving.

"No," he whispered, but then one of Spill's fingers twitched. "We have to get to him."

"Too exposed," she shouted over the scream of sirens and gunshots.

"Tabasco to Runt," crackled through the comms. "Come in."

Leif again touched his aching ear. "This is Runt."

"What's your location, over?"

"Northeastern corner of the shop."

"Copy."

"Spill's down but alive. What's your ETA?"

"Five mikes."

"Copy." They just had to hold their position for five minutes. That was doable. His gaze connected with the RTB leader, who shifted his head. Silent signals relayed through his eyes to get him out of there.

Leif patted Iskra's arm and pointed to the end of the alley. "Cover me."

After she gave an acknowledging nod, he sprinted toward Spill and grabbed his drag strap.

Fire blazed a trail down Leif's shoulder as he scrabbled backward. He growled but kept moving. Amid the report of Iskra's weapon, he hauled Spill to safety. The loss of heat and light as they fell into the shadow of the alley seemed strangely promising. He dropped next to RTB's chief and probed his wound—a round to the back had probably punched the breath from his lungs. His leg had eaten a bullet that struck his knee.

"Team's en route," Leif said, tearing off a sleeve to wrap the wound. "Just hang in there."

Spill nodded. "Dini?"

Leif hesitated. Glanced around. "Gone."

Scurrying back to them, Iskra looked distressed. "They're coming up the alley."

Crap. They had to get out of here. But without a vehicle and with Spill's leg messed up, they weren't going anywhere.

Unless . . . Leif eyed the roof. The wall. The dumpster. He turned back to Spill. "Keys to the SUV."

Spill considered him but dug them from his pocket.

Keys in hand, Leif said, "Stay here."

He launched himself at the dumpster a couple of yards away. Toed it. Bullets sprayed the building, chasing him up the corner he tic-tacked. He caught the lip of the roof and hauled himself over, rolling into a flattened position. He shimmied across the rough surface, tarred and dirty. Low-crawling, he avoided the section missing thanks to the grenade, and made his way to the front of the shop.

"Runt," came the preternaturally calm voice of Devine. "Two hostiles to your ten."

Frustrated, he stilled. "Need the truck. Spill's down."

"Hold position," she said.

Anticipating some Devine intervention, he lay there, tense about being out in the open on the roof, but also knowing that few people thought to look up when they were pursuing a target.

He heard booms seconds apart, and then came the telltale thump of bodies hitting the ground.

"Light and fast. More incoming, but you're clear for now," Devine said.

"Roger that." Leif rolled over the lip of the roof, dropped to the ground, and scurried to the SUV. Instead of using the fob, he unlocked the armored Suburban with the key and slid in through the front passenger side, staying below the windshield, and drew the door closed. He jammed the key into the ignition slot and cranked it. Rammed the shift into drive and punched the gas. Giving himself no more than an inch to look over the steering wheel, he gunned for the alley. Struck the wall. Righted the SUV and again nailed the gas. The SUV rushed to the end. The wheels groaned to a stop next to the dumpster.

Through the sliver of space, he saw Iskra look at the Suburban, startled, then smile. She came up. Her eyes went wide—her gaze locked on something else. He glanced to his nine. A man stood in the alley with a rocket launcher on his shoulder.

*Oh crap!*

Leif threw himself out of the truck just as a heated whistle streaked through the blazing afternoon. He dived into a roll and came up, sprinting for Iskra and Spill.

Fire erupted. He was lifted into the air. Suspended like some sick dream as the concussion whipped him around and flung him at the far wall like a toy soldier. Air punched from his lungs, he dropped hard. Groaned. Came up. Fiery daggers shot through his shoulder.

Across the alley, Iskra watched him, eyes a mixture of rage and worry. But she stayed with Spill, as she should.

Leif righted himself, growling and holding his injured arm close to his body. He staggered to his feet. Stumbled toward them.

Shots spit dirt and rock at him.

111

"Augh!" He shoved back. Flattened himself. Grabbed for his weapon, only to find it wasn't there. He cursed. Realized the futility of his situation, trapped on the opposite side of the road from Iskra and Spill. And shooters closing in on Iskra, who was out of ammo.

Rocks crunched. Whispers carried on the oppressive air.

*Move or die.* Leif rolled around the corner of the building. Eyed the ledge above. A bit high. He could do it, but his shoulder was dislocated.

Dislocated shoulder or dislocated head?

He hopped and grabbed the ledge. Strained as he drew himself up. Tried to reach with his bad arm—agony exploded. His grip slipped. He dropped. Stumbled back, grabbing his bad arm to keep it immobilized. Looked up.

Right into the business end of a rifle.

# CHAPTER 9

## DJIBOUTI CITY, HORN OF AFRICA

Though he knew he shouldn't, Leif threw himself at the guy. Dove into his stomach—shoulder ablaze—and drove him backward into the open street. A shot fired, but Leif had one objective: take the enemy down.

The gunman cried out and struggled. Pain rocketed through Leif, blinding him to anything but his injury. He slumped, growling, unable to think past it. When he rolled over, he again found himself staring at the man's weapon. Only this time the guy had a new addition—a dark stain on his shirt.

Shouts peppered the street. The gunman glanced toward his buddies.

Another report echoed through the steamy air as Leif reached for the weapon, unwilling to die like this, on his back.

The gunman dropped with a meaty thud near Leif, who scrambled up against the building seconds before he saw the hulking approach of an MRAP. It roared down the street and screeched to a stop. Leif tensed but then saw the rear door fly open. To his left, he heard another peal of tires and saw a second armored vehicle blocking the street.

Lawe and Baddar rushed to him and helped him to his feet. At the door of the MRAP, he searched for Iskra, relieved to find her hurrying toward him. He urged her inside first, then climbed up after her, moving aside as the others assisted Spill onto a cot they snapped into place over the seats.

Soon they were thrashing through the city and back to RTB.

"On three," Saito warned, holding Leif's arm with one hand and bracing his shoulder with the other.

Leif balled his fist and clenched his teeth.

"One, two—" Saito wrenched the arm back into its socket.

"Augh!" Leif went to his knees, growling. The pain slowly abated, leaving an angry reminder. Rubbing his shoulder, he lumbered to his feet. "You said *three*."

"Man up." Saito grinned.

Nursing his aching joint, Leif glowered, then turned his attention to Ghillie. "Where's Spill?"

"Getting stitched up now, but he'll be fine. He's had worse."

"And Dribbler?"

"He'll be back. I'll send him your way."

"Thanks." Leif spotted Iskra in the conference room near the windows. He went to her, slipping a hand onto her waist. "You okay?"

"We could have died."

There were, of course, measures in place for just

such a situation, but that wasn't her point. He slid his hand behind her neck. "I'll get you home." When she looked up at him, he felt his gut clench again, followed by a strange warmth. "I promise." He kissed her, as if that sealed the deal.

"Runt?" Mercy hung just inside the door. "Got a minute?"

"Sure." He gave Iskra's arm a reassuring squeeze, then focused on Maddox. "Did you find anything?"

"I haven't cracked it, but there's a file buried in there." She glanced back at the hub. "But I think we have a problem."

He waited.

"I think Jeeves is not who he claims to be."

Unsettling. "How's that?"

"He was able to track my every move, even piggybacked me. If I open that file, he'll see it—possibly destroy it—before I can download and back it up."

"Get it on your system, then—"

"No," Mercy said, her face pale. "That's just it. I think he managed to slip into my system."

Leif stared, unable to process that.

"Exactly." Her hazel eyes roared with indignation. "You can't do that unless you're *really* good. Remember how long it took DIA to even detect me when we were storm chasers?" She hooked her hands in her back pockets. "He did all that in less time. He plays dumb, but"—

she shrugged—"he's not. And I'm worried about what this file contains. Worried it'll vanish."

"Then just hold it for now. We'll figure out—"

"Figure out what?" Dribbler asked with a smirk as he joined them. But when nobody answered, he backpedaled with a nod. "Understood." He trained his gaze on Leif. "You asked for me?"

"Yeah, wanted to get your take on Fuji. Spill said you knew him best."

Dribbler gave a lazy shrug. "I guess. Shared a bunk room with him for a few months until things leveled out with the change of duty stations." He lifted a ball from his hoodie pocket and started snapping it against the wall, then catching it. Floor. Wall. Hands. Floor. Wall. Hands. "He was weird, if I can say that."

"How so?"

Another shrug. "Just all into that Jesus stuff." Dribbler wiped a finger under his nose. "I mean— nothing wrong with that, know what I'm saying? He was always watching preachers online and listening to that music."

"Hymns?"

"Nah," Dribbler said. "That's what was weird— it was pop songs or something. Had a beat. Good ones," he allowed, bouncing the ball over and over, "but it just seemed wrong for church and God. I mean, I can't see God rocking out, ya know?"

Leif wanted to smile. Dribbler probably had never been to a nondenominational church. "Was he acting weird in any other way before he went missing?"

"Nah. Same old Fuji. God, family, and country." Dribbler caught the ball. Looked at Leif. "Which is why this doesn't make sense. Why would he up and leave?"

"That's what I hope to find out." Leif decided to change tacks. "What about this Dini who ambushed us? Know anything about him?"

"He's always been this side of traitor. He'll sell you anything if it feeds his kids. But this—going all Rambo on Spill?" Dribbler scratched his head. "That's a new one."

It begged the question of whether Dini was just a local protecting his own against the evil West, or if he was colluding with ArC. Leif would need to work that out, but right now . . .

Christian. Jesus.

"Excuse me." Leif stalked out of the room, bugged about Dribbler's description of Kurofuji's faith. When a guy couldn't decide which god he served, was he playing it safe? Or . . . ?

"What's up?" Lawe trailed him down the hall to Fuji's room.

Leif stepped inside and eyed the bookshelf, wishing whatever was nagging at the back of his mind would just come forward and out itself. He strode over and grabbed the Bible again. Fuji had studied it. Even watched online sermons, according to Dribbler. The Bible had been a gift from his fiancée, which meant it was important. Right? Yet . . .

He shelved the Bible and moved to the tapestry. Strange. Buddha at the middle. A journey. Pilgrimage. And the surrounding images or whatever they were called seemed . . . familiar.

How could it be familiar? No, it was just that something about this bugged him. He touched the tapestry. All four corners were secured, firm. In fact, the entire perimeter was taut. Hard. He tugged it. The left corner swung toward him. He flinched as it shifted and began to drop. He caught the edge, muttering an oath at the weight.

"Holy secret ciphers, Batman," Maddox muttered, rushing up to him. "Look!"

Leif struggled to hold the tapestry, which felt more like a giant wobbly picture frame, then set it aside. He glanced back up and stilled, stunned. "It's a data wall."

Saito eyed it, too. "Most of that is Chinese—a festival, an article on Beijing, the People's Liberation Army." He motioned to a piece of paper. "That's an article on the spring festival."

"Those are blueprints," Lawe said, pointing to another pinned item. "For what?"

"No idea." Leif examined the corners of the schematic, looking for identifiers, but there were none.

"It's all related to China," Saito said, his tone heavy.

"So he went to China," Leif muttered, piecing it together. "His target is probably there."

"Whose target?"

Leif pivoted to Spill, who leaned on a crutch in the doorway. "You're up—"

"What's happening?" Spill's tone was hard, businesslike.

"Found this behind the Buddha tapestry," Leif said, nodding to the wall. "Articles, features, profiles, schematics."

"For China," Spill said. "That's what your guy said."

"It appears so."

"Why would Fuji have a target?"

Leif shrugged. "We don't know. Intel provided his name as a possible operator tracking a target. After learning he was MIA, we came here to find out who and why."

"What else?" Spill demanded.

Not answering, Leif stared back. No way could he divulge more, and the RTB chief knew that.

Spill's jaw muscle jounced. "I think it's time you and your team left."

"Agreed."

## 32,000 FEET OVER AFRICA

"Okay," Maddox said, adjusting in her seat aboard the jet, "to prevent any blowback compliments of Jeeves, I isolated the file from Fuji's system

119

at RTB and offloaded it to a separate, contained server and system." She bounced her gaze to Leif. "Oh, and I'm totally digging up his bio. That man is not just an analyst."

"Neither are you."

"Maybe, but while I'm HackerGirl, he's the Braddock Supercomputer. It was evil—tried to kill its own creator." Her lip curled. "Jeeves is sick enough to do that."

"Why? Because he managed to get that packet on your system?" Cell asked.

"Yes," she hissed. "His intentions were malicious, and that ticks me off. There was no call to try to crash my system."

"Maddox," Leif prodded. "What did Fuji hide?"

Her eyes hit Leif. "You realize he violated me."

"Violated your computer."

"Same thing," she insisted. "Opening the packet now."

Shifting his gaze from her to the wall, Leif watched the screen populate with a couple dozen icons.

"I've created a subroutine to send each of these to Command as they open," Maddox said quietly, "but I'm waiting for one to nuke my system."

"You said you moved this to a different system."

"Yes, but that doesn't mean it won't tick me off if it blows."

"Understood. Open them up."

Maddox went to work with the keyboard, then glanced at the wall screen. "That's . . ."

"Mandarin," Saito offered. "Looks like a list."

Leif had no knowledge of the language, so he'd have to get read up.

"Uniform, badge, rubber shoes," Saito read. "It's a supplies list."

"Print it," Leif said. "Next one?"

A document with an image of a man and a record of some kind. Again, all in Mandarin.

Saito lifted his chin. "It's the military personnel file for a Lieutenant Li Chongyang in the People's Liberation Army."

Four documents were extensive articles on the spring festival.

"Next," Leif said, a dead weight settling into his gut. They knew where they had to go, but this wouldn't be pretty, inserting into Communist China to stop an assassination. If caught, they'd likely get charged with attempted murder, not with interdiction of said attempt, and vanish like so many others into a prison camp.

Maddox clicked the next file. A collective gasp sped through the room as dozens of files filled the screen. "They were all in one folder," she said. "All pictures."

"Well, well, well," Saito muttered. "That's General Chang Xi."

Leif glanced at the image. "Who?"

"The executive of the Ministry of National Defense." Saito eyed them, looking a bit green. "He holds one of the most powerful positions in China's political system. He is an active military officer, a state councilor, a member of the Communist Party's Central Committee, and vice chairman of the Central Military Commission. Very influential in PLA decision-making." His expression darkened, and even though he was sitting down, he seemed to stagger. "If that is who Fuji is after, we *must* stop him. The wrong man in that position could be disastrous!"

"Let's get the director and Braun on the line." Leif nodded to Maddox. "Once you're confident those files are safe, send them to us. We'll divide and conquer before going in, so we know what Fuji knows."

"Leif," Iskra said from the side, "if Jeeves was really that advanced, if he was that determined to stop Mercy from recovering the files, do you think he is part of the Neiothen?"

He huffed. "Maybe. We'll send word to Iliescu, who can have him monitored, but we don't have the resources to spare on him right now." He tightened his jaw. "It's going to take a lot more than a potentially destroyed computer to stop us from getting ahead of these assassins. We can't be distracted and miss the chance to prevent the next murder."

• • •

"Have a minute?"

At the sound of Iskra's voice, Leif looked up from his device, then stood. "Yeah. Sure." He checked the tarmac beyond the hangar for the chopper they'd been waiting on for the last sixty-three minutes. "What's up?"

Iskra touched her forehead. "The explosion at the shop. It sort of worked me up."

Her voice had a strange quality that unseated his nerves. "Me too." Like time was short, and he needed answers now.

"I want to help the team, but I want to stay alive for my daughter even more."

He wanted to curse. He knew exactly where this was going.

"I'm going back," she said softly.

He felt his mood and expression darken, but couldn't stop it. Didn't want to stop it. "I thought—"

"Your family was brilliant to take Taissia, but I can't leave her indefinitely. She needs me. And I need answers of my own about my brother." She winced. "Besides, China has me on a kill-on-sight list after a botched mission."

"You said your brother's Neiothen. We could find him—"

"You're going to China. After a man who is *not* my brother."

Leif gritted his teeth, watching her rock-solid resolve slide into place.

123

"I have to return."

He'd fought enough losing battles to know when to surrender. "Okay." Then he huffed. "Fine."

But he couldn't fight the battle in his head that said, for them, this was the opening of a never-closing chasm.

# CHAPTER 10

## EN ROUTE TO BEIJING, CHINA

Civil disobedience had never been on his radar, but there were times when a man knew obeying orders wasn't in the best interest of the collective whole. It was a fancy way of saying their rules sucked. Like a giant vacuum in space. Or a giant vacuum cleaner in space.

Cell had gone to great lengths to secure his promotion within the DIA/CIA team, to get out of the field so he didn't see his friends die *ever again*. He'd had one dose too many of that pain.

And yet, here he was. Thirty-three thousand feet in the air, flying straight into another scenario that could leave him minus a few body parts, maybe even kill him or one—or all—of the seven other members of the team. That was why he'd named them Reaper. Because you couldn't kill Death. Right?

Heading into communist China wasn't exactly a vacation in the Caribbean. But they'd gotten wind of an event Kurofuji's Chinese target was hosting and Reaper would infiltrate.

But back to the treason at hand.

He drew in a long breath and stifled it. Fisting his hands over the keyboard, he braced himself.

Mercy was like none other—she could hack the best hackers. But she had ethics. A moral base that kept her this side of sexy. The notorious Mei did not. She was cruel and ruthless. Protecting Numero Uno was her soul conviction.

And she'd bought his soul.

Pressing his palms together, Cell touched his lips and stared at his laptop screen. Turbulence rattled it a little. Rattled him a lot. It was like a premonition, warning him not to do this.

He'd asked for help with the code names. The Book of the Wars had a series of code names written into its prophecy. Well, more like tucked in between the prophecies. They'd extracted the names, but it was like knowing the base code of computers was ones and zeros, but knowing nothing else. They had the letters, managed to compile them into the most probable order. Whoever had penned the cipher had foreseen that they weren't as enlightened as many in today's world believed and provided the letters in order. Otherwise there would've been a million different combinations. Not literally, but might as well have been.

So they had a list of names. Codes. And they'd only been able to match those to current identities. Three identities, to be exact. Nine code names. Three identities.

And therein lay the problem—the other six. Nobody named their kid Bushi. Well, he'd thought so until, upon searching, he discovered it was quite common.

So. Altogether, the book, though corrupted, had nine lines that contained code names. Therefore nine Neiothen. At least as far as the Book of the Wars and the falling-kings war was concerned. There could be more—a truckload more. Who knew? Due to the corruption and being unable to read them all, he'd made the connections slower than molasses in January.

But he still had to match the ones in the book to current names. And the military and intelligence branches complicated things by assigning their operatives or agents or officers—why were there so many terms?—unique names within their own communities.

Which meant Cell wasn't just sorting out an ancient code name. He was having to find some variant of it within intelligence communities and somehow—it felt miraculous at times—match it to a living person.

"Because matching two sets of code names wasn't confusing enough."

Even that work hadn't netted them all nine identities, just a lot of grief from the team and Dru, as well as accusations of slacking.

Great. Beautiful. What else was he supposed to do? How did he take the name Akin and sort the thousands of possible identities across the globe? Or Wu. Yeah, right. Wu who?

Cell sniggered at his inadvertent joke. But it was seriously messed up. There was only one recourse. He took his hunch and ran with it. If they were all warriors, it was possible they were connected to governments or militaries.

Then there was this very formidable queen of hacking named Mei. She never provided her last name, and good luck trying to track her down. Believed to have top-level clearance in some government, she'd saved many backsides and burned many others who asked for her help. Her services always came with a price: a person's soul.

Okay, maybe just their job or entire bank account, but it felt the same.

Her price when he posted a Mei-Day for help?

Well, it was pretty freakin' high. He had to give her all the intel he had gathered on the Neiothen, which could not only jeopardize the mission—what if she had ties to ArC?—but also his career or life. Maybe both. Especially when she realized he hadn't given her *everything*. Because there was something and someone else he feared more. The thing he only allowed himself to refer to as "it."

He couldn't think about that, or he wouldn't have the nerve to open the next packet. And they needed the names. Needed to track down the Neiothen.

Never in his job description when he'd re-upped

had he seen "track down and neutralize psychotic sleeper killers written about in a thousands-year-old text." And yet here he was. Staring at the screen doing just that.

*You're stalling.*

Yeah, yeah. So what? If Iliescu found out . . .

Exactly. If he found out about *it,* they'd never get the names. Or at least, not in time to stop ArC.

Cell double-clicked the next packet.

A tone sounded—Mei's signature, a sort of "the bell doth toll" thing. It reminded a person of the soul they were losing. This time, however, a darkly silhouetted head and shoulders appeared in the video. Ridiculous. Overkill.

"Here are the names connected to those codes," a masked voice droned. "Do not send me the other names."

*You just want to scare me.*

More like terrify. And it was working.

"These files are dangerous." Even with the voice masking, he heard a thick Asian accent. "I have too much to protect and will not sacrifice it for you. So I've added a subroutine to this package."

"No," Cell muttered, grabbing his screen as if it were her shoulders.

"I cannot have this come back to me. I can't risk it. So once the packet is opened, you will have forty-five seconds to record these names. Then they, along with your system, will be destroyed."

No no no. Cell snatched up his laptop and ran down the gangway of the private jet to the briefing room. Grabbed pen and paper.

"I am sorry," Mei went on, "but I must be sure you have not copied this to other drives or systems, so the program is already digging through and following every variant of this information. Any system with these names will crash, too."

"Son of a biscuit!"

"What's going on?" Leif stood in the door to the small briefing room aboard the transport, scowling at their harried comms expert.

Cell didn't look up from the pad of paper as he feverishly scribbled. "Nothing." He grunted, shaking his head. "Everything." His gaze again hit his laptop, and he twitched away. Frozen, brow knotted, he stared at the screen as color drained from his face.

"Cell?"

Whatever he'd read made him seem ready to puke, and he lowered his head.

"I can get you a barf bag," Leif offered as he slipped closer, eyeing the laptop.

Cell started mumbling. Though he hadn't looked up, his gaze flickered back and forth, evidenced by the twitch of his eyelashes.

"Cell." Leif leaned around him to see the screen.

Lightning-fast, Cell slapped his laptop shut. Straightened. Swallowed. "It's nothing. Just"—his blinking eyes weren't focused—"ticked. I got hit with a Trojan." He lifted his computer and the pad of paper. "Didn't see it coming. System's probably toast."

"I can fix that," Maddox said from the gangway.

"Not worth the time." Cell bobbed his head toward Leif but didn't meet his gaze. "Got a mission, remember? China." His half-hearted attempt at a smirk failed. "I have to get on the horn and requisition a new system. ASAP." He scurried out of the room.

It bugged Leif. He'd seen ticked before, and that wasn't ticked. That was scared.

Arms folded, Maddox squinted after Cell. "He's acting . . . odd."

Leif nodded.

"Cell?" Lawe said with a grin as he pushed into the cramped quarters. "He's always been odd."

"Yeah, but not like that," Maddox amended. "He's Barc-odd, but not . . . weird-odd. Maybe I should—"

"Leave it," Leif said and motioned to Saito and Culver. "Let's group up." They didn't need to borrow trouble—there was plenty to go around right now. When Cell was ready to talk, they'd listen. "Let's go over the plan for Beijing."

"Since Cell's laptop is fried, I'll get mine," Maddox said.

Five minutes later, the team assembled in the briefing room. Since Fuji had information on the executive of the defense ministry and the schematics to his home, he'd eliminated their guesswork on which location would be targeted. The executive's summer residence was situated in the mountains, just outside a nature preserve. Heavily wooded. That both worked for and against them. *For* because most of Reaper were Caucasian and would be easily noticed in that private setting. *Against* because it was very hard to get a line of sight on anyone through trees.

"This summer residence used to be a lodge at a nature preserve, but it was gifted to General Chang," Leif explained. "He doesn't own it, but it's his to use at will. It's remote, yet not too remote—a perfect location to host a party for his wife's birthday. They have armed security, as well as motion sensors. Lawe and Devine, intelligence suggests this spot"—he pointed to a location on the wall screen—"should give you the best vantage. However, if line of sight is obstructed, get where you need to be. You'll have twenty-four hours to slip into position without being seen or tripping those sensors."

Devine scanned the images, rubbing her lower lip, then nodded.

"We've learned that Chang requested a security assessment from local company Whole Solutions. Unfortunately that officer was exposed an hour ago for his involvement in a scandal. Saito will be replacing him. Maddox will pose as his date. Representing the company"—he indicated Saito—"Zhao Li will also have his security detail. Wise man that he is, he happens to have a few former American special operators on his payroll and will be taking this opportunity to show them off. That'd be me, Culver, and Baddar."

"Nice," Culver said. "Do we get a pay raise?"

"We get to live." Leif eyed Cell. "You'll be holed up in a security van. It's tricked out so you can set up shop to keep tabs on us."

"We're going in wired?" Culver asked.

"Private encrypted channel. They're expecting us to be wired, since we're security contractors for Zhao," Leif said, nodding to Saito. "Concerns, holes, or questions?"

"What will General Chang think about an Afghan commando working his property?" Baddar asked. "They ally with the Russians and are not very friendly with my people."

To say the least.

"If he questions your integrity," Saito said, his words suddenly heavy with a Chinese accent, "then he questions *my* honor. That is unacceptable." He glanced around. "Where is my sword?"

Laughter tittered through the room.

"If things go ape in there," Lawe said, "who do we shoot first?"

"We?" Devine eyed him, amused.

"It's a team effort," Lawe amended.

"Mm," Devine demurred.

"Just don't shoot us," Culver snarked.

"The legitimacy of our presence on-site is delicate at best, so do not fire unless being fired upon," Leif said. "Two hours till wheels down. We get in, find and stop Fuji, then exfil ASAP. This is a nightmare waiting to happen."

# CHAPTER 11

## EN ROUTE TO BEIJING, CHINA

The team had spent the last hour going over scenarios, contingencies, placement, and throwing barbs at one another. Mercy slipped out of the briefing room to use the lavatory, and when she emerged, she caught sight of Barc in the seating area, head in his hands. She went to her satchel and drew out her tablet. No way could she hand over Natalia, her laptop. But she couldn't stand to see him digitally handicapped. It was like he needed a pacifier to keep him happy.

She walked over to him and held it out.

He straightened and eyed the pad. Hesitated. "Thanks." Though he took it, he didn't access it. Didn't even try.

"Okay, Barc," she said, folding her arms and arching her eyebrow. "What happened?"

He snorted as if about to argue, then deflated and sighed. "I got stupid."

"Got?" She couldn't resist the taunt.

He almost smiled, but the heaviness lingering over him really bothered her.

"You do realize computers can be replaced, right?" she teased. "It's really not the end of the world."

135

"I don't know," he said. "We are, after all, trying to stop a group racing Armageddon. How much more end times can you get?" A shadow flickered through his face. "Never thought I'd see it, ya know? Where everyone wants to kill everyone. Where you can't tell friend from foe."

"Yo." Mercy turned him toward her. She pointed to herself. "*Friend*. Say it with me—*frieeeend*."

He squinted, his mind clearly not on her teasing. "Does it bother you that we're digging for names just to go kill these people?"

"You're Bruce Banner-ing me, Barc. I'm impressed, but I'm not going to date you." When even that didn't get a smirk, she eased down onto the seat next to him. "They're killers. And they will kill unless we stop them. We'll try to do that without lethal force, but Reaper is authorized and must use that force if necessary in order to stop this madness. They're targeting one person, but we know better. It's never just one person who gets injured. There's fallout."

Head back against the leather seat, he shook it. "I thought leaving the field would get me out of these situations." Sorrow tightened his features. "I don't like it, Merc. I don't like what's happening to"—his expression tightened—"the team. To us. This isn't . . . I can't . . ."

"Can't what?"

He gave another quick shake of his head.

"Never mind." He roughed his hands over his face. "I did something really stupid."

"You already said that."

"But I didn't say that I recruited Mei to help me with the code names."

Mercy punched to her feet. Drew back her elbows. "You *what?*" Heart crashing against her ribs, she glowered at him. "You are not that stupid!"

"I couldn't figure it out," he admitted. "I—"

She slapped his arm.

"Look—"

She slapped his head. His arm again. Smacked him in a rapid-fire revolution.

Cell scampered out of his seat, covering his head. "Mercy, stop. Stop!"

She shoved him. "You are the biggest idiot. I cannot believe—Mei's acid! She burns and kills everything. You cannot—how—*augh!*" She dug her fingers into her scalp and turned in a circle. "I knew you had some harebrained moments, but this—"

"Would you please just listen?"

"That—" She drew in a sharp breath. "*She* is why your system is fried!" Hand to her forehead, she paced. "Barc, how . . . why . . ."

"Because the code names in the Book of the Wars had no meaning. I followed a hunch, and it proved right. Each code name is tied to another code name, which is current-day, modern. Military. With Mei's help, I . . . made a connection. The worst of it is that she now also has the information." Grief clawed his features. "And now she is in danger for helping me."

Mercy widened her eyes. "She said that?"

Barc hesitated. "Not directly, but she came unglued in her last message. She'd promised to help—with her usual caveats—but this time she said no more." He raised his hands in frustration. "I mean, not that it matters. Without the book, we can't get the rest of the names anyway." He let out a long, painful breath. "It scares me."

"What? Being without a laptop?"

"No, being without the names," he growled. "Without a way to get ahead of ArC—and we have to do that or we're dead. Because they are some serious slag, ya know?" He looked like he'd eaten a bowl of pea soup.

Mercy touched the side of his face. "Where is my fun, quirky Barc?" It really worried her to see him like this. "You're so serious."

He pushed her hand away. Which was even more proof that something was seriously wrong. He never did that. Ever since they'd met, Barclay and his adorable, rule-abiding self had been champing at the bit for a chance to date her. They'd tried it, but . . . meh. Wasn't right. Yet he never gave up.

That was it. Rule-abiding. And with Mei, he'd outright disobeyed Dru.

This was worse than she'd thought. What drove a man to violate his prime directive? To go where no man had gone before? And how did she pull him back from the dark side?

"This is quite the role reversal," Mercy murmured. "You going against a direct order. Me sitting here wanting to slap you back in line."

"You did slap me. A lot."

"Apparently not enough." She planted her hands on her hips. "What's going on, Barc? There's more. I can tell. It's written all over your face."

Surprise colored his cheeks. "It's not fair."

"What's that?"

"That you can read me like that yet won't go out with me."

She lifted an eyebrow. "That was *almost* normal." She wrinkled her nose. "Wanna try again? Better this time."

"Try what?"

"To convince me you're okay," she scoffed. "Because I am not buying that lame attempt, *Dawg*."

Instead of rallying, he slumped. Shook his head as he looked at her, then over her shoulder. That shadow skidded through his brown eyes again. Concern. Wariness.

She glanced in the same direction and saw the team emerging from the small room. "You worried about this mission?"

"Yeah." His brown eyes seemed lost in memory or thought. "Guess so."

That was his worst lie yet.

## OUTSIDE BEIJING, CHINA

Getting down and dirty meant something entirely different to Peyton Devine. She'd served on the front lines of football games with poms, short shorts, enough makeup to cover an elephant, and glittery boots. But when her brother deployed, then died while serving, her priorities rearranged real fast.

She had no regrets—not even now as she low-crawled through a Chinese forest that was damp and reeked. Neither did she begrudge any of the girls back home still cheering on their teams.

Dressed in a makeshift ghillie crafted from local vegetation attached to a camouflaged flight suit, she had her face greased and patience tested. Rifle over her arms, she crawled, inch by inch, deeper into the vegetation.

*Low and slow.*

Leaving the poms behind and entering the Army had been a tribute to her brother. She'd felt like she'd picked up the torch he'd laid down. Joining hadn't been about besting the boys or proving anything. Until she met Adam.

He was behind and to her four. They'd been able to slink half the distance, but the last six hours required painstaking precision as they approached the sensor perimeter. Each heartbeat, each centimeter strangled her breath in fear that they'd misjudged the line placement.

And though she would never admit it to him, she was tense about being alone with Adam for an entire day. Granted, they were sneaking into position, so there wasn't much room for discourse. Amazingly, he hadn't broken their necessary silence.

Okay, that wasn't entirely fair. Adam Lawe was a tough mudder when it came to operations. Intensity radiated off of him. He might mouth off or hand out jibes like candy, but when it came to the team or mission, there was no soldier more loyal. Then there were his eyes. Blue in some light, green in others. To top it off, he'd never treated her like a sex symbol like a lot of grunts, especially when they found out she'd cheered for the Eagles.

The GPS/communications device strapped to her forearm thumped. Though she'd only advanced a yard in the last hour, she paused. Blew a breath hard enough to stir up dust. Her breath caught as the dust danced along a previously invisible-to-the-eye beam less than six inches from her arms. Inches closer than she'd anticipated.

With extreme slowness, she moved her fingers toward her opposite arm, taking painstaking effort not to rustle a branch or grass. To her knuckles. Then just above her thumb. Eventually her wrist. A minute later she felt the strap of the device and began the arduous task of angling her head in that direction to see the readout on the device DIA had rigged. It would have taken her ages if she hadn't been crawling with her arms in opposing $L$ shapes. Gripping the edge of the device, she drew it out a millimeter at a time, careful to avoid any motion that would lure attention to her position.

She felt more than heard Adam slink up behind her. They had taken parallel courses to assure the slight depression in the grass created by the weight of their bodies didn't compound and mark a path straight to them.

She uncoiled the long wire and wafer-thin conductors. It took her ten minutes to stretch the wire out to its full length, flicking fingers not holding the wire to cover it in dust and debris. Once the wire was taut, she pressed the near-solid stem into the ground directly beneath the sensor. She barely had two inches of space between the beam and the ground.

On its own, thanks to the wafers veined with circuitry, the interrupter would count down thirty seconds, then snap up into the beam, at which time it would conduct the sensor line through the thin cable to the other wafer. If it worked properly, then the security system wouldn't register an interruption, and there'd be a gap just wide enough for them to ease through single file.

Peyton trigged the wire, and it deployed as expected. She held her breath before testing the gap. Relieved when nothing tripped, they began the hurry-up-and-go-slow journey through the gap. An hour later, they were both inside the perimeter and two feet from the sensor.

Peyton stared down the hillside toward the house, garages, and parking area. Two more hours would plant the team on-site and her in position—six feet from her current location. She eyed her goal—behind the knoll where three trees formed a natural barricade.

Her thumper tapped out a Morse code message: *U OK*.

Adam.

It was nice of this job to give her a solid reason not to talk to him—twenty-four hours of silent treatment. A girl could get spoiled. Instead of replying, she focused on reaching the location. They'd be side by side there. That was bad enough.

She didn't hate him. Not really. But if she gave him the time of day, he'd take the whole year, too. And she just couldn't do that again. He'd shattered her heart when he walked away.

Shouts erupted from the walled compound. Peering over her arms, Peyton stilled and eyed the half dozen soldiers darting toward the walls. One guy pointed up the hillside.

Silently, she cursed. They'd been spotted. Compromised.

The soldier lifted a weapon and fired.

Peyton's heart jammed into her throat. In her periphery, she saw a plume of tree litter erupt—right where Adam lay. But no sound. No movement. Panic tempted her to call out to him, to turn her head.

*Don't move, don't move, don't move.* It was a silent plea to both her and Adam. If he was grazed, they could deal with it. But it would leave evidence, and that would be a problem.

Another man shouted and pointed farther east, having seen something there. Two guards shot that direction.

She waited until the men gave up, apparently deciding they were mistaken, and retreated to their stations, then continued the arduous task of relocating to the nest. Very slowly, she drew over nearby brush to better conceal her position, weapon, and body. Adam was doing the same, and though she could see his subtle moves, she doubted—prayed—nobody else could.

She eyed him as he settled next to her. And startled, breath stuck in her throat, when she saw his face. His cheekbone oozed an angry, bloody trail. Grazed. By the bullet. Her heart danced a frantic jig, thinking of how that could have ended differently. A fraction more to the left, and it would've gone through his skull. She swallowed, marveling that he hadn't made a sound. Not even a grunt. He'd protected their position even when a bullet had skimmed his face. Man, that had to sting, not to mention scare the snot out of him.

His gaze hit hers. His eyebrows lifted as if to say, "At least I'm alive."

She mentally shook her head. That was Adam. All warrior.

The longer he knew Iskra, the more Leif learned about her. That was the way it should be. But the things a guy normally learned in a relationship weren't the same ones he'd sorted with Iskra. For her, they included the fact that she'd killed two Hungarians who'd trafficked women and tried to add her to the number. Or that she was more proficient with a 1911 than he was. She still hadn't let him live down that day at the range when she'd outshot him. Neither had the range master, which had nothing to do with why they'd started going to a new range. She'd also once swum to the bottom of a small inlet off the coast of France in order to reach a tunnel and gain access to the estate where her target had been hiding. So it surprised him when she'd insisted she couldn't go to China because she was wanted by authorities after a botched mission.

And it bugged him. He knew an undercurrent of her decision was his own excuses and absence while he'd been looking for answers. He'd tried to fix the mess, tried to move on and act normal. But normal was wrecked.

He hated that she wasn't here, because it should be her wearing the sleek navy blue gown, hair done up, and neck glittering with diamonds. He'd kill to see that. Instead, Mercy was dressed to the nines, and while she was a formidable woman, she wasn't Iskra.

"Can I keep the diamonds?" Mercy wrinkled her nose. "They're kind of working for me."

"You'll be working a gravel pit if you keep them. They're on loan from the agency."

"Spoilsport."

"Okay, Reaper," Cell calmly said through the comms from the Whole Solutions security van lumbering behind their black SUV, "we have a clear connection, and Coriolis is in position."

They slid through the gate checkpoint without complication and aimed for the parking lot atop the hill.

"Copy," Leif said.

There was a reason he'd signed up to be a soldier, not a spy. He hated this stuff. Put him in ACUs and slap a carbine in his hands—the world was right. But this pretending to be someone else and walking into the devil's lair, where a known terrorist was intent on killing a target, potentially endangering the entire team . . . And don't forget the Chinese who, if they discovered who Zhao Li really was, would make Reaper disappear so fast heads would spin. It was enough to make him long for ISIS-led combatants.

They parked and exited the vehicle. At the side entrance, they were met by grounds security, who collected their IDs—conjured by some whiz back in the States and executed by an in-the-know local—and took their time verifying identities.

Five minutes later, Saito challenged the guard, shouting in Mandarin.

*Should've read a book on Mandarin before infiltrating.*

Mercy stood one step behind Saito, her gaze on him like a good, doting girlfriend. Leif, Baddar, and Culver arced behind their "boss" and presented a strong front, glancing around to verify they were safe, but also to warn these goons that they would act. There was a whole lotta trust placed in Saito to pull off this charade.

The guard clapped hands to his thighs and gave a curt bow.

Saito grunted his disapproval at being made to wait, then stalked toward the house.

Extending a hand in Maddox's direction, as if to guide her along, Leif once more eyed the compound. Saw the van where Cell was hunkered. His gaze hit the hills, knowing somewhere among that vegetation lay the last two team members. Probably staring right back at him.

"Remember," Cell muttered as the team stalked

into a marble-lined hall and yet another security checkpoint, "I need to piggyback their feeds, so be sure—"

"Quiet," Leif subvocalized. The last thing he needed was someone cluttering his hearing and attention. Reaper knew the mission. Knew what they had to do.

"Welcome. If you please," a very petite Asian woman greeted them and inclined her head in respect, "we must check you in and give you security cards that will provide access to restrooms and the bar."

Once Saito and Mercy had cleared without hang-up, Leif took the lead and set his phone on the counter within inches of their computer. Thankfully, technology had advanced enough that a device did not have to be plugged in directly to gain access. Complying with the woman's instructions, he pressed his finger to a pad, praying the false fingerprint he wore did its job.

"Thank you, Mr. James." She reached toward a card maker, where she tugged a small plastic card from the dispenser and handed it to him, eyeing Culver and Baddar. "One for all, yes?"

"No," he said. "Three, please." That way they could each move around unhindered. A limited number of cards were available for the evening and provided privileges based on notoriety. Thanks to Zhao Li and Whole Solutions, the team

148

should have full access to the grounds, save the residence wing.

Her expression tightened, but she gave a quick cock of her head in agreement. Culver and Baddar went through the same process without grief.

Next they passed through scanners, which seemed futile, as the team was authorized for weapons since they were Mr. Zhao's guards. The narrow security corridor dumped them into a cavernous hall.

Soaring ceilings with candelabras snagged the attention, leaving the spectators in awe. The smartly organized space had a massive fireplace along the far wall, but the central focus was a slick fire pit. Settees and tables were clustered facing the pit and held couples talking and toasting one another. In the middle of the hall, two semicircles formed a full-service bar and were nestled by tables offering hors d'oeuvres. The far right side of the luxurious space had a dance floor. Guests were clustered here, some dancing, others watching and talking, all drinking bubbly.

That was where Leif finally spotted Maddox, her hand hooked over Saito's shoulder. The imposter was talking with a man in uniform—a colonel.

A dozen jokes popped to mind, which told him his stress level was a little high.

"I'm going to do my walk-around." Leif stalked the perimeter, leaving Culver and Baddar with Mercy and Saito.

The flow of kitchen staff entering and exiting a door drew him over to check it out. He scanned the stock rooms, his security card accessing places most couldn't. He checked the restroom, not surprised that, since this place had once been open to the public, the bathrooms were segregated.

"Mercy, check the ladies' room when you can," he said into his comms, glad they'd given her an invisible earpiece.

He tested a set of double doors, spotted the access reader on the wall, and swiped his card. The red light blinked, refusing admittance. He tried again. Visually tracing the doors, he spied a small camera in the upper right corner.

Was this the residence portion of the estate? He backed up and glanced down both ends of the hall before returning to the main ballroom. If he couldn't get in there, he'd bet most attending tonight's birthday gala couldn't either. And they hadn't seen their target yet.

*Come out, come out, wherever you are, General Chang.*

Saito guided his entourage toward Leif, probably so Mercy could excuse herself. The two sure played the cozy thing well. Leif's gaze bounced to Baddar, and he nearly smirked at the commando's missing smile. Must be frustrating. Leif would probably lay out Saito if that were Iskra instead of Mercy.

Baddar inclined his head to Leif and hung back as a colonel approached Saito to talk.

Leif monitored those around them, searching for Fuji. Where was Chang? This was his gig, his celebration, and while there were easily a hundred guests here, he hadn't shown.

What if Fuji wasn't here for the killing? What if he'd set a device, a bomb? Heat shot down Leif's spine and forced him to walk a wide arc around Saito to get a better view. Was that possible? How did that make sense, to activate assassins to go in and kill—but they didn't "go in"?

Nursing a drink, Maddox wandered over to him, but her gaze never left Saito. "He is so droll, talking to all these people."

Expecting the hall to be bugged and every guest watched, Leif said nothing, even when she deposited her glass in his hand with a smirk.

"Be a dear and hold this for me." She glided past him and aimed for the restrooms.

Trailing her, Leif made eye contact with the other three of their team to be sure they knew his location. As he parked himself outside the restroom, he felt a buzzing start at the back of his head. Something was off. He skidded his gaze around the hall, surfing faces and expressions, hands.

"Heads up," came Cell's voice again. "Something's going on in the kitchen."

"Need my attention?" Leif asked, as Mercy exited the restroom, retrieved her glass, then returned to Saito. He glanced at Saito, who gave a curt nod of understanding as Mercy sidled back up to him with Baddar not far behind.

"Uh . . . negative. There's some kind of altercation," Cell said quietly. "Can't tell what it's about. Bad angle. Sending you the feed."

Baddar wandered in that direction, bisecting Leif's line of sight. Even as the Afghan commando entered the kitchen, Leif's phone buzzed with a live video. After verifying Saito and Mercy were keeping the brass entertained, he focused on the feed. A tall guy and a chef were arguing. The lanky guy backed up, hands lifted in mock surrender. Even as he turned to leave— never giving his face to the camera—he glanced back down a hall.

"Smiley, give me eyes on what he's looking at," Leif ordered, shifting so his back was to a column so nobody could see over his shoulder.

The food locker. What was he looking at in there? Canisters. Plastic containers of vegetables, trays of desserts . . . "He was worried about something," Leif muttered, recalling the man's expression. "Find out what."

"Trouble comes in pairs," Culver said. "Chang incoming."

152

Leif looked toward Culver, saw the direction he was staring. General Chang and his entourage were emerging from the door Leif hadn't been able to access, confirming his suspicion that it was the residence wing. Mobbed by the thanks and greetings of his guests, Chang made slow progress through the crowd.

"Copy, eyes on Chang," Leif confirmed. Now that Chang was on-site, the situation had escalated. It was all the more likely that Fuji would make his move.

What if Fuji wasn't coming? The thought bred frustration and confusion, but his sixth sense told him Fuji *would* be here. He couldn't explain how he knew. Just did.

"So, Mr. James."

Surprised to be addressed by the general, since he was nothing but a lackey on this gig, Leif turned toward the voice. He inclined his head. "General Chang."

"What do you think of my celebration?" he asked in broken English. "A good event, yes?"

"Yes, sir."

The round-faced general squinted at him, eyes nearly disappearing beneath thick folds. For a general, he wasn't exactly trim and fit. "Zhao Li say you were in the military."

"Required for Whole Solutions, sir. We all were."

"What branch?"

"Navy."

"So if my guards hold you underwater"—he motioned out the floor-to-ceiling windows to an Olympic-sized pool glimmering blue in the dark night—"you would not drown."

"No, but they would."

Chang barked a laugh. Gripped Leif's shoulder. "I like you."

"That is not a requirement." Leif managed a smile. "But it is appreciated."

The general aligned himself beside Leif and waved toward the crowd. "Tell me what you see, security expert."

It was part of the game. And again, this was why Leif had been a SEAL, not a spy—he hated that the man beside him was responsible for untold atrocities. Hated that if he just lifted the tactical knife from his boot, he could end a serious threat to peace. But even if he did, another would take Chang's place. "I assume you don't mean the scantily clad women or the men sucking up to you."

Another boisterous laugh. "No."

"Your system is weak, sir."

The man objected. "But you could not get into the corridor to my home."

"I didn't try." He let his meaning settle. "The doors were old—hinges off by a fraction. Makes it easier to break down. I had no reason to do that." The general's probing eyes held his, and

Leif pushed on. "The restrooms are a problem, as they're close to the gas line that feeds the fireplace—a very easy target for flammables or explosives."

"But you walk the hall, yes? You saw none."

Absorbing what the general had just revealed, Leif held his gaze. They had been watching Reaper. "None." He kept his hands at his sides, ready. "You have vulnerabilities. Some can be remedied. Others would require reconstruction."

A string of Mandarin flew off Chang's tongue as he turned to Saito, whose smirk deepened. Saito gave Leif a quick nod of approval, and the two walked away.

"We have trouble," Baddar said, his accent thickened by his concern. "I just bump into Fuji come out of supply room. He accessed heating closet behind the kitchen. There are purifiers for the air conditioners—and one of the canisters is not the same. I think he will release gas."

Air purifiers. Leif eyed the vents in the ceiling. Large. Abundant.

Even as he did, plumes of mist snaked out.

# CHAPTER 12

## BEIJING, CHINA

"Gas attack. Get him out of here!" Leif shouted to the general's security detail. He pointed to the ceiling. "Go! Out!"

Culver darted toward Baddar, who was staggering, coughing, slowing. He hooked his arm under the commando and around his shoulder, then pulled the fire alarm.

Claxons screamed in shrill warning.

Guards swarmed the general, throwing their jackets over him as they tugged him into a protective hold and rushed him to the exit. Guests started coughing, gagging. A woman near the fireplace slumped to the ground, vomiting blood. The Chinese barreled out with their general, bodies falling around them.

Shouldering out of his jacket, Leif pivoted to Reaper. "Move!" He tossed his jacket at Mercy. "Cover your face."

Instinct made Leif head to the full glass walls. A glance over his shoulder told him it was the right way—the security halls were clogged with people trying to get out, falling as they did. Screaming. Coughing. Vomiting.

He lifted one of the small bar tables, and

Culver and Baddar—blood slipping down his chin—fired as they ran. The windows cracked and spider-webbed beneath the barrage of bullets, then surrendered when the table careened into it. Glass crunched beneath their shoes as they sought the refuge of clean air. But the haze encircling the residence thickened. A woman tripped into him. He narrowly avoided her vomit as she collapsed and breathed her last.

"Reaper, van is idling and ready," Cell reported, his voice laden with worry. "Authorities and rescue squads are notified. Where are you?"

"Rear of the facility."

"What chemical?"

"Unknown." Throat raw and tight, Leif hiked back around the property to the vehicles, folding into the throng of guests, some coughing and gagging, but nothing worse than that. "Sarin is clear, but maybe something he used to deploy the gas made it visible. Symptoms are the same. Baddar saw Fu—"

*Crack!*

Not slowing but recognizing the report of a sniper rifle—Devine—Leif did his best to avoid looking at the hill as they rounded the building.

Saito widened his eyes.

"Target down," Devine calmly reported.

"Mercy—get to Cell. Get into their feeds." Leif glanced toward the residence where the guests—what was left of them—staggered around, confused. Panicked. Screaming. Some running down the drive, away from the middle of the parking lot. Away from the body of the man who'd received some Devine intervention.

Coughing and throat raw, Mercy slipped into the van with Cell to monitor cameras and see what she could learn. Find out if there was a way to draw the toxin out of the air. But she was a hacker, not a scientist. Her gaze hit the monitor, and with a shaky breath, she absorbed the chaos of bodies and movement. She lifted a hand to her mouth as guests tumbled out of the house. The ones who exited later didn't make it far before vomiting and collapsing, thereby blocking the path of others trying to escape.

"What a nightmare," she whispered, tears stinging her eyes, grateful that Leif had given her his jacket for protection. How many guests were stuck? Was there a way to seal off that section of the house? She looked to Cell. "You already called it in, right?"

He nodded, forlorn. "Command, where's containment and medical?"

"En route, two mikes," Braun said, "and we've looped in the local authorities, so they'll be on scene soon. Clear out ASAP."

It was horrible and brought back seismic waves of dread that reminded Mercy of Ram's death amidst others dying on a battlefield. But this was especially cruel because the people here weren't combatants. They were guests at a gala.

Tears blurred her vision. She had to do something, but going out there could contaminate her. Until officials cleared the air, she couldn't help. And that was the most wretched thing of all.

"This is messed up," Cell muttered, shaking his head. "At least Peyton got Kurofuji."

Swallowing hard, Mercy's gaze involuntarily went to the body in the parking lot. "What drives a person to do this, to participate in a mass killing?" Monitoring the frenzy, she noticed Leif and the others were farther out of sight. "They're almost at their SUV."

"They need to get to a medic and get checked." Cell hissed a curse. "And sarin—if it is that—is communicable via skin contact, so they need to keep a safe distance to avoid contamination."

Numb and grieved, Mercy scanned her own arms, then looked at the crowd, wishing away this night. Wishing—

With a gasp, she jerked straight and blinked. "No," she breathed, clicking on the feeds to home in on the parking lot. Where . . . where . . .

"What's wrong?" Cell asked.

She'd seen him, right? It wasn't just her imagination. Couldn't be. But where? She switched cameras. Scanned and zoomed. He'd been . . . Squinting at a person on the far side of the crowd, she leaned in. He shifted—yes!

Mercy spun and threw herself at the back door of the van. Flung it open and leapt onto the concrete, stumbling. Ditched her shoes. Came up running, ignoring Cell's shout to come back.

Andrew was here. And he was not getting away. Not this time. Running, she crossed the parking lot in a wide arc, away from the infected. She skittered around a man who lurched and vomited.

Scanning as she ran, Mercy refused to accept defeat. Andrew would be hers. He'd give her answers. He would not get off scot-free like he had in Angola. There was no power-giddy general here to stop her. She would have his name and identity. Not that he'd readily give them up, but if she tackled him, she could maybe pickpocket his phone. Hack that. Unearth every dirty little secret about the too-slick operator.

She saw his brown-haired self bobbing through the crowd.

With a skip, she sprinted after him. She wanted to yell for him to stop, but she was not giving this guy a chance to make a run for it.

A woman in front of her staggered and collapsed, her husband catching her, pitching the couple into Mercy's path. She hopped over them, startling the man, who yelped.

Andrew glanced back. His eyes widened, and he flung around. Bolted into the woods.

Adrenaline coursed through Mercy, giving her ample fuel to pursue him. Going ninety to nothing, she was closing in on him. *Yes.* She would take him down. Make sure—

She registered something in his right hand. A gun?

A dozen feet separated them.

Unwilling to let the weapon deter her, she continued. Refused to let him get away. He was connected to these deaths, and he would pay. She ran harder. Pushed herself.

Eight feet.

She wished for Leif's endless energy or his parkour skills, though they wouldn't do much good in this sequined number. She would shove off a tree and plow into Andrew's back. It'd be great to be Storm and call down lightning. Zap him in the head.

But he stopped and pivoted. "Don't!"

Seizing her chance, she dove at him even as he yelled, "No!" They went down, the leaves and dirt softening their landing.

Mercy grabbed his arm.

He flipped her onto her back. Extricated himself unbelievably fast and leaped backward. He glanced at her hand, muttered an oath, and dropped to kneel. Using his knee, he held her to the ground and gripped her wrist.

"Get off me," she shouted, trying to wrest free.

"Stop. Look."

Her hand—red, blistered. The sight slowed her. She gaped at her skin reacting.

Gas. She was contaminated. How? She'd checked! She looked at his arm and saw blisters. Even as she did, she noticed the syringe he slid into her thigh.

Dumbstruck, she barely felt the prick of the needle. "I—"

His arm hooked her throat in a chokehold, cutting off her air. She struggled against him. Writhed. Slapped. Tried to drop free. Nothing worked.

"Easy," he muttered, a strange sound to his words. "I'm sorry."

Her vision went gray, like curtains being drawn over her senses, pulling her into a dark void.

Shouts hauled her back from the emptiness of unconsciousness. Groaning, Mercy peeled off the ground. Squinted, momentarily lost. Where was she? Woods. Okay, but—

Andrew!

With a gasp she whipped onto her feet—and the world spun. Her vision jiggled. She canted and caught herself on a tree.

Leaves crunching to her right helped her home in on Andrew. She would wring his ruddy neck! She pushed herself toward him, aware she had no weapon but her hands. Rounding a tree, she saw his form. Drew up sharp.

"Mercy," Leif breathed in apparent relief. "Reaper, this is Actual. I have her. Rendezvous in five." His expression darkened. "You okay?"

"No, I'm not okay," she growled, feeling the stinging of her hand and the thickness of her tongue. "But that doesn't matter."

Leif assessed her. "What happened?"

"Andrew." She sounded petulant but didn't care. "He was here. I went after him, because I could not let him get away again. He spotted me and started running. I gave chase. Tackled him and he—" Those moments crawled through her brain with painstaking slowness. His shout to stop, his *don't,* the panic in his tone. "He was warning me," she whispered in disbelief.

"Come again?"

How did that make sense? "Nothing."

"We need to move before the authorities show up." Leif led her to a dirt road, and they hurried to the van. Climbed in, everyone clustered at the front.

Seated, she let out an exasperated sigh. She'd been so close. Her thigh throbbed, and she rubbed it. A lump rose beneath the skin, and she recalled him injecting her. Peering down, she wondered what he'd stuck her with. How had he known what antidote to have? Was he involved? Mentally, she probed herself for sickness, fever, nausea, dizziness. . . .

"Mercy?"

She flicked her gaze to Leif, who was watching her way too closely.

Then she saw the body bag on the upper bunk,

zipped up to the face, a mask covering the nose and mouth. The strong forehead. "Baddar!"

When she punched to her feet, Saito restrained her. "Stay back."

"Why?" She visually traced the few inches of Baddar's body that she could see. Eyes closed. Oxygen mask. No new holes. Was he alive? A face mask meant alive, right?

"He's contaminated," Leif said from the bench. Sirens screamed past them, heading in the opposite direction—toward the residence. "We're headed to the airstrip, where a medical team has been waiting for us with a medical quarantine."

*Has been waiting.*

Her gaze struck Leif's as his meaning pushed her into her seat. Because she had been missing, Baddar's medical treatment was delayed. "How long was I . . ."

"Found you in fifteen." Leif's answer held no condemnation.

Fifteen minutes. They could've already been at the airport. Baddar would be getting treatment. Instead, he was here.

She reached for him.

"No," Saito said, then started. "Your hand!" He frowned. "You blistered, but . . . nothing more?"

Withdrawing her arm, she shook her head.

"Arriving now," Cell called from the front. They cleared the private security gate and barreled toward the waiting transport jet, its engines whining. At the base of the ramp, a team of doctors waited with a gurney. They were hurrying toward the van as it rolled to a stop.

Bereft, Mercy watched Culver and Leif hustle Baddar up into the plane.

"Mercy," Leif called with a nod. "Come on. Since your hand is affected."

She swallowed and obeyed, every ounce of petulance wiped out of her. She'd failed on two fronts—she hadn't gotten Andrew, and she'd kept Baddar from getting help. Trudging after them, she was met by a woman in a full hazmat suit.

Brilliant. Not just a failure—a contaminated failure.

"Hey." Cell trotted up behind her but kept his distance. "At least you have more in common with Bruce now."

"That—he wasn't . . ."

Oh, never mind. It was useless to explain that Banner was bombarded by gamma radiation, not poisoned with sarin gas. He got superpowers out of it. She'd only gotten heartache.

The video popped to life and showed the Reaper hub and the deputy director. "Okay, Braun got waylaid and will be here in a minute, but let's get started. Tell me what you know," Dru said as he settled in at the desk in the hub.

"Mercy saw Andrew again," Leif said as the jet

rumbled down the runway. The nose tipped up and lifted off. "Said she was chasing him."

"Was she contaminated before that?"

"No, she was in the van with me," Cell said. "No gas exposure."

"But she ran a virtual minefield of infected guests," Culver said, his voice hoarse from the gas. "So if anyone touched her . . ."

"We had a team recover Kurofuji's body," Dru continued, "and it's en route to American assets, so we'll run an autopsy. We've heard from China that General Chang was spirited away." The director's gaze met Leif's. "Good work. It would've been nice if you had set eyes on Fuji before Devine had to take him out."

"Baddar saw him, but too late. And what would've been nice is preventing the release of that gas," Leif said, frustrated. "This wasn't a win. We didn't get intel, and people got hurt, including three of our own."

"Granted," Dru agreed.

"Both killings were chemical in nature," Saito said. "Do we think this will be the MO going forward? Maybe it's a good idea for me to be prepared with antidotes—which might be how that Andrew dude had what he needed to help Mercy."

"If we actually had the book," Culver bemoaned, "we could see if that's what the second war was about. You know, like the first war was about storms."

"Technically," Cell said, "it was about a type of cloud seeding—"

"Easy, Purcell," Dru chided, then glanced at the team. "We're working on re-securing the book and have a couple of leads. By the way, Maddox was suspicious of Jeeves at RTB, but I've confirmed he's a nonthreat."

Leif leaned forward. "Hold up. 'We're working on re-securing the book'? What leads?" Why hadn't the director included him on that?

"Yeah, I thought that was *our* primary objective," Lawe added.

"Yet we got sent to China," Culver grumbled.

"Kind of hard to secure something when you don't know where it is." Devine crossed her arms and settled in her chair.

"Dial it back, guys," Dru said. "You were in China, working a legitimate lead. That meant you couldn't be doing everything. When you return, we can debrief fully, hopefully with Kurofuji's test results. So rest up, and we'll see you back here."

Though the screen went blank, images danced in Leif's mind. Like the expression on the director's face when he'd been called out on outsourcing leads on the book. Was he trying to hide something?

As the team cleared the room, Leif wondered who Dru was using to go after the book. Why exclude him? Was there someone better? Sitting alone, the drone of jet engines a loud white noise, he had a thought. Retrieved his phone and dialed.

A mechanized recording answered, saying the number couldn't be reached but to leave a message. Iskra had never changed the pre-programmed recording that came with the phone. It was one less way for people to know who they'd reached. Ending the call, he tightened his lips. If she wasn't on a mission with them, why couldn't she answer the phone? He'd called three times and never once gotten her. No return calls.

Tapping his phone on the table, he rubbed his lower lip. Instinct told him to forget it. She was a big girl, and he didn't need her.

But he did. Which was crazy. He'd been a loner all his life. As the baby of six children, he'd made his way in the wake of the Metcalfe legacy. Watching all their mistakes and learning how to navigate life without inflicting stress on their mom as his siblings had. His oldest brother, Stone, had married, and then his wife ditched him for someone else. Brooke escaped an abusive husband. Canyon married Dani, following a rocky first start because of conflict with Range, who'd tried to date her first. And Willow— Bohemian Peace Corps and a lot of drama but unmarried. They weren't exactly stellar role models on relationships, though Canyon came close.

Love and relationships were just too messy.

He didn't want the trouble. Especially after the Sahara.

He pocketed his phone and stood, haunted by a dark thought: he might not want trouble, but he wanted her. And they seemed to come hand in hand.

# CHAPTER 13

## REAPER HEADQUARTERS, MARYLAND

Adam had screwed up a lot of things, but nothing as painful as his relationship with Peyton Devine. Damage pervaded his life, his past. He was like the notorious bull in the china shop trying to hold a priceless gem in hooves that crushed concrete.

But he'd had her. They'd been an item. Yet with every day that passed, he had known he'd never be good enough. He knew that. Heck, every guy back in A-stan told him that when he and Peyton hooked up. He knew he'd eventually hurt her, and that thought, compounded by the brutal reality of deploying and being separated—What if he got killed? Left her a widow?—killed him. Besides, she wouldn't leave the military, and neither would he. It was impossible. They were headed to Heartache Central. So he had broken it off.

But hot dang, he'd kill the guy who tried to step in. Ghillie had about met his maker, which was why Adam had removed himself from RTB's hub, where the intruder and Peyton were laughing and connecting. When they were on the roof, he'd gone up to check things out and found them entirely too cozy as they stretched out and peered through their scopes.

Flexing and unflexing his fist, he kept an eye trained on the deputy director's closed door, where Pete was having a one-on-one. A steady drone of conversation filtered out, though words were unintelligible. Because she'd neutralized Kurofuji in China, the questions were detailed, the debrief more thorough.

Back at Bagram, when trips outside the wire resulted in her neutralizing a target, it always hit her hard. Every kill shot had. That was why he'd planted his hairy backside right here, waiting. She didn't need him—Pete was tough as they came—but she had a good, soft heart. And maybe, if he showed he could be there for her, always would be, she'd listen. Give him that second chance.

*Keep dreaming.*

Out in that field beyond the Chinese mansion when he'd been grazed, she'd acted like she cared. Flashed those bright eyes, tangled in concern. Man, he wanted to believe that. A guy could go a long way on those truths. He leaned forward, resting his elbows on his knees and rubbing his palms together.

Light bloomed, wakening him to the fact someone had turned off the lights in the hub and that Peyton was exiting the director's office, her attention on the man behind her.

Adam rose slowly, watching. Anticipating.

When she pivoted, she spotted him. After a

slight hesitation that jammed his pulse into his throat, she headed his way.

His heart did that jiggy thing it always did around her.

"You always sit in the dark?" she asked.

"Helps me think." Adam scanned her face, then glanced at the office. "You okay?"

Irritation skidded through her features, but her jaw twitched, apparently restraining the retorts that had been so quick on her tongue since he'd messed things up. Instead, she shrugged. "It's . . ." Her gaze skipped off.

"Yeah." With a nod, he tried to let her know it was okay. That she didn't have to talk. He got it. Though he guessed what she'd probably say, he still asked, "You want company?" He touched her elbow.

She tugged away.

Accepting that answer, Adam stepped back.

"Yes."

He blinked. Froze. "Yes?" He wouldn't let her rescind that yes. "Okay."

She angled toward the exit. "Tomorrow I'm going over to Belvoir."

"Why?"

"Found out Carsen Gilliam's unit commander while he was in Afghanistan is there now. I have an appointment." She chewed the inside of her cheek for a second, pausing. "I'd like a second set of ears on this," she hurried to explain. "That's all."

"Sure. Makes sense. I can pick you up." At least they'd be together.

"No, I'll pick you up. I want to arrive in one piece."

"You saying something about my driving?"

"I'm saying a lot about your driving."

## MCLEAN, VIRGINIA

"Hey, thanks for letting me barge in." Leif tucked himself inside the foyer of his brother's home.

Canyon shut and locked the door before guiding him back to the living room. "Glad to have you over. Doesn't happen enough."

Legos and cars were strewn around five-year-old Owen in the den. Agitation scratched at Leif for coming. This was a bad idea.

His sister-in-law came around the corner with a little girl perched on her hip. "About to start dinner—tamales." Dani cocked her head. "You staying?"

"Yes, he's staying," Canyon asserted.

"Leif!" Gray-green eyes brightened as the child on Dani's hip reached for him.

Recognition registered. "Taissia." Confused, he took her, and something corkscrewed when she latched onto him, tight. Hugging her, he gave a laugh he didn't feel and shot his brother a look. "Is Isk—"

"Taissia's having a sleepover with Tala," Dani

said. "The girls have had a tea party and been to a movie so far."

Leif tried to hide his frown. Where was Iskra? Should he be alarmed that she still wasn't answering his calls?

"Taissia," Tala called. "Come play!"

"Guess you'd better hurry back," Dani said as the little girl scrambled out of his arms and raced toward the bedrooms.

He swiped a hand over his mouth and turned to his brother. "What is that? Why is she here? Where's Iskra?"

"Didn't you tell Iskra being around our kids would be good for Taissia?" Dani challenged with a shrug. "She's having fun, and it's a pleasure to have her here while Iskra is doing something work-related."

"Work-related."

"What? Did she break some rule, not contacting you first?" Dani shot back. "Was she supposed to check in?"

"Check in?"

"You're doing that annoying thing where you repeat my words." Dani arched an eyebrow at Canyon. "Might want to intercept your brother before I ruin dinner by dumping it all over him."

Leif scowled. "What—"

Laughing, Canyon stepped out the back door onto the deck. "C'mon. Out here."

Dani had always been direct and forthright,

174

which was the only way she'd managed to catch Canyon.

But Leif felt like he was walking over an IED. "What's going on?" he demanded as he closed the door. "Where'd Iskra go? It's unlike her to leave Taissia. She wouldn't go on the mission with us because she was worried about leaving her daughter."

"I don't know," Canyon admitted. "She had to leave for a few days and asked if we could help. If I didn't know that Iliescu was aware, I'd have been reluctant."

"Dru knows?" Leif squinted. "You're saying Dru sent her out?"

Canyon held up his hands. "Whoa, chief. No." He huffed. "You are uptight. No, my point is that Iskra can't go anywhere without Iliescu knowing because she's in his protective custody, right?" He sat on the back step.

Leif joined him. If Dru knew, why hadn't he told Leif? "So you don't know where she went?"

"If I did, I'd tell you."

"Would you?"

Canyon's lips tightened.

"Because it seems like you're real good at buddy-buddy secrets with Dru."

His brother's eyes blazed. "We're *real* good at watching your six, Runt."

His brother had always been there for him and didn't deserve the careless accusations he was

175

throwing around, so Leif hauled his annoyance into check. "You're right." He nodded. "Things have gotten so whacked between me and Iskra. I don't know what to do or how to fix it." He ran a hand down the back of his neck. "She's not talking to me or answering my calls. So to find Taissia here—"

"She said you were gone for a while, wouldn't answer her calls."

Leif startled. "She told you that? Yet she won't talk to me?"

"She might, if you'd told her what was wrong or where you went."

But he couldn't. He realized the truth, the inflection in his brother's words. The subtle accusation, along with the hammering guilt over that trip. They didn't want him looking for the past, but they weren't doing anything to help fill the missing gap, though they'd promised they would.

"You're digging again," Canyon said quietly.

Leif let out a sigh. "It's wrong. . . ."

Canyon studied him—something he was really good at, peeling back the exterior and finding what lay beneath. Mom had dubbed his brother her silent tormentor because he'd go quiet for such long periods and never complain. Yet he always called it like it was.

"*What* is wrong, Leif? What is going on with you? I don't need Iskra to tell me something's off with my little brother." Canyon's blue eyes, so like his own, pinched. "I can see it. Have seen it. What's got you lit?"

Peering across the yard the family called the back forty, Leif shook his head. Eyed the green grass and shrubs that lined the fence. "Something's going on with Iskra, and when she bailed on me and the team, that"—another shake—"wasn't right. Then this book . . ."

Canyon had been there after they'd retrieved it and captured the infamous Viorica. Crazy how things had changed. "Still haven't found it?"

"Nope." Leif studied his shoes. "And Dru's not sending us to look for it. Instead, he's having us track down people."

"People mentioned in the book."

Leif started. "I shouldn't be surprised you know that."

"Neither of us can change what DIA is doing." Canyon smirked, another Metcalfe trait. "But the power is in your hands regarding Iskra. You need to fix it, or it's just going to get bigger. It's like potholes in the road of your relationship. The longer they're ignored, the bigger they get, the more damage they inflict—and that will infiltrate the rest of your life, including your job."

A gnawing started in Leif's gut. "I know. I just . . ."

"You're scared."

"Yeah." Something zipped through him. "But

not for me," he clarified. "For her. I don't—"
He hated talking about this. "I don't know what
happened to me before the Sahara, and I don't
want that hurting her somehow. Just . . . I have
this feeling it will."

"You assume it was bad."

"Are you kidding?" Leif snorted. "Six months
of my life are missing, like someone erased them.
How can that not be bad?"

"We don't know for sure that someone erased
them."

Why was Canyon arguing this? "It's the only
answer," Leif countered. "The markers in my
bloodwork with interferons, the scans—my
parietal lobe was altered so that pain—"

"Which"—Canyon cut in—"the specialists said
could have been from a head injury."

"Or from an experiment."

"Leif," his brother said with a heavy sigh. "I
hear you, man. I do. You want that gap to make
sense. You want it to have significance, but we
have no proof."

"*I* am the proof!" he snapped. "And what if—"

"Dad?" came a small voice from behind.

Canyon looked over his shoulder. "What's up,
bud?"

Beneath a shock of blond hair, Owen was
blessed—cursed?—with the Metcalfe blues.
"Mom said she needs your help, and I'm stuck on
my homework."

His brother tapped Leif's shoulder. "See if you can help Owen? I think I'm on KP."

Kitchen patrol. "Yeah." Sure. Why not? There wouldn't be answers out here either. And he wouldn't have to endure more of Canyon telling him to leave it alone. Tucking away his frustration and questions, Leif moved toward the door and flipped his nephew up over his shoulder. "What's melting your gray matter, squirt?"

After depositing Owen on the kitchen floor, he followed him to the living room, where a folder waited on the coffee table with a pencil. He eyed the worksheet. "Math."

"Yeah, Mom says I'm good at it, but I hate it."

"You and me both," Leif muttered. "Wouldn't you rather learn about tactical—"

"No!" Dani snapped from the kitchen, where his brother was setting a steaming casserole on the island. "Do not corrupt my son, Leif."

"Corrupt? I'm training him up in the way he should go—"

"And he won't be able to calculate how far and fast he has to hoof it to safety without math," she said with a warning smile. "It's dinnertime anyway. Owen, go wash up and tell the girls to do the same." She pointed a spatula at Leif. "You too, Runt. No arguing."

After a delicious meal gathered around the table with family and Taissia, a constant reminder of her missing mother, Leif played a game of catch and then football with Owen before his mother declared it time to finish homework, then bedtime.

Canyon skillfully avoided continuing their conversation. Leif guessed it didn't matter. There were only questions on top of questions, and he knew answers weren't going to magically appear. He'd have to extricate them from the past, out of whoever was hiding them.

Yawning, he watched the news with Canyon for a while and let the negativity of the world drown out his own chaos.

About midnight, his brother slapped his thigh. "Guest room's yours, if you want it. Thought maybe we could head to the range in the morning, work off some steam."

It was an invitation for more family time, more talk. Or was it more avoiding the elephant in the room? "I think I'll head back. Want to get a workout in before I crash."

His brother gave him a sidelong glance. "You avoiding me?"

"Pretty sure that's your tactic." Leif stood. "I'll catch you in the morning. Thank Dani for dinner for me."

Back at his place, he changed into workout shorts, shed his shirt, and blasted music through the open-concept space. Of the two-thousand-square-foot flat, he used one-third for living and the other two-thirds as an obstacle and workout area. He started with jumping rope, then burpees. From there, he worked on tic-tacking the corner and the salmon ladder. A good hour in, he was back to the salmon ladder and had reached the top. His hand cramped, and he was tempted to release.

*"Chief, let go!"*

Leif blinked. Shut out the memory. The cleft. Krieger. His face, sweaty, dusty, tangled in panic.

*"Let go!"*

The words slapped his ears. His concentration broke. He dropped to the floor with a grunt. Hung his head, eyes closed. Fought back the memory. He staggered back to his bed and fell against it. Cupped his hands over his face, waiting for the memory to recede.

*"We got trouble."*

*"I think we crashed."*

*Gunfire. Shouts.*

*"Call it in!"*

The incident refusing to leave him alone, Leif flopped back against the mattress with a grunt.

*"Grenade!" Krieger shouted and ducked.*

*It thunked against the large boulder protecting them, then clattered around the rocks. The explosion punched Leif's chest. Pitched him forward. He caught himself and felt the shower of rock and debris. Dust clouds plumed.*

*As the air cleared, Krieger grinned. "I'm too pretty—"*

Crack! Crack! Crack!

*Krieger froze. Eyes wide. He glanced down.*

*Leif realized a fraction too late what was happening. He lunged as a chasm opened below Krieger, who clapped arms with him. Rocks rumbled beneath his feet. Easily fifty to seventy feet yawned below Krieger, who saw it, too, then swung back with bulging eyes.*

*With both hands clamped onto him, Leif tried to haul him up. Rock cracked and surrendered, widening the chasm. The more Krieger fought for a toehold to push up to safety, the more rocks fell away. The massive boulder that had provided protection groaned, as if its burden was too great to bear any longer.*

*"Let go. Let go!"*

*Metal clanged. "Always remember"—a voice came through, tinny, uncertain—"I will rise."*

*"Taking fire! Taking fire!"*

*They were on the valley floor, fleeing insurgents. Avoiding eating lead.*

*"Chief, it's no use," Krieger shouted, struggling on with Harcos, who now had no legs. Blood draining out.*

*Leif strangled a shout.*

*"Do it again. Over and over," that tinny voice said.*

*"I will rise." Leif swung around, aiming his carbine down the plain to the barreling fighters. This didn't make sense.*

*Now Guerrero was falling. Falling. "Let go."*

"No!"

*"Not worth it. We can't save everything. Let go."*

"Leif?"

"No," Leif ground out, turning to the voice. *Kappi. He was walking, tripping because a lone tendon held his leg together. He reached a broken hand toward Leif. "Nooo!"*

"Leif?"

*Someone tackled him with a primal shout. Leif shot out his arm. Cuffed the throat. Flipped the guy.*

"Leif!" *Frantic eyes.*

*But it was no good. He wouldn't be weak.* "I won't let you kill them!"

"Leif, please! It's me!"

*The eyes . . . familiar. He knew them.*

He blinked. Sand and rocks gave way to a gray blanket. Soft bed. Black hair and wide, beautiful eyes. Throat in his hands.

"Iskra!"

Thoughts slingshotted through the dark. His apartment. He was in his loft. On the bed. Leif threw himself off her, heart jamming. Mind burning with the image of his hands strangling her.

She shifted, hand going to her neck.

Stricken, he sagged onto the mattress. "I . . . I'm sorry." Shame shoved his gaze down. He didn't want to see how he'd hurt her.

"Hey," she said softly. "It's okay."

He reached for her—and she came. He pulled her spine to his chest and tightened his arms around her. Crushed her close. Anything so he didn't pummel her with apologies and let her see his brokenness, the terror that had claimed his soul.

This was not how she'd imagined being in bed with Leif Metcalfe. He hauled her against his bare chest and wrapped his hold around her. Her heart writhed at the restriction, the familiar sense of panic from when she'd lived with Hristoff. But this was Leif, and his touch was strangely calming.

Ragged breaths came hot against her cheek. They were frantic, exhausted. Lying there, she recalled his pale blue eyes. Wild and dark, they'd been hostage to whatever nightmare had him shouting in the night.

A clock in the living room ticked off the seconds, droning into minutes. She didn't dare push him, and she had no idea what to say. What surged to life in his dreams obviously tormented him. And he needed time to emerge from that. Reset.

She smoothed a hand along his arm, sensing his frenetic heart rate slowly even out and his trembling quiet.

"I could've killed you," he breathed against her ear.

"Don't flatter yourself," she taunted. The

violence of his actions had been real and startling. But she couldn't voice that, not after the agony in his tone when he apologized.

His arms were a perfect cradle hold. This wasn't about passion, but security. About being there for each other, being a refuge. When Taissia had been in danger with Hristoff, Leif had come. Now she wanted to do that for him. Even though he was the most capable operator she'd ever met. From the start, his lack of fear warned her that he'd been through a lot. Only an experienced person rushed *into* an unknown situation without hesitation. But the demons hiding in the dark passages of his memories . . . those had them both terrified. Leif was skilled. Unafraid. What did it take to make a man like him quake?

Silence cocooned them as night lumbered on, defying dawn to break its power. Much as Leif had, apparently, been fighting whatever specter occupied his dreams.

"You didn't call," he said, breaking the quiet around them.

"I couldn't." When he inquired about her whereabouts, why she hadn't responded to his calls or texts, she would have to lie.

No. She couldn't do that again. Not after the last time, the way he'd looked at her. The anger and hurt that wreaked havoc with her ill intentions. She must find a way to explain without compromising.

Or she could just tell him. But then Director Iliescu would be livid.

Leif's hand twitched, his hold weak yet steadfast. His breathing soft. He'd probably fallen asleep. Relaxing, she let herself drift off, too.

Amid a strange chill, her mind sprang awake in time to feel Leif vacating the bed. He plodded to the bathroom. It was a nice view. His v-shaped, well-muscled torso, the black workout shorts, his long, tanned legs. She nearly laughed at the irony that she'd slept with him without *sleeping* with him.

Iskra sank into the warmth of the bed, surprised she wasn't bothered by being here with him. That she'd lain in his arms and didn't find it constricting or repulsive as she had with Hristoff. This was beautiful. This was . . . hope. She snuggled into it and drifted off.

The sounds of cooking coming from the kitchen drew her back to consciousness. Sunlight poked through the window over the sink, amplifying his beautiful physique.

Startled that she'd fallen back asleep, she scooted off the bed and made her way over to him. Around a yawn, she eyed his still-damp hair. His scruff was gone.

"Eggs?" he offered as she slipped onto a barstool at the island.

"Please." Chin on the heel of her hand, she

watched him, still drowsy. A little drunk on being here in a domestic, casual sort of way instead of the intense live-or-die way.

Last night had surprised her. What if it had been Taissia who'd awakened him? More than once, Iskra had imagined being married to Leif. With his training and work, she had to respect the warrior in him. Just as he'd respected her.

But . . . did he?

Unease sifted the quiet of the flat. He clearly knew she'd been somewhere. But he wasn't pushing it. At least not yet.

"Taissia will be glad you're home." He moved the eggs onto a plate and slid it over to her with a fork.

"Mm, I can't wait to see her." She made quick work of the eggs. "What about you? Are you glad I'm home?"

Amusement crinkled the edges of his eyes. "Home?" He chucked the pan in the deep sink, then pivoted and palmed the island. Stared at her. "Why did you come here?"

She set down her fork, surprised at the quick turn in conversation. But not really. This was Leif. He never played dumb. "Last night, I called your brother as promised to let them know I was back. Canyon was still up, said to leave Taissia for the night. He mentioned you'd been there. That you asked about me."

Leif snorted. She could almost read the "so if

Canyon hadn't said to come here, you wouldn't have" in his expression.

"Your brother didn't tell me to come, but I saw the number of times you had called—and didn't leave a message." She tried to make a point, but his face remained impassive. "So I . . . came over."

"Where have you been?"

That tone went sideways through her. "You sound like Hristoff." She hated the words as soon as they left her mouth. Teeth gritted, she swallowed.

"This isn't about me controlling you," he bit out. "It's about what I suspect."

"Jealous lover already?"

He scowled. "How long do we dance around this?"

"Why am *I* getting the third degree?" Hurt plucked at her that he wasn't glad she was here. That she'd stayed with him last night, slept in his arms. That she'd allowed him to keep her in bed. He had no idea how hard that had been. How in retrospect it so nearly paralleled being held down by Hristoff. But his touch, her desire for him, had settled that panic. "Why don't we talk about you shouting and screaming in your sleep?"

Leif pitched his plate in the sink and stalked out of the kitchen.

She let him. Hugged herself, arms resting on the island, and followed him with her gaze. He vanished into the closet.

She expelled a painful breath. After what she'd been through with Hristoff, she had no inclination to pander to a man. To placate his moodiness. But that wasn't Leif. He wasn't moody. He was intense yet funny. But something was . . . off.

When he reappeared, he had on jeans and was threading his arms through a black T-shirt. He grabbed his wallet and phone, stuffing them into his pockets before plodding to her on still-bare feet. He planted one hand on the island, the other on the back of her chair, and leaned in close.

And God help her, she felt herself collapsing beneath those sparkling blue eyes.

"I'm not trying to control you." His gaze searched her face. "Tell me you know that."

She nodded. "I also know you want answers from me but aren't willing to give them yourself."

He clenched his teeth, his jaw muscle bouncing. Then a nearly imperceptible nod. "Two operatives make for an interesting relationship. Both with secrets we can't or don't want to uncan."

"You know I can't tell you where I was."

"So you *are* working for Dru."

"But you can tell me where you were," she challenged, speaking of his trip to who-knew-where.

"No." He drew in a hard breath and snorted it out. "I . . . can't figure out what's in me, so I can't explain it."

She shifted on the barstool, peering up at him.

"Let me help. I want to be there for you."

He cupped her face and tilted it forward. Kissed her crown. "Soon." He snatched his keys. "My brother asked me to go to the range with him. You ready to see Taissia?"

Curse the man—he always knew how to negotiate his way out of conversations he didn't like.

"Yes. But when you're ready, so am I."

# CHAPTER 14

## FORT BELVOIR, VIRGINIA

After clearing the main gate and security checkpoint of the building, Adam strolled up the main hall to the commander's office. It was good to be working with Peyton again, but he felt like he was walking on eggshells. "We wasted half a day waiting for this guy to call."

"At least he called." Peyton strode to the receptionist's desk and handed over her creds. "We're here to see Captain Brigham."

Hair in a slicked-back bun and her ACUs crisp, the airman nodded. "Have a seat. I'll notify him you're here."

Adam turned toward a row of butt-numbing plastic chairs and wanted to groan.

"Right here," a man said, his voice the nasally kind that made Adam want to punch him. He extended a hand. "Lieutenant Devine? And . . . ?"

Seemed he'd deliberately forgotten Adam's name. Usually happened when guys saw Pete.

"This is Staff Sergeant Adam Lawe," Peyton introduced. "Special Forces, multiple tours, plenty of medals to cover that thick chest of his."

Adam stilled at the way she rattled off his record. What was that about?

"Right." Withdrawing his wary glance, Brigham nodded over his shoulder. "Come on back. There's a conference room we can use." He led them down a hall, banked right, then angled through a door. He took a seat at the head of the table. "So, you have questions about Gilliam?"

Peyton lowered herself onto a brown vinyl chair and crossed her legs. "We do," she said sweetly. "You may have heard he's AWOL."

"I looked up his record when I was made aware of your appointment."

"We're trying to establish a history for him. We were told you were his unit commander when he was last in Afghanistan."

Brigham, hair trimmed close on the sides and back but not quite a high-and-tight, scratched his head. "I'm sorry, but isn't this the job of the MPs or CID? I've already talked with them."

"Does it bother you to answer our questions, Captain Brigham?" Peyton asked, patronizingly calm.

"It bothers me to take time from my duties," he said with a nervous laugh.

A glint appeared in Pete's expression. "Is your duty not to your fellow soldiers and those under your authority, as well as your country?"

"Yes, but"—he shrugged—"soldiers go AWOL every day, wracked with guilt or struggling with PTSD."

"He had PTSD?" she asked.

"I didn't say that," Brigham said, obviously aware of the legal ramifications of asserting a soldier's state of mind and what that could do to a soldier's chance for advancement.

She cocked her head. "Did Carsen have a hard time when he returned from his last tour of duty?"

"Sure." Another shrug. "We all do. It's hard to come home and find things different. Life goes on here while we're out there fighting for freedom and the innocent. You return, and your friends have new friends and jobs are hard to find—where do sharpshooter skills fit in with society?"

"Sir," Peyton said leaning forward, "you saw our credentials, proof that we're not with CID. Sergeant Lawe and I have no interest or desire to prosecute or otherwise charge Sergeant Gilliam. Our intent, plain and simple, is to find him. Maybe find out why he disappeared."

The granite expression of the captain never faltered, but something in his eyes did—and yet still forbade him from opening up.

Adam had dealt with things like this many times in the field, convincing privates to cough up intel that could get their buddies in trouble. "Look." He shifted to the edge of his seat. "I get not wanting to rat on one of your own, but that's not what we're after. We have cause to believe Carsen may be in trouble or caught up in something he probably wouldn't do on a normal day. That's what we want to stop. I've been in the field, seen things nobody wants to talk about. Done things most would never admit. I'd do anything for my team, anything to protect them. Even if it meant protecting them from themselves." He narrowed his left eye. "I think you're the same breed of soldier."

Brigham sighed. "I swear, if you turn what I saw against him or me—"

"Give it to us," Adam said. "It stays between us."

Brigham looked at the door and swallowed. "Carsen did come back . . . different."

"Moody, irritable?" Peyton offered.

"Yeah." Brigham hesitated. "No. I don't know. He was irritable, but it seemed . . . He wouldn't talk. Even his AARs were off."

"Off?" Adam repeated. "How's that?"

"Incomplete, vague." The captain straightened and swiped his lower lip. "It was like he was afraid of telling the truth."

"Did something happen out there that he wanted to protect or hide from superiors?"

"That's just it, no. Nothing." Brigham tapped the table. "I mean, what happens out there, we want it to stay there, but he didn't do anything worth getting run up the flagpole over. But when I applied pressure on him to fix the report, he got mad. Told me to back off—indirectly, of course."

"Just one report?" Adam pressed. "Or on several?"

"A few," Brigham admitted.

"Was he always sloppy with reports?"

"Never. He was by the book, and one of the best I've worked with. And he had it together, ya know?"

"When did he change?" Peyton asked.

"I don't . . ." He seemed to be searching for information. "Maybe two, three weeks before we came back."

"Was there a trigger?"

"No."

Adam nodded. "Can you tell us which mission the vague reports started with?"

Brigham bounced his shoulders. "Not off the top of my head. I could research it and let you know."

"We'd appreciate that," Peyton said with that killer smile. "Anything else you can think of about Carsen? Anything he mentioned that upset him—"

"No."

"—or worried him? Made him not want to come back?"

"No." He stilled. Frowned. "I haven't talked to him since we came back because I got reassigned here, but last I saw him, he was worrying about his sister."

"Sienna?" Peyton supplied.

"Yeah." Brigham sniffed. "Carsen was a gruff

son of a gun, so you'd never expect him to have a hot sister like that."

"She's a cultural support team member, a valuable member of the military," Peyton stated flatly.

Brigham blanched and donned a contrite expression. "Right. Of course." He hunched his shoulders. "Sorry."

"If you recall anything else, Captain," Adam said, standing, "you have our contact information. We'd appreciate your call."

"Of course." He shook their hands. "I hope you find him and he's okay. Nothing worse than finding out someone you worked with became one of the twenty-two."

Adam tensed. It was no secret that every day twenty-two veterans committed suicide. "You think he was that bad off?"

Brigham hesitated. "I don't know. None of us ever knows, do we?"

"I thought you were going to take a bead on him," Adam teased as they left the base in her crossover.

"In my mind, I was," Peyton admitted as she pulled into traffic, still furious over how hard her fellow cultural support team members had to work to prove themselves and not get treated like meat. "He mentioned nothing about Sienna's abilities, only her looks."

"Cad."

"You mocking me?" She whipped a glower at him.

"Never." A grin peeked from his thick beard. "Maybe a little."

Her pulse thrashed. "So you think it's okay for him—"

"No!" He grunted. "Not at all." He hooked his arm over the back of her seat and gripped the headrest. "I hope you know that I appreciate you for more than your gorgeous looks."

Did he seriously—

"I mean, if you had any." He flinched. "See? This is why I don't do politics. If I were in government, I'd accidently sign over the country somehow."

The man was hopeless. "It's not *political,* it's *politically correct.*"

Adam threw up his hands. "I can't even get that right."

Okay, she had to admit she felt bad for him. He tried. Honest to God, he did. But he was so immutably alpha and, well, *male.* Peyton tried to hide her smile, knowing he'd seize on it. She shifted her attention to traffic, to Brigham's information.

She wanted to get things written down before she forgot what he'd said, but traffic was a bear, as usual, heading onto the Beltway. "Mind if we grab dinner to avoid rush hour and so I can write things down while they're fresh?"

"I'm always up for food."

That was one thing they'd always done well—dinner. She wasn't one of those ounce-of-dressing-and-pile-of-leaves girls. Give her pizza, burgers, and cheesecake all day, every day. She could put away a steak with the best of the guys.

Seated in a booth near the back of Mozzarella's, her favorite American grill, she tugged a small notebook from her purse and started jotting notes. The waiter took their orders and soon brought glasses of water and a basket of bread for them while they waited for their meals.

"I'm surprised you defended Sienna," he said quietly.

Peyton hesitated, pen poised over the bullet journal. "I didn't defend Sienna. I defended CSTs." She dropped the pen and sat up straight, pushing her bangs from her face. "Go to any social media site or website that talks about our role in the combat theater and check the comments. The majority are male veterans belittling our work, questioning our medals— saying they aren't earned—and disputing that we're heroes, too."

For several long seconds, he studied her, then glanced down at the table. "It's wrong." He scratched his beard, looking abashed. "I was one of them. Until I met you."

The girl who'd fallen hard and fast for a special

operator was feeling a bit giddy right now. But the one who'd been crushed by said operator tightened her abs, ready for a sparring match. Was there a *but* to his statement? Or was he just sweet-talking her, hoping to get her back?

"Don't scowl at me like that," he said. "I mean it."

"Okay." She managed that word without it shaking her. "Tell me."

He looked like a scared schoolboy. A really well-built, smart-aleck, tatted schoolboy with a thick beard and gray-blue eyes. "Tell you what?"

"You said you thought the same way until you met me. What changed your mind? And know," she said, trying to barricade her heart and hope, "that I'm not convinced your mind is changed. I think you still see me as the cheerleader."

"I'm a guy, Pete," he said, using the nickname that drove her crazy. The one he'd whispered against her ear, butchering her real name in an intense romantic moment. It had stuck. "We are visually based. I can't help it. You *are* beautiful."

She let out a disgusted sigh. "S—"

"Back up," Adam said, motioning. "Forget I said that." He ran a hand over his beard and leaned into the table. "The first time I saw you line up a shot on a Taliban leader and nail him at nearly a mile, I was sunk. Then, seeing you enter that hut and ferret out the scoundrel literally hiding behind women's skirts, I had mad respect for you." He shifted toward her. "You were the total package. I never thought I'd find someone who liked to take a carbine to the range and massacre the target, then doll up for a night on the town. That woman?" He shook his head. "Didn't exist—until you marched into Bagram. Help me understand why that is a bad thing. Why can't you be both a kick-butt woman and a beautiful one?"

"It's not that I can't—and I am, by the way—but that you see the cheerleader and your brain stops working."

He studied the table again. "Can't help it if I'm crazy about you."

Her heart tripped over that statement. Over the man sitting before her, lost in his own masculinity. Which also wasn't bad. Because Adam Lawe was a powerful presence. Maybe that was what scared her. She was afraid of losing herself. Of giving herself to him again and having him stomp the life out of her. She wanted him. Wanted to be with him.

But Adam . . . Adam was career first and only. If she became an obstacle to that pursuit, he'd walk. Again.

"What am I doing wrong?" he asked, his words pleading. "Tell me. How do I get you to give me another chance?"

It was a cruel answer, but the only one that would tell her where she stood. "Walk away."

At his confusion, she breathed the fatal words. "From the Army and from Reaper."

A frown slithered through his expression and pushed him back. "You serious?"

"It's the only way I'll know you want *me,* just not an excursion or entertainment while we're on missions."

"Pete, I walked away from you because if we did this, if we made it official—"

Made it official? Her heart rapid-fired.

"—and we both stay active, there is no guarantee we'll both come home. I can't guarantee I will make it back to you, and the thought of hurting you like that—"

"So it's okay to hurt me *now?*"

"That's not—"

"That's *exactly*—"

"What if *you* don't come back?" he asked, stabbing his hand at her. "How am I supposed to recover from that?"

"Okay!" Their server appeared with steaming plates of food. "Bacon-bacon cheeseburger with sweet potato fries?"

Swallowing, Peyton sat up as the waiter set down her meal, then delivered the other to Adam. Her ears were ringing with words she'd never considered. He worried about leaving her a widow. They'd never talked about having kids—it was just too weird to imagine the brawny operator trying not to drop a newborn—

but it hung at the back of their minds. It was too complicated. Too . . . domestic for Adam. But the words that had her struggling for air, unable to think about anything else . . .

*"How am I supposed to recover from that?"*

The soldier who'd had enough brass on his Class As to supply an entire war effort, the man who rushed into danger without a second thought, the man who'd faced down commandos and terrorists with near irreverence—that soldier was *afraid*. Afraid of losing *her*.

# CHAPTER 15

## REAPER HEADQUARTERS, MARYLAND

"Where is she?"

In his hub at the Reaper headquarters, Cell looked up from his bank of monitors to where the deputy director stood, being faced down by Leif.

"She's working," Iliescu said.

"This is like the second, third time you've sent her out. She has a kid here." He lifted a hand. "She was back, what, two, three days? And already—"

"She has a rock-solid focus on the Book of the Wars."

"You're sending *her* after it?"

"Leif, I'll talk to you, but right now I have something else to deal with."

"We will talk." Leif pivoted and left.

Iliescu blew out a breath, then turned and entered Cell's office. "Got a minute?"

The gyro from lunch plummeted to Cell's toes and threatened to vault right back up his throat. "Um, sure," he said as the deputy director entered and closed the door. Locked it. "Do I need to make arrangements for my body?"

"Depends," came the director's terse reply.

Mentally, Cell traveled the monitors surrounding him, wondering if he'd left some of his guilt up for the director's viewing pleasure. "On what?"

"You." Iliescu leaned back, an ankle resting on a knee as he rubbed his chin. "Anything you need to tell me, Mr. Purcell?"

Formal address. Meant he was annoyed. Which crime was Cell supposed to confess? His system nearly crashing? Using Mei when he'd been told not to? Digging into Above Top Secret files to get a lead on suspicions that were only hunches? That alone was enough to turn the director's anger into a hydrogen bomb.

"I got nothing," he lied.

"What happened to your computer on the plane?"

Well, crap. "It crashed. A Trojan was attached to some . . ." His pulse jiggled. He glanced at his screens, mind racing. "You're monitoring my system."

"That," Iliescu said, his anger finally sparking, "has nothing to do with why your system crashed."

"You're freakin' monitoring me? *Babysitting* me?"

"You're new in this office, so I'll forgive your disrespect and rudeness," the director said, his face reddening. "What I won't forgive is your disobeying a direct order." He rose to his full height. "You might be a genius where it comes to computers—"

"Might be?"

"—but there are analysts who could take you down in a heartbeat."

Cell snorted. His screens blipped. Words started sliding off the screen, falling to the bottom as if they were resting on a floor. Then they vanished. "Son of a batch of cookies." They were toying with him, mocking him.

"There was a reason I told you not to reach out to Dragon Mei."

"I had a hunch—"

"And it has devastated our ability to move forward."

Cell blanched. "No. It was just my system."

"I wish it was, but your system—"

"Devious foul betrayer," Cell growled. It made sense now. "Because you were monitoring and jacking my system, they got into the agency's computers. That's what this is about, isn't it?"

"Do not put this on us." Iliescu's brow furrowed. "Had you obeyed orders, respected my instructions and agency protocols, we would not be struggling to get the problem isolated."

Gaping, Cell considered his screens, which were now functioning again. Cursed himself for not thinking the agency would spy on him. "Holy out of the fire and into the spying pan." They were spies. What else would they do? And why wasn't the director outright livid? "Why are you so calm? That's a sick calm, not a good calm.

What's wrong?" he asked, feeling as if menthol filled his aching lungs.

Iliescu considered him, his eyes dark with reproach.

"You're not yanking my clearance or having me escorted out—which is completely within your rights."

"I don't need you to tell me what I can do."

"So something's happened or"—he tried not to gloat—"you need me."

"We will deal with your negligence and defiance later." Iliescu checked the door, then lifted a device from his pocket. Clicked it. A jammer? "The information Mei sent you may have also been relayed to certain parties whom I have gone to great lengths to conceal things from." He stared at Cell for a long time.

A really long time.

Cell shifted. Grew uncomfortable and knew where this was going. What it was about. *Who* it was about. Leif. "Okay" was the only word he managed to drag through the thick sludge of ominous silence and a guilty conscience.

"I think we understand each other. What you've done not only compromised Langley and this division, but it has put him at *great* risk."

"I . . ."

"I think you consider him a friend."

"I do."

"Then I need what you have, because if he's

compromised, you have no idea the storm you've unleashed on him." Iliescu stood. "Fill me in. Completely. Or we may lose our only hope for stopping ArC and keeping our assets alive."

## ITALY

Iskra strode into the upscale Italian restaurant in a silk pantsuit and heels. Her attire wasn't for the company she would keep in these walls, but to play the part, she had to dress the part. She approached the lectern where the host stood with an apathetic expression.

"Yes?" he droned.

"Miss Todorova?" a deep, gravelly voice called as two men in suits approached, arms resting comfortably at their sides—near weapons, no doubt.

"Ah," the host said, shifting on his feet. "Forgive me, *signora*, I did not realize—"

"Please." The burly man spoke again and motioned her past the foyer, irritation tugging his pocked but chiseled face. He might not be muscled like Adam Lawe, but he was clearly experienced in getting his way.

She inclined her head. "You kept me waiting," she said, sauntering past him and praying he could not detect the twitch of her heart.

In a quiet, secluded area of the restaurant,

two guards were posted at double doors, which opened upon a command from her escort. As Iskra entered, her nerves strangely unsettled, she saw someone—a woman—exit through a side door.

A dozen elegantly decorated tables adorned the lavish room that held one customer. Impeccably dressed, his hair tousled slightly and threaded with silver, Ciro Veratti sat like a king holding court.

His gaze swept her as she approached. "Miss Todorova, had I any idea that you would one day be free of Hristoff . . ."

"What would your supermodel girlfriend say about you flirting with me?" She slid into a chair across from him.

His laugh was light and far too relaxed. "That she knows my character and my admiration for capable, beautiful women."

As a waiter placed a black linen cloth across Veratti's lap, Iskra noted there were no utensils on her side of the table. "Afraid I have a vendetta?" She sent him a demure smile as the staff poured glasses of red wine.

"I am amused by you but not foolish." A shadow passed over his deep-set eyes. "And you are not here to eat, but to listen."

"I am curious," she said. "Why come to a restaurant when you have ample staff at your estate who could do what these employees do?

Would it not have been simpler and more private to meet there?"

"Presence brings notoriety, Miss Todorova. Not everything I do is for myself. By frequenting Giuseppe's, my name and money are associated with this fine establishment. That will bring him business, and he, in turn, graciously allows me a fabulous porterhouse."

"And scares off his own business, too."

"Those who run are not worthy of such a place. And this is a brilliant setting with capable staff and exquisite food." Veratti sipped his wine. "Have you tasted Claude-Pierre's skill before?"

She had no appetite for food or idle talk. "What do you want, Mr. Veratti?"

"Cooperation."

Now Iskra laughed.

"Oh, please," he said, waving a hand. "Do not doubt yourself, Miss Todorova. I realize you failed Hristoff on two occasions and even assisted in the murder of your patron, but I trust you and believe in you despite those failings."

Furious, Iskra would not play games anymore. "Last time," she said with a tilt of her head. "What do you want?"

He held up a finger, waiting until the server delivered their salads and departed. "Not until after our meal."

Iskra gritted her teeth, fisting her hand in her lap. She had been a man's pawn before, forced to pretend, to endure too much time with someone who only sought to control where she went and what she did.

This was Hristoff all over again. But with a gun all but pointed at her head—she could see the imprint of the burly guard's weapon beneath his jacket—she had no choice. Which infuriated her.

"Anger looks good on you, Iskra," Veratti said, forking his leafy greens and tomatoes.

The tone was insulting—a mix of master and lover. But she would never again sell her soul to a man.

"Hristoff said that as well." She lifted her wine glass. "Look how he ended up."

Veratti's eyes glittered as he sipped his wine. He took another mouthful of salad, a smile never leaving his gaze. "Abandon that vitriol climbing your throat before it gets you in trouble, Iskra. I may not have had the pleasure of you, but I know your kind. I know what drives you, what controls you."

"Nothing controls me," she hissed.

With a guffaw, he stabbed his fork at the door. "I know you want to stay alive to protect that precious daughter of yours, and that *does* control you. It keeps you from tempting fate and leaving this room. Not that my men would allow you to leave."

Was that a challenge? "I never knew you to be so wasteful with resources."

He tipped his wine glass at her. "You have *never* known me, Miss Todorova." A sip, and he swirled the crimson liquid in the goblet. "Do not fool yourself into thinking I am like Peychinovich, weak man that he was, though brilliant in business." His face enlivened as their main courses arrived and Iskra's untouched salad was whisked away. Once the waiters exited, he leaned forward and narrowed his eyes. "But absolutely feckless when it came to you."

Why that made her feel bad or guilty, Iskra could not say. But it stoked her hatred of this man.

"Hristoff cost me a great deal," he said, cutting his steak. "In fact, I think his debt now rests on your shoulders."

Dread curdled in her stomach. "I owe you nothing."

"Uh-uh," he said, shaking his finger. "Who was it that did not secure the Cellini?"

She stared back defiantly.

"And who lost the Book of the Wars?"

"That was not my fault—your thugs interfered, and that had colossal ramifications."

"You were there!" he roared, slamming down his knife. He bent forward, elbow on the table, and skewered her with a glare. "I tasked you with *one* objective—find out the name of the facility. Just the name. No doubt existed that you could do it. And you did. You got inside, and"—his hand and eyebrows raised—"did you deliver that information to me? Did you call and say, 'Ciro, I have what you want'? No! No, you did not."

She had no regrets over choosing Leif over Ciro in that situation.

Veratti sucked his teeth as he lifted his fork and studied her. Then grinned. And laughed. "I see," he said, carving off another chunk of steak. "I see why Hristoff was so very distracted."

"And now he's dead. Would you like to see that, too?"

In a blur, a weight clamped the back of her neck and slammed her face into the table. Pain crackled through her head. Training had her shoving back the chair. Gaining her feet. Palming the table and twisting, driving her foot into the back of the guard's head with a wicked-fast round kick. He staggered.

Freed, Iskra hopped away and landed in a fighting stance. "If you have something to say—"

"Had you not so rudely interrupted me," Veratti said, never slowing in eating his meal as he pointed to the table. "Please. Sit."

Another guard righted her chair and palmed his weapon.

"I'll stand," Iskra said. "Let's get this over with."

Veratti huffed. "Indeed. You are ruining my dinner."

She dared not speak the retort on the tip of her tongue.

"We have a mutual enemy, Miss Todorova."

"Only one?"

"One," he said with emphasis, glowering up through his thick eyebrows, "who is causing me a great deal of trouble. I want your help persuading him to . . . step aside."

This was interesting. Not what she'd expected from the notable Ciro Veratti. "You have assassins and lackeys at your beck and call, Mr. Prime Minister. Why draw me into your problems?"

"Motivation."

She arched her eyebrow.

"Find the right one, and you are the master of the soul." He set down his napkin and eased back in his chair. Hands resting on either side of his plate, he studied her. "It is true that I had the book—or, more accurately, I had control of it, though it was not directly in my possession. That would create problems, draw attention. So it was held for me. But it seems that recently a certain enemy of ours—a man supposedly loyal to me—has taken it upon himself to recover the book."

Her heart skipped a beat. "Recover."

"Indeed. You know of whom I speak."

"Rutger Hermanns." Saying the name felt like consent.

Veratti tilted his head in a nod. "You will take care of this problem."

"Why would I do that?"

He eyed her. "Weren't you looking for some-one? A . . . brother?"

Breath trapped in her throat, she stared back, disbelieving. He couldn't know about Mitre.

"Do this thing with Rutger, and we will talk."

## REAPER HEADQUARTERS, MARYLAND

. . . garbed in authority lost their lives, breath snuffed like lamps doused. Rage in the right hand, vengeance in the left, there was naught but blood upon the lands. Kingdoms shifted. Countries collapsed. Chaos seized and reigned in answer to the summons of the enemies of kings. Upon those from below is marked the quest that tethers their soul in darkness . . .

*Rage in the right hand. Vengeance in the left. Upon those from below . . . marked . . . tethers their soul in darkness . . .*

Leif ran his thumb over the scar on his right hand. He'd gotten it in the crash, from the fire.

Fire.

His mind bungeed back to RTB, that explosion. Seeing the aftermath of the fireball. The scorch marks. He dug into his laptop and the files. Pulled up the photos he'd taken from news footage. From his visits to the site. Studied the dark smudges.

Phone in hand, he placed a call.

"Spill."

"Hey. It's Runt."

"What can I do for you?"

"D'you have pictures from the explosion at the shop that you could send over?"

"Sure," Spill said. "I'll have Ghillie shoot them your way."

"Cool, thanks. Take care."

"Is that it?"

"Yeah. Thanks." Leif ended the call and stared at the photos, itching to see the images from the shop.

"Hey," Devine said, joining him. "You got a minute?"

Leif closed his laptop, extricating himself from the past. "What's up?"

"When Adam and I visited Brigham, Gilliam's unit commander mentioned there were some AARs that he bugged Gilliam to fix, said they were vague."

"Okay."

"He sent them over, and I noticed a pattern. Each incomplete AAR was from when he and his team had dealings with a particular unit." She handed him four separate files, each with highlights.

Leif eyed them. "Typical," he said, recognizing a special-ops unit designation. "A lot of times those are classified, so he might've been told to be vague."

"Yeah, I just . . ." Peyton shrugged. "I dunno. Just seems odd that his team would keep getting picked to work with the same unit."

"If it works and ain't broke," Leif said with a smirk.

"But what if it's more?"

Leif eyed her. "Like?"

She folded her arms, skating a glance behind him—toward Lawe, if he guessed the trajectory of her gaze right. "I dated this guy once. A Marine."

"No wonder it ended."

"It ended because I picked up on something in his texts and emails. He was vague. I got a hunch that he was leaving stuff out, and turned out he was leaving out his other girlfriend."

"Ouch."

"So," Peyton said, "what if Gilliam was leaving stuff out because he wanted to hide it?"

"You saying he was shady?"

"Or the unit was, or someone on his team." She shrugged. "It's possible, right?"

"Maybe." Leif had to consider what she'd said. It happened more often than anyone wanted to admit. "Can I keep these?"

"Yeah. I have the originals."

"Okay, people," Braun said as she strode into the hub. The team gathered for a briefing. "We have a serious problem. I just got off the phone with the commander of Indo-Pacific Command. Apparently, Chinese authorities are claiming the attempted murder of General Chang was carried out by an operative for Taiwan."

"Come again?" Leif objected.

Lawe snorted. "Are they out—"

"According to the Chinese, one of the men involved in the attack—"

"*One* of the men?" Culver repeated, looking at Leif.

"—killed himself when authorities stormed his home," Braun continued, unfazed.

"Kurofuji worked with someone?" Lawe asked, frowning. "Did we miss a memo?"

"Negative," Leif said, confounded at how things got twisted when a government implemented a wag-the-dog scenario and used a bad situation to advance agenda or policy. "We had one man on location, and that—"

"PLA provided footage of the apprehension in Beijing the day after the attack at the palace," Braun said, tersely plowing past their objections. "Mr. Purcell, if you please."

The wall screen sprang to life, a scene unfolding across its surface. Outside an apartment building, a line of SWAT stood ready. Shots exploded through the door. The camera—apparently an officer's body cam—swung away for protection, which provided a bird's-eye view of the parking lot several levels below. Light danced and glinted, and then the camera shifted back as the sea of black-clad bodies flooded into the apartment. A volley of gunfire erupted. Shouts rang out.

Saito leaned forward, then yanked his gaze from the screen, tapping into his phone as the confrontation continued. Had he figured something out?

"Inside," Braun explained, "they found a computer with emails to and from a notorious and much-sought-after Taiwanese operative. After barricading himself in his bedroom, the target killed himself."

"That's convenient," Lawe grumbled.

Nodding, Leif roughed a hand over his mouth. "Now he can't confirm or deny the accusations. But this isn't just about an assassination attempt."

"Precisely. Establishing an attack on their soil hand-delivers China justification to attack Taiwan," Braun growled. "We all know they've been looking for a reason to do exactly that for years, but according to them, trying to assassinate one of the most powerful men in China and killing a half dozen notables means it is not only their right, but their duty to respond."

"I think they spelled *duty* wrong," Lawe muttered.

"This makes no sense," Leif countered. "If we're hunting names from the Book of the Wars, why would these operators be working for other countries?"

"Actually, if you think about it, the prophecy," Peyton said quietly, "doesn't say who the Neiothen are, nor does it list their country of origin. Simply that they will rise up."

*I will rise.*

*I will rise.*

*I will rise.*

Leif shook his head, plugging the dam on whatever that was. "But still—"

"You said that's Beijing?" Saito asked.

Braun frowned, then nodded. "The video came from the Chinese embassy here."

"Someone is lying," Saito said. "That footage is either faked or it's not connected to what happened at the palace." Unflinching, he set down his phone.

"How do you figure?" the admiral asked.

He pointed to the screen. "At the beginning of the raid, when the body cam panned away from the insertion to avoid the light and shock, the footage showed the road below." He instructed Cell to freeze the frame. "There were puddles all over the street. Rain." He looked at the others. "According to weather tracking, it hasn't rained since before we landed in Beijing." He squinted at the paused image. "China wanted someone to blame and a reason to go to war. The attack on the defense minister is the perfect excuse for an escalation of aggression."

"Which is what we suspected," Braun agreed with a nod.

"But not stopping that attack isn't our fault," Culver noted, then hesitated. "Right? I mean—"

"Fault isn't our concern," Braun snapped. "Preventing a fallout is. If China attacks Taiwan . . . this is classic dominos falling here."

Cell shifted. "Or, like the text foretold, kings falling."

"Right. One country falls, then another in response, and so on, until all that's left standing is whoever toppled the first domino," Braun said, her tanned face severe. "We're assembling intel and, within the week, hope to send you after the next name on the list."

Frustration coiled in Leif's gut. They were seriously getting away from their primary directive. "What about the book?" he asked. "Why aren't we doing more about that?"

Dru glanced at Cell, who focused on his laptop.

That ticked off Leif. "Am I missing something?"

"We've had a . . . complication," Dru admitted but didn't expound.

"I-I'm close to unlocking the next name," Cell said. "But without the book, this may be the last one."

"Which means we should be looking for the book," Leif asserted.

"Just because you aren't out there running around like chickens with your heads chopped off," Dru said, "doesn't mean we're not working on it. You aren't the only team or operators at our disposal."

"We have another contact connected to Carsen Gilliam," Braun said, ignoring Leif's challenge. "His psychiatrist, Dr. Lilah Sheng."

Leif pinched the bridge of his nose, hating the way they kept bulldozing over him. And that they were still searching for Carsen. It bugged him. Worried him. "Why haven't we seen notes from this doctor?"

"Because she's a civilian doctor," Dru said. "No records, and patient-doctor confidentiality buried it. We were able to back-source from bank records where he made a payment to her. But it seems they met more than once—consistently, in fact."

"Civvy doc means he didn't want it on his records," Culver suggested.

"How sure are we about this, that he really visited her so often?" Lawe asked.

"Hacked his car locator records," Cell said. "He was there every week since he returned from his last deployment."

"I want Leif and Iskra to talk to this doc," Dru said.

"Wait," Leif said. "She's back?"

"She's en route now."

Irritation crawled through Leif's veins, but he shoved his thoughts back to the mission at hand. "Okay, wait—if we can hack Gilliam's car and figure out his movements, how are we not able to track him down? He's a freakin' soldier, not a spy. How is he hiding so well the agency can't find him?"

"That's what we'd like to know," Dru said. "Get out there and find an answer. By the time you return, we hope to have things sorted to send Reaper after the next target." The director sent a heated glare at Cell. "Isn't that right, Mr. Purcell?"

"As you wish."

# CHAPTER 16

## BALTIMORE, MARYLAND

The forty-minute drive was made in near silence because Leif didn't trust himself to speak to Iskra. They were headed out to the medical center where Dr. Lilah Sheng had met with Carsen Gilliam. A shrink. They were going to see a shrink, and it was hard not to feel like this was one of those nightmares where he'd forgotten to wear pants. Top that brilliance-of-a-mission objective with the fact that the woman beside him had been away on a mission to find the book without him. Again.

About halfway there, Iskra shifted in her seat to face him.

Hand up, Leif kept his gaze on the road. "Save it."

"What?"

"It is what it is, so let's just leave it."

"You cannot know what I was going to say."

He slid a glance toward her. "Right then, when you turned, you were about to say something about where you've been, or maybe why."

"And what else?"

He nodded, eyeing a rig in the rearview mirror that was bearing down on them. "Either that you know I want to know about the mission, but you can't tell me, so you're sorry. Or that you want to know what the dreams were about." He checked her expression to verify his accuracy, and when she arched an eyebrow, he grinned. "I've been able to read you from day one."

"Why is that?"

He lifted a shoulder. "I guess because, as Dru told me once, we're the same. We think alike."

"Well, I *am* sorry you were not on that mission with me. I wanted you there."

"Seriously?" He veered toward the off-ramp.

"I always did things alone before because it was easier, but with you . . . it is different. Like you said—we're the same. So it makes things simpler to work together. I wanted to talk things through with you. Then, coming back and finding you shouting in your dreams, drenched in sweat . . . I hated it."

He clenched his jaw. "You and me both."

"This last mission, I just . . . I really could have used your presence."

Okay, that surprised him. "Why's that?"

"I met with Veratti."

Leif nearly missed the red light. He nailed the brakes. *"What?"*

"It wasn't part of the plan, but"—she hunched her shoulders—"it had to be done."

"Is that where you got the knot on your cheek?"

"I expressed an opinion he did not like."

Leif's mind screwed up every which way from Sunday. She'd told him about the mission and that piece-of-crap Veratti had roughed her up. Iskra wasn't a woman who needed protection or pandering. She was tough and resilient. Yet she had a softer side that was as sweet and sticky as honey, drawing him to her like a bee. "You're good at holding your own with guys like him."

She smiled. "He admitted he had control of the book but lost it. Implied Rutger Hermanns has the book. Veratti wants me to find it."

Pulling into the medical complex, Leif darted her a look. "You're working with him?" This would be some kind of messed up.

"No, I'm working with you," she said firmly. "But I must give the appearance of placating him."

"Why?" He slid into a parking spot and checked the clock on the dash. They had a few minutes, so he angled toward her. "He got something on you?"

"No, but he has something I want."

"What?"

"My brother. He said if I did this, we would talk about Mitre."

"And you believe him, that he knows where your brother is." He wasn't accusing or questioning. Just curious. *Could* Ciro Veratti have information on her brother? He wasn't sure why, but her search for Mitre had worrisome rip currents.

"I cannot risk *not* believing him and missing

the opportunity to find Mitre." She touched his hand. "You know what will happen if I walk away simply because Veratti is dangerous."

"It takes longer to find your brother." Really, he wasn't seeing the bad side of that scenario.

"Is twelve years not long enough?"

Who was he to argue? He'd spent the last four years searching for his past. "You're right." He nodded. "I hear you." But man, it made him sick to think of her tightroping that fine line with Ciro Veratti. "Did you tell Dru about this?"

She nodded. "He is working on a few things, and so am I—and I will not give up." Vehemence dug into her features.

Leif admired her grit and determination that nearly contradicted her beautiful façade. He nodded, scanning the parking lot and entrance. "Well, we better get in there."

When they approached the appointment desk, Leif checked the time. On the nose. "Leif Metcalfe for Dr. Sheng."

The studious brunette nodded to a side door. "Go on in. She's expecting you."

Moments later, they were seated at a round laminate table with the much-younger-than-expected Lilah Sheng. "As you know," she said sweetly, a leather-bound notebook in hand, "patient confidentiality prohibits me from divulging much of what Mr. Gilliam said to me."

"Actually," Leif said, sliding a letter from the

deputy director across the table, "this will help loosen the details a little."

Wariness barged into the doctor's confidence. She scanned the letter, then sighed and wagged her eyebrows. "Well, that does change things. So, you think he's committed a crime?"

"Yes." Going AWOL was a crime, so Leif wasn't lying. "And we are concerned he might commit another."

Iskra threaded her fingers. "We simply want to find him, and to do that, we need your help."

"Well, like many veterans I speak with, he wanted to fix the symptoms but wasn't willing to look at the problem." Dr. Sheng leaned back in her seat. "Most come in wanting me to help them get rid of, say, angry outbursts. Or to lessen their responses to unexpected noises. But they do not want to delve into what caused their heightened state of vigilance."

It took everything in Leif not to shift in his seat.

"Carsen asked most often about a single recurring nightmare. He wanted to know if it had significance, what it meant. He hoped that once he understood it, it'd go away."

"*A* nightmare? Only one?" Man, that was hitting a little close to home.

"Yes, and the strangest thing was that while military in nature, it wasn't real."

"Dreams . . . aren't real," Leif said, confused.

Sheng gave a placating smile. "What I mean

is that for most veterans who come see me, the nightmares are based in truth. Something that happened in combat. A distortion of some traumatic event that significantly impacted them," she explained. "Carsen said this dream seemed like he was having someone else's nightmare—with things that didn't happen to him—and while it was terrible and terrifying, he somehow felt distanced from it."

There was this side of Leif's head that, when he flew, felt like someone was trying to extract his gray matter from his skull. That was what it felt like sitting here listening to this. But he had to get his thoughts back on terra firma. "Did you, um, see anything in Carsen that gave you concern?"

"Do you mean did I think he could turn violent?"

"Sure." Not exactly, but okay.

"Never." She shook her head, glancing at her notebook. "Carsen was a gentle young man with a fervor for his country and fellow veterans. Never once was I worried for his safety or those around him. And trust me, I see plenty that does give me concern."

Good to know. Reassuring. "Did he ever mention wanting to leave the country?"

"No," she said, smiling again. "Recall that I said Carsen was very much about serving this country. He was a patriot. A healthy one, physically and mentally."

• • •

After meeting with Dr. Sheng, Iskra noticed Leif was strangely quiet on the way back, even while picking up Taissia from kindergarten. Back at the loft, Taissia was content to munch on pizza while watching her favorite snowman-and-sisters cartoon.

"I want a sister, Mama," Taissia announced without preamble.

Startled, Iskra tried not to eye Leif, who was standing on the rooftop terrace, looking out over the city. "Eat your pizza," she said, deflecting the topic. Hopefully he hadn't heard that pronouncement, his mind already occupied. "I'll be right back."

She came up behind him at the rail and slipped her arms around his waist. Rested her cheek on his muscled back. Here. Here she was safe. Happy. Despite the tension between them.

"Do you want more kids?" His question rumbled through his torso.

"You heard," she said. More than a little embarrassed by the topic, Iskra shifted to his side and watched a cab roll around the corner below. *Did* she want more kids? "I do not know," she finally admitted. "Before you, I vowed never to end up in that condition again."

Taissia had not been planned, and since Iskra had feared what Hristoff would do when he learned of the pregnancy—especially since

Taissia wasn't his—for many months, she didn't want the baby. It was a cold, unfeeling truth. Not wanting more children after all that seemed a natural progression.

"You still never call her 'my daughter.'"

"I do," she said. "But it is hard to let her exist and thrive when for so long I feared we would be ripped apart."

Leif had transformed a lot of things in her life. With him, she might just be willing to face pregnancy again. But that was leaping far, far ahead. She was not even sure about marriage. Or if he was interested.

"You've been quiet since we got back," she murmured. When he did not answer, she peered up at him. She wasn't an expert, but he'd been especially focused on one thing the doctor had said. "When she mentioned the dreams, you seemed curious."

Leif shifted on his feet. "Yeah."

Sometimes, Iskra felt like she needed a sledgehammer to open his personal vault. She propped her hip against the rail, debating whether to push.

Gripping the bar, he sighed. His gaze bounced over the horizon. "She said Carsen told her the dreams felt like someone else's."

The tension squirming through his expression concerned her. This time she knew to wait, because whatever he was thinking, Leif was fighting it or wrangling it into something manageable.

Frowning, he met her eyes. "That's how my dreams feel. That one nightmare that nearly had me take you down? I couldn't figure out how to describe them, but what she said is right—they seem like someone else's." He clenched his jaw, lips flat. "But they're not. They're mine."

She wanted to make it go away, to ward off the evil that had infected his life and stolen his gregarious nature—well, what she suspected was once a gregarious nature. His intensity had worsened to a dark shade since he'd saved her and Taissia. "Tell me about the nightmares."

His gaze snapped to hers, then he tucked his chin and looked back at the city. And as if he'd flipped a switch, lighthearted Leif was back. A smile touched his eyes. "My mom had six kids," he said, bending to lean on the rail. "We had a big family, and I never thought twice about it. In fact, I assumed it'd always be big and tight." He shrugged, something weighted in his expression. "Things sure change. We've all gone our own ways. Canyon and I are the only ones within driving distance now."

Anger cloyed at her tolerance, tempting her to rage over his change of subject. But there was a storm consuming his life, one seemingly left over from the mission that had brought them together.

She could be that nagging voice in his head, or she could simply be here for him. "So." She forced a smile into her voice and face. "Do you want kids?"

His gaze bounced over the city as quiet settled between them. Perhaps that was his answer, which stung. She lowered her head. She just couldn't win. Maybe she wasn't strong enough to bring him back from this vortex devouring his life.

"I do." His words were barely audible. "I want it all," he said louder. "Marriage, kids—the whole shebang." His expression tightened, pulsing through his jaw muscle.

Surprised, she wondered what the problem was. What kept him from that dream. Was it her?

He glanced down at her with a huff. "Think about what I did to you the other night. How can I—" He shook his head and looked away again. "I will not have a family just to end up harming them."

"Leif," she said, slipping her arm through his and pressing into his space. She rested her face against his chest, forcing him to hold her. "There is time. And answers will come."

"They've been telling me that for four years, and I'm no closer to the truth." He wrapped his arms around her.

"It hurts me to see you like this."

"Like what?"

"Pulling away. Sad, angry." She shrugged. "You've changed a lot since Russia." She wanted to be for him what he had been for her with Hristoff. But for him, the abuser was the nightmares. There must be a way to alleviate the desperation in the voice of a man rarely vulnerable.

"I can't risk having a nightmare and hurting you or Taissia. I just can't." He kissed her head, and they stayed there for a while. "Do you have nightmares? You went to hell and back under Hristoff's grip. Does that plague your dreams?"

"No," she said quietly, guiltily. She could not explain why she didn't, and it made her feel bad. As if something was wrong with her. Then again, hadn't Leif told her once that she was broken? One of Hristoff's lackeys had called her damaged goods.

Leif let out a long breath. "How do you not have nightmares?"

"I don't know." But she did know. Besides compartmentalizing what she had gone through, it was the man standing before her now. She glanced up and touched the side of his face, aching for the reassurance of him. "You." She smiled, her gaze falling to his lips.

As if reading her thoughts, he caught her mouth with his, and urgency sped through them both. Relief pushed her deeper into his arms. Savored the strength of him as passion roared and tethered them to each other. He was an anchor for her, and his touch proved electrifying.

He kissed a trail across her jaw and down to the crook of her neck, sending skitters down her spine. He buried his face there, crushing her against himself. "That night," he murmured over her throat, "with you in my arms . . . it was the first time I slept without nightmares."

Cupping the back of his head, she ached for him to know peace. "I wish you'd tell me. Let me help. I want to be there for you."

"That'd be nice . . ."

"Tell me about them."

He sighed. "I can't."

"Convenient."

"But true," he said and slumped back against the rail.

"Then you will understand my silence about what I'm doing for the director."

He considered her for several long seconds. "Understand, yes. Like, no."

"Likewise."

His gaze slid over her and into the living room. He shifted around her. "Where's my Taissia?"

He moved inside and scooped her daughter into his arms and blew raspberries on her belly, eliciting peals of laughter.

Yet grief tethered Iskra to the spot, sad that Leif still did not trust her with whatever was tormenting him. They had made an agreement, one that did nothing to soothe the ache.

An hour into another animated movie and more of Leif's avoidance, his phone buzzed. Then hers. They didn't need to look at the screens to know they were being called in. She wrapped Taissia in a hug and kissed her, knowing she could not keep rushing off to save the world when *her* world was right here in her arms.

# CHAPTER 17

## REAPER HEADQUARTERS, MARYLAND

"Okay, listen up. Short and sweet," Iliescu said. "We have new intel on the next possible Neiothen." He nodded to Cell, who moved his laptop.

"We're still working with piecemeal information from the corrupted USB that Iskra gave us, but combining that new intel and painstaking research—"

"Are you wanting a pat on the back?" Lawe asked.

"More like smack on the head," Saito countered.

"—we've managed to tie," Cell ground out, "the code name found in the Book of the Wars, Wu, to one Arlen Dempsey. We have not been able to figure out much except that Dempsey holds dual citizenship—Ireland and U.S. Similar to Kurofuji, Dempsey has been doing contract work with a cybersecurity company in Taiwan—convenient, considering the Chinese maneuvering. This after six years in the Defence Forces of Ireland."

"Okay, explain to me," Culver said, stroking his beard, "how we're tying these guys to the Book of the Wars again? This is making my brain hurt, because I know the name Arlen Dempsey wasn't in the book."

"It's not us connecting them," Cell said. "Recall that in the Book of the Wars, we found random letters. We took those letters and discerned they were in order, creating a series of what we believed were code names. And then we used that code name mentioned in the book and plowed through file after file until our eyes bled to find a connection in some military or government database."

"Do you ever get multiple hits?" Devine asked.

"Unbelievably, no. Not yet." Cell seemed pleased.

"Anyway," Iliescu said, "Leif and Saito will deploy as the advance team to scout the sites and last-knowns, then the rest of the team will head down so that if we're unable to weed Dempsey out, you'll all be boots on ground." He pinched the bridge of his nose. "Ideally, we want to intercept him before he's either initiated or activated. I wish we knew more about how that worked."

Lawe shrugged. "If they don't know when they're activated, how on earth are *we* supposed to tell?"

"At this point, we can't," Iliescu admitted. "We just need to interdict, hopefully before anything happens."

## BALTIMORE, MARYLAND

Sitting on the shag rug in her apartment, back against the sofa, Iskra cradled a sleeping Taissia, who had clung to her from the moment she'd been picked up from school. The missions were getting harder on both of them.

The innocence and sweetness of her daughter—ha, take that, Leif—did something strange to her on the inside. Tracing Taissia's face, she could see so much of Valery—the fair skin, the temper, but also his intelligence. While living in Hristoff's house, she never had the chance to sit and cuddle her daughter, because she had done her best to convince him that Taissia did not matter. Otherwise, he would have used Taissia as a pawn. In the end, that was exactly what he had done.

Mercy brought the cupcakes and cookies from the island and set them on the coffee table, where her laptop was still humming. "How do you handle it? I don't think I could if I had a little one."

Iskra smoothed a hand over Taissia's forehead, brushing back brown strands. "I've promised to finish what I started. So I will do this only until the Book of the Wars is recovered." Would Leif be ready then?

Mercy slumped onto the floor next to her. "Okay, so what are we hacking?" She lifted a chocolate-frosted cupcake and peeled the paper away.

"I met with Veratti—"

"Wait. Is he alive? You're alive." She screwed up her face. "I'm confused."

"I did not kill him." Iskra sighed with a rueful smile. "He wants me to find the book."

"But Reaper wants it."

"Yes."

Mercy's brows dove toward her pert nose. "So, are you a double agent?" She frowned. "Or is that triple . . . ?"

Iskra propped her arms on her legs to thwart the aches in her muscles, but the bite of pain was worth this moment with her daughter. "It works to my benefit that he wants the book as well, but it does make it harder, because there is no doubt he monitors my every move."

Face white, Mercy gaped. Her gaze skipped around the room.

"I meant digitally. He knows I have resources, so he set me on the hunt. And he will have someone track my movements to see if he can preempt me."

"Why would he do that if he asked *you* to find it for him?"

"Because he doesn't trust me, and I am certain there is someone else looking, too."

"This makes so much sense." Mercy's hesitance was frustrating but understandable. "So, where are we starting?"

"Can you show me the footage from that secret facility near Cuba, when the storm came and the book disappeared, possibly with Andrew?"

"Sure." Mercy tugged her laptop closer. "But

you know my vendetta against Andrew, so I've already been over this a million times. None of the angles caught him taking or escaping with it."

"I want to see him enter, leave, and everything in between."

"Probably should've brought a bigger stash of sugar," Mercy said with a laugh as she pulled up multiple files. "This is going to take a while."

"I am going to put her in bed." With Taissia in her arms, Iskra struggled off the floor, onto the couch, then upright before delivering her daughter to the bedroom. She took a moment to admire this precious child, then kissed her cheek. "Soon we will be free of this, my sweet. Until then, forgive me." She returned and settled beside Mercy, reviewing the files.

Over and over she watched the footage.

Mercy eventually started working on a second laptop she'd brought. Iskra focused on the facility files. Then she asked for the satellite images of when Andrew had shown up in Burma, stills that were grainy and unhelpful.

"Did you want this, too?" Mercy offered, angling her screen toward Iskra. "It's of him in the Bahamas watching the guys. Nothing important except him getting into a vehicle."

"Wait." Iskra's heart staggered. "Look!" She pointed to the green truck.

"Right," Mercy said, giving her a frown, "getting into a vehicle."

"And here," Iskra noted, "when he and the men are spotted in an Army truck at the facility— they're unloading these plastic crates."

"Okay . . . ?"

"In Burma—check the crates."

Mercy gasped. "You have to be kidding me! How did I not see this?"

The truck in the Bahamas. The crates at the facility. The food stores from Burma. All marked with the same logo of a bird in flight with an arrow in its beak.

Mercy's fingers flew over the keys. "Got it. Logo belongs to Worth Your Salt, a company that's been doing a lot of charity work in third-world countries to help supply potable water and nutrient-rich foods."

"Which is probably why we had their supplies in Burma."

"Mm."

"Who owns it?"

Long auburn hair dangling as she leaned forward, Mercy narrowed her eyes, searching. "Okay, it looks like Salt is a subsidiary of Frankfurt & Stuttgart Biologics, with an office in—boom!—New York City." She pinched her lower lip as she rifled through the information. "They have numerous locations around the world, but I can't find who . . ." She sucked in hard. "Owned by Rutger Hermanns."

"That man is a plague. He is part of ArC, but

I wonder about that, since Veratti called him his enemy and has me going after him to get the book." Iskra nodded at the laptop. "Can you get into his company's system?"

Mercy was typing. "Already on it." She slowed and grunted.

"What?"

"I . . ." She paused, still working and navigating, then shook her head. "I can't do it from here. It's a SCIF—Sensitive Compartmented Information Facility. Means it's not connected to the outside world." Dropping back against the sofa, she shoved her hair from her face. "I have to be on-site and get into their server room."

"Then I guess I'm going to New York."

"Don't you mean we?"

"I must do this. Veratti told me Rutger has the book. If he has it, then perhaps it's there. Or maybe something in their system will lead us to it, or to this Andrew who keeps showing up at the same time that logo does." Iskra squinted, thinking. "There are too many connections to this company and Rutger not to pursue it."

"True," Mercy said, "but unless *you* know how to hack a system, I'm going with you. All I need is a few minutes at a terminal and we can dust that place." She indicated the hall. "What about your little one?"

Iskra cursed herself. She kept promising not to leave. "I . . . I can ask Leif's family if they can help again." Her stomach churned at the thought. "Since we'd be in and out quickly, we could be back before nightfall tomorrow." The trip had to be short and fast. Not only because of Taissia, but because in two days Mercy and the team headed to Taiwan.

## NEW YORK CITY, NEW YORK

"This place is entirely too people-y for me," Mercy muttered as they hurried up the sidewalk, skating the eastern edge of Central Park. She nodded to the thick green vegetation. "And that's mind-blowing. You get deep enough in there, and you don't even know you're in a city with millions of people and cabbies who honk more than geese."

"Stay on task," Iskra said. "Remember—stumble and lift. Most men will miss the obvious when you lean into them."

"You do realize I'm not you, right?"

"But you're still beautiful. Just be light and fast."

"You should—"

"Be confident, like you belong there." Iskra focused on the objective. "Okay, let's split up."

"We still have four blo—"

Without another word, Iskra hustled across the street, leaving Mercy. She could feel Mercy's nerves, which was why she had separated sooner than planned.

Iskra squared her shoulders and lifted a phone from her purse. She put it to her ear and started chatting like the majority of people in this dirty, cluttered city. People raved about the wonders of New York City—and there were a lot of them—but Mercy was right. There were too many people. Which made it perfect for operatives. This wasn't her first mission here, and it probably wouldn't be her last.

Even as Frankfurt & Stuttgart Biologics came into view, Iskra spotted Mercy entering through the front.

"In the building," Mercy whispered through the tiny short-range comms piece that would not emit electronic signals. At least, that was what Mercy promised. They were about to find out if she was right.

Iskra reached for the brushed nickel handle and opened the door. Armed guards flanked four hubs where security processed a line of people, including Mercy, who was a few people away from entering. Hovering over the foyer was an arching catwalk fed by an escalator. Head down and staring at her phone, Iskra started for the stairs.

"Ma'am?" a guard said, nodding to her bag and the small scanner.

Pausing, Iskra gave an annoyed glare—wasn't everyone annoyed by everything these days?—to another security guard walking toward her. Mercy came up behind, bumped into him while he was distracted with Iskra, then flashed him a coy smile. A silly grin lit his face as he watched Mercy hustle through the checkpoint and out of sight. With the all-access badge she'd relieved him of.

His attention finally found Iskra again. "Need you to clear the scanner, ma'am," he said.

"Fine." Iskra set her bag down and stalked forward, holding her breath as she passed beneath the sensor. The guard waved her on, and another returned her purse. Which, of course, had cleared, because she really didn't need a knife to be lethal. A pen and the flat of her hand both worked fine. Not that she would do that . . . today.

She strode to the reception desk.

"May I help you?" the receptionist asked.

"Yes, I have a ten-fifteen with Dr. Hansen."

The receptionist looked at the computer monitor and clicked something. "Miss Munroe?"

Iskra smiled. "Yes."

"Sign in here," she said, motioning to the clipboard sheet, and then slid a tag over. "Take the escalator to the upper level, over the catwalk"—she pointed overhead—"and it's the second door on your left."

"Thank you." Iskra signed the clipboard, attached the badge to her lapel, and started for the escalator.

"Found a terminal at the back of the facility. Logging in now," came Mercy's whisper.

Iskra reached the upper level and strode over the catwalk, eyeing the lobby. She opened the door into a smaller, more intimate reception area, and crossed the room. "I'm—"

"Miss Munroe," a woman behind the counter greeted. "If you'll have a seat, Dr. Hansen will be with you soon."

"Thank you." Iskra moved toward a chair with a view of the atrium and catwalk.

As she turned to sit, something triggered in her brain. She stilled, then jerked back to the windows, catching sight of a man barreling past people on the escalator.

*He's in a hurry.*

Then his build, familiar from the footage at the facility, smacked her.

Iskra rushed for the door. "He's here," she breathed into their comms as she broke into the open. "Andrew's here."

She darted for the escalator and scurried down it. Her heels hit the floor and slipped, but she caught herself, gaze on the man exiting the building. By the time she had the brushed nickel in hand again, he had reached the sidewalk.

No no no. If he got away in that traffic, she'd never find him.

Iskra hurtled into the open and raced across the small terrace to the steps, locked on the tall frame in a sports jacket weaving through the crowd. At the foot of the steps, she couldn't see past the sea of bodies. She growled, scanning. New Yorkers filed through the busy intersection, swallowing him into their numbers.

She shifted, searching the sidewalk. Up one side, down the other. Where . . . where . . . ?

He was gone.

"Excuse me," an older woman said. "Did you know that man who hurried out of here?"

Iskra glanced at the bent woman, wondering why she asked.

"He looked like he did something wrong, something nefarious." The older woman thumbed over her shoulder toward the building. "Do you work in there? Did he take this from you?" She held out her palm, where a dark vial lay.

Iskra felt herself startle. "Yes," she breathed, amazed at this encounter. What were the chances? "Thank you." She took the vial and clutched it. "You saved my life."

The elderly woman patted her hand, then shuffled away.

Iskra glanced at the vial—blood? poison?— then toward the street where Andrew had vanished. She turned to look back toward the woman, only to find her gone, too. What . . . ?

When she saw Mercy across the cobbled terrace, Iskra slid the vial into her purse and met her with an exasperated sigh. "I lost him in the traffic."

"But he was here? You're sure?" Mercy said, watching the crowds.

"Positive." The vial felt like an anchor on her conscience. Why was she hiding it? Why not just tell Mercy?

"Then we definitely need to get home so I can dig into their system and find out what he was doing there. Maybe even track his movements on their security feed, assuming they record things, even if for a short period."

"So, obviously, you did whatever was necessary?" Iskra asked as they headed to the car park.

"I did. And I got a guy's number."

"Let's hope he thinks you're forgettable."

"Thanks," Mercy muttered.

"If he remembers you, he can tell security what you looked like."

Mercy swallowed. "Forgettable is good."

# CHAPTER 18

## TAIPEI, TAIWAN

Since Taiwan did not have an American embassy—something the Chinese had vehemently objected to because they considered the island a breakaway province—the American Institute in Taiwan was where Leif and Saito were headed. Officially, the AIT was a government-linked nonprofit established with the help of the American government to serve its interests in-country. The de facto embassy was their best shot at digging the newest name Cell had unearthed—Arlen Dempsey—out of hiding.

Their vehicle swung up the arcing drive to the new facility that had opened in 2018, stirring tensions. Marines guarded the site and ushered Leif and Saito past the checkpoint without a hiccup, thanks to the cooperative effort of the CIA, DIA, and DoD. As they strode into the building that still smelled new, Leif noted that while there were American guards and workers at the location, the employees were largely local.

After checking in at the front, they were instructed to wait in a glass-enclosed area, where a TV streamed news from multiple channels, the sound muted. Two other people were waiting, noses glued to their smartphones.

Leif positioned himself with a clear line of sight on the front door and reception desk, while Saito sat shoulder to shoulder with him, his chair facing the opposite direction, toward the rear of the facility.

"Do you ever think it'll be you next?" Saito asked as they waited for their contact.

"Next for what?"

"One of these Neiothen," Saito said, thumbing absently through a magazine yet staying eyes out. "I mean, if you think about it, couldn't any of us be one? And that is *crazy*. They have no idea they're assassins, but then they cut ties with sanity and deliver death in a handbasket." He tossed aside the magazine and huffed. "What if we suddenly go ape?" His brown eyes nailed Leif.

"You're not in the book."

"We don't know that," Saito hissed. "The code names are ancient and only matched with current names in piecemeal. It could be us, man."

With a sniff, Leif had to admit he'd wondered. It was hard not to. "It's messed up. Freaky, thinking you could be a preacher in the pulpit on Sunday, then unleashing chaos on Monday."

"Like something out of a movie."

"Definitely a B movie." Leif monitored those in the building and the guards, keeping tabs on movement and demeanor.

"How d'you think they're doing it? Triggering them?"

"That recording—remember?"

"But that was initiation, according to Ibn Sarsour. How do they start it? How do they get activated? Maybe the Neiothen"—they shouldn't use the official name in public—"are already triggered, just biding their time . . ."

Leif shrugged. "Seems unlikely. Risky if someone turned chicken."

"But Ibn Sarsour didn't even realize he'd been activated, yet he was there, poised to kill. What if someone remembered between being activated and initiated? What if they decided to bail? They could blow . . . whatever it is ArC's doing."

Leif arched an eyebrow at his buddy. "If I go whack—you know what to do. I don't want to be hunted down like some dog out of his mind."

"Your wish is my command."

Leif shook his head, not wanting to think about it.

Through the front door came a man in a trench coat, black slacks, and a blue button-down shirt. His sandy brown hair needed a trim—but he should start with a comb. If he'd ever owned one. As he walked toward reception, he patted his chest, hips, then thighs like an absent-minded professor. What was he searching for? He wheeled around.

Electricity zapped through Leif as gray eyes met his. Grateful for perfect recall, he stood. "Dempsey," he muttered to Saito.

Though the man looked right at Leif, he wasn't seeing him. Dempsey's gaze was . . . distant. Unfocused. Wide with panic—no, paranoia.

Saito glanced toward the reception desk, lifting his phone to call it in. "Eyes on Dempsey."

Dempsey stumbled through the foyer. Went to a table with pens, paper, and forms to fill out. He stood tapping a pen against the table as he glanced around the lobby area. His gaze hit the main entrance, a side wall, then another door with a sign over it.

*Scouting exits.*

"Think he's been triggered?" Saito asked as they started toward the door of the glassed-in area with no idea what they'd face if they confronted him now.

"Either way, our response is the same."

Someone else beat Dempsey to the desk, forcing him to wait. He crossed his arms over his chest. That paranoid tick at least told them he likely wasn't wearing a suicide vest. But he had way too many nerves bouncing off him to be here just for a visit.

Saito casually strolled to a water fountain, then made his way to a Marine stationed on the far side, no doubt warning him to sound a silent alarm and be ready.

"Excuse me," Leif said, angling up to a sweating Dempsey, hoping his ruse of distraction would work.

Wide bloodshot eyes, pupils dilated, fixed on Leif. Not in his right mind, which made him a danger to everyone in this building, suicide vest or not.

Leif had to distract him. "D'you have a pen I could use?"

"I . . ." Dempsey's gaze wandered the building, as if seeking a home base.

Leif checked Saito, who'd wandered back. "Get everyone out," he ordered under his breath.

"Mr. Metcalfe." A woman strode toward him all casual and ease, no idea of the maelstrom she and her crisp gray suit had stepped into. "I'm glad you could stop by."

Dempsey looked between the woman and Leif as she continued her introduction.

"I'm Mary Mansour."

Holding a stalling hand toward her, Leif kept eyes on Dempsey. "Easy," he said, and it seemed Mansour finally keyed in to the situation.

Dempsey shuffled back.

Leif cursed the distraction of Mansour, which had given Dempsey time to put twenty feet between them. Too far to interdict.

"You don't know . . ." His hands and lower lip trembled. "They . . ." He gripped his head hard with a shrieking groan. "My head—it's—they're—"

"Easy, easy," Leif repeated, noting the din in the AIT grow, nerves jamming common sense and calm.

Saito must've relayed the threat to the Marines, because they were quietly guiding people to exits.

Dempsey's gaze tripped over the departing. "What . . . ?"

Time to shed pretense. "Dempsey."

Frantic eyes bounced around and finally landed on Leif.

"You okay, Sergeant?" It was a risk, using Dempsey's former rank, but from boot camp on, grunts were trained to respond quickly and decisively to direct questions. "You seem confused."

"My head," Dempsey murmured, frowning. "I keep having these thoughts. . . ." Suddenly, his gaze sharpened. "I need help."

Leif nodded, slipping closer, erasing inches at a time yet careful not to alarm his target. "I'm here for you, man. What can I do?"

"It's just . . . I . . ." Fingertips to the side of his forehead, Dempsey flattened his lips. "The things I keep thinking about . . ." His face screwed tight. "It's not me. I was—Distinguished Service Medal. Service Medal. Up for Military Medal for Gallantry with Distinction." Confusion flayed his features. "This . . . what's in my head—it's not me!"

"I get it, man." Less than six feet separated them. "Been there. Serving, seeing combat, engaging the enemy—it does things. Messes with you."

Dempsey nodded absently. But then his gaze

drifted to the tiled floor. He squinted. "No." His head began swinging back and forth. "No, no, it's not right."

"You're right—it ain't. But—"

"They're not my thoughts." His words sounded strangled, as if they were hard to push past the chaos erupting in his brain. "They're not my thoughts." Now he was more forceful. Distraught. Angry. The red in his eyes seemed to glow with fury. His hand moved, and somehow he produced a weapon.

"Whoa!" Leif's pulse backfired, and he wondered how Dempsey had gotten that in past the scanners. He held up his palms, taking a mental step backward, as those still here on the main level twitched and whimpered at the sight of the gun. "Easy, Dempsey. No need to hurt anyone." This had gone south fast.

Torment careened through the man's face, his hand still lifting the weapon.

"Listen to me!" Leif paced options, scenarios. None of them good. "Nobody will hurt you. We just want to help."

Dempsey pursed his lips as if fighting back the rage. "They're not my thoughts," he said, agony replacing his anger. With a growl, he tapped the muzzle against the side of his head.

"Dempsey." The bark of Leif's voice in the near-empty reception area startled even him. "Put it down. Put the gun down."

"I can't. I can't do what they want me to." His expression twisted. "You understand ossi, don't you?"

What was *ossi*? "You're in control, man. Nobody will force you to do anything." Heart thudding, Leif worked to erase the distance.

Furrowed brows heaved over tormented eyes. "I can't let them make me. And they'll try. I saw. Saw the others do it. I can't . . . I have to stop it."

"That's right—let's stop it, Dempsey. Give me the gun." Leif extended his hand. "I'm here to help. We'll do it together—climb this hill. Scale the rise and conquer it."

Arlen Dempsey blinked, focus hitting his gray eyes. It seemed he finally saw Leif. He straightened and gave a sharp nod. "Yes. *Ego semperer ex profundis.*" He snapped the weapon to his chin.

"No!" Leif lunged too late.

# CHAPTER 19

## 20 NAUTICAL MILES OFF CUBA

With snorkeling and dive rigs littering the sea, Iskra was confident her rented boat and hired local wouldn't draw attention. She straddled the dive prop bobbing off the port side, started the small waterproof camera attached to her shoulder, and verified her regulator was feeding her oxygen. After a wave to the boat driver, she opened up the throttle. The black torpedolike hull slipped beneath the surface.

Hours reviewing the footage from the facility where she and Leif had nearly killed each other, where the book went missing, had handed her a tip. A man rounded a corner and disappeared from the camera. Though an idea had formed, she was too disconcerted to voice it, even to Mercy.

Now she was back in the sea that had nearly drowned her. But this time—armed with oxygen tanks, a KA-BAR tactical knife, a Glock with an underwater firing adapter, a waterproof camera, and a multifunction GPS strapped to her wrist—she was testing her theory. A dangerous one.

The prop maxed at twelve knots, so the two-hour dive to her destination provided plenty of time to run through contingencies if she met trouble. It also made her wish Leif were here. As a former SEAL, he was better with underwater endeavors. And there was the little fact that she always felt safer with him around.

Searching for his past was tearing Leif up. Add to that the way the director handled the situation—even she could tell he was keeping something from Leif—and Iskra was doing her best to give Leif room to sort things out. It was likely the only way to get past this point to marriage and family.

Perhaps she should try to help him find those answers? It would mean derailing her attempts to locate Mitre. That vial she'd received in New York—she'd handed it off to a trusted asset and phlebotomist who verified that it was blood and promised a complete work-up soon.

A vibration against her wrist drew Iskra's attention back to her surroundings. The water wasn't as dark. She let off the throttle a little, glancing at her gauge. A few hundred yards to shore still, but it was definitely lightening. And not from the sun penetrating the surface. She was still too deep for that.

In the inky, wavering distance, light gathered at a lone central source. She aimed her shoulder cam in that direction, sure she was about to find proof. Another few minutes, and the brightness grew into a distinct bright spot. Manmade, not bioluminescent.

Darkness cocooned the light, confusing her. How was that possible? But another hundred yards cleared it up—a cave. A large swath of the ocean floor descended into a very large cave. Filled with light. Several lights.

*I knew it.*

Victory saturated her muscles as she swung the prop around to get another view of the cave, wary of getting too close and risking discovery. Slowly, she drove in closer . . .

Movement bisected the light.

Her pulse spiked—a shape was coming at her. A rivulet through the water registered a second too late. Fire seared across her thigh, and she felt something thunk against the prop. The subtle thrum of the engine beneath her died.

Pulling her Glock, Iskra let the prop fall and started swimming away from the cave, trying to let the darkness swallow her. But she'd gone in too close. A strange vibration rang through her spine. Realization struck—her tank. Had they hit it? She checked the gauge. Fear turned to clawing panic at the plummeting indicator.

Thrusting upward, she raced for the surface before her oxygen ran out. Water churned near her neck. Another shot! She took a gamble—went limp. Eyes open as she sank.

The guy came at her with his prop.

She had one chance. Underwater, the Glock would not chamber another round after she fired it without being racked. She was fast, but . . .

He was there. Checking her, reaching for her.

Iskra fired center mass.

The man jerked.

She racked the slide as he lunged at her. She fired again. His momentum carried him into her. She shoved him off and treaded water. He was sinking. He'd gone still.

She scrambled for his prop, which was dropping fast. Swimming, she caught sight of her gauge. Her heart tremored. Would she have enough time to get the prop? Maybe. Maybe not, but she definitely could not reach the surface in time without it.

Her fingers snagged the handle. She pulled her leg over the hull and let out the throttle, holstering her Glock. She wouldn't be able to manage both. This wasn't Hollywood—it wasn't a fast-dive prop. But it was faster than fins and hands.

The light in the water flickered, drawing her gaze back.

Oh no. Another diver. At least he couldn't go faster than her, but if she went straight up, she'd never lose him. But going farther out could drown her.

Frustrated and out of options, she headed away from the island, toward the dark waters. Glanced at her $O_2$ gauge. Her heart thudded. Empty. She tapped its face and tried not to panic. Tried to slow her breathing. Already the deprivation tightened her chest.

She had to rise. Had to. Darkness or not.

*If I don't, I'm dead.*

But if she did, he could find her easier.

Iskra compromised. Angled up and out. It felt like a weight sat on her chest. She focused on reaching the surface, on slowing her breathing. Something made her look back—just in time to see the other prop closing in.

What? How?

He threw himself off the prop and at her.

In a fluid move, Iskra whipped her KA-BAR from its sheath and slashed at the man's oxygen hose. Crimson bloomed in the water. He thrashed, hand going to his throat.

Kicking to rise, she forced herself not to open her mouth. But her chest squeezed. Temples throbbed.

Her depth gauge showed she was nearing the surface.

This sea would drown her after all. Terror seized her. Tears leaked out, and Iskra knew she needed to calm down. But it didn't matter. She was going to die, and Leif would never know how. Taissia—no no no. Oh God, please . . .

She wheezed, struggling. Her head felt like it might explode. Gray ghosted the edges of her vision. Leaning on the prop, she felt life slipping from her body.

Everything went black.

Then light exploded through her eyes. Iskra jerked up and vomited water onto a sandy stretch of beach. She coughed and gagged, blinking up at several locals gathered around her.

## CIA SAFE HOUSE, TAIWAN

This whole thing wigged Mercy out and reminded her too much of Matt Murdock, who'd battled the Hand for his entire career as the Daredevil, but then—crazily—became the Hand himself. And only later realized he'd been possessed by the Beast of the Hand. In a moment of supposed clarity, Daredevil had killed himself to keep from being used. Elektra later revived him.

If only Arlen Dempsey had an Elektra.

Mercy's gaze wandered to where Leif sat with the team. More like simply occupying space.

"The doctor said one more week and antibiotics, then I can resume duty," Baddar said over the live feed, drawing her attention back to the handsome commando.

" 'Bout time you quit slacking," Culver teased. "My back got burned, and I've returned to duty. You get a burn *inside* and get to sleep and have beautiful women catering to you all day. I got cheated. Again."

Mercy slid another glance toward Leif, hating how weighted his expression had been since the suicide at AIT. He might have washed the blood and gray matter off his face and changed his shirt, but Dempsey's life was all over Leif. And the teasing banter among the others wasn't helping.

Baddar smiled. "When you are as handsome as I am, maybe you will have better luck."

Laughter rattled through the small Taiwanese flat where they were holed up after the Dempsey debacle.

"You guys are cads," Mercy said, nudging them away from the camera and taking the center seat. She had to admit—she'd missed the commando. His constant presence had been a stabilizer. She'd thought she needed something wild and exciting, like Leif and Iskra had, but she found a sense of rightness in the calm stability that was Baddar Amir Nawabi.

She smiled into the camera. "Hope you feel better soon."

Seriousness washed over his expression, replacing his sarcasm with sincerity. "Me, too. I would be with you again."

Why was it that when he sounded eager and focused on her, she had this compunction to shove him away? To push him back? She stifled it and retrained his thoughts on the team. "Reaper needs you." When he deflated, she hated herself for the obvious deflection. "It'll be good to have you with us." *Why* couldn't she just say it? "Take care, Baddar."

"And you, Mercy."

The transmission ended, and she turned, eyeing Leif, who hadn't moved. His hand framed his mouth, and his expression was tight. Ankle over his knee, he looked comfortable for a frozen guy.

"Ya know, I knew you were hard-core, but I never figured you one for torture," Adam taunted her.

"What?" she asked, knowing he meant Baddar.

"Tell the guy you got a thing for him or free him. You know, fish or cut bait."

"You mean like you trying to win Peyton back?" Mercy challenged.

"He's making progress," Peyton said, hoisting an eyebrow at him.

"Wait," Adam said, "did you just defend me?"

"Well, he *was* making progress."

More laughter. And still, Leif hadn't moved. Wasn't joking the way he normally did, the way he loved. When was the last time he'd told a joke? Of the eight team members, he was the one known for his bad jokes. His very bad jokes.

"Mercy, you are cracked." Adam wrapped an arm around Peyton. "Between me and Pete, we got all we can handle."

"True, you are hard work," Peyton joked, allowing the big lug to kiss her cheek.

Mercy wandered over and slapped Leif's shoe. "Hey. You still breathing in there?" She snorted when he started and met her gaze. "You look as frozen as Batman and Robin when they tried to escape Black Lantern."

He lowered his hand but said nothing. His gaze hit something across the room, then skittered away to nothing in particular. Mercy tried to figure out what he'd looked at. Culver, Peyton, and Adam were at the table. Beyond them, Cell was working with two computers.

Leif dropped his foot to the floor and scooted forward. "Can you get me the files on Dempsey and Gilliam?"

Lazily, she shrugged. "Don't you already have those?" They'd all been handed the condensed dossiers with need-to-know intel compiled from the full CIA file. "Ah," she said in realization. "The *full* file." That was what he wanted.

Her heart skipped a beat. Sure, she could get that. She had the skills to extract most anything she wanted. But she had put herself on probation from digging into her employer's systems, because staying gainfully employed—and alive—was a good thing.

She took a deep breath. "Why?"

His gaze traipsed around the floor, the plastic chair, the others. "I think I'm seeing a pattern. But"—again, he scanned their hideout—"I'm not sure *what* I'm seeing. I can feel it lurking right under the surface."

"What kind of pattern?"

His blue eyes nailed her. "Can you do it or not?"

"We both know I can. It's a matter of *should,*" she said, never one to be bullied. "I could lose my job and all the respect I've earned, including self-respect. Just because one has the ability doesn't mean one should."

He shoved both hands over his head, then straightened. "I hear you."

"This may not be the best job on the planet, but I like it and the people I work with." She tweaked his ear. "Even you."

After a nod, he stood and stalked into the kitchen, where he retrieved a water bottle, then vanished into a back room.

So much for her attempt to draw him out. She might've made things worse. With a huff, she deliberated doing what he'd asked. If she started hacking just because one of her friends asked her to, she'd get a reputation. Maybe she already had one, and that was why Leif had asked her to break all kinds of morality codes.

She moved until she could see him in the back room and felt her heart pinch. He sat on the edge of a bed, leaning forward, bottle in one hand, cap in the other, staring at the floor.

*Do not go all wounded-hero on me, Runt.*

Mercy wasn't the type to be girly emotional and stuff. Unless it came to her own. Her own program, her own people. Over a year and a half ago, Ram had been killed, and she'd missed the signs of what he intended to do. So much she'd let him handcuff her to a bed in Russia, thinking he had *other* intentions. She hadn't seen him again until the night he sacrificed himself.

Now it was happening with Leif, who had run the *Danger* banner up his personal flagpole. Over the weeks they'd been hunting these Neiothen, he'd grown more irritable and foul-tempered, then more introspective and moody. A near one-eighty from the lighthearted, sociable guy she could've easily been smitten with.

She would not make the same mistake twice.

Mercy retrieved her tablet and went to work. Having clearance within the system made things easier, but since she didn't have full access she had to bypass barricading protocols. The easiest route was to slip into Dru's system using his password, which meant not only breaking the law, but breaking his trust.

Did the ends justify the means? She had no idea this time, but they were pretty short on patterns and tips to chase down these ArC guys.

"Barc."

"Yeah?" he answered, more a grunt than a word, his gaze on his laptop.

"Barc." She wanted his full attention.

He scowled and glanced up. For two whole seconds before his gaze smacked into the screen again. It was like a zombie thing where he couldn't look away from fresh blood.

"Barc, do you have the primary files on the

Neiothen we've already gone after? I have one on Kurofuji, but not Dempsey or Gilliam."

"Why?" he asked, typing away on some file or coding.

Irritated, she snatched her laptop and sent a harmless but annoying virus to his system that would slide hippos dancing amid flames across the screen. She waited a couple of seconds.

"Mercy," he growled, coming out of the chair. "Get rid of it."

She smirked and hit a key. "Gone." She raised her eyebrows. "Now that I have your attention, Amadeus . . ." With him, it always took longer than the average bear to realize her references.

Too long. He returned to his work.

Annoyed, she got up and slapped his laptop closed.

"Hey!" he barked.

"It's rude to ignore me when I hand out superhero cards."

He huffed. "Amadeus Cho. I get it." He shook his head, gaze already sinking back to the laptop. "Not the first time you've called me that either."

She placed a hand on the laptop. "The Dempsey and Gilliam files."

Confusion rippled through his unnaturally young face, then cleared. Followed by eyes widening then narrowing. "Leif asked you for them."

Great. Somehow she'd just betrayed Leif's trust, too. "So?"

Barc caught her hand. "C'mere." He led her to a quiet corner.

"I already told you I'm not interested," she demurred, knowing this wasn't romantic but unable to resist taunting him.

Arms crossed and hands under his armpits, he hesitated. Soon, he stroked the nonexistent facial hair around his mouth. "Don't give it to him."

Mercy twitched. "I'm sorry?"

"Just . . . trust me on this," Cell whispered. "Don't give him the files. Not yet."

"Why?"

Sighing, he peeked at the others. When his gaze drifted to the back rooms, conflict held a battle on his face. "I can't explain it. But I think . . . I think it'd be dangerous to give him the files."

Mercy recoiled. "Dangerous? He's our team leader! He's responsible for intercepting the Neiothen before they can act. I have never felt more confident in anyone—well, except Tox and Ram—but Leif is right up there. Remember, he gave you this job. Why would it be dangerous?"

Contrition looked great on everyone but Barclay Purcell. On him, it looked puke green. "I can't answer that, but—please." His brown eyes begged. "Trust me on this one."

Frustration encircled that restriction he'd just placed on her. "How long?"

He frowned, then shook his head. "I don't know."

This reeked, and she hated it. But Leif's unusual behavior was the wedging factor in her indecisiveness. "For now," she relented. "I'll hold off *for now*. But if I think this could help him—"

"It won't. Trust me, Merc. Trust me, please."

"I—"

Her phone intoned the arrival of an email. She checked it and frowned that the FROM heading was empty. About to dismiss it—she wasn't stupid enough to open an attachment from an unknown source—she spotted a five-word message preview that changed her mind.

*Sorry about the gas poisoning.*

Chest hiccupping, Mercy gaped at the message. Then her hatred of the man had her typing back a reply.

*You mean sorry you failed to kill me?*

She hit send before she realized the idiocy. Too late to retrieve it, though.

A tone signaled another message.

*Never meant to harm you.*

Why apologize? Why talk to her? Mercy did what she always did when she got a strange message, even those marked SPAM. She traced it.

Of course, Andrew was too good to leave a trail. Even in places where there should be a trail, he'd left none. The location ping bounced around—as expected—from city to city. Yeah, he was too good. *Can't you just once screw up like the rest of humanity?*

And he obliged. Mercy stared drop-jawed when the ping stopped. The location pin ballooned in and out.

No way. After arguing with herself over whether this was a trap or not, she took a screenshot and sent it to Iskra.

**Possible sighting of Andrew. Check it out?**

Iskra texted back:

**He's too good to leave a trail.**

Great minds thought alike. Mercy smiled and nodded. Considered the trace location icon.

**Maybe he messed up?**

**ISKRA**
**Or maybe he's baiting us.**

MERCY
So . . . leave it?

ISKRA
If he's baiting us, then he has a message. Gotta follow.

*Atta girl.*

# CHAPTER 20

## CIA SAFE HOUSE, TAIWAN

*Ego semperer ex profundis.*

Grateful for his near-perfect memory, Leif recalled the phrase Arlen Dempsey had uttered right before he killed himself. He'd looked up the translation on his phone: "From the depths I will always rise."

*I will rise.*

*I will rise.*

*I will rise.*

He gritted his teeth, those haunting, taunting words tearing through the empty spaces of his mind. What did it mean? Every time he shut it out, convinced himself the words were from a movie or TV show he'd watched, they crept back up like some menacing ghoul.

Fingers to his forehead, he rubbed. It felt like the midnight hour of his life was about to yield to the break of dawn—memories. It made his head ache, so much like Dempsey. He'd do anything to know what was behind the redacted parts of his life. The things someone had hidden from him. In light of what they were chasing, in light of what Saito had asked—*"Do you ever think it'll be you*

273

*next?"*—he didn't like where his thoughts were going.

Dru and Canyon would be ticked, but Leif couldn't look away any longer. The missing fragments were there, waiting for him to take a leap of faith. Jump after them. Haul the past into the present.

If he did, there'd be no going back. He had more than one scar from trying to dig through that pile of dung the Army had used to backfill his life. His records showed no lapse in service, no missing days. Yet he had a six-month gap that nobody could explain. According to them, there was nothing wrong with his brain, no swelling, no damage. He'd been convinced at one time that part of his gray matter was missing, but the VA said it was all there.

But it wasn't, figuratively. And it ticked him off.

His mother was a devout Christian. She wholly believed in the Bible, its inerrancy, and the truth that when people blamed God for one situation or another, they were only looking at it from one perspective: theirs.

What other perspective was he supposed to have when it was his life missing six months? When his career had nearly tanked? When his men had died and he hadn't?

Someone had messed him up. Stolen his life. And he was ticked. It was time to turn the tide.

Mercy had shown her hand when she mentioned the full file. It confirmed what he'd guessed: there was more intel. Why were DIA and CIA holding back? His own team was holding back as well. Why?

Thoughts crowded his head. Too many coincidences. Too many voices screaming from the past. He had to change that. Somehow.

His phone chirruped. He flipped it over, and the screen lit up with an email notification. He unlocked it. His inbox had a dozen emails, but one had no subject or sender. But it did have an attachment. He checked the message preview: *Thought it only fair you had this . . .*

Hesitantly, Leif opened the email. Nothing nefarious or notable happened. It could be rooting through his system, but agency security protocols should shut viruses down. Hopefully. In addition to the attachment, the email had two lines:

*Thought it only fair you had this as well.*
*Since we have the same end goal.*

The attachment was a video file. He accessed it.

In the recording, a man stood backlit by the sun. "I know sending this to you is an extreme risk, but voice triggers an integral part of the stimulators. The general insists you'll figure it out, but I think the clock has run out on that happening. Netherwood is in danger. There are moles trying to undo what needs to be done to advance the agenda. If you haven't awoken, it's time to rise. We need your help. Look for Akin and Bushi—they're key. Don't try to find me. I'll find you." The figure leaned toward the camera, and for a second, his face was clear: Carsen Gilliam.

Leif played it again. And again. Who were Akin and Bushi? Buddies? Neiothen? Both? His thumb hovered over his phone, thinking to shoot a message to—

No, no records. They'd be all over him otherwise. Maybe he could talk to Mercy, but she wasn't cooperating either.

"Yo, Leif."

He flinched toward the door where Culver stood.

The redhead frowned. "You okay?"

"Yeah." Leif tucked away the phone. Played good Boy Scout as he'd done for the last four years. "What's up?"

Culver indicated back down the hall. "Command wants a briefing before we head out."

On his feet, Leif started down the hall. "Head where?"

The director's voice boomed a greeting over the live feed, followed by Braun. "You're on the next transport out of the area."

"Destination?" Cell asked.

"Afghanistan."

Grumbling tittered through the team.

"Why A-stan?" Lawe asked. "We were all pretty glad to get out of there last time."

"We've identified two of Gilliam's special-ops buddies who are currently attached to units in-country—a Sander Brandon and Cyrus Block. They're outside the wire right now, so we weren't able to make contact directly, so I'm sending you to put boots on the ground to talk with them. Find out what you can on Gilliam and if they've had contact." Dru glanced at his desk, then back at the camera. "We've had a stroke of luck, thanks to Mercy and Iskra."

Leif glanced at Mercy and couldn't help but feel betrayed.

"How's that?" Lawe asked.

"They followed a tip that led them to a New York City firm. Mercy dug around the secure server, and through that, Cell was able to extract more names and pair those with possible connections to the Neiothen."

Cell. Another traitor.

"And the names?" Leif pressed, anxious to know if they were the ones Gilliam had handed him. He should probably mention Gilliam had contacted him. . . .

"First one is Harald Elvestad—he was designated 'Dreng' in the text," Dru said. "He's

Scandinavian, and we have no intel on his current location. He is, however, a member of the Särskilda Operationsgruppen, Sweden's special operations task group. We reached out to the SSG, but they are nonresponsive at this time. As soon as they tell us, we'll tell you."

"So, not American," Leif verified.

"Obviously," Dru said, glancing off camera and nodding. "The second name is Turi Vega, code-named 'Kampfer' by the book. His dossier is showing very similar to Elvestad's—part of Spain's army, in particular the Mando de Operaciones Especiales."

Culver grunted. "I'm digging how that sounds—*especiales*." He grinned. "Dudes, I think we're *especiales*, too."

"The GOE was very responsive—with a string of rhetoric and accusations a mile long. Seems Vega was a top operator in La Unidad Boinas Verdes, the equivalent of our Green Berets."

"Hooah," Lawe grunted.

"But he's off-grid as of a week ago."

"Think he's been activated?" Leif asked.

"Unknown. Again, we are not a hundred percent certain these two are legitimately Neiothen, but we have no other actionable intel at the moment, so we're moving on it."

"Sir, what about the book?" Saito asked. "I mean—why aren't we kicking down doors to get it back?"

At least Leif didn't have to ask the question this time.

"And what doors would you have us kick down, Mr. Saito?"

"Someone has to know where that thing is," Devine said. "Everyone and their dog was looking for it a couple of months ago—and what? Suddenly nobody is interested in it?"

Leif folded his arms over his chest. "Has Iskra found out anything?" It was a gutsy question, one replete with implication, but he couldn't ignore it any longer.

Cell laughed, then frowned, looking between Leif—whose gaze locked onto the director—and the screen. "Wait. What?"

"I mean, since you have her hunting for the book and Veratti told her to go after Hermanns . . ."

"Oh, heck no," Culver said. "Tell me he's not right."

Dru scowled. "We use assets to the best of our abilities. Right now—"

"I want to go wherever she got sent," Lawe said. "I need to give certain people some serious payback."

"Bet Baddar would agree if he were here," Saito added.

"You're going to Afghanistan as instructed," Braun barked. "If we needed you in another location, we'd send you there. Of all people, I would expect former JSOC operators to understand how delicate situations can be and the need for precision, for the right people in the right places."

Straightening, Leif lifted his chin. "Nobody understands the need for this book better than Reaper, since we were sent after it in the first place. Since our team is hunting down situations and people mentioned in that text." But even as he spoke, he felt the sinuous threads of secrecy vibrating beneath the surface of conversation. Again.

"Jet's on the runway in ninety," Braun said, ignoring him. "Get moving."

## PARIS, FRANCE

It had taken only a little ingenuity and a lot of legwork to connect the dots that Mercy found in Frankfurt & Stuttgart's system to the location lock they'd gotten off Andrew's email. Iskra had no view of the Eiffel Tower, which was fine, since she wasn't sightseeing. Using the list of business addresses that Mercy had scooped, she'd narrowed down her target to two within the area, but only one belonged to Rutger. An art gallery in an old building that looked more like a hotel than a trendy spot for modern art.

What a perfect place to hide an ancient text, in

a location with airtight containers and bulbs that did not wear down ink and history.

Iskra eyed the building, knowing full well that if she went in there, she would be identified. Rutger would know she was here. She was not afraid to dig around in that art gallery, but getting caught complicated things unnecessarily. She had a five-year-old waiting at home for her now. Her chest tightened at the thought of something going wrong.

*Then make sure it doesn't.*

That was what General Varvarinksi had taught her during her training at the Kremlin. Being caught didn't have to be "getting caught." It was merely an opportunity.

Right. She had to get her mind in the game.

Iskra left the car and crossed the small park that separated her from the shop. She'd made the necessary changes—short blond bob with a lot of makeup and expensive clothes. Iliescu would have a screaming fit over the small fortune charged to the agency card, but he would understand. As long as she found the book.

Which was a long shot.

And really . . . she was after Andrew, her starting point.

She stepped up to the door of the gallery and tugged the handle. It jarred, metal rattling and sending a strange jangle of nerves up her arm. Closed at this time of day? She glanced around for a posting of the hours, but instead found a white button set into the brick. Pressing it, she eyed the camera, a black round bubble in the corner.

A grating buzz granted access. The door clicked free. She opened it, and a whisper of cool, scented air caressed her and drew her into the gallery. Elevator music wafted lightly through the open space.

"Ah, Miss Todorova."

Iskra's heart fled through her spine back into the open air as she met the eyes of a man she did not recognize. But he clearly—correctly—identified her.

"I'm sorry. How do you know me?" It definitely felt like she had walked into a trap. Right where someone wanted her. Rutger? Andrew?

He gave her a wry smile, then motioned around to the pieces displayed behind glass and art hanging on the walls, along with probably a dozen different security measures. "With valuables like this, I'm sure you understand that we make sure all persons entering the gallery are identified."

Right. "Of course." That did not make her any less on edge.

"Are you looking for anything in particular?"

Iskra eyed him, taking in his appearance, his posture, his pupils, the rise and fall of his chest. Nothing was out of order. His breathing was normal, since his chest wasn't moving raggedly. Was this the game? Be open about her nefarious motives, and he'd give her what she wanted? She nearly laughed at the absurdity. Then again, why not? What did she have to lose?

"Actually, I am."

"Have you seen this Leighton?" He indicated a lovely painting of a lady with long blond hair and a mounted knight.

Iskra skated a glance toward him, wondering at his point. "Uh, no."

He delved into the history of the piece, the significance, the interpretation of various elements, and Edmund Leighton's choice of colors and lighting.

"I was . . ."

On he went to the next piece, this time a small Van Gogh.

"I'm here about a book," she insisted. "I believe someone brought it here for storage, or perhaps it is on display."

His bushy brows furrowed. "We have no books here."

"It's called the Book of the Wars, but it is a scroll." Iskra felt the air shift behind her. Sensed someone moving—quickly. She peeked over her shoulder.

Dark leather jacket.

"Here is another," the curator said, gripping

her arm and tugging her back to the paintings.

But the impression had already formed. Instincts reared. Her mind saw what she needed. Jeans. Black rubber-soled shoes. Lanky form. Rushing out of the gallery as he tucked his head and donned a helmet.

Andrew!

She spun around, but the curator held her. She stepped back, yanked her arm up and over, snapping it down across his, breaking the hold and possibly even the bone. He cried out and went down.

Iskra pitched forward, only then noticing the windows were blackened to protect the art. Which meant she could not see which way Andrew had gone. She burst through the vestibule and out onto the street, nearly toppling an older woman with a wheeled wire basket filled with shopping bags.

"Watch it!" the woman cried in French.

Glancing right and left, Iskra searched for Andrew. His helmeted head.

Helmet. Was he on a bike? She searched for one and spotted it across the way. She swirled her focus wider and found him hustling toward it.

She sprinted across traffic, pumping her arms hard to reach him before he drove off. When he hiked a leg over the seat, she cursed herself for being so slow, for not paying more attention.

Ahead, he revved the engine and swung the

bike onto the street—and came around to fly past her—on the wrong side!

Iskra spun and darted back to the old lady and her wheeled carrier, who stood peering into a trinket shop. Iskra snatched the cart and shoved between two parked vehicles, then pitched it into the road. In that split second as it sailed at him, she saw the leather crossbody satchel he wore.

*He has the book!*

His tires screeched. The back wheel lifted as he tried to prevent a collision. He struggled, distracted. Iskra lunged, punching his helmet as he narrowly avoiding sailing over the handlebars. The strike knocked him sideways. The bike fell, engine wailing. Tires spinning.

He bounced at her.

Iskra stumbled, not expecting that maneuver. But she should have. If he had the book, he would be vicious in defending it.

In a blur, he pinned her against the hood of a car. Gripped her throat.

Iskra shoved her hands up between his and twisted, catching his right arm. Her other went to the satchel, straining to reach it. She wrenched at it and stabbed a knife-hand strike at his throat with her other hand. It should have dislodged him, but he was animalistic. Enraged. He tossed her to the concrete at the base of a step.

She tucked her arms and thrust with her shoulder, forcing herself into a roll. She came up out of it and hopped onto her feet—just in time to see his fist coming at her. Ducking only changed where the punch landed—it nailed her ear.

Trained to focus on not her own injuries but the ones she inflicted, Iskra pummel-punched his gut. Drove him back, his helmeted head thunking against her shoulder. She rotated and jammed her elbow into his stomach. He shuffled. Then rushed her. Stabbed his hand into her lower back. A vicious blow to her kidney.

Pain exploded, blinding her, and she crumpled to the ground. She growled, struggling to focus. Peering up at him and his black helmeted head, she glowered. Tried not to foam at the mouth from the radiating fire. She sought her next target—his leg.

Pushing herself up, she felt something beneath her hand. Solid. Cold. Like a pipe. She closed her fingers around it, a new idea forming. Whipped it around at him, stunned to find a cane. It would have to work. She switched to a quasi-bo-staff grip and snapped it at his helmet, then his leg. Helmet again. A crack splintered in the visor, giving her a delicious sense of victory. Again. She struck again. Advanced.

He was backing up. Good, he was scared. She'd win. She'd find out who he was and why—

But like lightning, he snatched the stick. And snapped it at her. Struck her temple.

She dropped into darkness. Felt her ears

ringing. She heard sounds but could see nothing. On all fours, she groaned and felt sticky warmth slide along her earlobe and down her neck. Warbling sounds clamored around her. She groaned, and then her hearing cleared.

Just in time to hear the *twang* of a fleeing motorcycle.

# CHAPTER 21

## JALALABAD, AFGHANISTAN

"You couldn't have come at a worse time." Major Hank O'Neill stormed into the concrete structure surrounded by six or seven other buildings.

Two guards eyed Leif as he followed O'Neill down the dank corridor to an open room with a large tactical hub and several doors branching off to the left. O'Neill aimed for the farthest one, and Leif shot a glance over his shoulder as he entered the major's office. The team was bunked two deep in the fifteen-by-twenty space.

"Why's that?" Leif asked the major.

"SOCOM's drawing down the number of special operations forces, which means they're watching us with a microscope." O'Neill swiped his high-and-tight cut. "Had two soldiers die in a Daesh ambush last week, and yesterday an adviser was killed." He huffed. "Tensions are high and personnel short."

Daesh. Leif sighed. Essentially, it was the new name for ISIS, using an Arabic acronym from the group's previous Arabic name, *al-Dawla al-Islamiya fil Iraq wa al-Sham*.

"Daesh getting the upper hand?"

"When haven't they?" O'Neill planted his hands on his tactical belt. Then nodded to the door. "Close it."

Anticipating the major had something to share with him that couldn't get out, Leif did as instructed.

"Lost contact with Brandon's team. They're two hours overdue reporting in."

"That could be a lot of things." Leif knew how things could get muffed in a hot zone and make it hard to keep to timetable.

"It could." O'Neill gritted his teeth. "But in light of the ambush and the ambassador's adviser—"

"I'll go out there."

O'Neill's sharp gaze penetrated Leif's words. "You do that and don't come back? I'll have DIA breathing down my neck."

"And if you don't let us, you'll have them breathing down your neck," Leif said with a smirk. "Better to send us out and see if we can render aid to your guys." When the major didn't argue or refuse him outright, he pushed on. "All we need are weapons, comms, and a vehicle. We can handle the rest."

O'Neill roughed a hand over his face.

"Like you said, you're under a microscope. We're not attached to your command or this unit, so it has no bearing on you. Say we took the things. Disobeyed your orders."

"No need to lie," O'Neill said. "Jackson!"

A sergeant trotted into the room. "Sir?"

"See this gentleman and his team to the motor pool. They need gear and a vehicle."

"Yes, sir."

Leif felt the thrill of the fight plume in his chest. "Thank you, Major."

"Thank me by coming back alive—with Brandon and his unit, also alive."

"Do my best, sir."

After securing weapons and tac, Reaper was delivered to the motor pool, where they geared up and checked weapons. Leif had Mercy pull up satellite images of the forward operating base where Sander Brandon, Cyrus Block, and their unit had been hunting key assets to assist them in bringing down the Daesh insanity out here. The village was remote and a veritable fortress. Both were points of concern. Ten structures huddled around several others, forming a circle—a choke point with one road in and one out the back.

"Watch this hut," Lawe said, pointing to a small building along the road in. "Probably has lookouts or artillery."

"Agreed," Leif said, eyeing the surrounding sloping land.

"This is a problem," Devine suggested, pointing to a cluster of shrubs and small trees roughly a klick outside the village. "It's elevated and perfect for concealing a lookout or sniper."

"About the only thing making me happy is that it's getting dark." Leif expelled a thick breath. "Okay, Mercy, monitor radio and satellite traffic from here. Devine, we'll drop you and Lawe here"—he tapped a spot on the image—"so you can get into position and scout it as we go in. We can't afford to get into a chokehold out there." He palmed the table. "We'll split it into a three-part grid." If Iskra and Baddar had been here—or even Cell—they could do four and do this a lot faster. "Clear the buildings and scoop around to the back. No one in the middle." He looked at each member. "Clear?"

Once their affirmations came, Reaper headed to the vehicles and went outside the wire, Culver driving and Leif in the jump seat.

"Crazy to be back out here, huh?" Culver spoke loud enough to be heard.

"That's a word for it."

Culver shook his head. "It's . . . different, ya know? On one hand, coming back is like breathing. You don't forget. Senses are buzzing. The vigilance returns." His gaze skidded along the rooftops as they barreled farther from the base. "And the smells. Hot dog, this place can stink when it wants to."

"O'Neill said things are heating up with Daesh."

Lawe snorted and called over the drone of the vehicle, "If it ain't the Taliban, it's ISIS. If it's not ISIS, it's ISIL. If it's not them, now it's Daesh or Haqqani. New names, same mess."

It was true. It seemed like any time things were normalizing—as much as they could in a combat theater—a new threat emerged with the same endgame: kill US-led NATO forces. And now they had another entity to fight, one that couldn't care less who they slaughtered as long as they won.

"Heard anything from Iskra?" Lawe hollered.

Leif shook his head and peered through the side slat in the armor-plated MRAP. He had no desire to talk about Iskra. Seeing that look in her eyes on the balcony, knowing she wanted the same things—marriage, kids—but was hurt and disappointed because he couldn't go there. Not yet. Too much risk. And Dru had her searching for the book, which led Leif to one conclusion—he was afraid of what Leif might dig up. That was it, right? Otherwise, he'd send the one person who had more to gain and therefore more motivation to succeed: Leif.

Knowing she was out there, hunting the book, that she'd already been confronted by Veratti . . . it all meant she was in danger. And that wrecked him. What would happen to Taissia if she died? What would happen to him?

*Nice thoughts, Runt.*

"You and I are dirt when it comes to women, ya know that?" Lawe's smirk split his thick beard.

Truth. "Comes with the uniform. Like all that facial hair." Leif studied the road and landscape, glancing at the map on his watch. He eyed the road again. The terrain. The rise in the east. Heat wakes rippling in the late-afternoon sun. "Slow down."

Culver glanced at him, concern replacing his smile as he lifted his foot from the accelerator. "What?"

"Devine," Leif hollered over his shoulder, then ordered Culver to stop. "Behind that copse of trees."

Culver eased the MRAP into a tangle of shrubs and trees that effectively hid them. Saito and Lawe went eyes out while Devine clambered toward the front and shouldered in close.

"Mercy, you seeing anything?" Leif asked over the comms.

"You passed the collapsed structure?"

Leif glanced at Culver, who shrugged and shook his head. "Negative."

"But . . . how . . ." Mercy muttered. "Satellite shows you did." She growled. "I think things might be fudged."

Devine peered out the front. "We'll drop here," she suggested. "We can hike up the hill, clear that shrub area, then set up on the overlook. Maybe get vantage on what's happening in the village."

Attaching the strap of his M4, Lawe nodded. "Always did love me some Devine intervention."

"Light and fast," Leif said. "Eyes out. This could be nothing—"

"Or it might be exactly what has your spidey senses tingling," Lawe said, heading to the rear door.

They slipped into the night, following a ravine around the back side of the copse. A dried-up creek guided them eastward in a twisting path.

Culver aimed the MRAP back onto the road and let it lumber along.

"Got a problem," Saito called from the rear. "Signal keeps dropping."

The words pushed his gaze to the circular village. Dropped comms could be from jamming tech, or they were too far from a tower. Either way, once they were in there, it was trouble.

"Base, this is Reaper Actual, come in." Leif waited, anticipating there wouldn't be a response, then keyed his comms again. "Coriolis, what's your sitrep?" They rolled along the hard-packed road without a response. "Coriolis, this is Actual. Come in. Over."

When more distance vanished without a response, he eyed Culver.

"Jamming, and I don't mean with a rock band."

Which meant someone knew they were coming. Was Brandon's team okay?

Saito hovered between the front seats. "What're you thinking? We still going in?"

Squinting, Leif considered their options. With

Devine and Lawe on the hill, there was no way to notify them if they retreated. But entering that bottleneck with no obvious or safe exfil . . . He rubbed his jaw.

"They could shove an RPG right up our noses on approach," Culver offered.

"This thing is a blazing beacon begging for explosives," Saito said. "With comms down and us just walking in there . . ."

If they ditched the MRAP, they'd have to hoof it. Which meant being exposed and open. But it'd be easier to get out of a city individually than in a big vehicle that screamed *I'm an American soldier—shoot me!*

"Let's go to ground."

Once they'd low-crawled up into position and set up, Adam noticed something. "MRAP isn't moving." Tracing the anti-mine, anti-IED armored vehicle with the lenses of his nocs, he frowned. No movement. The side windows were no more than slats, so he couldn't detect shapes in there. Trees and shrubs hid the front end.

Draped in a ghillie with local shrubbery attached to it, Peyton lay atop the hill. She nestled her weapon against her shoulder and peered through the scope, angling slowly in the direction of the others. Seconds fell off the clock. "Not seeing anyone in front. Glass is intact, but no sign of them."

Adam shifted to key his comms. "Reaper, this is Badge. Come in." Flattened with elbows propping his torso, he swept the area before repeating the call. "Reaper, what's your situation? Over." He tugged out his sat phone and nearly cursed. "No signal."

"You always have a signal," Peyton said, her eyes wide. "That's why you have that phone—so we aren't hung out to dry."

"Someone's jamming us," he grunted. "Let's hope Runt figured that out or anticipated trouble in the village. Check it—see what you can find there. I'll look for Reaper."

He searched the outlying terrain, searching for the team, for sign of—"Got 'em. Right below us to our six. Looks like Samurai."

Focused, Peyton used her long-range scope—the same one she'd begrudgingly let him use when they were on the mountain in Burma. The one he'd bought her as a peace offering that had only aroused more anger and irritation.

She adjusted the dials, scanning the village.

He liked this. Always had. It might seem messed up to some guys—in fact, some men at the base had given him grief for being her spotter, since they felt *he* should be sniping—but he liked it. Liked being with her. Liked being there for her. She was a piece of history and a work of art. Lame saying, but it made her smile. Man, she had a nice smile. Glowing. He'd rather be stuck on a hillside with her in blazing heat than watching a game with the guys at a bar.

What did that mean? That he loved her?

*"If you love something,"* his gran had always said, *"let it go. If it comes back, it's yours. If it doesn't, it never was."*

Pete was here. They weren't on the best of terms, but things had started to shift. Swinging back toward good. Maybe. She tolerated him now, a big leap from a month ago. He considered her beneath the ghillie, memory filling in what the camouflage concealed. The smooth complexion and her full lips, so soft. She knew how to kiss. Would he—

"You're staring."

Adam grinned.

"Which means you're not working," she chided. "I'm not seeing anyone in the village." Her movements were graceful, slow, and so perfectly stealthy. Even her calm, sultry voice was stealthy, sneaking under his radar. "Switching to infrared."

He went back to poring over the terrain to find Reaper. "Spotted another." It took him a while, but he finally located the others as they regrouped, hoofing it to the village. He relayed their location to Peyton. They weren't obvious, or he'd have seen them right off the bat from an elevated position, so he wasn't worried someone on the ground would see the team breaching the village.

Peyton uttered an oath.

Stunned, Adam couldn't process what had come out of her mouth. Then his pulse spasmed, knowing that if Pete had cursed, it was *bad.* "What?"

"Unknowns holed up to Reaper's three o'clock inside gate. There's easily twenty armed combatants."

"Brandon's guys?"

"Not likel—wait." She went silent for a minute. "I think our objectives are alive, but not in control," she hissed. "Reaper's walking into a trap."

# CHAPTER 22

## JALALABAD, AFGHANISTAN

Shoulder to the wall of the main structure that formed the village gate, Leif tucked his head and listened behind him as Saito and Culver brought up the rear. A soft *thump* on his shoulder indicated their readiness. He did a look-see, then rounded the corner and rushed to the next one. Slammed up against the plaster, he waited for the guys. The fortress-like village was ominous through his NVGs. In the center, vehicles were parked around what looked like a once-thriving well. But no people. No lights. Quiet.

Too quiet.

After the next tap, Leif hustled right and slid along the back of the square hut that formed the main gate. At the corner, he slithered into the dark shadows that separated the hut from a larger, multistoried building. He pressed his shoulder to the wall, probing for signs of life. Glanced back to signal his team.

Green flared in his goggles, startling him. He froze. What was that?

It repeated. Glared in his sight. It was a lot like the infrared they used to paint a target—

not visible to the naked eye but noticeable to someone wearing NVGs. It repeated, flashing—a pattern.

He grinned. Almost laughed. These fighters wanted to silence communications, but they didn't realize who they were trying to cut off. He swung his gaze to the overlook and through his NVGs saw the infrared beam streaking down the hill. Devine intervention.

His pulse jacked at what she relayed using Morse code. *Twelve guns. Four civilians. 0300.* To his three o'clock. Mentally, he tracked that with what he knew of the village layout. He gave Devine a nod, indicating he'd received her message, then shared the intel to Culver and Saito. He swiveled and went to a knee, drawing in the dirt to update their plan.

The crunch of steps in the street stilled him. Leif snapped up his weapon and motioned the others back. Cheek to the stock, he focused on the gap between two buildings, anticipating a confrontation. He strained to hear past his drumming pulse to figure out how many were inbound. Did they know Reaper was in the fortress?

He only detected one set of steps. Hurrying. Sneaking. This guy was probably a lookout, which meant if he didn't return, the combatants would know they had company. As the footfalls drew closer, Leif slid his M4 aside and unholstered his suppressed SIG P226. Unless someone was following this guy, neutralizing him was unlikely to be heard, but still a last resort.

Leif crouched in the darkness.

The man blurred into sight, rushing toward the front building where they'd come in. Leif eased farther into the alley, burying himself in shadows but keeping eyes on the target. Watching down the line of his SIG, he saw the guy peer around the corner, then glance over his shoulder toward wherever his buddies were holed up. He reeled about and started back.

Sensing the approach, Leif held steady. If the lookout entered this alley, he'd go down. Fast steps came . . . and went. The shadows were too heavy to see his face.

After switching to his M4, Leif peered through his scope to get a line on which door the guy opened. A face peeked out before the door closed—and somehow the guy looked right at Leif. His eyes widened.

Leif fired, clipping his shoulder.

The guy stumbled backward, leaving a clear bead on another man.

Leif eased back the trigger again. When a barrage of shots vomited from the doors and windows of the hideout, he sprinted to a vehicle and took cover. Checked the windows—curtained. They hadn't boarded them up.

Relocated to the middle of the village, Culver

and Saito had engaged the fighters but kept their fire controlled to avoid harming Brandon and his unit.

Leif hustled a wide circle around the fountain and came up on the opposite side, sliding from one structure to another. Sticking close to the wall, he kept his head on a swivel. The next building was the hideout. Shots volleyed, pinging off the vehicles where Saito and Culver were keeping them distracted. Leif snatched two flashbangs and pulled the pins. He tossed one through the curtained window and rolled the other at the door near the shooters.

Fire streaked across his bicep. He bit off a curse and yanked back, turning away in anticipation of the bright detonation. He closed his eyes and opened his mouth.

Light exploded. Smoke plumed and billowed on the hot breeze.

Ignoring the sticky warmth on his arm, Leif jerked around, throwing himself forward. Sighted the window. The curtain fluttered and gave him a view inside. Two men with weapons slumped against the wall, clutching their faces and coughing, disoriented, trying to see through the haze.

With that split-second recon, Leif lined up the shot and fired. Two short controlled bursts.

Shouts and screams echoed in the night.

Culver and Saito targeted those stumbling

out of the house, coughing and shooting indiscriminately. They fired and took down the combatants, then scurried into position on the opposite side of the door. They nodded, and Leif barged in.

Shots went wild.

Leif snapped right and fired. Dropped a man. The crack of weapons' fire outside rattled the air as Culver neutralized the last two. "Clear," Leif called and waited for the same from Saito and Culver.

"They're down," Saito said. "Two wounded but alive. The others are gone."

"Who's Brandon?" Leif assessed the four soldiers against a wall and one on the floor.

A wiry guy cough-grunted and lifted an arm. "Here," he said, then pointed to the soldier next to him. "He needs a medic."

"Medic!" Leif called Saito over, who knelt at the injured man's side and shouldered out of his ruck.

"You. It was you they were waiting for!" Brandon accused. "Why? Who are you? What did they want you for?"

"They wanted *us* dead?" Leif said, unsettled at the proclamation. Why would these terrorists be waiting for him? How could they even know Reaper was coming?

"Hey." Culver nodded to something in the corner and hurried to it, flipping a switch.

Crackling erupted in Leif's ear—the base, Devine, a chopper. Relief hit him.

"—ound. Repeat, helo is inbound!" Mercy's voice sailed into his ear.

"Understood," Leif replied. He turned to Brandon and indicated the dead terrorists. "Why'd they take you hostage? How they'd know . . . ?"

"Have no idea, but it wasn't random. They knew our names." Brandon saw Leif didn't like the answer and shrugged. "They just came in, guns blazing, and rounded us all up. Spoke a language I don't know."

Leif swiveled over and knelt. Tugged back a balaclava. Brown hair, but not dark like most around here. He checked another body. Blond, not Middle Eastern. "What the . . . ?" He eyed Culver. "Check the others."

"Shoved us all in here and took our weapons and comms," Brandon said. "Said if we talked, we died."

"Half look local," Culver said as he finished checking the dead. He thumbed the courtyard, where a steady thunder vibrated the ground. "Chopper."

"Chief, your arm." Saito pointed to Leif's bicep.

"Just a graze."

"Very big graze."

"I'm fine." Leif considered Brandon with narrowed eyes. "Who's Cyrus Block?"

304

Fiery hatred spewed through Brandon's expression. "Over there, dead," he growled.

Stadium-bright light exploded through the center of the fortress as the chopper descended. Dust whipped up, peppering them even in the relative safety of the house.

"Can you walk?" Leif asked Brandon, who nodded. Leif extended his hand and helped Brandon to his feet, steadying him. Two Pararescuemen took over with the more heavily injured man, Saito giving an account of his vitals and situation, as well as what measures he'd taken in prepping the soldier. On board the helo, Leif wasn't surprised to find Devine and Lawe had already been retrieved.

Back at the base, they were met by O'Neill and several officers, all demanding to know what had happened. They spent the better half of an hour breaking down events, actions taken, and justifications.

When the brass left, O'Neill glowered at Leif. "I told you I didn't need trouble."

"And I didn't need to get shot," he countered. "If you don't mind, I'm heading to the infirmary to talk with Brandon."

After a wary, confused glance at Reaper, the major nodded. "I have heat to douse after this fiasco anyway."

Reaper crossed to the medical hub, where they entered the urgent care area. They made quick work of locating Brandon on a gurney, shirtless and freshly bandaged.

"Thanks for the extraction," Brandon said with a lopsided grin. "Who the heck are you guys? You nailed that infiltration."

"It's what we do, right?"

"Hooah," Brandon affirmed.

Leif tried to figure out how to frame the questions that buzzed his brain.

"What?"

"What d'you know about Gilliam?"

"Carsen?" Brandon's voice pitched. "He's a good friend and a darn good soldier. Why? Why're you asking about him?"

Something about the way he asked told Leif beyond a doubt that Brandon knew plenty. "Because whoever those people were who tried to kill me and my team didn't kill you but knew your identity." He let the meaning settle thickly between them. "Since you're not wearing name tapes, that tells me *you* have something they wanted. And since my team is probably after the same thing, I'm going to guess you know something about Gilliam."

Brandon swallowed, his gaze traveling to the door, then back to Leif. Reticence tugged at his features, but he said nothing.

"I don't think you understand the situation, Sergeant," Leif ground out.

"What I understand is that people—you included—have thrown around a lot of weight and firepower to locate one of my guys." Brandon pursed his lips. "Not exactly a warm invitation to dialogue, if you ask me."

Frustration tightened Leif's muscles, making him check his bicep, where the graze was already scabbing. It wasn't big, but it stung.

"You should get that checked." Saito frowned, eyeing it. Then outright scowled. "That looked bigger in the dark."

Leif homed in on the sergeant. "I get that you're watching out for your guys. When we're in charge of a team, we take that responsibility seriously. We protect our men, in good and bad times." He squared his stance. "Even when it calls for breaking the rules or fudging the truth—for the sake of the team. For the mission."

Sandy-haired Brandon shifted beneath the blanket draped over his waist and legs.

Leif leaned on the edge of the gurney, craned his head closer, and lowered his voice. "But what you're protecting—it's not Carsen. He's a pawn in a much bigger game."

The sergeant's cheek twitched. "He said as much."

Leif wanted to reach down the guy's throat and yank out the secret. "I need to know, Brandon. My team is tasked with helping him and others like him."

"Others?" Face drained of color, Brandon eyed Reaper. "That's what she said."

Now it was Leif's turn to be confused. "She?"

"A woman—real piece of work," Brandon said, shaking his head. "Pretty, walked in like she owned the place, and I think she did. Then the fighters started arguing, and she told the men to get it taken care of so they could deal with the others."

Leif studied Brandon, whose expression guarded more intel than had passed his lips. But the sergeant wasn't being defensive. It was like he wanted to tell Leif. "I want to help him—protect him against that woman, whoever she was." He lowered his voice. "What d'you know?"

Brandon sighed. "I know where he is."

Two failures. Two near-encounters with death. Well, maybe not death, but enough to make Iskra realize two things: she wanted to make it home to her daughter more than ever, and she didn't want to do another mission without Leif.

"I almost caught him—and he had it, the book," Iskra complained into the phone. "In the last week, I've been shot underwater, nearly drowned, and now thumped on the head." The knot Andrew had put on her temple fueled her determination to make good on her new vendetta. "I'm going to rendezvous with Leif and the team."

Director Iliescu huffed. "I don't—"

"You're not hearing me," she asserted. "I'm doing this—going to be there for him. I want him watching my back, and I want to watch his. Then I'm going to rethink this whole operative thing." She grunted. "Actually, I'm already doing that."

"Iskra . . ." The tremor in his words warned of his concern over losing someone as skilled as her. "Yes, go to Leif. Cell's here with me and is already scouring security feeds at airports, train stations, and ports to find Andrew."

Iskra sighed. "He knew I was coming."

"Because of New York?"

"Must be—and he sent Mercy that email, so maybe he wanted us there. Maybe I got there before he anticipated." But she wasn't buying that. Her actions had been sloppy, predictable. Another reason she should team up with Leif— he would keep her sharp. She felt the plane descending and ended the call so she had time to prepare herself.

MPs escorted Iskra to the building where Reaper was holed up. As she entered, she ran into Culver and Lawe, who grinned and welcomed her back.

"We're heading to the mess. Chief's down the hall," Culver said.

"Thanks." She strode toward a lone light in a glassed-off area.

Palms on a table, Leif was studying whatever was strewn across its surface. A red mark on his bicep, slipping under the sleeve of his black T-shirt, strained for attention. With his tactical pants, blond hair, and strong jaw, he cut an impressive figure. His eyes were torrential, threatening to drown her just like that storm that nearly killed them a few months ago. Never had she imagined she'd want a relationship with a man, and it wasn't his looks that convinced her to attempt one with Leif. It was *him*.

Iskra tugged open the door, surprised when he didn't even flinch or look up. She eased into the room. "Leif?" When he didn't respond, she angled her head and noticed that, while his gaze was on the papers, he wasn't focused on them. There was a distance to his eyes. A weight. What had him so distracted?

She slipped to his side and touched his arched back. "Leif?"

Jerking upright, he pivoted to her. Blinked. "Iskra." The way he said her name stirred a smile in her—which fell away when a cloud passed through his features. "What're you doing here? Where have you been?"

The past roared to the fore, and she didn't want to answer that, didn't want to feel controlled. But she tempered her reaction and decided to go for everything. "I needed to be with you."

He started at that, and then his gaze lit on the knot on her temple. "Who do I need to kill?"

"Is this you being romantic?" She tried to laugh, but weirdly her eyes stung.

Leif drew her into his arms. Crushed her

against his chest and buried his face in her neck and held her for several glorious minutes. This was what she had longed for, ached for. Relief sagged through her, and tears slipped free.

Leif angled back and cupped her face. "You're nearly trembling. What happened?" A ferocity lined his question. "Whoever did this to you—"

Appreciating his protectiveness, she eased away. Held the hand still cupping her face. "Thank you. I'm better . . . now." She let the meaning resonate. "And you?"

He frowned.

"Your arm."

Leif shrugged. "A graze while trying to extract a connection to Gilliam." He raked a hand over his short crop and leaned back against the table. "What happened to you?"

She shook her head. "Too much." Overwhelmed and unsure where to start, she huffed.

His expression darkened. "Fine. I—"

She touched his arm. Slumped into him and rested her head on his shoulder. "Please. No fighting."

He hooked her waist, and they stood in the quiet, lonely room, holding each other.

The falling away of tension allowed her to process. "I got close to the book. And got knocked on the head for it." She moved to a chair.

A thousand questions glinted in his pale blue eyes. "Veratti?"

"Not this time," she admitted. "Andrew."

He dropped into a chair and studied her. "You can't tell me?"

"No," she said, and his expression tightened. "But I'm going to."

Surprise popped his eyes wide.

"Before Reaper headed to Taiwan, Mercy and I went to New York. We noticed a company there was owned by Rutger Hermanns, and when she couldn't access it from home, we figured it had information he wanted to protect."

"So you got curious."

"Mm, quite. We got her on-site to gain access to their system, and when we left, I spotted Andrew but lost him." She left out the woman and the vial. "Before that, I'd reviewed footage of the chaos in Cuba when the book vanished. Something kept bothering me, and I haven't really shared it with anyone, but I grew . . . well, a theory. The Cuba footage hinted that I might be right."

He scowled, probably at the mischief she knew to be dancing in her eyes. "About what?"

"There is an underground facility a couple hundred feet below that mountain facility."

"That's your theory?"

"Actually, now it is fact. I was nearly killed confirming it."

Leif lurched. "Come again?"

She smiled. "I really do love when you act

312

heroic, but relax. I am fine. Remember what I do for a living."

"Used to do—what you were supposed to be leaving behind."

"Someday." She brushed her hair off her shoulder. "Now, my *theory*—this one unproven—is that someone from the belowground facility retrieved the book and went deep into the mountain with it. I saw a guy round a corner in the surveillance footage, but he never appeared on the next angle, and there were no doors he could've used." She hunched her shoulders. "No obvious doors. I dived down there a week ago and discovered a cave access. So it *is* there."

He grunted, scratching his jaw. "That's why we couldn't find it, why there was no trace of anyone leaving with the book."

She nodded. "Because it never left. I think that guy used a hidden panel to slip out of sight."

Leif frowned. "But how do we verify that?"

"I have no idea," she conceded. "What I want to know is who this Andrew is—I mean, he's obviously connected to Rutger, but how? And why?" She shrugged. "I doubt that is even his name, but I've had two encounters with him. He is very good, very fast. And always—always—two steps ahead." She dug her fingernails into her scalp. "If we can find him, we'll get all our answers."

"You think he took the book from the Pearl of the Antilles?"

"No, not according to the footage, but I think—like us—he was looking for it. It was taken by that man who disappeared in the passage."

"So we find that guy."

Iskra sniffed. "He doesn't exist."

"You already checked." His face screwed up. "So, if Andrew was looking for it, why do you think he's the one with the answers?"

"Because he had the book in Paris."

"You saw it?"

She grimaced. "No, but he had a leather satchel, and I am sure it was in there. He's tied to Hermanns. Veratti told me to look to Rutger for the book, and he was right."

"You trust Veratti?"

"Again, no," she said, tempering her frustration. He really was so much work right now. "But Veratti was right about the book. And if I can get it, I might be able to find my brother. And that will be a massive leap toward the super-army. When I told the director all this—"

"So you went to him but not to me."

"After all I just told you, you want to be petulant?"

He flattened his lips and looked away.

Iskra sighed. "I went to the director because he tasked me with finding the book. It was my job to go to him. And can we not do this again? Please."

She peered up at him. "I need your help, Leif. I think we are very close to finding the book, but it's all a swirling molten pile of goo right now."

"Yeah." He nodded. "Let's run through it again."

An hour later, having reviewed her intel and told him about her adventure in the sea, she received a text from Dr. Gradeless, the phlebotomist to whom she'd given the blood sample. Earlier, she'd made a commitment to be open and honest with Leif, to try to turn this thing between them toward better ground. Already she wanted to break that.

She pocketed the phone, feeling his gaze on her.

"Dru?" he asked.

Iskra faked a smile. "He never quits. But you know what I think?" When he didn't answer, when his expression remained flat, she forged ahead. "I think it's time the whole team saw the intel we dug out of Frankfurt & Stuttgart's servers. I want to know what Andrew was after."

He ran a hand over his hair. "Agreed. What one person misses, another will notice. More eyes, more chances."

A man entered the room.

"Brandon," Leif said, coming to his feet. "What can I do for you?"

The guy hesitated, glancing at Iskra.

"It's good," Leif said, reaching toward her.

This was her out. "I'll take a break. Use the restroom." She nodded at Leif. "Want coffee?"

But he saw through her. Smirked. "No, I'm good." His gaze shifted to the newcomer.

Slammed with guilt, she swallowed. Regretted the decision she'd made and the secret she chased. Yet not enough to stay. Or apologize. Shame pushed her out the door.

"What is it?" she heard Leif ask the guy.

Once his voice faded, Iskra retrieved her phone. Dialed. "Dr. Gradeless?"

Once alone, Leif lifted his jaw to Brandon. "This about Carsen?"

The sergeant handed him a throwaway phone, then walked out.

Leif glanced at it, surprised to see a call already in progress. He put it to his ear. "Hello?"

"Why are you looking for me?" Carsen.

Leif told himself to breathe. "Your name showed up on a list."

"You know more than that."

"But not much."

"I can't . . . time's short. If you want to stop this thing, go to The Hague."

He paced to the wall and palmed it. "Why would I do that?"

"Because Brandon said you were a soldier—"

"SEAL."

"We can't all be perfect."

Despite the tension, Leif smiled. "Or failures."

Carsen barked a laugh. "You have a team. Spec ops. Go to The Hague. That's where they're sending us."

"Us?"

"I can't say more right now. But go. You'll know."

"Know what?"

"If you see me—shoot. Shoot to kill."

# CHAPTER 23

## THE HAGUE, THE NETHERLANDS

It seemed almost ominously prophetic that Carsen had said to come to The Hague at the same time the Quantum Technology Conference was happening. It wasn't a coincidence. Couldn't be.

The conference was the most significant event happening in The Hague at the moment. Leaders around the world could learn about the latest quantum technology opportunities in areas such as aerospace, specialty chemical, automotive and transportation, R&D, government . . . and defense.

That smelled a lot like the Neiothen.

Standing at the window of a hotel that overlooked the North Sea provided the perfect view to clear his mind. But Leif couldn't shake the nagging at the back of his head after examining the photos Spill sent over of the explosion in Africa. It was wrong—not that explosion, but the other one that didn't make sense. The one without scorches or a crater.

Yet he could still see himself waking up, staring at the sky and the geysers of fire. The wreckage. It didn't add up.

But he couldn't do anything about that. Not

right now. He had to get his head back in the game. This Quantum Tech conference would draw politicians, nobles, and military alike and had a registration list longer than a roll of toilet paper. There'd be more brownnosing than drunkenness and exploration of quantum advancements.

His mind skipped back to his conversation with Iskra. Her trust in him had both anchored and unmoored him. Her confidence and desire answered a deep longing in him. But it also terrified Leif that someday, coming out of a bad dream, he'd seriously injure her or . . .

Saito had a point. Any one of them could be one of the Neiothen.

Things were coming to a head. At least, Leif hoped they were. He'd had enough games. It was time for answers. Not just about this mission, the book, or these so-called Neiothen, but about his own life. About the constant buzzing in his skull that wouldn't quit. That grated and irritated him until he was on the verge of ripping someone's head off. He'd been petty with Iskra because that vibration never quieted, despite holding her, talking to her, and hearing all her progress.

At least someone had made progress.

"Hot dog," Culver said, striding out of the adjoining room of the suite. He tugged the edges of his tux jacket. "This is slick, but it ain't me."

"Doesn't have to be you." Leif went to the mirror above a side table and tied his bow.

"Dude." Lawe appeared from the bathroom in a gray suit that probably cost more than he made in a year. "I look *good*." He nodded, sliding a hand down the silk blend of the jacket. "She won't be able to resist me now."

Leif snorted. "If you're staking your relationship on a suit, I have bad news."

Unrepentant, Lawe grinned. "Look at me, man." He held out his palms and thrust his chest forward. "I'm freakin' irresistible."

"I think you mean irresponsible," Cell muttered from behind the three laptops he had going.

"You're only jealous you ain't got a woman."

"Neither does Culver," Cell asserted.

"You should get changed," Culver said. "Maybe drown yourself in the tub while you're at it."

"I only meant—"

"I know what you meant," Culver growled. "I'll find the right girl when I find her."

"And technically," Cell said, "Lawe doesn't have a girl either. He's just wishful-thinking himself into that relationship."

"After tonight, there will be no doubt," Lawe said. "Seeing how you're so good with computers, why don't you conjure yourself up an AI girlfriend."

Culver snorted.

"You are *sick*." Cell's lip curled.

"All right," Leif said, shaking his head, appreciating the guys and their camaraderie.

Hoping he didn't let them down again. "We need to be on the terrace in ten. Head out in intervals."

Lawe shrugged. "I'm ready."

"I'll wait for boy wonder," Culver said.

Leif nodded.

"Going live with the comms in five." Cell stroked a few keys, then gave a thumbs-up. "All set. See you on the beach."

Leif and Lawe left the suite of the Amrâth Kurhaus. The luxurious five-star grand hotel was a beautiful historical and monumental building elegantly situated on the coast of Scheveningen. More palace than hotel, its rich history dated back to 1818 and had been remarkably well preserved. With two-hundred sixty-five rooms, a restaurant, terrace, and spa, it was an exquisite setting for the conference.

"Crazy," Lawe whispered as they waited for the elevator to the main level. "Always heard about The Hague, but never thought I'd see it."

"Too political for me—I'd hoped never to see it." Leif entered the gilded elevator, catching his reflection in the mirror as he turned to press the button.

"Since you're Mr. Encyclopedia," Lawe said, squaring his shoulders as he checked out his reflection, "what do you know about this place?"

"The Hague or the hotel?"

Lawe snorted. "The Hague. I mean, we hear about it all the time with NATO."

Leif shrugged. "It's not the capital of the Netherlands—that's Amsterdam—but The Hague does seat several government entities like the cabinet and the Council of State. It hosts most foreign embassies and a hundred or more international organizations."

"Doesn't the Netherlands have a king or something?"

"The king and queen live here," he confirmed.

Lawe smoothed his beard. "Think they'll be at the party tonight? It's huge. Whole hotel is blocked out."

"Doubtful." Leif checked the backlit floor numbers as they descended.

"Can I ask a question?"

Leif eyed his friend, noting that question had weight to it.

"You ever think about marrying Iskra?"

Leif started. "Yeah. Why?"

Sincerity tugged at the big guy's features. Gaze intense and serious, he retrieved something from his pocket. Held it up.

Seeing the ring, Leif felt one-upped. "You sure about that?" His buddy had been crazy about Devine since they met, but the two hadn't exactly been on good footing since Reaper set up camp in Maryland. "I mean, you two . . ."

"Things are on the upswing."

"Meaning she hasn't punched you recently."

"Meaning we're talking—nicely." Lawe

shrugged. "Well, most of the time. I have to convince her." His beard twitched. "I made the biggest mistake of my life walking away from her last time. Won't do it again."

"Don't tell me that—tell her."

"I have. A hundred times."

Hearing the pout in Lawe's voice, Leif tried to hide his smile.

"Sometimes I wonder if she's not willing to go all-in with me because she's hot for someone else."

"I think Devine wants to believe you, but you hurt her. Bad. You were talking rings and weddings when I last saw you." When Lawe nodded, he continued. "You start talking rings and weddings again, she's going to wonder when you'll bail this time."

Lawe stilled as the elevator came to rest on the lobby floor. "So, what? Don't talk rings?"

"No ring. Just get to know her—favorite food, favorite color."

"Lasagna and teal."

Surprise lit through Leif. "Good start, but my point was more about nuance," he said as they exited and strode over the marble floor. Down a set of steps and across another open area, a wall of glass pocket doors had been opened so the interior bled onto the terrace. At a table, Mercy stood chatting with Baddar, who'd rendezvoused with them here at the hotel.

"There." Leif slapped Lawe's gut and indicated the commando. "Follow Smiley's lead. He's crazy about Mercy, but you don't see him buying or talking rings. He's there for her. Talks to her. It's not about you, man. It's about *her*."

"When did you become Dr. Phil?"

Leif shook his head, just as surprised the words had fallen off his lips. "I can hand it out, but I can't follow it." It wasn't that simple, but . . .

"Maybe you should, because Iskra"—Lawe nodded behind them—"is a whole lotta woman that a whole lotta men would like to get to know."

Irritated at the challenge, Leif glanced back in the direction from which they'd come and stilled at the goddess gliding down the steps with Devine.

"Ho-lee crap," Lawe whispered, apparently having seen his girl, too. "I need a bigger gun. And I gotta get a ring on that finger soon." He stilled. "But no ring talk tonight."

Leif was dumbstruck at Iskra. She wore a wine-colored velvet gown that accentuated her curves and tossed color into her cheeks and eyes, which were bright with amusement as a smile traipsed onto her lips. Hair swept up with those maddening tendrils dangling along her face and neck, she truly did look like a goddess. And the way she was smiling at him made him dizzy. Cemented the tentative alliance that had

324

arisen out of the information they'd shared last night. Crazy how all that swelled into a heady concoction, mixing her attraction with trust. Made a guy want to man-up. Figure out how to make this work.

"Well." Iskra gave him a coy smile as she curled into him. "You clean up nicely."

He took the kiss she seemed to be offering. "Not that anyone will notice while I'm standing next to you."

"Nice," she said around a smile, accepting the compliment. "Ready to enter the fray?"

Sun glinted off her eyes as they approached the retracted glass doors and moved onto the terrace. Adorning the fifty-by-forty-foot area, tables offered wine glasses and champagne flutes, which guests were welcome to fill from fountains placed every twenty paces that poured a variety of wines. Beyond the stone steps, the beach cast a glittering backdrop. Ivy climbed lattice planters that formed a barrier on the sides, ensconcing the party of roughly three hundred in intimacy and privacy.

Iskra took a wine glass and handed one to him. "No."

"Take one," she murmured. "Nobody likes prudes at these gatherings." Hooking her arm through his, she sauntered to a fountain that looked as if blood spilled from its spout. She tucked her goblet beneath the stream, filled it halfway, then switched glasses with him and repeated it. Turning, she straightened and smiled.

He could get used to this view. Though her smile didn't fall and her expression didn't change, something in her eyes did. "What?"

"You should relax."

"D'you see what I'm wearing?" he teased. "How does one relax in an ape suit?"

Iskra leaned against him, adjusting his bow tie and throwing his mind in all the wrong directions. "Veratti is here."

Reality crashed hard against his thoughts. He wrapped an arm around her, playing cuddly—such a sacrifice—and skated a glance around.

"His assistant just showed," she amended. "He checks to make sure things are okay before Veratti enters." She slid a hand up around his neck. "Maybe we should dance."

"Thought you'd never ask." He grinned. "I saw one of France's ministers near a fountain."

"King Ahmad's only surviving and uncontested heir is here as well," she said.

"Quite the who's who," came Cell's voice in the invisible piece tucked in Leif's ear. "So far, representatives from Palestine, China, Syria, the United States, Britain, and Saudi Arabia have cleared security."

"And if Veratti sees me . . ." Iskra whispered.

"Game over."

"We're lucky they didn't put me by the chocolate fountain," Mercy said as she handed a plate of petit fours to a guest.

"It is not good?" Baddar worked beside her, decked out in a black suit and tie, as were the staff, yet he stood miles above them. Dapper.

"You kidding me? You'd have to roll me out of here like a hippo." She wrinkled her nose, scanning the crowd and chaos. "Or I'd figure out how to hook up an IV for myself."

Baddar laughed. "You like chocolate?"

"Wrong again."

He frowned.

"I *love* chocolate. I've been unfaithful to many a confection when it comes to chocolate."

"I am not sure whether to laugh or be sad that you speak of chocolate the way you would a person."

She delivered more food, then eyed him. "Don't worry. I have my priorities straight—chocolate! People are too fickle and too mean. Chocolate never fails me."

"I would like to think that maybe I do not fail you."

Her heart ka-thumped right into his eyes, brown like a dark chocolate truffle. She took in his gentle smile and demeanor. It was so hard to remember he was an experienced commando.

That persona just didn't match the chill dude who always greeted her.

"Careful," Mercy said softly, nervously—which was strange and awkward. "Talk like that . . ." She fidgeted with the napkins, realizing she'd been about to tease him about taking her to dinner.

It scared her to go down that road again. Maybe it had been long enough since losing Ram. Some would say more than enough. But opening the door to Baddar was like freeing a dam.

He'd homed in on her jitters and touched the small of her back. "I make you nervous."

"No," she lied. She glanced up to smile and shrug him off, and got snared in those truffles again. *Oh Mercy, have mercy! Date the guy already.*

"I would like much to take you to dinner." The waver of his smile, indicating his nerves, unleashed jellies in her stomach. "Would you go with me?"

No no no. "Yes."

His eyes brightened. "Good." He shifted. "I mean, thank you."

"Right." She touched her forehead, turning. "Now—um, cheesecakes."

Eagerness ever his motto, Baddar went back to work, sliding her sly smiles that made every junior high phase she'd skipped come roaring to life. The thought of a normal life seemed strange. It had always been out of reach.

Smiling, she handed a plate of *nougat glacé* to a woman with a small tiara nestled atop a mountain of curls. And over the woman's shoulder, she saw him. *Andrew.*

Mercy was halfway across the terrace before she realized she hadn't told Baddar what she was doing. After a moment's hesitation, she glanced back—found him being his typical happy self, smiling as he delivered cheesecake to another guest—and barely slowed.

"Maddox, where are you going?" Iliescu commed.

At his intrusion into her diversion, she skipped into a jog and cleared the decorations.

"Maddox, report!"

Down a concrete stairwell, she saw a door flap shut—a side entrance into the hotel. She hurried and yanked it open. Threw herself into the hall.

The door cracked shut behind her, snapping her into darkness. Mercy gasped and spun back, only to feel a sharp pinch at her neck.

"Do you think Mercy is okay?" Iskra looked at Leif, noting he seemed unusually agitated. "She left her post."

He grunted, circling the power couples and dignitaries as they danced. "She's smart. Maybe she's taking a bio break."

Iskra took a sip of wine and her gaze connected

with a familiar tanned face. "Ah, I'm noticed. Rutger."

Leif, to his credit, didn't turn to see Hermanns.

"I hate that man. So very much."

"Only because he beat you."

"More than once."

"Is that what I have to look forward to?"

She laughed. "Beating me, or my hatred?"

He frowned. "Beating you."

"You can try."

"Worried Hermanns will say something to you?"

"I am convinced he knows I am onto him after all the encounters with Andrew. Though he is a formidable man, he is not dangerous like Veratti."

"But he's a Veratti lackey, isn't he?"

"That is what they say, but I do not think the two get along."

"Don't have to get along to work together. Look at me and Cell."

"Heard that," Cell commed.

"Always butting in where he doesn't belong."

"Always watching over those depending on him to guide their sorry carcasses out of dangerous situations," Cell corrected. "If I like them."

A man stepped into their path.

Iskra felt the world tilt at the presence of Ciro Veratti. She drew on the strength that carried her through a dozen years tethered to Hristoff Peychinovich. "Mr. V—"

"I am surprised to see you both here," Veratti bit out. "I vetted the guest list, and I know for certain neither of you was on it." Though he smiled, there was a lethal warning in his words.

"You must've misread," Leif said, not cowering before one of the most powerful men in the world.

"I did not," Veratti countered. His gaze slid to her. "Viorica." The nickname was intentional, reminding her where she'd come from. That he held sway and control over her. "I believe I gave you a task."

"I believe," Iskra said around a rampaging heart, "you *asked* for my help and tried to hold it over my head with information on my brother." She shrugged. "But I'm wondering why a powerful man like yourself can't seem to rein in someone under his influence. Rutger answers to you, does he not?"

"Unless you want to be unceremoniously tossed out, I suggest you amend your tone, Miss Todorova." Veratti shouldered into her.

Iskra tensed, not because of a threat Veratti posed, but because of Leif.

Who cut between Iskra and Veratti. "You're a gentleman," Leif said in a low tone, his gaze sliding to the four security suits that manifested around them. "You and I know she's earned the respect you aren't showing her."

Veratti's dark eyes bored into Leif, and his chest drew up. Leif had hit a nerve, and no doubt ArC's founder was conjuring ways to hurt him. He lifted a hand, and Iskra half expected Leif to end up dead.

Instead, the Italian prime minister rested a hand on Leif's shoulder. Swiped his lapel. Then patted his shoulder. "We'll talk, Mr. Metcalfe. But not yet." His gaze skidded toward Iskra. "I'm holding you to our agreement. Find it. I told you what you needed to know."

Too many games. Too many unanswered questions. Veratti's insinuation about talking later stirred Leif's curiosity. But then, at the far side of the terrace, something caught his attention. He directed himself and Iskra out of the prime minister's range.

"Harcos." The name was a breath on Leif's tongue.

"Who?" Iskra asked.

He stiffened. Frowned—why had he said that? "Vega," he corrected. "I have eyes on Vega."

He rushed across the terrace to the beach, the sand deflecting his steps. He pushed between two sections of the lighted lattice. Saw Vega rushing toward the front of the hotel.

Leif gave chase, but the Neiothen moved like the sand wasn't there, as if he were some kind of sand spider. And his speed was ridiculous. They ran for what felt like forever, but Vega never slowed or faltered. Never lost ground.

Unbelievably, Leif struggled to catch up, but finally closed in. He launched into Vega. They went down hard, dust pluming in his eyes.

Flipping Vega over, Leif drew his fist back—and froze. The ground shifted—rocky, hard. Not sand. Then the beach returned beneath them. The face registered. Harcos.

What? Harcos—from his dream? No, intel said this was Turi Vega.

Leif's confusion created a deadly hesitation that left him open.

Vega flipped him. Nailed him in the side, knocking the air from his lungs. Leif collapsed with a groan, vaguely aware of Vega escaping. He watched the guy's legs disappear. Holding his side, he staggered up.

Someone leapt in front of him.

Leif flinched, expecting trouble, and caught the guy's shirt, noting the tac vest beneath it. "Carsen."

Gilliam's warning to shoot him on sight rang in Leif's head. However, something else tremored through him. He released Carsen's shirt. Slapped him on the shoulder. But even as he did, a pang jarred his skull. Leif stumbled back, clutching his head. "Augh!"

Gilliam surged forward. Grabbed his shoulders. "Do you remember?"

"To shoot you?" He should be reaching for his SIG. "Yeah."

"No, you *have* to remember ossi."

Leif shook off the pain. "What are you talking about? Who did this to you? Tell me!"

"I won't betray her. We can change this!"

"Betray who?" Leif blitzed for a second—a flicker of a memory, a ghost of someone else imposed itself over Carsen's visage. *Shoot to kill.* He palmed his weapon.

"You *must* remember!"

Confused and disoriented, Leif felt hot air stroke his cheek.

Gilliam let out a gurgled cry and pitched forward.

Leif startled, registering the report of a weapon as he saw a dark stain spread across Gilliam's shirt.

Despite the wound, Gilliam turned and flew up the embankment.

Leif stared after him, dumbfounded. He should not be moving that fast or unencumbered. He should drop, bleed out. Any second . . .

Gilliam kept running.

Leif shouted, "Stop him!"

# CHAPTER 24

## THE HAGUE, THE NETHERLANDS

Urgency threw Iskra over the beach behind Baddar toward a frozen Leif, who stared after two men running into the hotel. Culver and Saito were hot on their trail.

It wasn't right. Leif wasn't right. Why wasn't he going after them? She was still a half dozen paces away when Baddar reached him.

Leif flung around, throwing off Baddar's hand as he unleashed a stream of vitriol that was lost to the wind. Iskra slowed, surprised at the wildness of Leif's expression, the fury of his response.

"You nearly shot me!" Leif yelled.

Hands raised, Baddar shook his head. "It was not me. I did not shoot."

"Who were those men?" Iskra asked. "What did he do to you?"

"Nothing. He—he was crazy." A few blinks, and Leif seemed to come together. "It was Carsen Gilliam." He started jogging. "We need to take them out before they're initiated."

*That was a delayed response.*

"Go, go!" Culver shouted to Lawe as the two

hurried past, sparing Leif the briefest of glances.

Leif keyed his comms. "Carsen Gilliam and Turi Vega are on-site. Repeat, they are on-site. Stop them before they initiate."

"I think Gilliam is dead," came the quiet voice of Adam. "Sprawled just inside the hotel lobby across the street. A lotta blood. Going to guess a sniper hit. Heading back."

"Did Ha—Vega shoot him?" Leif paused, gaze flickering back and forth across the sand. He lowered his gaze. Scowled.

"Unknown," Cell barked.

Intensity roiled off Leif like a heat wave on a blistering hot day.

Iskra touched his side. "What's wrong?"

He glanced at her, then back toward the latticework, then up the buildings.

"Leif?"

He jerked toward Baddar, his demeanor all business as he took in their surroundings. "Put your gun away. Now."

The commando complied, but his brows drew together.

"What's wrong?" Iskra repeated, a pervasive dread coiling in her stomach. She had never seen Leif like this.

He keyed his comms. "Any eyes on Vega?"

"Negative," Cell replied calmly. "We're reviewing security cameras to find out where he went. Authorities are swarming the lobby."

"What about Elvestad? If Vega's here, is Elvestad?"

"And who is their target?" Iskra asked. "There are hundreds of VIPs here."

Leif muttered something to himself. "It's not just one target. It's several. That's why there's more than one Neiothen."

"Okay, authorities appropriately detoured," Cell said. "I put in a call saying I saw a man with a gun on the west side of the garden, heading back to the street."

"Everyone keep a low profile," Leif ordered. "Eyes out. Find Vega and possibly Elvestad."

"And Mercy," Baddar said quietly.

Leif started. "What?"

"She is missing," Baddar said with frustration.

Anger detonated through Leif's expression. "She's *what?*"

"We were at the dessert table and, um . . ." Baddar swallowed. "She just leave. I thought maybe she go to use lady room, but she not come back."

"You had one job," Leif shouted. "One job— protect her. The one person on our team who doesn't have tactical training. She needed your protection. What is wrong with you?"

"Whoa." Iskra stepped in. "Leif," she pleaded. "Stop."

"Get off me, V."

The nickname shoved her back, making it impossible to hide the wound he created.

He saw it. And shrugged it off. "Mercy's the weakest link. She needed protection. And he can't pay attention long enough to keep her safe. This whole team—I have no idea why I even put it together."

"That's uncalled for," Iskra chided, surprised at his acidic response. She touched his chest, as if she could reach past the fabric, past his skin, to the organ pulsating between his ribs. "These men are extremely loyal to you."

His lip curled, and his blue eyes seemed to fade to gray. "Yeah? Well, loyalty doesn't get the job done." He cursed and jerked back toward the event.

"What is wrong with you?" Iskra called after him, but he never slowed or responded.

Hurt and anger spiraled through her veins.

"Something is wrong," Baddar said.

"Agreed," Iskra said, monitoring him but unable to bring herself to give chase. To talk to him. She realized only as the distance grew that this was so much like Hristoff's tirades. And by the saints, she would not cater to such a man ever again.

An ache bloomed in her breast, watching Leif's taut shoulders and fists slip back behind the lattice. Something *was* wrong.

No, something was broken—in him. She'd seen fragments over the last few weeks, but since these missions to stop the Neiothen, he'd become

progressively worse. It scared her, but worse—
it worried her. He was truly the best man she
knew, and she did not want to see him become
something else. Something terrible.

*Can't breathe. Can't breathe!*
Mercy jerked awake with an intense feeling
of suffocation. She reached for her mouth—but
her hands yanked to a stop. She glanced down
to see what she'd caught on, only to find duct
tape, rope, and a strap coiled around her hands—
tightly. She couldn't even separate her hands
from each other. They were anchored to her feet,
and her whole body was curled around a marble
column.

What . . . ?
It all came back in a torrent. Seeing Andrew.
Following him around the hotel and in through
that side door. Hearing something and turning—a
pinch. Mentally, she probed the spot in her
shoulder, the one she was lying on. Yeah, still
tender.

*So where am I?* She swiveled around the
column, taking in a borderline gaudy hotel room.
Massive four-poster king bed with drapes. Cold
marble floors. She scooched around some more
and found the windows.

In particular, the man standing behind a long-
range scope, staring out the window.

"Sorry about taping your mouth," Andrew said

339

without turning. "Couldn't have you shouting and giving me away."

She'd give him shouting.

Mercy screamed at the back of her throat, thrashed against the floor, and tried to bang the column to generate some noise to annoy the rooms above or below so they'd contact hotel security.

After several minutes, her throat was already starting to ache, but she persisted and thumped her hands on the column.

She wasn't sure how long she protested and attempted to stir a commotion, but when she finally looked at Andrew, he was bent over a computer and wearing noise-canceling headphones.

She throat-shrieked more. Jerked but only ended up thudding her head on the marble. Defeated, she slumped on the floor and considered her bonds. Was there a way to get them off? Maybe if she had Vision's stone, she could use a blast of solar energy to free herself.

Ha. Forget the bonds. She'd send a blast through that arrogant skull bent over his work. Being a villain suddenly had very real appeal.

She scooted around the column, this time taking in her environment for a different purpose—tools. She hesitated, eyeing the sofa. Too far away, but there was a brass lamp standing sentry over the seating group. What else . . . what else?

Cords. There were cords nearby, but the way he'd tied her . . . Ugh! She deflated against the marble. Darkness fell over her, and she flinched. Glanced up. Her heart jumped into her throat—he was squatting over her.

Head cocked to the side, he smirked. "How you doing, Miss Marvel?"

A high-pitched alarm squealed through her mind. No. There was no way he could know about her affinity for Marvel superheroes.

"What?" he chuckled. "You can hunt me down and learn everything about me"—he wagged his hands—"or so you think, but I can't return the favor?" He was backlit by the light from outside, throwing him into shadows. "Admiral Manche handed me good intel on you. From there"—his shoulders bounced—"it was easy work. What I can't figure out is you and the Arab. Never saw that one coming. He's not in your league, Ar—"

She shrieked, not wanting to hear that name. Not wanting it spoken. Ever again.

"You imagine that girl is gone, yes? That you're someone new." Andrew brushed a strand of her hair aside. "I get it. I do. We can put on nice clothes, we can cozy up to the rich and powerful, but in the end, we are what we are, Marvel. It doesn't matter who people think we are as long as we get the job done, right?"

There was a lot of "we" in that speech. He included himself?

"I'm curious, though. Will you ever tell them?" He scratched his jaw. "Or are you so wholly immersed in this identity that you can't remember who she was? Who you were, not so many years ago?" His fingers swept her cheek, and she jerked away. "I am sorry for what they did to you. Maybe you should let her out, let her return for one last stand."

Something beeped, and he returned to the window, his tablet in dark mode to prevent it from giving him away. She noticed a small cable running from the device to the window—camera. Why was he watching from up here?

He lifted a phone from his pocket and typed into it. Repocketing it, he removed the scope from the tripod and tucked it into a bag. From the corner, he retrieved something and moved back to the window.

With the backlighting of—lights! There were a lot of lights out there! Music drifted into the hotel room, and a gentle breeze rippled the curtain. The gala. They were overlooking the gala!

When he shifted, she saw it. Saw the way the lighting from the event caressed the long black barrel of a rifle.

Mercy's heart backed into her throat. She couldn't move as he settled behind the weapon. He was going to shoot someone. Murder them right in front of her, and she could do nothing to stop him.

She shrieked and thrashed.

"Quiet," came his condescending and ridiculously calm voice, his focus unbroken from his task.

*Please. Please, please, don't . . .*

Hotel security was upped after Gilliam's death. What Adam couldn't figure out was why the event continued unaffected. Maybe that was what rich folk were like—flaunting their ability to be stupid but look good.

"Cell, what's the intel on the shooting?"

"Nothing," Cell said. "Management wanted to shut down the event, but Veratti convinced the royal house to keep it going."

Adam grunted. "No kidding. Body's been removed, lobby cleaned—after photographs were taken, of course. Never seen anything like it."

"And I've never seen anyone move the way those two did," Saito said.

"Yeah," Culver said. "Dude, he had a hole in his chest and ran as if he had a jetpack."

"No chatter on the scanners," Cell continued. "They don't want anyone not already on-site getting wind of the killing. Security brought in more badges to search for the shooter. And—hold up." He went quiet. "We have Elvestad on-site. He just slipped onto the crowded dance floor."

"Move, people," Leif said. "Blend in. Dance—whatever looks normal and puts you in place near Elvestad. Don't draw eyes."

Adam took Pete in his arms and led her around the dance floor, the ring burning a hole in his thoughts. He reminded himself not tonight. But he was starting to feel like if he waited for the perfect time . . .

*Not the time, idiot.*

"You're quiet." Peyton smiled at him, her gaze surfing the crowd. "Nice change."

"Ha-ha."

"Got anything?" Leif asked through the comms.

"Negative," Cell responded. "DIA and CIA have analysts working on the footage I'm feeding them, but there's nothing. They think the sniper must've been elevated."

"The hotel next door?" Leif suggested, gaze swinging up the multistoried building.

"A SWAT team is checking it out."

Nestled against Adam, Peyton had her arm draped over his shoulder. "I see at least three different vantages. This hotel, the one next to it, and a building about three-quarters of a mile out. Any are viable options for a sniper."

"Stay sharp, Reaper," Iliescu said. "We'll keep you posted."

Peyton met Adam's eyes. "I should be higher."

Man, he loved her focus. "We can do that when it's time."

"That may be too late." She huffed and shifted her gaze, then stopped dancing. She frowned over his shoulder.

"Now what?"

Color filled her cheeks. "Dance us closer to that group," she said, resuming their rhythm and circling quickly toward the side where men in U.S. military uniforms were clustered around a wine fountain.

"Why?"

"Because I'm pretty sure that's General Elbert. He was Sienna's godfather—she always bragged about him, and honestly, I think that's how she got most of her promotions."

They left the dance floor, and Peyton broke away.

Peyton lifted a glass and aimed it at the golden fountain stream near the officers.

"I can't believe it," General Elbert said. "I watched that kid grow up and even worked with him on his last mission. He was as smart and intelligent as they come. To hear he was here and shot . . ."

"I heard he was here to kill someone," a three-star stated.

"No way. Not Carsen."

Peyton deliberately made eye contact with the general. "I couldn't help but overhear you, General Elbert."

Strangely dark brows against a mostly silver head of hair frowned at her. "Do I know you?"

"No, but you know one of my cultural support

team members, Sienna Gilliam." She tilted her head. "And clearly you knew Carsen as well."

"Like a son."

She gave him a sad smile. "I'm sorry about what happened. I was surprised, but then, I've heard he was having trouble with anger and depression. Someone"—she didn't need to mention it was Sienna—"said he cracked."

"It happens to the best of them," a colonel murmured.

"It does, but it didn't to Carsen." Anger etched the general's eyes and tone.

"But he went AWOL," Peyton argued. "Because he was struggling with PTSD."

"He was struggling, all right, but not with that." He scowled at her. "I thought you said you were friends with Sienna."

"No, I said I was teamed with her as a CST." The truth seemed to be taunting her, just out of reach. "Why?"

"Because it wasn't Carsen who cracked. It was Sienna. Carsen took leave to take care of her, but when he came back . . ." He shook his head. "The thing is, she's assigned to Colonel Nesto as his attaché."

The truth struck Peyton like a gong, sending reverberations through her bones and up her spine. "Sienna." *She* was the one who cracked?

General Elbert eyed her.

"I hadn't heard. Wow."

"What are you doing here?" he demanded.

"Tell him he'll need to talk with Admiral Braun about that," came Iliescu's quiet, assertive voice. "Good work, Devine."

She repeated the message, which drew surprised glances from the officers, then excused herself. Her knees felt puddly as she returned to Adam's arms and leaned heavily against him. "Dance," she instructed.

"You okay?" he breathed against her ear.

"Just a little more shaken than I expected." Resting against his chest, she focused on the strength of Adam, the warmth of his touch.

"That was a lot of brass you stared down."

Something jabbed her arm. Cheek to cheek with Adam, she reached into his coat pocket and felt a small object. She traced it. Circular. Her breath backed into her throat. She lifted it from his pocket, held it up behind his back, and gasped.

Adam looked over his shoulder. "Well, crap. You weren't supposed to find that."

"*What* is this?" She gaped at him.

"It's an engagement ring."

"*For?*" Her heart thundered. Was this for . . . her?

"The right time."

"For whom?"

"Are you freakin' kidding me?" he balked. "Who else would it be for?" He roughed a hand over his face. "It wasn't supposed to be like this. Leif told me to—"

"Heads up," Leif barked into the comms, "Elvestad and Vega spotted."

The speakers cranking out lively tango music crackled. A voice intruded on the event. "Dreng. Two. One. Four. Initiate rise. Rise. Rise."

Leif stilled, the words ominously similar to the recording they'd heard when Ibn Sarsour killed the Saudi king and crown prince. A thick, heavy ache pulsed behind his ear, making him grimace. His thoughts swam in a thick, hazy quagmire. He planted the heel of his hand to his head, squinting.

"Kampfer. Two. One. Six. Initiate rise. Rise. Rise."

"That's two initiated," Saito said.

Culver commed. "It just got real, y'all."

"Cut off that mic to the sound, Cell!" Iliescu ordered. "Do it now!"

Leif started toward the sound system, wanting to find whoever had spoken the words. Halfway there, mind addled with the growing throb in his skull, he noticed chaos around the sound board. Uniforms were shouting at the DJ, who was shrugging and lifting his hands at the angry men. Though he couldn't explain why, Leif turned his gaze to the far side, where a cluster of guests were buzzing and chatting, all looking to one man for guidance. One calm man who seemed almost apathetic about the strange words still reverberating in Leif's head.

Sipping wine, Ciro Veratti held a casual pose, as if none of this was happening. As if someone hadn't just charged the air with bizarre words through a PA system. As if a man hadn't been shot and killed in the lobby.

When their gazes connected, Leif felt a strange trill run through his veins.

"Runt!" came the director's bark.

Leif blinked. "Ye—" His throat caught, so he cleared it. Shook off the stupor. "Yeah. Here."

"What's happening with our Neiothen?"

Someone slapped his shoulder and whizzed past—Lawe.

Leif fell into a lope behind him, scanning the strangely still dance floor. The scene was macabre.

A scream shot out from his ten. Like the Red Sea, the crowd parted. Guests scattered away from something—right into Leif's path. He negotiated the insanity, propelled by a sense of urgency.

"Whoa, whoa," Lawe snapped. "Hold it. No need to do this."

Leif broke around the last few guests and saw the object of Lawe's concern. Turi Vega. *And* Harald Elvestad. Weapons trained on each other. Leif's mind whiplashed. Shooting each other didn't fit the Neiothen MO. Something was off.

A weird taunting tapped Leif on the shoulder and told him to look back. He fought the urge, then finally surrendered to the lure. Visually

349

surfed the crowds. Saw uniforms. Suits. Gowns. VIPs. "Get back!" he shouted, wondering who the targets were. Warmth hit his gut. If Elvestad and Vega were here, why were they delaying with each other?

Unless they were each other's target.

No way. You didn't hardwire triggers in assets and activate them just to have them kill each other. Unless they'd already carried out their mission.

People started running, some clearing the area, others lingering in morbid fascination. A woman staggered. Her hip struck a wine fountain. She faltered—seized in rigidity—then collapsed amid the wine's crimson stream.

Leif's gut tightened. They'd missed it—poison. The missions were complete. The assets now liabilities, which was probably why they were killing each other.

How did they carry out their mission? Poison the guests? How many poisoned?

Leif thought back to the Book of the Wars. The way the Saudi king and crown prince were killed. The attack in China.

Chemicals. They were always using chemicals. His gaze hit the wine and champagne fountains. "Cut the fountains," he muttered into the comms, then more stridently, "Cut the fountains!"

Peyton joined him, nodding. "I think we all had a glass."

Her words forced him to wet his lips, thinking

of the sips Iskra had insisted he take. "They weren't after mass casualties," he said, trying to convince himself they weren't all about to bite it.

"What's going on here, Devine?" A star marched toward her.

Devine straightened. "Not sure, sir." She frowned. "Are you okay? You look a bit peaked."

The general's lips were discolored.

Leif started. "Sir." Surged forward, needing to know why he was targeted. "What is your job?"

The general gaped. "I beg your par—"

"Where do you serve in the Army?"

"I'm retired."

"He's the SECDEF," someone supplied.

Crap! "Samurai, I need you here. Now." Leif pointed to a chair. "General, sit down." He touched the older man's shoulder. "Command, we need medical services here."

"Excuse me?" The general still wasn't cooperating.

"I think you were—"

*Crack! Boom!*

Sensing the line of the bullet aimed at his back, Leif dove into the general, knowing he was too late. They landed in the sand, and he searched for piercing pain.

"Sniper!" Lawe shouted. "Down, down!"

Curses flew. Leif heard two thumps.

Once convinced he wasn't hit, Leif glanced toward the commotion.

Lawe raced to Elvestad. "Stay with me!" He grabbed fistfuls of sand and packed the wound. Another uniform knelt beside Vega. "Gone." Beneath Leif, the general was gurgling.

# CHAPTER 25

## THE HAGUE, THE NETHERLANDS

The unmistakable *crack*—albeit quieter than expected—robbed Mercy of any hope that this wouldn't happen. That she wouldn't witness a murder.

Maybe he didn't shoot a *person*. . . .

*You are not that dumb.*

She couldn't think. Refused to move. Realized that perched at the window was a monster. He swept away, packing equipment with experience and precision. Just as he had killed.

Surely authorities would be banging down doors soon. Once they figured out where the shot had come from. How long would that take? It required experts and measuring. In other words, time. Enough for him to get away.

Deflated, she slumped against the floor. This was entirely too familiar . . . memories lurked in the dark shroud of her childhood.

No. No, it wasn't the same.

She reached out and coiled her finger around the thin thread of faith to which Nonna Kat had encouraged her to cling. Closed her eyes and begged God to help her somehow make this right.

*How, Merc? You can't bring people back from the dead.*

The air shifted, and a crisp scent teased her nostrils. She looked—and flinched to find him squatting over her again.

"Hate to love you and leave you," he taunted, "but I have to bug out."

When he lifted a knife from a holster at his belt, she tensed. Searched his eyes for intent. Would he kill her now, too? Fear tremored through her muscles.

"Come now," he scolded. "You've chased me enough to know I'm not a cold-blooded killer."

*Um, beg to differ, Loki. You just sniped someone!* Her gaze bounced to the window.

He smirked. "Things are never what they seem. Neither are people." He rotated his stance and went to a knee. Raised the knife.

Mercy cringed.

He stabbed it past her shoulder. A resounding *thunk* made her yelp.

"You're a smart girl. Find a way to get it and cut yourself free." He pushed to his feet.

Mercy glanced over her shoulder and found the dagger embedded in the leg of the lampstand. When she looked back at him, she caught only the last glimpse as he exited the room and closed the door.

· · ·

"Medic!" Leif called. The threat of the sniper very real, he dragged the general to the side and upended a table for cover.

Saito dropped to a knee, accessing the general's swollen air passage. With no doctor on-site and the general dying, he ran an IV, then did an emergency tracheotomy to open his airway.

In minutes they were hurrying the general toward the street where an ambulance met them. Moving on the blacktop was easier than the sand, making their task faster. The EMT vehicle swung to a stop, and the rear door opened. They loaded the general in, his face splotchy. Saito relayed the one-star's medical condition, vitals, and what had been done.

When Leif turned back, he spotted a group of local uniforms coming toward him and stiffened, feeling oddly responsible for what had happened. That was how it might look to the locals, since Reaper was here without authorization. Explaining they had foreknowledge of the attack but were not behind it would be, at best, difficult.

"Easy," Leif said to the guys, hands still bloody from helping save the general.

"Are you Admiral Braun's people?" the local policeman asked.

He eyed their combat gear and the tac vests they carried. Warily, he said, "We are."

The officer handed over the gear. "Some

protection until we get this locked down. Two targets are dead."

Vega and Elvestad.

"Nothing like putting on a vest *after* a shooting to make you feel safe," Saito muttered.

Unsure if the officer knew who those targets were, Leif kept his thoughts to himself. "Both expired?"

"Yes, which means we can't get anything out of them." The officer didn't look especially frustrated. "At least they won't be hurting anyone else."

Lawe shifted forward, frowning. "The guy I worked on, you sure? I—"

"EMTs verified," the officer said. "They removed the victims to avoid having bodies laid out with this many spectators."

"You moved bodies out of a crime scene," Leif repeated, disbelieving this level of stupidity. But when the officer squared his shoulders, Leif shifted tactics. "Who is the woman who fell in the wine fountain?"

"Amalia Willems," the officer stated. "She was the NATO Secretary General."

Leif mentally backtracked, rifling through the files he'd read on The Hague and NATO. Something like oil simmering in a pan filled his gut as he retraced her file. Willems had been the chair of the North Atlantic Council, the main political decision-making body within NATO.

Which meant she'd overseen the political and military processes relating to security issues affecting the whole Alliance.

And someone apparently didn't like the job she was doing. Or Veratti simply wanted her replaced.

"Who is the deputy secretary?" he asked.

The officer smiled. "Italy's Matteo Trevisan."

Italy. Why did his suspicions always have to be correct?

Leif inclined his head. "Thank you—for the gear and the intel." He thumped Lawe's gut. "Let's head inside and clean up."

"Clean up?" Lawe complained. "Have you—"

"Seen my hands?" Leif held them up. "I have." He glowered, raising his eyebrows in meaning, hoping the big lug would get the point. They were well across the beach when he shook his head.

"What was that about?" Lawe asked, keeping pace as they reached the hotel.

"Willems is dead, so the deputy secretary takes over—that's Trevisan. Who's Italian." Leif balled his fists. "And who's prime minister of Italy?"

Lawe growled. "Ciro Freakin' Veratti. So all this—you think it's connected, that Trevisan is a puppet. This attack is ArC."

"Of course it's ArC." Leif gave a cockeyed nod. "It'd be a colossal coincidence otherwise. Think about it—Trevisan is now NATO's key player, putting all that power in Veratti's hands."

Leif stalked to the back of the hotel, his mind

rattled. Why had Gilliam come here? Only two initiation codes went live. And Carsen seemed to know what was going on instead of being brainwashed like the rest. How? Did he have a target here? Had that person survived?

"Here," Culver said, stuffing sanitizing cloths into Leif's hand.

Leif made quick work of cleaning up, but his mind wasn't doing so well with the intel or the nagging that said something was off. How on earth could they know if Gilliam had been here for a target?

"You got that same buggy feeling I do?" Lawe asked as they entered a side entrance of the hotel.

"Yeah." Leif deposited the cloths in a bin, deciding that would have to be good enough for now. Where was his team?

The noise of a vibrating phone made him glance at Devine, who'd fallen in with them. She lifted it from her small purse and eyed the screen. Sucked in a breath.

"What?" Lawe asked, every protective urge no doubt rising up.

"We must be getting close," she murmured, her face white.

"Why?"

She showed them the screen.

Stop interfering or you'll be next.

Ticked, Leif keyed his comms and motioned them into the hotel. "Cell, can you track the message that just hit Coriolis's phone?"

"Uh, on it."

He spotted Iskra walking toward them, blinking rapidly. She hesitated. Frowned and looked back in the direction from which she'd come—a long hall with flowery wallpaper.

"Iskra?"

She met his gaze.

"You okay?"

She lifted her jaw. "Are any of us?"

Something in her gaze was off, too. There was a lot of that going on around here. "You sure?"

She sighed. "No. I thought . . ."

"Runt! Runt!"

The shout drew him around.

Face flushed, Mercy flung herself across the south entrance lobby, wild and frenetic. In the two seconds before she reached him, he saw the bruise on her cheek and wrists. A trail of blood.

Rage rose up inside him. "What happened?"

"Andrew," she heaved. "Andrew was here. When I chased him, he drugged me. He tied me up and held me hostage in the window." She screwed up her face and shook her head. "No, he didn't hold me in the window, *he* was in the window, watching. But he tied me to a column and duct-taped my mouth. I couldn't do anything. Couldn't stop him." Eyes glossy, she gulped air, her face flushed—wait. She'd said duct tape. What he thought was a flush could be tape burn.

"Slow down, Mercy. What—"

"Andrew shot them!" she shriek-growled. "Right there. Right there in front of me. One second he was watching, and the next he was pulling the trigger and and and"—she waved her hands, brows tangled in despair—"he shot them!" She flung her hand toward the door, tears sliding free. "The two men on the beach."

"Mercy, they weren't shot by a sniper. They shot each other."

She blinked. Jerked straight and scowled. "No . . ." She drew out the word. "I was there. He fired a shot. Then he left me—well, he left me with a knife, then fled."

"A knife?"

She held up her hands. "To cut my bonds."

"So he didn't hurt you?" Leif eyed her cheek.

"Yes, he hurt me!" she nearly screamed, then sagged. "But not really. He just"—she squeezed her shoulders and shuddered—"held me there while he did the deed. He said I was getting in his way."

Leif had no idea what to do with this information, though his gaze probed the surrounding darkness, the elevated angles. Andrew wouldn't be up there still. "Where was his nest?"

She pointed across the beach. "Third floor."

"Why didn't he shoot her, if he was willing to snipe someone?" Lawe asked.

Baddar came in through the door, and when his gaze fell on Mercy, the knots and tension in his expression vanished. "Praise God," he exclaimed as he went to her. "Are you okay?" He cupped her face. Stepped back to visually inspect her. "What happened?"

"I'm okay," she said, apparently embarrassed by the attention. But her mojo returned. "He's here, Leif. He's here, and we have to find him. He can't get away with killing those men."

Frustration tightened his muscles. Mercy claimed Andrew was responsible, but Leif's instinct said he wasn't. "He didn't kill them."

Too many things to process. Too many things that didn't make sense. Too many people dead. Too many losses. He balled his fists, feeling this thing sliding completely out of his control.

"How do you know? Were you there?" Mercy demanded.

"Yes!" he barked.

She flinched. "You were?"

"You said Andrew fired 'a shot.' One." He narrowed his eyes. "Just one?"

She hesitated, wondering at the question. "Yes."

"*Two* men went down. You're sure Andrew only shot once?"

"I . . . yes." She glanced at the others, confused.

"I don't understand. If not them, then who'd he shoot?"

"That's what I want to know," Leif huffed.

"Mercy." Iskra's voice was soft, strained. "What does Andrew look like?"

Mercy shoved her hair back. "Are you kidding me? I've told you a dozen times."

"Specific, please," Iskra insisted, peering down that hall again.

"What?" Leif asked, pouncing on her tension and the direction of her gaze. "You see something?"

She stared back at Mercy. "Eye color, nose, jawline, anything."

Hands in a wild dance, Mercy tried to explain. "Strong, square-but-not-quite jaw. A slight rise in his nose." She considered Leif. "Sort of like yours, but not as much."

"Eyes?" Iskra pressed. "Were they light green, maybe go—"

"Golden." Mercy drew back when they both spoke the same word. "He had a beard. Could be Clint Eastwood's son."

Iskra's chin lifted.

"What's going on, Iskra?" he asked.

"Here," Lawe said, angling in with his phone, on which he'd pulled up a picture of the actor. "That's Eastwood."

Iskra sucked in a breath and turned away.

Leif stepped in front of her, surprised when she

362

lowered her forehead to his shoulder. "Talk to me."

When she straightened, tears spilled down her cheeks. She looked around as if she couldn't find a safe haven. Red rimmed her eyes. "I think . . ." Her gaze collided with his and revealed a twisting agony there. "It could be my brother. Andrew could be Mitre." She whimpered. "I chased him—twice. He fought me. Hit me." She shuddered. "I did the same to him."

"Your brother is Mitre," he countered, knowing a name had little meaning in the covert world. "Why now? What makes you think this now when we've been chasing him for months?"

She bunched her shoulders. "I do not know. Something just triggered—then Adam showed me that picture. I saw Mitre in that face, too." She choked back a sob and covered her mouth with the back of her hand. "Vasily told me the book would lead me to Mitre. He knew." She muttered something in Russian. "Vasily knew Mitre was a Neiothen, not just part of some big army."

"And a sniper, apparently." Leif tucked his chin, thinking. Recalling. He started for the side door, his thoughts roiling and champing for confirmation.

"What is it, Chief?" Lawe asked, trailing him.

Leif trudged across the sand to where the forensic team was still processing the scene. He approached the officer who'd provided the tac vests. "Hey. Got a minute?"

The policeman stood. "Yes?"

"The weapons from the victims," Leif said, "are they bagged yet?"

"Let me check." The officer trudged over to where others were collecting evidence and taking pictures.

"What're you thinking?" Lawe asked quietly as Culver joined them. "I mean—we were right there. We saw them both get shot."

"Yes," Leif said. "They were both shot."

Lawe looked at him as if he'd lost his mind.

"Hang on." Moving to a photographer, Leif pointed to the painted outline where Vega had fallen. "That victim. Do you have photos of his body?"

The photographer pulled them up.

Lawe scowled. "What's this? I was there—"

"You were with Elvestad," Leif said as they studied the images.

"Well, butter my butt and call me a biscuit," Culver muttered. "Mirrored."

Leif nodded as the officer returned with another policeman—apparently the one responsible for the weapons being properly secured—and two bags.

"Please do not touch the weapons themselves," the second officer said.

Nodding, Leif opened the bag, lifted it to his

nose, and sniffed. Just gun oil. He handed it back, then did the same to the other, marked as the gun from Victim 2. He sniffed and caught a strong chemical odor. This gun had been fired. "Whose was this?" He handed it back.

"Second victim. ID'd as Harald Elvestad," the tech said, pointing to the farther position.

"Thanks." Leif headed back toward the hotel.

"What did you figure out?" came Cell's voice in his comms.

"Vega never fired."

"Come again?" Lawe said. "I still have Elvestad's blood under my fingernails. It's obvious—Vega shot Elvestad, who was shot by Mercy's sniper."

"Do not call him *my* sniper," Mercy snapped.

"That's not what happened," Leif said. "Angles and wound damage are wrong." He kept moving, as if it would help him solve this. "I think there was a second sniper."

# CHAPTER 26

## THE HAGUE, THE NETHERLANDS

"I think we need to back that villain up." Cell linked to the satellite in the suite later that night. "First—what you all just went through? That would be why I'm on the safe side of the combat theater nowadays."

"You mean the cowardly side?" Culver taunted.

"There is *nothing* cowardly about protecting my assets and keeping them attached," Cell countered. "Besides, I like being your superior."

"Superior pain in—"

"Easy," Leif warned from the couch. He propped his head back and closed his eyes, still thinking. Processing.

"But suggesting there's two snipers? That's a stretch. And you figure that on guesswork?"

Leif didn't take the bait. He knew what he'd seen. And the distance and trajectory math didn't work.

The din of Reaper's banter was replaced by a strange, mechanized voice in his head—the initiation voice. He sat forward and roughed a hand over his face, then went to the mini fridge.

He tugged out an OJ, uncapped the bottle, and leaned against the counter, guzzling.

Cell powered up the system. "Incoming call from Command." The screen came to life with the images of Braun and Iliescu.

"How're you holding up, Reaper?" Iliescu asked as someone out of view handed him a folder.

"Alive," Leif said, not willing to consider more than that.

"That's what counts," Dru said. "Let's review a few things about today's events. From what we could discern from surveillance images, Gilliam *was* shot when he was with Leif on the beach but died in the lobby. Leif, we considered your concerns about the shooters and number of shots. Analysts agree that Vega didn't shoot anyone."

No surprise. He'd felt the passing of the bullet that hit Gilliam. Mentally walked it back, tracking himself on the beach. The trail of heat near his face. High. The shooter had been high. Mercy's sniper. No . . . Mercy had left her post only minutes before. "There was a second sniper," he said. It would confirm his suspicions about how Elvestad died.

Wary eyes held his before Dru said, "What's your reasoning on that?"

"Mercy went MIA before Carsen rammed into me, then ran off. Andrew wouldn't have had time to haul her to his nest and line up the shot that hit Gilliam. Means there was a second sniper."

Dru nodded. "That's what our analysts are saying, too."

"Autopsies should prove it," Saito said.

"We've yet to get access to the bodies, but once we do, we'll hopefully have more definitive answers."

"Moving on," Braun said, peeking over her reading glasses at the notes she held. "Okay, again, reminding you that our intel is based solely off videos and images captured, since we cannot examine the bodies, which I've filed a grievance over. After the initiation announcement, it appears Turi Vega was shot through the back. Bullet exited the chest wall. Analysts guess the bullet either ricocheted internally, causing massive internal hemorrhaging, or it nicked an artery for him to die so fast. He was also shot through the neck." That fatal moment appeared on the screen, showing the blood spray from two wounds. "Second bullet was from Elvestad's weapon, straight on."

"So, shot twice," Leif expounded.

Braun's head bobbed, but she didn't divert from her notes. "Elvestad was struck through the chest as well."

"So Runt is right," Lawe said, his arm hooked around Peyton where they sat on a loveseat. "Vega didn't get a chance to fire, so there must've been a second sniper."

"Ballistics confirm Turi Vega did not fire his

weapon," Braun reaffirmed. "Plausible explanation is that one sniper bullet hit them both."

"So why were the Neiothen targeted?" Culver asked.

"Didn't want them talking," Lawe offered. "They did their job taking out the two targets, and ArC didn't want witnesses."

"Veratti was pretty calm through it all," Leif noted. "He knew what was coming." But what if . . . "Another possibility: someone thought they could get ahead of Carsen, Vega, and Elvestad to stop them." But who? Andrew? Was he there to prevent the killings? Why?

"True," Saito agreed. "It wasn't until after they targeted each other that Willems and Elbert showed symptoms."

"You seriously think someone tried to stop them?" Culver's brow furrowed in thought. "Like we were doing?"

"Yes, just like us," Leif grunted as he leaned forward. "We all failed. He just did it more violently." And one step ahead. Reaper had come here on Gilliam's tip but unsure of what they would face. Andrew was there with full knowledge, as evidenced by the setup in his nest.

*"He?"* Braun repeated. "Do you have someone in mind, Mr. Metcalfe?"

Leif glanced at Mercy, then slowly shifted his attention to Iskra at his side. It was her story to tell.

"I believe so," Iskra said, adjusting on the sofa. "I am not certain because I have not seen his face up close, but I have reason to believe the sniper may have been my brother, Mitre."

"Except he said his name was Andrew," Mercy said, offering a thin thread of hope that this wasn't what Iskra projected.

"Director," Iskra said, "I would talk with you privately—"

"No, hold up," Culver said. "We keep this on the table. All of this. We have lost in some heinous ways. No more flippin' secrets and running off on private missions."

Startled at the acerbic tone coming from the laid-back cowboy, Leif considered the others. Did they feel the same way?

"My brother . . ." Iskra drew in a slow breath and let it out. "Since I have not seen Andrew's face, I have no proof that he is Mitre, but their descriptions are eerily similar. Also, I know my brother was involved in something very dangerous. Vasily told me Mitre was part of a super-army, that I had to find it to find him."

"Super-army," Saito repeated. "That's the Neiothen, right?" He narrowed his eyes. "We're down, what—four? So six are left? Eight?"

"Six down," Leif corrected. "The book had nine lines, so three remaining, if nine is the entire complement. We haven't been able to confirm that a hundred percent." He focused on Iskra. "If

Andrew is Mitre, then—according to your own account—he's working for Rutger Hermanns."

She paled. "I hadn't thought it through that far yet." She swallowed. "But yes. If true, then . . ." Hesitation tugged on her features. "Yes, he's under Rutger's thumb." She lifted her head. "Each guardian's mission represents a radical shift in policy or politics and means Ciro Veratti has more power. Veratti controls Trevisan, who—with the death of Amalia Willems—now occupies one of the most pivotal roles in the world: secretary general of NATO."

"All right," Culver said, jerking forward, elbows on his knees, fingertips pressed together. "Let's say all these Neiothen pull off their assignments. I mean, it's possible—we can't seem to get a leg up on these super soldiers. If they succeed . . . what does that mean?"

"But Gilliam—we have no idea what his mission was. He died"—Leif shrugged—"for what?"

"What do you mean?" Culver growled. "He was going to kill someone."

"Their success means the end of the free world," Iskra said, glancing at Leif, her brow diving toward her pert nose. "Bible prophecy about the end times mentions the inability to purchase food without a mark—"

"Heck no!" Culver balked. "Ain't nobody giving me the mark of Satan."

"He's trying to beat it, not implement it," Leif said. "But with his actions, it's starting to look like he's determined to revolutionize commerce. That would mean there'll be a unified community that forces countries together for global trade and economy." He met their gazes evenly. "It has been suggested before that the UN and NATO would be part of that."

"And now that Willems is dead and Trevisan in power," Iskra said, "Veratti sits atop that tower."

"So maybe it's time for all of us to go after that book again," Lawe muttered.

"How can we do that when we can't even get ahead on the names?" Saito asked. "Gilliam gave you those names, right?"

"I found them," Mercy asserted. "In the Frankfurt & Stuttgart servers."

"Gilliam tipped us to The Hague," Leif said, still withholding the names Akin and Bushi.

*You must remember!*

"So we haven't really gotten anywhere, except more dead Neiothen," Saito pointed out. "How'd Gilliam know who else was a Neiothen?"

"We should check into that," Lawe said. "We're the only ones chasing this information."

"Already looked into the connections—same results. Nothing new," Cell said. "But now that we're back to ground zero, I'll go through it again. Another option we haven't considered is Iskra's friend."

"Her brother?" Adam asked.

"No, the guy with the yacht."

"Vasily," Iskra supplied.

Cell nodded. "What if he gave a USB to someone else, too? What if somehow that got to Gilliam?"

"No," Iskra said, too strongly. "Vasily would not betray me like that."

"Would he betray you," Leif asked quietly, "if he thought, in the long run, he was *protecting* you?" His phone vibrated, and he glanced at it, seeing a new message notification.

Her wide eyes held his, and he could see in them that she didn't want to answer. She sagged. "He might."

"Then we have to consider it," Leif said and stood. "I'll be back." He went into the bathroom, locked the door, and opened the waiting video from someone who was supposed to be dead.

Iskra was losing this battle. And they were right—she had no proof Vasily had not given someone else that information. She sat in the bedroom, deliberating. There *was* someone who might have convinced Vasily to share the information. But Iskra was not sure she wanted to open the portal to that woman any more than absolutely necessary.

Which was foolish. Bogdashka had been a lifeline in dark times. And yet there was something about her that always unsettled Iskra, something she couldn't pinpoint.

Was it worth it? What good could come out of asking if Vasily gave her scans of the book? Bogdashka was known across the Eastern world for her passion in sheltering young girls. And Bogdashka would never admit she had that information. She was a veritable vault. If she had the scans, it was for her use to protect the girls under her care.

*And I am no longer under her care.*

So Bogdashka would not help.

But did Iskra need to try?

Unsettled by the video from Carsen, Leif shut himself in one of the bedrooms to think. On the edge of the bed, he ran his hands over his face and head. Aches wound through his shoulders and neck, squeezing and compressing nerves, throwing throbs up into his temples.

*Two. One. Six. Initiate rise. Rise. Rise.*

They were numbers. That was all. Just simple numerals.

Dru. Iskra. They'd conspired to keep this from him. He'd tried to let go of that, of being cut out of the chase to find the book, but Carsen's video changed that decision and unleashed the dregs of nightmares. Made him recall a conversation that now seemed to be an entire fabrication.

*"This book," Iliescu said after a lengthy pause,*

*"has information. I don't know much more than that."*

*"But you do know more."*

Conflict teased the edges of the director's mouth. *"I do,"* he admitted.

*"And you're not going to tell me."*

*"I can't. Not yet."*

*"Just like the things in the shadows."*

He recalled Dru's words as if they were being spoken to him right now. The inflection. The intonation.

*"This book has information. . . ."*

Thinking, Leif pulled himself off the mattress and wandered to the window. Heavy realization thudded against his irritation. Dru *knew* this book talked about the super-army. That was why he hadn't told Leif.

That was why . . .

It wasn't just the Neiothen. It wasn't just the super-army. It wasn't just ArC's pursuit to control the global economy and form a one-world system.

*It's about me.*

No. No, no. That couldn't—

*From the depths I will rise.*

*I will rise.*

*I will rise.*

Breath trapped in his lungs, Leif tried to reach for the hazy threads of the past and grab hold. Those six months. Wreathed in black, they

375

echoed down the long dark halls of his mind. Tossing himself back over the queen-sized bed, he held an arm over his face and eyes. Tried to shut out the events, the betrayal. Especially the voice echoing those words over and over.

*Two. One. Six. Initiate rise. Rise. Rise.*

It was similar to the chant he heard in his dreams, his own voice and that of many more echoing into infinity: *I will rise. I will rise. From the depths I will rise.*

Haunted, hating the phrase that would not vacate his thoughts, he yanked himself off the mattress and pushed to his feet. He moved to the window again and folded his arms.

Why had he called Vega "Harcos"?

*"Do you remember?"* Carsen had demanded, voice like tumbling rocks and panic. *"You* must *remember!"*

Leif heard the subtle click of the door. Someone stepping into the room. Another click—the door shutting.

"You okay?" Iskra asked quietly.

He felt her presence but didn't know what to do with it or with her. She was an enigma. He'd helped free her from Hristoff, and she'd had ample opportunity since to cut tail and run. But she hadn't. In fact, she'd even come clean about her activities with Dru. Shared openly.

Why? What was her endgame?

His thoughts took a dark turn. Maybe Dru

wanted her keeping tabs on him, monitoring him. Dru and Canyon had always been afraid he'd snap again. Come unglued. That was why Dru had gotten Canyon involved, to keep him under watch. Out here in the field someone had to look after the problem child.

The thoughts lit his anger. After four years of being sober, of getting his stuff together, they still expected him to crack.

Leif stared through the sheer curtain to the churning ocean beyond. Coming in, receding. Coming back in. Receding. Like the missing six months of his life, taunting him with closure, then rushing away with maniacal laughter.

Iskra slid around in front of him. Her hair was down—a deliberate act. She'd had it tied back earlier. But he liked it down, and she knew that. He returned his attention to the windows.

"I've been on the receiving end of your anger before," she said, "and it scared me. Once I experienced it, saw that look in your eyes, I knew I never wanted to see it again. Not aimed at me."

That twisted up his thoughts. "You don't have to be afraid of me," he said, touching her upper arm.

She stepped closer, sliding her hand around his waist. He held her but could not look at her. There was a reason Iskra Todorova was known as Viorica, the Wild Rose, a fierce assassin and operative: she knew how to work every angle and every weakness a person had. And she was his weakness.

"I think we should go to Germany," she said.

Leif gritted his teeth. Was this a plan she'd concocted with Dru? *Why are you so freakin' paranoid?* "You've been gone for a week this time. I thought you'd want to get back to Taissia."

"More than anything," Iskra said, resting her cheek against his shoulder, "but what good is it to go back with so much still hanging over our heads?"

*Our heads.*

"Why Germany?"

Iskra shifted and leaned against the glass. "That's where Rutger Hermanns lives, and he seems irrevocably tied not only to Mitre, but also to the book, which I believe he has."

Leif scowled. "Hermanns."

"He has been my nemesis for as long as I can remember, so it does not thrill me either." She shook her head and stepped away. Why was she putting distance between them? Was it a psychological thing?

"But he was here tonight," Leif said. "Why go to Germany when we could probably track him down here?"

"He would not have the book here. Which means it is likely hidden somewhere in his estate. I . . . my brother . . ." Her words trickled off her lips as her expression hollowed. Tears glossed her eyes.

"What?" Instinct moved him toward her.

She touched a hand to her throat. Swallowed. "I've been hunting *my brother*. He is Rutger's operative who has repeatedly beaten me to targets and artifacts. He got the Cellini. He took the book." Her cheeks flushed. "*My brother* stole the book! The brother I've tried to save, the one I've tried so hard to pull out before it was too late. *He* is the killer. He's working against you, against me."

"Wait." He touched her arm again, something strange rattling through him at the change in her attitude about her brother. "Hold up. Remember, Mercy said he *didn't* get the book. They ran the feeds at the facility. He wasn't the one who got away with it."

"But he had it in Paris . . . I think. And he has been one step ahead. At the gala—he was ahead of us. And Mercy said he fired his rifle."

Leif didn't want to talk about this. Irritation clogged his brain.

She drew in a sharp breath. "Why would he send Mercy those texts and save her in China if he's working for Rutger? Why?" Again her eyes widened. "To lure us into a trap? How did my brother become this? He was a good person."

"He's ArC!" Leif barked. "He's never been good." For some reason, he needed to believe that. Because if her brother had been good, then turned . . .

She stiffened, then sagged. "Mitre and I have been separated for more years than we were together." Grief scratched at her features. "Maybe I never knew him. I mean, I knew his skills, encountered them regularly working for Hristoff. I just never knew . . ."

"You *think* you know his skills. There were two shooters tonight."

"Right," she scoffed, "which still means he killed someone."

He held up his hands, conceding, seizing another thin thread of hope. "You went rogue on Hristoff, turned against him, and made something bad good." He studied her, searching for some hope. "Maybe your brother is doing the same."

She drew back, mouth open as if to argue, but said nothing.

"What? It's okay for you to turn good, but not him?"

Scowling, she glowered. "I never said that. You just don't know—"

"That's right," he shouted. *"I don't know!"* The roaring in his head was as loud as his voice, and he had no idea why. "I don't know because you keep holding things back. You act like I'm not grown up enough to handle things. As if you need to *handle* me."

Iskra eased back, gaping. "When have I *ever* treated you like that?"

Guilt pushed his head down. He spun back to

the window. Flung aside the curtain and placed his palms on the ledge. Stared down at the sandy stretch of that taunting shoreline. But for every positive thought, two negatives invaded. "I overlooked you using me once, but I can't overlook your continued defiance of any trust I've tried to build with you."

"Defiance!" Iskra stomped forward. "Do you remember that night I slept in your arms after your nightmare? Can you possibly imagine what that was like for me after what I went through with Hristoff? But I trusted you—wanted to be there for you. How about the fact that my daughter is with *your* brother because I *trust* you. I trusted when you said it would be good for her. Do you know how hard it was for me to do that? To leave her and come out on this mission with you?"

"*With* me?" He whipped around, the world bleeding red. "You didn't come out here *with me,* remember? You diverted from some other mission. So don't act like you're making big sacrifices for me. Keep your freakin' secrets if you want."

She huffed and rubbed the spot between her eyes.

Her pain and frustration smacked him. What was wrong with him? Why was he so amped? He rubbed the back of his neck. Wished he could just jump into the ocean and never return. But if she could so easily turn against her own brother, after believing for her entire life that he was good, how much more quickly would she turn against him? Or maybe she already had.

No. He had no grounds to think that. Yet his thoughts were thick and aggressive.

"Mitre is six years older than me," Iskra said in a soft, shaky voice. "Already he had escaped our father by the time I was sold to Hristoff, but Mitre did not find freedom. He found something far worse—an addiction to danger and violence. The last time I located him, it was to beg him to go back to Bulgaria, to our mother's family. But even then he was not the same brother I had known, and I was not the little sister he knew."

Leif really didn't care about family squabbles. Rage vibrated through his blood, begging to be unleashed. He felt a dark desire to feed on weakness and more anger. He planted his feet, wishing they could dig roots into the marble floor, and closed his eyes.

"Next thing I heard, my mother's brothers and sisters in Bulgaria were slaughtered." She shuddered through a breath. "On my father's encouragement, Mitre made a last visit to our mother's family . . . to silence them forever so they could never again try to influence him. I tried to save my brother and killed my family instead." Her touch was firm but soft along Leif's spine. In the glass, her reflection seemed so perfect next to his. "I was already too late to save him. Yet I will not give up on him. I cannot not try."

His heart thundered, banging in the dark recesses of his conscience, searching for that elusive hope. What if she found out the truth about *him?* Would she do the same and not give up on him?

Iskra wedged in between him and the glass, forcing him back. Words that sought release perched on her lips. She searched his gaze, as if looking for permission. Or maybe reassurance.

He couldn't give it. Didn't care. He should. The man he was *should* care. The soldier he was should care. But Leif Metcalfe didn't. Not anymore.

"I think," she said softly, "the answers you are looking for may be with Mitre and Rutger."

# CHAPTER 27

## THE HAGUE, THE NETHERLANDS

The hotel suite was wickedly quiet. Cell sat at the dining table, glad the team was grabbing rack time in the three bedrooms while they waited for direction from Iliescu or Braun.

Until he got that order, Cell would sit with his back to the wall and his eyes open. He might be crazy, but he wasn't stupid. He could read. He could interpret data. And videos. With headphones on, he didn't need to worry about anyone overhearing.

Except him. He had no business in this file or the others he'd accessed over the last several hours, but he was a veritable pit bull when he got a hunch. Granted, his hunches were notorious for being wild and out there, but they were—more often than not—accurate.

And holy traitors, he did not want to be right.

*What if you are?*

Then . . . then he'd need a plan. A really good one. Another reason he couldn't front his theories, because using a separate system and different server, among other things, to hide his trail, he'd be strung up if the director found out he was still digging.

It was a risk. One massive step backward for Cell-kind. Like, right into a federal pen. His curser hovered over the play icon on the video. *Please please please be wrong.* He liked the guy. A lot. Most of the time. He considered him a friend, so that chucked the bad in with the good. But being a traitor . . . being a danger . . .

*Stop guessing and get answers.*

He clicked it. The first few seconds passed in relative silence, and the angle on it was bad, but that happened with piecemealed feeds. On the screen, Leif was hoofing it from the dance floor set up on the beach. He'd broken through the lattice to catch up with Vega. And the speed of these two—on sand!—was crazy. Leif dove into his back. Took him to the ground. Rolled. Straddled him and lifted a fist to coldcock Vega.

Only he didn't.

Leif froze. Vega pummeled him, then spirited away, only to have another guy jump into the mix—Gilliam. Again, no confrontation. Leif released the guy's shirt. Slapped at him. No, not slapped. It was one of those guy-pats. Like, *I didn't realize it was you.* What . . . ? Wind garbled their words, but they were definitely talking. Cell backed up the video. Enhanced the audio, weeded out background noise—the ocean, the music, the shouts, screams—until he could make out some of the conversation.

*"Carsen."* That was all Leif said when he saw the other man's face.

Then Gilliam had the upper hand. Grabbed Leif. *"Do you remember? . . . You must remember!"*

Cell flinched, aware that was the moment Gilliam had been shot. But what did Gilliam want Leif to remember? Clearly he hadn't been referring to his name, since Leif had spoken it. So, what? And why was he so adamant that Leif remember whatever it was?

Okay. No answers to that. Not yet. But he'd find them. For now, he'd save this puppy on a separate drive. Trolling through various emails and videos, he saw a new one populate the server. Strange. Where had that . . .

Oh snap. It was from one of the team's phones. He checked the address. Leif. He moved his cursor away—but must've had too much pressure on the trackpad because the video opened. Played.

*"I don't know why you haven't figured it out yet, but you're the one who can stop this. You're probably thinking I'm one of the Neiothen. I'm not."*

Cell's heart thudded—that was Carsen Gilliam speaking. Why was he sending Leif messages?

*"Well, I was. I went through the training. But I failed, started cracking. So they tried to wipe my memories, tried to make me forget. That didn't work either, though I let them think it had. They dumped me—"*

The file blacked out. His screen blipped, and the video closed.

Cell backtracked to reopen the file, but it wasn't there. Where had it gone? He searched the recent downloads. Not there. He frowned. Where—

Movement swept in front of him.

Cell strangled a cry, and his blood fled to his toes. Leif stood over him. *Where had he come from?* He could feel the color draining from his face. "Hey," he managed shakily. "Scared me."

Leif rapped on the table. "Know how you said once that you could find"—he motioned to the system—"anyone?"

"Well, n-not *anyone*-anyone." Why in blazes did the question make him so nervous? *Maybe because you were spying on his phone?* Not on purpose, but still. "I mean, there are limitations to what even I can do." A nervous laugh skittered through his teeth, and he wanted to punch himself. "Why? Who'd you have in mind?"

Distance grew in Leif's gaze as he stared at Cell's laptop. Had he seen Cell watching that video?

"Chief?"

Leif pursed his lips. "Never mind." He walked the five paces to the kitchen, pulled a bottle of OJ from the fridge, and started for the bedrooms.

"Runt," Cell called, feeling bad for spying and acting so stupid. And insanely curious who Leif wanted to track down. "Try me."

Again Leif hesitated, glancing down the hall. Finally he closed the gap. "I only have a last name—Gilliam said it when I confronted him."

Gilliam had said a name? Had Cell missed it in the feed?

"Harcos." Leif took a swig of juice. "Think he might be one of . . . them."

"You mean a Neiothen?" Cell wrote down the name.

"Kind of hard to know, since we don't have the book, but he said the name, said I had to remember."

"Huh." Cell hadn't heard Gilliam say anything like that. Maybe he hadn't cleaned it up enough. "So, someone named Harcos."

"Yeah." The haze in Runt's eyes was telling. And creepy. "Military. The name might be Hungarian."

And he knew this all because Gilliam had said to remember? Maybe that made sense—how else would Leif know a possible Neiothen named Harcos if not through the military?

Cell made more notes—anything to avoid looking at Runt's jacked expression. "I'll check on it." He tossed down the pen. "Let you know what I find."

Leif nodded. Took a step, then leaned closer. "Keep this between us."

Great way to amp the strain. "Sure." Shrugging felt like dead-lifting three hundred pounds. "I mean, as much as I can without the agency knowing, since this is their system and they

388

see everything." He laughed, but Leif didn't. "I mean—"

"Ya know what? Forget it."

"No, it's okay—"

"No." His gaze sharpened. "I'm good."

Concern carved a hard line through Cell's betraying self. "What? You don't trust me now?"

"I never trusted you." There was no smile or mirth in Leif's expression. Just a dark shadow. "You're just good at what you do, and we need that."

"Wow. Don't spare my feelings or anything."

"If you're worried about feelings, you're in the wrong gig." Leif stalked down the hall.

Cell swallowed. Glanced at the notepad. Then his laptop. The video. Verifying Leif was really, truly gone and not lurking in the shadows, he checked again for the Carsen Gilliam video to no avail. Had Leif deleted it? But there should be something left on the server. Nothing deleted from email was truly deleted.

Which meant . . . He swallowed. There was no way Iliescu and his minions knew what he had on this laptop. He'd protected it.

Trying to shake the feeling of being watched, Cell replayed the feed video from the beach. Over and over and over. Trying to make out the full conversation. As far as he could tell, Gilliam had not mentioned a name.

Could it have somehow gotten caught on the

389

comms chatter? The video was scratchy in a couple of places.

And there it was—Harcos. But not spoken by Gilliam.

Veratti: *"I'm holding you to our agreement. Find the book. I told you what you needed to know."*

Leif: *"Harcos."*

Iskra: *"Who?"*

Silence. Leif: *"Vega. I have eyes on Vega."*

*Leif* had said the name. So why had he lied about where the name came from? They were a team, right? What in the name of all the motherboards was going on?

"Thanks for enduring an early wake-up."

"This isn't early, Dru," Mercy grumbled, fingering the tangles from her hair as she plopped onto a chair at the table. "This is downright indecent."

"We need to talk about your statement."

Mercy paused and frowned. "My statement? I assume we're not talking about my fashion statement." She glanced at Cell, who looked like he hadn't slept. Had he been up all night?

"What's goin' on?" Lawe slurred from the couch, where he was laid out.

"Maddox," Iliescu said, "confirm for us that you heard Andrew fire a shot."

"I did. I'll never forget that moment and how

powerless I felt." She'd told them that before, along with the hefty dose of nausea that swept through her at the memory. And they were questioning her about it? "You don't believe me?"

"On the contrary," Iliescu said. "We're just trying to be as precise as possible with this puzzle."

"What puzzle?" Lawe asked. "I thought the whole situation was pretty straightforward." He pulled himself off the couch and hovered behind Mercy. His deep, obtrusive voice drew Baddar and Culver from the bedrooms.

"I'm not sure I'd go that far, Mr. Lawe," Iliescu said with a sigh. "This entire mission from day one has been one-upping us, and Andrew is no different."

"Come again?" Culver asked, scratching his red beard.

Braun huffed, looking as haggard as they felt. "The trajectory is wrong," she said. "Marking the room Ms. Maddox referenced, our analysts ran the scenario, and every time, the trajectory is off. Not just by inches, but *feet*."

"But—" Mercy stuffed her hair behind her ear. "But I was there. Andrew fired the shot. The curtains even rippled with the tiny explosion from the barrel."

"Perhaps," Braun said with a nod, "but it wasn't his shot that killed the Neiothen. And it couldn't have been the one that killed Gilliam, because there was no clear line of sight."

"Then . . ." Holding her forehead, Mercy was sure her brain would fall out if she moved or leaned forward. "Then he *missed?*" That seemed unfathomable.

"Negative," Braun said. "We had a team at the hotel using metal detectors to look for casings, and they turned up absolutely nothing other than a wedding ring, bottle caps, and an earring. Nothing matching the caliber of a rifle round."

"I'm with Mercy," Cell muttered. "The more we dig, the less sense this makes."

"To top it off," Iliescu growled, "this morning we received a credible tip on another name."

"I'm not liking this," Lawe said. "Someone is puppet-mastering us."

"What's the name?" Saito asked as he joined them, looking determined.

"Before we give that to you," Iliescu said, "can someone get Leif and Iskra? We're going to send Reaper out."

Saito frowned. "I'll get them." He stumbled down the hall to the bedrooms. He peered into one, then another, then swung open the bathroom door. "Houston, we have a problem." He held up both hands as he returned. "They're not here."

Lawe and Culver shared a look.

"Think they went out for breakfast?" Devine

offered. "I was thinking about it—too cooped up in here."

"Negative," Cell objected. "I've been up all night. They couldn't have gotten past me."

"But they *did* get past you!" Lawe smacked the back of Cell's head. "They're gone."

On the screen, Command's end had blacked out. The bigwigs were obviously having a conversation without letting the children in on the secret. Mercy peered down the hall, wondering where Leif and Iskra had gone. When had they left? What did they know?

The screen flared to life again with Iliescu in the forefront. "Due to heightened security reasons, we want you out of The Hague immediately."

Alarm spirited through Mercy's stomach. "Heightened security?"

"Great," Lawe muttered. "It's called they're looking for dumb Americans sitting around waiting to be arrested. Am I right?"

"Close," Braun said. "You'll have the itinerary on your devices. Once you're en route, we'll relay the intel. Until then, heads down and move fast."

# CHAPTER 28

## STUTTGART, GERMANY

He was a Navy SEAL. He had mastered HALO jumps. But this—sailing off a building atop a hillside, letting the wind carry them across a thick forest toward the fortress-like estate of Rutger Hermanns—yeah, it amped Leif's pucker factor.

Air tore at the wind suit, grabbing the edges and shaking it like someone trying to snap a bug from a sheet. Cold bit his face and nipped at the nylon he'd zipped into like an overripe banana. Landing in the right place wasn't as easy as navigating a chute down, in his opinion. As his glider tipped and threatened to send him into a spin, he glanced at Iskra, who was all ease and elegance sailing above the trees.

He gritted his teeth and focused on not dying or being shown up. A plus would be landing with all body parts intact. Bruises and scratches he could handle.

She angled her left arm down and veered toward the trees. Close. Very close. His pulse seemed to shudder—or maybe that was his body in the buffeting air.

She'd said they would land in the woods, but

he hadn't given much thought to what that meant. That was what he got for being hung up on a name.

Harcos. Why had he called Vega by that name? Harcos was dead—in his dreams. Vega died in The Hague—someone different. But it wasn't just a mistake. Something was . . . familiar. Like a song he couldn't remember the lyrics to, but the tune played over and over in his skull, driving him mad.

"Leif!"

The ground rushed up at him. Too late he recalled her instructions. Saw his position. Knew he was dangerously low. He canted his arms, and tree limbs snatched and clawed at him, slicing through his suit. He growled but focused on aiming his feet at the ground, ready to run.

He touched down but still had too much momentum. He pitched forward, the wind flipping him over, ticked at him for tempting her power. He tumbled and rolled, tangled in his glider. Slammed into a tree. Air punched from his lungs. He tried to suck in a breath—but couldn't. He slid to the side and coughed, forcing air back into his lungs.

"Runt!" Iskra flew at him, forest litter dusting around them. "Are you okay?"

Holding his ribs, he gritted through the pain.

"*What* were you thinking? You never—"

"I know," he bit out, not wanting a lecture.

Or her pity. "I'm fine." He struggled to stand.

"You sure?" Breathless, her face flushed and eyes black with worry, she assisted him, unzipping the suit and freeing him.

"Admit it, you've always wanted to undress me." If he'd wet his pants, he wouldn't be more humiliated than right now. He climbed out of the suit. Mad at himself. One hand held his aching side, the other rubbed the knot forming on the back of his head.

Iskra rolled her eyes, then slapped his shoulder. "You idiot. You scared me. Do you realize what—"

"I just wanted you to worry about me." It was a bald-faced lie, but it broke the tension.

"Worry? I am *furious!*"

"Does that mean you'll kiss me now?"

She glowered, but there was a glimmer of a smile in her tight expression. "Seriously, how is your side?"

"Healing."

"You always say that."

"It's always true." In more ways than one.

She grabbed his shirt and jerked up the hem, baring his abs and side.

"Hey, I was kidding about undressing m—"

She probed the injury, and he nearly headbutted her when she pressed his ribs. "You may be the bravest idiot I know, but you are an injured one, too. It's possibly fractured."

"It's not," he argued. "I can breathe and move. Bruised."

"You cannot kn—"

"C'mon. We're on a tight schedule." He nodded toward the structure at the base of the incline. "Let's get this done."

But instead she cupped his face and planted a kiss on his lips.

Leif had no brains when it came to Iskra and leaned into the kiss.

She broke off. "See?" She held up her hands. "Idiot."

"For you, yeah."

She gave him a wide smile. "Then I will let you live this time, even though you nearly got yourself killed and ruined this mission."

After burying their gear, they shouldered into their rucks and hiked down the hill to the property. The perimeter security here was nothing like China, and Leif bypassed it without a problem. Guarding his side, he hustled behind her to the stone wall that embraced the estate of gray slate with decades of ivy twining through its mortar. Near a heavily treed part of the wall, they climbed over and dropped into shadows. Four yards separated them from the side entrance of the garage. Thankfully, the guards didn't seem worried about this side of the estate, apparently.

Leif and Iskra sprinted to the garage. Iskra went to work on the keypad while he monitored the patrolling guards. When minutes ticked by and they still hadn't moved, he glanced back at her. "Mercy's hacking would've been helpful here," he said, referring to the keypad that'd get them inside the detached garage.

Iskra's expression darkened. "I am more than capable of handling this."

"Didn't mean anything by it."

Rolling her eyes, she arched a brow as the lock disengaged. She slipped into the darkened interior. She held the door for him to follow, then eased it closed. Leif shook his head, realizing there was no smell of oil or exhaust. Instead, this was more a showroom for six vehicles, including an antique Rolls holding court in the middle.

They hurried through a barely shoulder-width wooden door and descended a dozen or so steps. Dank, the hidden tunnel probably had rats and other vermin scampering through it—just like Leif and Iskra. It snaked under the driveway and gardens and up into hidden servant corridors of the centuries-old estate. Thick stone walls made for a cold, musty experience. He had memorized the floor plan Iskra secured of the main structure. She navigated the passages as if she'd been here a dozen times, turning with confidence from one to another. Her lack of hesitation at each turn made him *more* hesitant.

A glimpse of light between wooden slats—a door, he guessed—stopped him. "Iskra."

He strained to see through the gap. Based off research photographs of that unique inlaid floor and the massive stained glass window that framed the door, he guessed they'd reached the far end of the main foyer. They were headed to the main library, which sat off Hermanns' study.

"What are you doing?" she breathed. "We must hurry." She tugged his arm. "Come on."

Since she'd gotten them this far, Leif shut down his paranoia and followed. It wasn't that he was afraid they'd get caught. Hermanns and even her brother, Mitre, were in The Hague, possibly en route back—it was why he and Iskra had hurried into the night, to beat them to Germany.

*What're you afraid of, then?*

That she was betraying him. The realization told him to go back, but voices on the other side of the wall shoved him forward.

*"The security measures are ridiculous,"* Iskra had said as they plotted their insertion on the flight over. But she'd vowed she'd long been working on a way to defy those measures.

*"Why?"*

*"He infuriated me the first and only time I was there—on business for Hristoff. He had this casual candor about his ability to keep out any burglar and how he so effortlessly beat me to the Cellini. I've wanted to break into that library ever since—to show him I could."*

"Where?" came a stern voice.

"The garage. A door was open."

Iskra flashed wide eyes at him, filled with accusation. But hadn't *she* closed it?

"Shut it down and walk it," a voice ordered.

"Yes, sir."

Was she setting him up? He hated the thought but couldn't shake it. Knowing he had no other options now and that their timeline had just been cut shorter, Leif hurried on. Boots scratching against the concrete floor, they turned a corner— right into a stone wall. *Ambush,* his paranoia accused.

"Here," she whispered, hand tracing the surface.

It was hard to believe they could get anywhere in this concrete coffin, but he told himself to chill. Wait it out. Iskra wasn't going to sacrifice herself, her career, or her chance of seeing Taissia again by screwing this up.

Unless that was her price—him for her and Taissia's freedom.

At the seamless gray wall, Leif's misgivings thickened. He skidded a glance at her, but she wasn't looking at the wall. She was staring at the floor.

"What're you doing?" he asked.

She ignored him, tapping her toe against the slabs. Which made Leif step back and study the ground, half expecting it to fall out from under him. It struck him how clean it was back here. Someone tended this. Regularly.

"Ah," she said, and hopped onto one square.

His breath stuck in his throat, waiting for something to happen. But . . . nothing. "Wh—"

"Here." Eyes alive with mischief and deduction, Iskra caught his sleeve and tugged him. "Stand there."

Disconcerted, Leif stilled on the spot she indicated.

Again, nothing.

"Over one," she said, assessing the wall, then him. "Yeah, one more."

"Are you—"

"Do it."

Irritated, he adjusted to the right.

With barely a whisper of noise, the floor dropped an inch. Then rotated like the well-oiled hidden door it was. The entire wall moved with it, switching them from the interior of the passage to . . .

The floor hoisted, sealing the gap as if the mechanism hadn't changed sides of the wall.

Now they were surrounded by a wall of black boxes with numbers and different shapes. The lighting was low and strained the eyes, likely to preserve the paintings that hung in what he guessed to be hermetically sealed boxes. Originals were labeled with the artists' names— Van Gogh, Leighton, Matisse.

"Holy wow," he whispered, scanning the room.

"Now," Iskra said, her voice a mixture of awe

and frustration, "to find where he stored the book."

Yeah, he got why she expected it to be here. Were these treasures stolen? Or had Hermanns bought them? Maybe both? Wouldn't he want to display them? Maybe some nice ones graced the walls. Perhaps his staff rotated them out. He had enough to do that each week for a year.

Looking around for the Book of the Wars, which Leif reasoned would not be on display but hidden away, he went to the wall of boxes.

"They're touch activated," Iskra explained. "Just the warmth of a fingertip will add light so you can see what's inside. But once we find it, getting the box open will be a different story."

"As long as we can take it," Leif said as he tested her instructions and tapped a box. The black faded to gray then clear, revealing a heavily bejeweled diadem. Mentally, he whistled, recalling the mission with Tox and the team when they'd found those gems near the lamassu.

"Taking it will pretty much happen," she promised. "Hurry."

"You'd think with pieces worth millions, Hermanns would go to greater lengths to protect them." Coming in through the garage, then the passages. It had been easy. "Too easy," he murmured, nerves jangling as he turned a slow circle.

"Don't be paranoid," Iskra muttered.

"I'm usually the one saying that." No, this *was* too easy. Way too easy. He studied the vault door that—according to their research—was at least two feet thick.

Two feet thick there, but not at the passage?

Leif glanced back to the swiveling door. His heart stuttered. "We have to get out—now."

Iskra scowled. "What?"

He nodded to the wall. Flanking the swiveling door were dual two-foot-thick steel doors. They were slid back. Closed, they would have prevented the door from swiveling. But they were open. Someone was already here.

Iskra cursed.

A gust of air drew Leif around. Two men emerged from behind curtains on either side of a Van Gogh. They lifted weapons at Leif and Iskra and fired.

# CHAPTER 29

## STUTTGART, GERMANY

"Sir, they are secured in the library as instructed."

Rutger Hermanns nodded as his head of security ducked out of the solar where he was working on the final assault. When he shifted back and found the young man shooting daggers at him, he could not help but smile. "Relax, Andreas."

"It is too dangerous!"

"It is necessary," Rutger countered.

"She is too close—"

"She knows, Andreas. Iskra already knows who you are. No more pretense. You must face this. Accept her wrath," he insisted with a quiet laugh, "because we all know well the wrath of Viorica." He lifted an eyebrow at him. "Do we not?"

"Veratti—"

"Will be informed." Rutger glanced at the schematics spread over the table. "For now"— he thumped the paperwork—"this is our priority. And they are our puppets."

"What if they won't cooperate?"

Rutger snickered, nodding at the monitor where the security feeds had been accessed. It was really too brilliant, having Iskra and Metcalfe think they were pulling one over on him. "They have bitten into the rotten apple like greedy children." He shrugged when uncertainty slid across the young man's brow. "They want what we have. What else will they do but cooperate?"

Andreas eyed the feed and his tenacious, sharp-tongued, sharp-witted sister. If only *she* had gone back to Bulgaria. Perhaps she would have a chance to live. But as it was, Rutger knew Andreas feared for her.

"They know we have the book."

"Yes, Veratti did just as expected," Rutger murmured as he indicated the plans. "I have told you, it is not foolproof, this method. I cannot guarantee—"

"What of Huber?"

Rutger lifted a shoulder. "One must hope."

"It is not enough!"

With an upheld palm, Rutger nodded. "It is all we have, my young friend." His gaze flicked to the monitor. "Ah, good. It's time."

Emerging from the dregs of the drug that he and Iskra had been shot with, Leif prowled the library, looking for a way to remove the metal cuffs that zapped him with angry darts of electricity when he got too close to the door and window sensors. He paced to the door, testing the current again. Fiery pain snaked around his wrist and up his arm, nearly sending him to a knee. He growled and jerked back. Shifted to the window and felt the cuffs zap him. There must be a way. . . .

"Just stop. It's useless." Also cuffed, Iskra sagged in a chair, holding her head. "They set us up. Now we wait to see what the monster wants."

The cuffs were steel, so he couldn't break them. But what if he found something to interrupt the current? At a bookcase, Leif searched for something to short-circuit it.

On both cuffs?

He rotated his forearms, eyeing his inner wrist where the cuffs had zapped him. A thin red welt stared angrily back. His gaze hopped past his burnt flesh to the small telephone table. On it was a bifold painting, both panels no bigger than his hand from heel to fingertip and painted into three rows with different depictions in each section. He lifted it from the table, eyeing the macabre images.

Shrieks and screams stabbed his brain as he stared at the middle image on the left panel—a king surrounded by eight or ten other kings, all laid out and bloody. Sick.

He set it down, unsettled. Turned to the bookcase.

*"We can do this, Chief."*

*I will rise.*

*I will rise.*

His skull ached from the leftover drug and the assault of words rushing in, luring his attention back to the diptych. He reached toward it but hesitated. Squinted.

*"You're pushing too hard."*

*"It's what I do."*

Not sure where the words came from, Leif grunted, feeling as if someone had just poured lemon juice on a cut. He cocked his head, trying to fight off the burning. To sort the chaotic messages his brain was digging up and throwing at him in no specific order.

"Ah, Miss Todorova."

At the voice of Hermanns, Leif snatched up the painting. Not sure why, except that he felt this compulsion to study the panels more, better. He slipped it into the pocket of his tactical jacket.

When he turned, he found Iskra rising. Color infused her cheeks as she glowered at Hermanns. No, not at Hermanns—the person behind him.

"How *dare* you," she growled at the younger man.

Startled, Leif recognized him from the Meteoroi confrontation in Angola.

Iskra trembled with anger. "You defile our name by working with this . . . this demon!"

"Are you talking to me?" Hermanns asked with a laugh. "Or your brother?"

"This is not my brother," she spat.

Before he could react, she flew at Andrew. Punched him. Kicked him.

Leif rushed forward, trying to grab her cuffed

407

hands as she beat her brother. It was not the precise, focused violence of an assassin, but the wild, angry rage of a sister betrayed. Leif caught her arm and drew her back, but her elbow connected with his jaw. Sent daggers of pain down his neck and shoulders. Though he stumbled, he maintained his hold.

"Get off me," she demanded.

"Now, now, Miss Todorova," Rutger said, all too patronizing as he crossed the room and sat in one of the leather high-backed chairs. "This is not what I expected from such a skilled operative as Viorica."

"She died with Hristoff." She shrugged off Leif's hold and straightened her shirt.

Hermanns lifted a pipe and tapped it against his palm. "Quite right," he said, as if he were a proper gentleman. "In fact"—he pointed the mouthpiece of the pipe at her—"it is said you have gone soft since he died, that you have lost your chutzpah, as they say."

"Wrong tack," Leif warned, seeing the fire hit Iskra's gaze.

"Oh, that's right," Hermanns said, eyeing him. "You're the lover now, aren't you? Did you find a ring among the items in my vault to give her?"

Leif gritted his teeth. "Why are you trying to tick us off? You want us to splatter your gray matter?"

Hermanns guffawed, then stuffed his pipe. "I

would like to see you try, but we will defer that pleasure until later."

"Why?" Iskra growled, molten hatred pouring off the iron gaze she aimed at her brother. "You were so smart, so good!"

"So good at what, Iskra?" Andrew asked, and his accent was different than it had been in Angola. "You don't know me. You haven't seen me—"

"I know the real you," she asserted. "The boy who brought me chocolate for my birthday."

"You were ten! And it wasn't for you," he said, his voice losing its potency.

The little girl she'd once been appeared in her fragile expression. "What?"

Andrew looked miserable. "I was home, trying to get our father to join a business venture. It could have solved . . . so much. But he—" A leaden breath drew him up sharp. His gaze fled hers and, apparently, the truth. "He told me what he planned . . . for you." He heaved a sigh. "I argued. Tried to stop him. But he wouldn't listen. He said there was no other way. That's when I saw you in the back room."

"I remember," Iskra said hollowly, her gaze distant.

"No," he argued, shaking his head. "You remember a romanticized version. I gave you the chocolate to keep you quiet, but it was supposed to be for Father's paramour."

"No."

"I thought if you could just stay out of his hair, if you could stay quiet, he would . . . forget." He lifted a hand in frustration. "But you . . . you were Iskra. You were our mother reborn. You could not let it be."

Her eyes widened and blazed. "You blame me? For being sold?"

"N—"

"A child, Mitre! I was a child!" She pounded his chest. "Innocent, pure. Was I an easy kid? No, but neither did I deserve what Father did, what I went through." Just as quickly, her confidence drained from her posture. "Or . . . did I? Was I that bad of a—"

"No," Leif barked, inserting himself into their history. "Nobody deserves that. No living, breathing human deserves that. Ever."

They both considered him as if just remembering he existed.

"Touché, Mr. Metcalfe." Rutger Hermanns clapped, pipe dangling between clenched teeth as a lazy tendril of smoke rose from it. "Well said. Well said."

Leif twitched, surprised to hear his name. Then irritation, so sweet a poison, rushed through him again. "What is this? What do you want?"

Hermanns crossed his legs and smiled, cupping the pipe. "Isn't it obvious?" He grunted as he came to his feet and started for the door. "Come with me."

"No way," Leif called after him, knowing the cuffs would zap him.

"It's quite safe, I promise. We have no ill intent."

Leif held up his wrists. "Except to drug us and zap us crazy."

"Oh yes." Hermanns chuckled, then nodded to his man. "Release them."

"This is not a good idea," Andrew countered.

"What are you afraid of, *brother?*" Iskra growled. "That I won't be *quiet* enough for you? Or are you going to kill us, too?"

"They're dangerous," Andrew said to his master.

"I understand," Hermanns replied, his voice and gaze softening. "But it is time. We need them."

Andrew turned, considering Leif. Wariness possessed most of his presence, but there was also anger. Uncertainty. He lifted his phone and swiped the screen a few times, gave them one last glance, and pressed it.

The cuffs clicked open, and with a quick flick, Leif freed himself. Of the cuffs and inhibition. He rushed Andrew.

Who produced a gun, leveling it at Leif's face.

Leif drew up short.

"Stand down." Confidence and willingness to pull the trigger seeped through Andrew's every pore.

"Can you shoot us both? In time?" Iskra asked, sliding up next to Leif.

"Yes," Andrew said without flinching as two more guards drifted into Leif's periphery. He cocked his head. "Hands where I can see them, or you'll take a nice long nap."

"Do we have a bead on Leif or Viorica?" Lawe asked once they were thirty-two thousand feet above sea level and racing east across the globe.

"Not yet," Iliescu said. "But we tagged them in London boarding a plane for Germany, which created some initial alarm and confusion, as we'll soon explain. They landed, but we lost them in a crowd. They didn't exit the airport, so we're reviewing footage to find out where they went next. We hope to track them down and get them to rendezvous with Reaper in Taiwan."

"Roger that," Culver said.

"We've matched the name of another Neiothen. We have eyes on this individual, so we might actually be ahead of this one."

"Heard that before," Lawe said.

Braun nodded. "The Neiothen this time is Herrick Huber, a German lawyer."

"Thus your alarm and confusion," Devine said with a nod. "Leif and Iskra land in Germany, and we have a German sleeper agent to hunt."

"Correct," Braun said. "We thought Leif and Iskra had a head start on Huber. Either way, we now know their arrival there was irrelevant, because Huber comes from old money and has his own plane."

"Let me guess," Saito proclaimed. "It's missing."

"It is. And its transponder is not working."

"I think I'm going to die of not-surprise," Culver muttered.

"Dude, that's from a kid's movie."

"Back on track, Reaper," Cell said. "Two matters of interest. The first is that we have credible intel from a source who sent us this image." A picture appeared on the screen of a merry-go-round with gilt etching splashed over its interior and exterior. "That is at the Taipei Children's Amusement Park."

"Come again?" Culver said.

"We've been in touch with Taiwanese authorities, and it seems President Kai Yi-Jeou is hosting a birthday celebration for his daughter there in two days."

"No." Culver slapped the table. "No, we are not doing a mission where kids are involved."

"That's mighty noble of you," Braun bit out, "but the enemy is, so you're going to leave these children out for slaughter?"

Culver uttered an oath.

"That is where you're headed," Iliescu asserted. "It's a big tourist attraction, so you'll be able to integrate without being obvious."

"What about the text I got at the party?" Peyton asked.

"Oh!" Cell snapped his fingers. "I did some digging on that. Whoever sent it was not very savvy about hiding tracks. The IP address belongs to Bagram."

"Bagram?" Culver repeated, gaping at the others. "Like, on base?"

"As far as I can tell," Cell said with a nod. "It didn't bounce after that, so that's it."

"Hold the freakin' bus," Lawe said, his face crimson. "You're telling me someone on *our* side is threatening Pete?"

"More accurately, it's entirely possible that someone on our side," Iliescu growled, "is involved with ArC."

# CHAPTER 30

## STUTTGART, GERMANY

"End these games," Leif demanded.

"*End* them?" Hermanns scoffed. "My friend, they are just beginning. You think you are armed with knowledge and know what's happening?"

"You don't have a clue." Andrew's sneer morphed into disgust.

"Mitre," Iskra said, her voice unusually soft, quiet. "Please. You cannot believe that working with Hermanns is right—or that carrying out the work of Ciro Veratti will bring any good to this world."

Her brother punched to his feet and turned to Hermanns. "I told you this was a waste of time. Let me get the gun."

"No," Hermanns said, motioning for his apprentice to calm down. "Not yet." He seemed distressed by Andrew's agitation, but then something changed in his expression at those last two words. Resignation? Regret?

These two were quite the pair, and Leif couldn't figure them out.

"We do not have time to wait for—"

"Andreas." Hermanns raised his voice, and it

seemed to startle him as much as it did the rest of them. "Please." He let out a long-suffering breath. "You must forgive him. This has been a most difficult time for—"

"Why are you even listening to him?" Iskra railed at her brother. "He is with Veratti, with ArC. You are better than this, Mitre. You are—"

"I am not Mitre!" Andrew yelled. "I have not been him in a decade."

"Our mother—"

"Is dead!"

"—gave you the name Mitre."

"And our father gave me the name that carries me today—Andreas."

"You are not this stupid," Iskra shouted, her face riddled with a pain so similar to her protective anger regarding Taissia.

Leif decided to try deflecting to a less personal subject. "Why have you been tagging Mercy, luring her?"

"I never intended to harm your asset," Andreas said. "But she . . ."

"She's very good at getting in the way when she wants answers," Leif said, his internal alarms trilling. "Like your sister."

"Bright and beautiful," Andreas affirmed. "It is what they look for." He glowered at his sister. "Isn't that right, Iskra?"

Wait. What? Who *looked* for . . . ?

Her face flushed. "Do not think that I had any choice in what happened to me."

"We always have a choice."

"No!"

As their war continued, Leif's mind migrated to the bipanel painting in his pocket that felt heavy. Or maybe that was his conscience for taking it. What if it was a million-dollar piece? He nearly snorted. Then he'd sell it on the black market and live comfortably with Iskra for the rest of his life.

The thought alarmed him. Startled him. *Live* with Iskra? Marry her? They were so far from that, it wasn't even funny. She with her assassin fury, he with his black-hole secrets.

No, the world was too volatile, their futures too uncertain, to entertain indulgences. He could never settle until that gap in his memory was filled.

*And what if you never figure it out?*

The bigger fear—what if he already had figured it out?

Still, it just couldn't be done, him and her. It was like trying to ride a bicycle without a seat. It would be painful at best, dangerous at worst.

His mind retraced the painting. The man in the gazebo with bodies strewn around it, some half in the ground, some skeletal. He internally winced at the dark images that connected to another scene to the right of a cemetery, littered with corpses that had made a mass exodus from some twisted crypt at the top. And to the left of that—

"Are you with us, Mr. Metcalfe?"

He yanked his gaze to Hermanns, irritated with himself for being distracted and with Hermanns for noticing. "Where else would I be?"

"I think it is time for some honesty."

The thrum of hissed conversation between Andreas and Iskra quieted, both looking to the older man.

Her brother swung into the chair next to the German. "You said—"

"Trust me, Andreas." Rutger Hermanns was used to getting his way and did not seem the kind of man to be easily maneuvered or manipulated. Indeed, he was probably the one who did the maneuvering and manipulating. Like now.

Hermanns drew on his pipe and squinted at Leif over the hazy coils of smoke. "There are some things you should know," he said. "First, what is shared here must remain within these walls." He smiled around another exhale of smoke, looking like a wizened wizard from some movie, save that his mustache and hair were not yet white-gray. "I should start at the beginning, with the Book of the Wars of the Lord and how I found it."

"The first pages," Iskra said. "They were found in the salt mines and—"

"But before that," Hermanns said. "How did I know where to find those?" He was smiling like a child in a candy shop. "A painting. I happened upon a small paneled painting that told me how to find the book."

Guilt pulsed through Leif, the bifold frame burning against his aching ribs.

"Since the discovery of the first piece of the Book of the Wars of the Lord, I have been intent on retrieving its entirety. I put untold resources to work in locating it."

"Why not ask Veratti?" Leif challenged.

Another breath of smiles and smoke. "We are not as connected as it might appear," Hermanns confessed. "It is true that I report to him, that I must answer to him regarding endeavors for the coalition." He gestured to Leif with the pipe. "I will, for example, make him aware that you broke into my estate."

Uncertain what that meant or what would happen to them, Leif glanced at Iskra.

"Come, come," Hermanns said around a laugh. "I am too busy enjoying my pipe and conversation to be bothered with lifting a phone at the moment, which would put you both at risk."

Was that supposed to comfort them? Leif regretted losing his Sig and KA-BAR to the guards. Did Iskra still have hers? Mitre was armed. Could Leif snag it and turn the weapon on them?

"As I was saying, yes—I must placate the

master." Sadness seemed to etch Hermanns' brown eyes. "Keep him happy, which keeps his gaze turned away from us, unconcerned."

"Sir—"

Hermanns again motioned for Andreas to be quiet. "Tell him about the facility. What really happened there."

A hard edge slid into the young man's face. He considered his mentor for a very long time before finally dragging his gaze to the floor. "I was at the facility when"—he glanced at Iskra—"you took her to the Pearl."

Pearl of the Antilles. When Leif still didn't think he could trust Iskra. When the book had been stolen right out from under them. When the Meteoroi killed one of his men.

Andreas continued. "We used the tracking devices on her and her phone to pinpoint the location."

"I had no tracking devices!" she said.

"You did. Vasily put them there."

An objection perched silently on her lips.

"Thankfully, I was closer than Veratti's men."

Thankfully? Closer? They were both tracking her?

"Getting into the facility wasn't a problem, but—"

"Why not?" Leif resented Andreas's cavalier attitude. "That facility—" Wait. "Mercy said she saw you on the *Mount Whitney*. That Admiral

Manche basically told her to leave you alone." He glanced between the two men, disbelief stoking the embers of anger. "Are you *controlling* the vice admiral somehow?"

"Let him finish," Hermanns said, puffing smoke rings into the air and chuckling at his trick.

"There is a lot you will not understand and things I cannot explain," Andreas admitted, "for security reasons."

"Security? I have the highest clearance—"

"You do not," Andreas countered. There was no arrogance or defiance in his words. Just fact. "If you did, we would not be having this conversation."

Something snapped off, a piece of Leif's confidence in Dru, in the system that had promised to find answers to his past. To fill those gaps.

"I got into the facility to retrieve the book, to bring it back here," Andreas said, nodding to his mentor, "but it was already gone."

Leif recalled what Iskra had told him about that underwater access, but the question—did Andreas know about it? One way to find out. "Who took it?"

Green-gold eyes held his, but there was an icy quality to them. And familiarity. They looked like Iskra's.

No. No, Leif *knew* these eyes. Or maybe it was just the terse glower brother and sister were so skilled at shooting his way. But there was a message here. A question. A . . . warning.

"Nobody entered that facility without authorization," Leif continued.

"There was a perimeter breach, if you will recall," Andreas said, all too confident in what he knew. He sniffed, a hint of a smirk in his face.

And now, paired with what Iskra had told him, Leif understood. "But there was no breach."

Andreas juggled a smile as he returned to explaining. "Like I said, there was only one way that book vanished."

"Someone on the inside."

"A powerful someone on the inside."

Leif folded his arms, digesting that juicy tidbit. It echoed what he'd begun to sense about this whole mess.

"So you took the book from him?" Iskra hissed. "I shouldn't be surprised—you've let me chase you all over the place. How could you do that? Why did you not—"

"You were dangerous," Andreas snapped. "You not only put yourself in jeopardy, you played right into Veratti's hands. Had I not intervened, he would've had the book. Earlier you said I was not that stupid, but you clearly—"

"I needed that book—to find you!"

"No, that's *not* what you were looking for," Andreas growled. "Is it?"

She recoiled.

"Is it?"

"Andreas," Hermanns said gently. "Peace, Andreas."

"She nearly ruined everything!" the younger man railed, his face reddening.

He was so different from the smooth operator Leif had encountered, which made him wonder if this reaction was because of Iskra. What had hardened him so much that he could not see how much Iskra longed to know and help him?

"The terror—the lives she has cost!"

Iskra lowered her chin, but not before tears filled her eyes.

That stirred Leif's anger. "Is that all she is to you? A measure of bodies?" He stood. "I've encountered you. Mercy encountered you. Skilled, smooth. Yet here, you're unhinged. Why? Is it guilt that you let your sister get sold like a piece of furniture?" His breathing was rough. "Or was the human side of you seared out by becoming a ruthless killer for ArC?"

"You have no idea what you're talking about," Andreas hissed. "If you knew—"

"Back off, man. She *didn't* know!"

"That is no excuse!"

"I said back off." Leif shifted into a fighting stance.

"My missions are tricky enough, going around Veratti and trying to find the Neiothen before—"

"Wait." Leif jarred, the words reverberating.

"*Going around* Veratti? Finding the Neiothen? Is that why you killed them in The Hague?"

Andreas ducked and expelled a very frustrated breath. "*I* did not kill them."

Leif stared, his mind hurdling over that doozie of a barrier to clear thinking. "You were there. Mercy saw you take the shot."

Andreas strode to the bar, glancing at his mentor as he went. A silent, unsettling conversation ensued between them.

"Now," Hermanns said, setting his pipe in a bronze tray before he threaded his fingers and eased back, "it is my turn to talk."

Leif felt as if fire ants were biting every last nerve. That and the stolen painting in his pocket. "I don't know what your game is—"

"My game, Mr. Metcalfe," Hermanns replied, his expression serene yet fierce, "is the most complicated chess game of my life. I am but an amateur playing against a master."

Wariness held Leif hostage.

"Ciro Veratti is that master," Hermanns went on. "A skilled, ruthless master. If he were to learn of my endeavors, I would no longer have a mouth from which to speak nor a head with which to so delicately weave a tapestry of espionage and betrayal that can only be detected by one intimately familiar with its fibers. I have labored on this effort for the last ten years."

"Do you want applause?"

"No, I want you to ask what effort."

Curse the man if he wasn't smiling. Leif just wanted an exit, and the quickest way was probably to play the very game Hermanns said he wasn't playing. "Fine." Either Hermanns had more guts than Leif gave him credit for, or this was one elaborate trap. "What effort?"

"The shot Miss Maddox saw Andreas take was not made with a sniper rifle." Hermanns grunted, then laughed, shrugging. "Or, I guess it was. Eh, Andreas?"

Lifting a snifter, Andreas answered, "A modified one." Then he took a swig.

Leif wanted to be mad, wanted to smart off, but this story was getting interesting. A modified sniper rifle.

"You see," Hermanns said, "we learned that the Neiothen are activated by a chip implanted in their brains."

A curse darted across Leif's lips before he could stop it. "Really? This is what you want me to hear? Watch any sci-fi flick out there, and that's their MO. That's science fiction." He rolled his eyes. "I'm done here."

"Bear with us a minute longer," Hermanns said, lifting a finger. "The weapon Andreas used, the one Ms. Maddox saw him fire? It did not shoot bullets but rather sent a high-frequency pulse. It had to be precisely aimed at the head, or it would not work."

"A pulse? But a sniper round went through both of their chests."

Andreas nodded. "I sent the pulse to Vega, but Veratti had a sniper on-site. Apparently he's been at every activation to make sure that, when the Neiothen complete their mission, they can't be taken alive."

"Which we try to prevent," Hermanns said. "You see, Andreas sends the pulse, and we have an operative waiting to intercept the Neiothen."

"How does the pulse work?"

"It disrupts the implant's ability to receive radio signals, which is how they've been activating the Neiothen," Andreas said.

"Wait, I don't—what about Ibn Sarsour?"

"Fortunately for him," Hermanns said, "there was an MI6 agent at the wedding, who took custody of him. But we try to get to them before anyone can kill them. Obviously, Veratti does not want these men talking."

Leif's brain hurt. He held up a hand. "So you shot Vega with the pulse weapon. What about Elvestad?"

"We tried."

"Bad angle," Andreas huffed.

Grief pinched Hermanns' eyes. "It took the activation of the first couple for us to realize the exact process. And, of course, intercepting the Neiothen alerted Veratti to our actions."

Leif rubbed his temples. "What is his endgame?"

"His singular purpose is to set up a caliphate to rule Armageddon, to prove to Christians that their belief in the end times is foolish. But while he pretends to care about eschatological concerns, his real priority is to put himself in control of trade and economy." Hermanns shifted to the edge of his seat. "He is three-fourths of the way to his goal. We cannot—*must* not let him finish the last one."

"Last what?"

"Country—Taiwan."

Futility seemed to be the main course tonight. "I don't get it. If all the other countries have been restructured, we can't very well undo all that by saving one country." He looked at them. "Can we?"

"No," Hermanns said. "But you saved the Chinese general, and while you are correct that we cannot undo what has been done, we can be a thorn in Veratti's side. Without Taiwan, his empire is not complete." Amusement seemed to camp in his features. "Did you know, Mr. Metcalfe, that the human brain is incredibly complex and yet susceptible?"

Leif scoffed. "What does that have to do with anything?"

"If one thing is off, if one neuron doesn't fire, it can singularly affect the body in a profound way."

"You mean like the implants?" Why did mentioning that make his brain buzz?

"I mean," Hermanns said, "that if one atom is altered, if one organ is affected, *everything* is affected. With the right steps, the right plan and implementation, we can be that one organ that affects Veratti's brainchild. We can be that thorn, that one misfiring neuron—or nation."

Leif snorted. "That sounds really nice and poetic, but it doesn't work in practice." And as much as it galled him . . . "He's won. Don't you get that?"

Anger tightened Hermanns' mouth. "I will *not* lie down in the grave before the last breath is stolen from my lungs. And I will not let Veratti easily take that breath!"

Leif had no response, no counterattack. There was no way to compel a man this convinced that he was barking to the wrong dog pound. "Fine. Protect your breath."

"I think our beautiful Iskra would ask when you became such a fatalist."

Iskra stared at her hands.

"About two dead Neiothen ago," Leif said.

"Do you know how many Neiothen exist, Mr. Metcalfe?" Hermanns pulled himself out of the chair and circled to stand with his hands on the back of the leather seat. "The one-fourth that Veratti still needs is not only a country, but the remaining Neiothen."

"Right." Leif glanced at Andreas, who swirled the drink in his hand. "So, what? You want me to help your boy find the last ones? Zap their brains so they don't complete their missions?"

"That's an interesting scar on your hand."

What? Leif resisted the urge to glance down or move. He knew which scar, the one from the explosion that had killed his men. He also knew men like this thrived on making others uncomfortable and scared.

Leaning against the chair, Hermanns held his gaze. "I would speak with Mr. Metcalfe alone."

Though Leif hesitated, he couldn't help but appreciate the alarm and concern that speared Andreas. And Iskra.

Hermanns stuffed a finger in the air. "Actually, no." He smiled at them. "No, I think I know you well enough, Mr. Metcalfe. It is with the eyes that you must see and believe." He started for the door. "Come. I will show—"

"This is not smart," Andreas asserted. "He does not know—"

"*Ja*," Hermanns snapped, then patted the younger man's shoulder. "I know, my friend. But . . ." His gaze traveled the room before it found Leif again. "I think he must see. He will believe. We must trust."

"I should come," Andreas insisted, hand going to his weapon.

"*Nein!*" Hermanns barked, expression stern. He patted the air. "All will be well." His smile lost its potency. "All will be well." He seemed to age decades right there. "I must tell him of my sister's work."

"Sister?" Leif frowned, following him.

"*Ja.*" His dark eyes found Leif again. "My Katrin."

# CHAPTER 31

## STUTTGART, GERMANY

"How can you do this? How, in all that is holy, can my brother be a part of an organization so foul, so . . ." Fingers clawing her hair, Iskra searched for a word that embodied the enormity of what she felt. Yet words eluded her. "Ugh! You fail me, Mitre."

Brows rippling with near amusement, he snorted. "Fail *you?* Are you stark raving mad? What I do has *nothing* to do with you."

"Wrong!" She closed the gap between them. "We may not have had a traditional family—"

"We didn't even have a dysfunctional family. We share blood. That's it."

The words stung as if driven into her heart by a dagger. "You can't mean that." She hated the tremble in her voice. "You came to me, you brought me chocolate. And the doll!"

Understanding washed over his taut expression, which then tightened. "Oh, for . . ." He swore and turned, then pivoted back. "It was a plant, Iskra. We needed to know what was happening in Hristoff's house." He swallowed, his face melting into regret. "It had a listening device."

431

"You gave me a doll so you could spy on him?" He might as well have committed an unpardonable sin, because she was sure she couldn't forgive this. "All these years, I thought . . . I stupidly, foolishly thought you cared."

"I had no idea—"

"No! You didn't. You do not know what I have done, what I have risked to find you. I risked my own safety and my daughter's to find you. Help you."

"Help me *what?*"

"Get away from the Neiothen and Hermanns."

He swung away, bringing a hand to his forehead. "Iskra . . ." He shook his head. Then frowned. "You knew of them before you met Metcalfe? Who told you about them?"

"Vasily."

"The father of your child."

"No, he was not." The pleasure of him getting that wrong was too fierce. Even if he had monitored her life, he had not stepped from the past to help her face the future.

He frowned. "But—"

"His brother, Valery, was Taissia's father."

"I mix them up."

"It is easy to do when you did not know them." She hugged herself. "Vasily and Bogdashka said if I could find the Book of the Wars, it would tell us about the Neiothen. Through them, I would find you."

His gaze sharpened. "Bogdashka."

Out of all that she had told him, he asked about the woman? Iskra crossed her arms. "Did you care nothing for me?"

"You misunderstand me."

"Do I?" she asked around a heavy breath. "I can't . . . this doesn't make sense."

"Many things changed about me when I entered the facility." He squared his shoulders. "I am not the same person I was then."

"Facility?" Her mind skipped to the waters that had nearly claimed her twice. Her heart spasmed. "What did they do to you?"

"What *didn't* they do to me is easier to answer." He snorted. "It was . . . brutal, but I have no regrets. It changed me, altered my body, improved my reaction time, sped up my healing—which fixed my hearing loss and my twenty-thirty vision," he said with a laugh.

"Your hearing," she muttered, her thoughts lost in the past, at a spring picnic at a small pond. "You got tangled in the lily pads. . . ." It had been the last outing their family enjoyed together. But his words about the chocolate, the doll . . . "You knew." She tilted her gaze to his. "You knew what was happening to me, what I was forced to suffer, and did nothing."

Studying the carpet, he fell silent. No rushing to explain or reassure. And worse—no denial. Finally, he said, "Look, I get that you want some great renewing or connection, but I can't, Iskra."

"That would be me getting in the way of your mission again. Is that it?"

"No, it would be you wanting something I can't give." Sorrow touched his golden eyes. "I'm not being figurative saying it changed me. The training, the treatments. When I say I can't give it, I mean that literally."

"Give *what?*"

"Emotion, connection, love—any of it. What they did here"—he tapped his right temple—"and improved? It fried that other side."

Her mind tripped over his words. She stared, disbelieving. "That's a convenient answer."

"Convenient?" He breathed a laugh. "Try catastrophic. I can never be involved with anyone because I will fail her every time. I will never understand what she wants, and I will not be able to provide what she needs—empathy, love, compassion. That part of me is dead."

Stricken by the severity of what had happened to him, she could think of nothing to say. He, too, had his own horror story. "I am sorry, Mitre."

"I'm not. It makes me one deadly soldier," he said with a gleam in his eyes. "And that's what I do. What I will do with my dying breath."

Startled by his vehemence and his ridiculous dedication to an organization that had death at the end of every sentence, she moved toward him. "After all they did, all they stole," she growled, "you would do this? Still work and kill for them?"

"Not *for* them, Iskra," he said, brows pinched severely. "My missions are to tear down that infrastructure. To find the Neiothen—my brothers—and free them." In his eyes glinted a fury that made her take a step back. "One way or another. What they did to me, I will use against them. Until they are dead."

"You mean until you both die."

His face was stone. "Do I?" The threat hung in his words—a dangerous one—but she wasn't sure why he said it to her. Why he looked at her as if he was making a point.

"Ready?" At the door, Leif stood with a leather satchel. Behind him came Rutger.

"No!" Mitre barked. "You cannot—"

Rutger shook his head. "Leave it, Andreas. It must—"

"No. You do this, we lose all control. We need it—"

"*He* needs it more. For now." Rutger settled a hand on Leif's shoulder. "For now, we have agreed."

Jaw muscle popping, Leif focused only on Iskra, a darkness clouding his pale blue eyes. "We should go."

Rutger patted his back. "We shall see you in Taiwan. To the victor the spoils, yes?"

# CHAPTER 32

## SOMEWHERE OVER EUROPE

"We should talk."

Immersed in coding and backtracking aboard the jet, Cell glanced up for the briefest of seconds, but his focus never left the program he was running.

"Mr. Purcell."

His brain glitched and yanked him from the electrical currents of the computer to the live feed flickering on the monitor to his left. He nearly cursed. "Director." He hadn't called. Hadn't allowed access. But he shouldn't be surprised. "Majorly uncool, spying on me again. But that's—"

"Close the briefing room door."

*Caught with my hand in the cookie jar.* Cell hesitated, then stood and did as instructed. He'd be home in six hours, so why couldn't this wait? His heart stuttered. Could he shut down the program without tipping off the director or drawing attention to his actions?

The deputy director leaned into the camera, his lips flattening. "I need you to stop."

Cell lifted his hands from the keyboard.

Threaded his fingers. Managed a fake smile. "Right." He folded his arms over the desk, curious if he could reach the keyboard without being—

"I need you"—the words were much slower, more intentional this time—"to stop. *Now.*"

How had they found out this time? It was a different system!

"Or we will stop you."

Cell froze. Stop *you.* Not stop the program and thereby stop him. But stop *him.* His body betrayed him and forced his gaze to the monitor. What? Did Iliescu have a freaking direct link to his brain? Maybe he did. "Right." He keyed in a string of useless letters, hoping he was buying—

"Understand that if you test me, you will find yourself buried so deep, no one will wonder what happened to Barclay Purcell and his sharp tongue."

"Wow." Cell nodded. "Got it." He backspaced and used both hands to quickly type in the code to pause the program. No way he'd kill it. It was getting somewhere. That was why Iliescu was breathing down his neck, right?

"I need to tell you a story, Mr. Purcell. One that, if it leaves this conversation, will—"

"Yep. Buried in a concrete coffin."

"No," Iliescu said. "If you persist after our talk, I'll have you tried for treason and dereliction of duty, then have you executed in record time."

Cell hesitated. Eyed the man who'd given him this job. Iliescu was a hard-nosed son of a gun, but he'd never resorted to threats of violence. It just wasn't necessary. Normal people usually got the point.

*Which excludes me, obviously.*

"I want to tell you the story of a young man who was dealt a very tragic and cruel blow. A man who had a promising military career ahead of him, just like his brothers, father, and grandfather before him. A young man who'd do anything to protect those he loved and his country. He was the kind of man with the true grit and raw courage found in old movies, a guy with a passion for protecting the innocent and defending honor and freedom. A patriot in every sense of the word."

"You sound like you want to marry him."

Irritation scraped at the director's sincerity.

"Sorry." Cell wiped his upper lip and nodded, hoping the director would come to the point sometime this century so Cell could get back to digging and sweeping.

"One day while running ops with his team, they were ambushed. Half were killed. The handful that remained came away scarred, either with missing limbs or missing pieces of their identity. It changed him so fiercely that he became a machine. One of the best and hardest-hitting sailors ever encountered. He'd always been at the top of his class, but now he was setting records. Getting noticed."

"Sounds like a legend." What else could he say when the director left the opening like that?

"There was a certain program ramping up, one that was so classified, the right hand never knew what the left was doing. Oversight was absurd, the secrecy lethal. They recruited that hero, convincing him that the men he lost shouldn't have been lost—and that he would never lose another man if he joined them. If he consented to enter the endeavor and never spoke of it to anyone. So, ready and willing to make sure nobody under his leadership died again, he signed on."

That was some heady insight. "Leif." His brain surged. "You're telling me you know for a fact that Leif—"

"Quiet," Director Iliescu warned. "Imagine the people behind this. Imagine the power they were given and the oversight. I know some of their protégés died. Some went crazy. Killed staff members. Killed each other."

Whoa. Hello, Science Fiction 101. "How do you know this? What if they—"

"You have questions."

Cell laughed. "A lot."

"Swallow them and your digging." Iliescu's eyes narrowed. "You are putting him in extreme danger, and I cannot—will not—allow that."

He let out a long breath. "In fact, I want you monitoring Leif, going after him."

"Whoa no. Hold up." Cell rose, feeling a tremor of turbulence. "No, I'm not doing that. Not to him. Especially if what you're saying is true. Besides, I have zero idea who was involved in this program or where they are—you've been really good at hiding that. And what could this mean to Leif? If he learns what I'm doing—I'm dead. And if I screw up, we could both end up dead."

Iliescu straightened. "And yet you didn't care about any of that when you were digging up classified intel on this—"

"I—" Had he just gotten punked? He sagged at the realization. "You had no intention of me going after him. Did you?" When the director didn't answer, Cell squinted at the screen. "How did you find out about my searching? I mean, I'm no newb. I know how to hide my tracks."

"Not as well as you think." Iliescu stabbed a finger at the camera. "We have the best analysts whose only job is to watch for keywords—sound familiar?" It was what Cell had done to find the Neiothen. "All phrases related to the intel I have on what he has been through. Their sole priority is to intercept those searches so I can prevent an asinine mistake from exposing him and putting him in dire jeopardy."

"Crap," Cell breathed.

"I get it," Iliescu said. "You have a gut instinct, and it's always right."

Eating his own words was putrid.

"But I need you to get your head out of your butt and quit thinking about yourself and your curiosity." Ferocity bled through the director's gray eyes. "Cell, I've been digging on this for nearly five years, and I still haven't gotten past the first layer of that crap you just mentioned. But what I do know is that there are very serious, very well-connected individuals involved who will come after Leif and kill him if they think *he* is digging."

"Kill him?" The thought shocked him. "Why would they kill him? I thought they'd want him back."

"Because of what he knows."

"But he . . . he has six months of his life missing. I thought he didn't remember things."

"It's way more complicated than I have time to explain. Not that I would hand you everything, but"—he glowered, then drew in a breath—"you'll find some scans on your system, Mr. Purcell. Review them and see if you can connect anything. Maybe a match to this mysterious program."

"Scans?"

"From the Book of the Wars. We received them an hour ago from the man we've been calling Andrew. You're going to Taipei with the team.

What I told you about our mutual friend is not for your benefit, Mr. Purcell. Information is a weapon. Use it."

Taipei? "Sir, I'm on a plane heading stateside. Remember, I'm not a field—"

"The plane diverted an hour ago."

## TAIPEI, TAIWAN

From the rooftop of the safe house, Mercy had a brilliant view of the Taipei 101 tower, its unusual but beautiful shape singular against the rectangular skyline. From its base, the tower rose in a series of eight-story modules, each flaring outward in a pattern reminiscent of a Chinese pagoda. A smaller tower capped the structure, forming a pinnacle, an elegant addition to the façade of double-paned green glass curtain walls. Just stunning.

Movement on the street drew her attention. A taxi pulled up to the curb and the door swung open. "I recognize that arrogant head," she muttered to herself, then went back inside and down a couple of levels to the team. She met Cell on the landing and grinned. "Miss the insanity?"

"Like a lobotomy." He struggled into the room with his ruck, equipment, and a satchel.

"Ha, what happened to your 'safe side of the combat theater'?" Lawe taunted.

"Got thrown to the wolves, obviously." Cell

seemed perturbed as he tossed the ruck against a wall. "I need to set up for an all-hands with the director ASAP."

Lawe alerted the others.

Helping Cell unload the systems, connect, and plug them in, Mercy didn't like what she saw in his mannerisms. "You okay?"

"Nope."

When he didn't elaborate, she grew worried. "You look like someone ate your lunch."

"Pretty much. Happens when you nearly get a friend killed."

Mercy touched his shoulder. "Barc."

He shrugged her off. "Leave it. I'll be fine." He powered up his laptop. "Going live in five," he announced.

"Cell—"

"Leave it!" Regret pinched his face. "Sorry." His smile was wan.

The door opened, and Leif entered with Iskra.

Cell's complexion now looked bleached.

"About time," Culver groused. "Where you been, Chief?"

"Working angles." Leif considered the equipment. "We have a briefing?"

Cell twitched but otherwise ignored him. "Here we go, people."

Concerned but unwilling to engage him further—for now—Mercy stepped to the side.

"Okay, listen up." Dru spoke via the live feed,

joined by Braun. "I've been contacted by Andreas Krestyanov, brother to Iskra. I'll queue him into the feed."

"Aka *Andrew*," Mercy said with more than a little bite to her words. "Saboteur, thief, rogue . . ."

"Guess we now add *double agent*," Peyton said, earning a nod from Mercy.

Andrew's image joined Dru's on the screen. *Andreas* either hadn't heard or didn't care what Mercy said.

"You should know," Dru said, "Krestyanov will be on the ground there with you at the park."

Andreas inclined his head. "Thank you, Mr. Iliescu. I will be quick with what I know, which is not much, but it is imperative that we share what we have to stop what is to come."

"Why don't you start with how you got into the facility in Cuba," Lawe growled.

"Or why you were on the *Mount Whitney*," Mercy demanded.

"Stand down, people," Iliescu said.

"I understand your reticence," Andreas said. "If our roles were reversed, I might feel the same. But we have a unified purpose—to be sure the Neiothen do not complete their task."

"Why you?" Culver asked. "Can't we—"

"I was one of them," Andreas said and tapped his temple. "I think like them, because I was trained and engineered like them."

He was one of them. A Neiothen. Mercy's heart

crashed into her ribs. Took a dive as if riding the Silver Surfer's board. In fact, Andreas reminded her of Norrin Radd, a frustrated galactic wanderer who was ambivalent toward earthlings, just like Andreas was toward them. That was the word. *Ambivalent.* That was why he could talk with such unaffected calm.

"What are you, freakin' Teslas?" Lawe asked.

"More like Humvees," Andreas said without a trace of a smile. "If it were not for the work and knowledge of a neuroscientist, as well as the help of Mr. Hermanns, I would not be here. And you would likely be hunting me, too."

"That makes me not trust you," Baddar added. Mercy knew Baddar was a good guy and found herself drifting closer to him.

"*Were* one of them," Culver said, emphasizing the key word. "So you're not now?"

"As said." Andreas shifted. "Thanks to the neuro-scientist, we have a means to disrupt the signal that activates the Neiothen. I will be at the park to do exactly that."

"One of them," Saito said, leaning against the table. "How do you know you're *one of them?* I mean, I could just announce I'm one, and how would you know I'm not?"

It was a good, if roundabout, question.

"Besides my chip, there are a host of reasons. We anticipated you would ask that," Andreas said, his gaze flicking to Leif, who folded his arms. "Which is why we sent you full scans of the Book of the Wars."

"So, you have it," Mercy said.

"No, I do not have it."

Stunned when Kolya didn't out him, Leif—

Wait. *Krestyanov*—that was his last name, not Kolya. Where had he gotten Kolya?

"Cell," Andreas said.

The tension in the room tightened as the team, almost in unison, turned to Cell, who was struggling not to yawn every five seconds.

"Have you had a chance to look at the scans?" Andreas asked.

Cell shifted in his seat. "I have."

"Can you verify the name Akin is in them?"

A long pause happened before he finally nodded. "It is."

Andreas met their gazes. "That is my code name."

"How are we supposed to know that's yours?" Lawe asked. "I mean, it doesn't say Andreas Crustynut is Akin, does it?" He high-fived Saito at the name joke.

Annoyance parked itself on the Bulgarian's face. "It does not."

"Krestyanov is right," Cell said quietly. "On the plane, I scoured the scans, found the code name, ran it, and"—he nodded—"Akin is Krestyanov."

"So, why haven't we gone after Huber until

now?" Culver asked. "Or even after this guy."

Leif wondered the same, but he felt the tremor in his veins, the same annoyance as Andreas.

"We did go after him," Mercy growled, nostrils flared.

"Because we only had a corrupted, partial scan of the book, remember?" The comms expert seemed irked. "If we'd had the whole thing, we could've been way ahead of this."

Culver eyed him. "And you verified—"

"Yes, yes, yes!" Cell barked. "He is Mr. Akin Breakin' Hearts." The smile never made it past his lips, and his gaze . . . drifted. Toward Leif. Yet never locked.

What did the kid think he knew?

"Can I proceed now?" Andreas asked in his superior tone that was probably digging him a grave with Reaper.

Nobody answered.

Leif just wanted to get this over with. "Please."

Andreas stared into the camera, meeting his gaze across thousands of miles. "If I can identify and intercept Herrick Huber before he makes his move on the president, then it is likely that any action by your team will be unnecessary."

"Wouldn't that be nice," Lawe said. "Y'all hear that? We can take a vacation. Where d'you want to go, Pete?"

"Not the Caymans," she teased. Their last trip to the Caribbean had been a fight for their lives.

"Do you need something from us?" Culver asked. "I mean, why share this intel?"

"Because I did not want you to misread my actions and think I am there to kill one of you." Krestyanov's gaze landed on Mercy.

She lifted her arms. "Hey, you had a rifle, you took a shot. If it looks like a sniper and sounds like a sniper . . ."

"Do you need help disrupting the chip in Huber's head?" Leif asked.

"Chip? What the what?" Lawe asked.

"The Neiothen have chips implanted," Leif explained but stayed focused on Krestyanov. "Can you give us any direction on the technology so we can assist you?"

Something fierce stabbed Andreas's green-gold eyes. "Just don't get in my line of sight unless you want your brain buzzed. Then again, maybe you'll find out what's really buried beneath your skulls."

"Wait," Cell said with a laugh, "are you saying we're Neiothen?"

"Nah, you're not that good," Culver snarked.

But Leif stared hard at the operative. Those words . . . *"What's really buried . . ."*

"All right," Braun interrupted, "we need to get to work."

"Yes," Dru agreed. "Thank you, Mr. Krestyanov, for your help and intel. Reaper will be on-site, and we'd appreciate it if you stayed out of their line of sight, too. They have a job to do as well."

Krestyanov gave a curt nod, and for the briefest of seconds before the screen winked out, Leif felt like Kol—Krestyanov was looking not at the camera, but at him.

"Okay," Iliescu said, his gaze down as he spoke. "Official target is Taiwanese President and KMT Party Leader Kai Yi-Jeou. His views were a shift toward conservatism, which is most likely the reason ArC wants him out of the way. If they can put one of their own in place, then they have the last piece of the puzzle to seize control and influence most Asian, Eurasian, and Mideast commerce and trade. We saw the destabilization in South Africa, then in Botswana and Angola."

"But it's *one* country," Cell muttered. "How is that going to stop whatever ArC is planning?"

"My brother had this Expedition that was sharp and slick," Leif spoke up. "He and Dani were driving down the highway one day when the truck just lurched and stopped. They got it to the shop and found out a coil had gone out. Know how many coils that truck had?" He held Cell's gaze. "Eight. One for each piston. But that one coil had them dead in the water." His gaze surfed the team. "We don't have to win big to affect ArC. We just have to affect them."

"President Kai is going to be at the amusement park in Taipei for his daughter's birthday party,"

Braun said. "They've rented the place for the celebration. We have no idea how the children's park will get hit, so eyes out for explosives and chemical weapons."

"Per the intel provided by Mr. Krestyanov and worked up by Cell," Braun said, "this is your target, Herrick Huber, code name Bushi."

A man's face flashed across the wall.

*Smoke from the crash stung his corneas and tickled his throat. He heard Guerrero cough again. "Need help, G?"*

*"I'll live. Check Krieger and Zhanshi. They don't look so good."*

*Leif spotted two of their team a few yards from his boots. They were piled over each other on a dark patch of the sand and gravel road. Coming to his feet, he got a better view—and cursed. That wasn't a dark patch. It was a* bloody *patch.*

*He lurched forward, jagged pain clawing his leg. With a growl, he grabbed it and negotiated the jagged terrain. His boots slipped and twisted as the rock gave way.*

*He dropped to a knee beside Zhanshi. Head and shoulders lay at wrong angles, lips blue against chalky skin. Beneath him, Krieger groaned.*

". . . MO is chemical agents," Saito was saying, pulling Leif back to the briefing. "Every one of the attacks so far has been chemical in nature. Food poisoning, air ducts, and drops in the drinks."

"Same but different," Lawe mumbled. "Distribution is different each time."

Leif nodded. "Probably to prevent anyone from developing a way to stop them."

Lawe placed his palms on the table. "What methods are left?"

"There are only two viable ways to disseminate poison—gas or liquid," Culver said.

"Too bad we can't count on him just killing Kai," Saito said. "After China, we have to be ready for a large-scale attack."

"Agreed," Iliescu said. "While we'll do everything in our power to make sure the president's daughter and her friends are safe, we will also send in agents to leave gear in case of an attack—masks, oxygen, antidotes to the most common toxins, and anything else we can dream up. They'll be placed in trash bins around the park, as well as at every station."

"How many kids will be there?" Mercy asked.

"The count we have is thirty," Iliescu said. "So we'll be prepared for fifty."

Leif shifted. "What's our ROE for Huber?"

"Same as for every Neiothen—stop at all costs."

# CHAPTER 33

## TAIPEI, TAIWAN

Amusement parks inherently begged for attacks. Blending in, Reaper had spread out around the Taipei Children's Amusement Park, concealing weapons and the necessary equipment to deal with a terror threat. Iliescu had alerted the Ministry of Interior and the National Police Agency, who sent undercover agents as well. The situation was a two-edged sword—the threat against the president and the fact that children were involved. That made them want to call off the mission. But President Kai refused to alter his plans because he'd had to arrange his entire schedule to be present for his daughter's celebration. He had uttered some gallant words about trusting his security to handle the threat. The truth remained: even if they changed the date, it wouldn't change the threat. The Neiothen was after the president. Whether here or there, the attack would happen.

"Let's get it over with," Leif had said.

Set on five hectares of land in the Shilin District, the amusement park was conveniently situated on the Keelung River. That meant twelve acres of potential for murder. Mercy and Baddar would enter as a couple of party guests, and Saito had been assigned to the president's security detail.

"Uh," Culver said as they pulled into the parking garage, "I thought this was an invitation-only party for Kai's daughter and family friends?"

Yeah. So why were there so many cars? This wasn't right. "Back up. Block the entrance. Don't let any other families enter—say you broke down," Leif said. "I'm going topside for a bird's-eye view. See what's happening." He climbed out and keyed his comms. "Samurai, this is Runt. Come in, over."

"Samurai here," came Saito's quick, quiet voice.

"What's going on? The barn is full of livestock." He stepped onto the sidewalk and eyed the concrete parking structure. Blue and white tiles adorned the lower half. Above and to his right were two walkways.

"Roger," Saito said. "Farmer's en route. Cannot get any hands to help or explain. There are four hundred head in the pen."

Leif nearly cursed. "Keep talking to them. Be the squeaky wheel. This can't happen."

He hopped and caught the garage's maximum-height indication bar, then hiked up to the sign above. Toed it and pitched himself at the edge of the first walkway. Concrete scraped his fingers as he dragged himself over it. He stood on the wrought-iron rail. Jumped for the upper rail.

Someone below shouted, probably telling him to stop, but he kept going. Hoisted up onto the top walkway. Even as he sprinted across, he saw the Ferris wheel turning, all the cabins full. At the inner lip of the garage, he peered into the packed twelve-acre amusement park.

"This many people here," Leif said into the comms, "means he's making a statement. So he needs a way to spread it big. Look for canisters, fans, or vents that feed into large areas."

Laughter spiraled up from a jungle gym area where two boys were chasing each other up the steps and down the slide. The Fly Bus, a jungle-design-painted bus, lifted children above the crowds, revealing a big black bear holding the vehicle high. Radial flyer swings painted like planets swung children in circles. Large and brown, a pirate ship swung from bow to stern, higher and higher, the children inside screaming in glee. Children. Everywhere. On every ride, and more waiting in lines.

*Dear God . . .*

Gut tight, Leif shoved aside his panic and the bile climbing his throat. "Overwatch, we have a situation. The barn is full."

"This is Overwatch," Iliescu replied. "What do you—"

"It's *full*."

"Magpie's on-site," Saito said, indicating the Taiwanese president had arrived.

No time for panic. No time for anger. Focus. Solve it. At the parking garage, Leif was elevated but with a limited view. He had to get farther in. Had Iskra and Andreas made it yet?

"Runt, how many innocents?" Iliescu asked.

"Hard to count everyone in twelve acres, but Samurai suggested four hundred." Recalling what Hermanns had told him, he glanced at the surrounding buildings. "Badge, Coriolis, watch the rooftops. ArC could have an eagle, too."

"Roger that," Lawe replied.

"Can we do an emergency evacuation?" Mercy asked quietly. "There's a *lot* of kids."

"Negative," Leif said. "Doing that could trigger early initiation or whatever delivery device they have. People clogged at the exits would be prime targets." He mentally turned to where Devine was nested atop the National Taiwan Science Education Center, another nearby building filled with kids. "We have to find the delivery device or source. Huber wouldn't be here unless he has to manually deploy it."

"That or he wants to go down in glory," Lawe suggested.

"I have eyes on target," came Devine's voice. "Am I cleared hot?"

"Negative," Leif barked again. "Not until

455

we know the location of that gas and have it secured." Holding his breath, he scanned the crowds, trying to put eyes on the target, Huber. Nothing abnormal and nobody moving fast, drawing attention. No, he would be too good for that.

*Think like him.*

"Target has entered the children's theater building."

Frustration soaked Leif's muscles. "Copy that. Samurai, Smiley, Kitty, tighten up on Magpie and his daughter." He had to get in there.

The sun glinted off something—a monorail. It ran the circumference of the park, elevated, loading and emptying right here at the garage. Perfect.


"I hated theme parks when I was a kid," Adam said, stretched out beside Peyton on the roof of the science education center with his binoculars at his eyes. It had been interesting getting onto the roof without drawing undue attention. "Too many people, too expensive, and I could never win one of those stupid shooting gallery stuffed animals for my girl."

"That doesn't surprise me," Peyton said, scanning the amusement park with her scope. "You're not a very good shot." A familiar shape bobbed into her scope.

"Baby—"

"Reaper, seven o'clock, Dragon's Pearl," Peyton said into her comms. They'd memorized the layout of the park to be able to talk quickly and accurately about locations. "Target is OTM toward the six of the Fun Hub."

"Copy. Got him." That was Culver, hesitating on the far side of the hub in gray work coveralls and a baseball hat set low over his eyes, posing as a park worker. He waited until Huber passed him, then lumbered behind the large gray trash bin he pushed that concealed weapons and a set of antidotes. "No obvious weapons. Engage?"

"Not yet," Leif said. "Unless you see him about to deploy the chemical agent, we need him alive and ignorant. Track him. If he makes a move you find threatening, take him. I'm boots down and en route to you, Tabasco."

"Understood," Culver replied.

"I have eyes on Huber and Tabasco moving north toward the Telecombat," Peyton reported. What an odd name for a ride with airplanes swinging in a circle, lifting and descending as children adjusted the controls.

Concrete and rocks dug into her as she stretched out behind her rifle, which was tucked against her shoulder, her cheek resting on the stock. Her left hand remained free to adjust dials, while her right stayed near the trigger.

She tracked Huber until he slipped into a building. "Target entered the ice cream parlor. I have no joy on the target." Meaning she could not assist at this point. However, she kept the reticle trained on the doors.

"Got the entrance near the gate," Adam said, observing with his own scope.

"Monitoring the north," Leif said.

Quiet draped them as they waited, nerves wound tight, for Huber to emerge. There was no way to know what he was doing in there.

"Eyes on target," Leif reported.

"So," Adam said to Peyton, expelling a breath after that tense moment, "you going to give it back?"

She nearly smiled. "You bought it for me, right?"

He huffed, which she always found adorable. Funny how a 110-pound woman could bring down a beefy, brawny 210-pound guy. "Yes, I bought it for you, but I didn't *give* it to you. And you didn't answer the question."

"As I recall that moment on the dance floor, you didn't ask one."

"You didn't give me the chance. You just took the ring!"

Peyton smiled. She had the ring on a chain tucked beneath her shirt and tac vest. "Why was it in your pocket in The Hague?"

"It's always in my pocket."

That didn't make sense. "Why?"

"You know, I'd really prefer to have this

conversation when you can look me in the eye, not in your scope."

"You brought it up."

"You stole it."

"Can't steal what belongs to me."

"Woman, you drive me nuts."

"Mutual."

Never had she intended to end up in love with a Special Forces operator. She'd gone into the military to *be* an operator, not love one. Somehow, falling for Adam felt a little like betraying the women she represented. But fall, she had. Hard and fast. Things had gone wonky for a while, but lately it seemed like maybe they could sort things out.

She hoped so. That ring would look really sweet on her finger.

The things she did on ops.

Sitting in the children's amusement park, Mercy tried not to think too hard about the fact that Baddar was with her, his arm stretched behind her, across the back of the bench. She glanced at him, like they were talking. But they weren't. They were watching for a terrorist, trying to figure out how he planned to unleash a toxic chemical.

And she'd done really well for the first little while. Until without the use of her brain—obviously—she'd slipped her hand into Baddar's.

He was surprised but just smiled at her with that thousand-watt smile and gentler-than-she-deserved gaze. It had been a mistake. She hadn't been thinking. It had just happened.

He hadn't yet released her hand. He seemed to enjoy it.

And laser beams and superpowers, so did she. Which scared her. So what if she was one of those people afraid of commitment? It wasn't the commitment. It was losing the person to whom she committed. Like Ram. Baddar had a different name and face, but he represented everything she swore she'd never do again—patriot, commando, active missions.

No can do.

But just try looking into those chocolate-truffle eyes and saying that. She'd break his heart. Admittedly, it was strange to be on this side of the breaking power.

She freed her hand to brush invisible strands of hair from her face, then shifted on the bench. From their location, she could see the front gate, where the president was having terse words with his detail. Apparently he'd finally figured out he wasn't safe.

"Looks like the president isn't too happy," Mercy muttered into the comms as if she were talking with Baddar.

"Huber seems a bit tense," Leif answered, his voice thick, probably from having to be surreptitious. "I'm going to back off and give him room. If we upset him, he could lash out and kill these kids. Slow and steady wins the race."

"Copy," Mercy replied.

Silence stretched as they waited, a nerve-numbing activity.

"There is so much," Baddar said, his comms off, "about you that reminds me of my sister."

Her heart did that trippy thing—tripping up her brain so she couldn't think. They had to sit here and blend in, and that required talking. Small talk, which Mercy really hated. It was pointless. But learning about his family . . . She had a strange, nearly morbid curiosity about his life before they met. "Armineh, right?"

He smiled. Really, she should just give his smiles ratings, because when wasn't he smiling?

"You've mentioned the resemblance before but never said how," Mercy noted, peering over his shoulder toward the front gate, where the president seemed to have been placated. What deal had been made?

"She was very tenacious," Baddar said, glancing around, "always make our mother very frustrated. But Armineh had sweet heart."

She loved listening to him talk. His English wasn't perfect, but it was far better than most Americans could do with a second language. There were small hiccups where he didn't pluralize a word or didn't use the correct tense or missed an article, but he was crazy intelligent.

"And she was beautiful," he added.

Cue the flaming cheeks. "Thank you," she said, tucking her head. She wished she wasn't prone to blushing, but with a gorgeous Afghan commando grinning at her like that . . .

His expression changed, locking on to something behind her. "Newcomers at the gate," he said, still smiling. "Suits."

"ID?" Leif commed. "Coriolis, you got anything?"

"Negative," Peyton reported. "They're under the awning. No joy."

Mercy considered the casual manner of the foursome. And something . . . else. A couple and their children walked over to them. "They might be joining friends," she guessed.

"Do you have family?" Baddar asked.

Man, she hated that question. "Doesn't everyone?" Somewhere. "But my parents are dead." She used to add sadness to the way she said that, but she hadn't really known her parents.

His dark eyes held hers as sorrow dug in. "I am sorry. No brothers or sisters?"

"Nope." She shifted her attention around the park, the front gate, the children with balloons skipping along. Determined not to fall down that well of darkness she'd climbed out of almost ten years ago.

When she checked the gate again, Mercy

hesitated. The foursome was now talking to members of the park security who had broken away from the president's main entourage. Security agents swung their gazes toward Mercy.

Her stomach plummeted. "Time to move," she muttered. "We have either been made or reported."

"Come again?" Leif asked.

She kept her face neutral. "Security is headed our way."

# CHAPTER 34

## TAIPEI, TAIWAN

Leif paced Huber, pretty certain the Neiothen knew he'd been tagged by the team. But Leif would not give him room to move or kill hundreds of kids. Maybe it was time to call it. At least they wouldn't be sitting here waiting for the toxin to kill them. At least some people would make it out uncontaminated.

What if they didn't? What if the toxin somehow carried with the people and infected more?

Crap.

Leif had no idea what he was doing. He'd been on-site more than an hour and visually traced every pole for signs of tampering or devices. Cameras had been double-checked—all legit. Culver had checked all the trash receptacles for a device or canister. He had a handheld that detected noxious gases in his jacket pocket, but it hadn't registered trouble.

Twelve acres of property. But this wasn't like a theme park in Florida with tens of thousands packed in. Granted, kids would die and that was a heinous thing, but it'd be contained.

Hopefully.

464

*"You know. You know what I would say to you."*

*"Don't."*

*"I feared as much,"* Rutger Hermanns said *with a grieved sigh. "This is not something you can continue to hide from. As the saying goes—* ego semperer—*"*

"Ex profundis."

*Rutger nodded. " 'From the depths I will always rise.' It was a catch phrase ingrained in you to lure you back. To remind you of what you are. It's like a smell that triggers a memory."*

Augh! Why couldn't he get the memory out of his thoughts? He just wanted himself in his head. Not the fragments he couldn't quite pull together. He'd tried to shove it aside. Bury it. Hermanns hadn't told him anything he didn't already suspect, but they were ideas Leif had refused to embrace.

But he couldn't run from this anymore. Couldn't let the bad guys win. Not this time. Enough people had died on this sick quest of ArC's.

Andreas's lanky form swaggered into view, Iskra at his side. Though she had her arm around him, she seemed ready to kill. And he just looked bored.

Leif hadn't wanted her here—tried to convince her to act as part of Overwatch. Tried to leverage Taissia, but it had only made her angry. She hadn't come this far to sit out the big confrontation.

"Heads up," Culver said in his thick drawl from the Fun Hub. "Something's happening. Shops and rides are closing. Still no sign of a device or canister."

Leif blinked and checked Huber . . . who wasn't there. He cursed his distraction. "Huber slipped me," he growled, noting Iskra break away from Andreas and go to a refreshment stand. "Find him, people."

"You know what he'll do," came the very soft, very calm voice of Andreas as he joined Leif.

"Drive them into the open." Leif's gaze shifted out of the building to the park. The children.

"And there's only one way you know that."

Leif ignored Andreas. Keyed his comms. "Reaper, he's driving them into the open. Means his toxin will likely be gas. Anyone have eyes on him?"

"Negative," Culver reported.

Then the others. No one had Huber in sight.

Leif balled his fist, moving quickly, searching frantically.

Andreas stayed with him. "Stop panicking. Think like him."

Pulling up short, Leif glowered at him. "Get out of my head."

"No," Andreas said in a low voice. "Get *in* his."

Peyton peered through her scope, scanning the park, trying to reacquire the target. With no joy,

466

she adjusted down and spotted Leif with Andrew.

Then she saw someone dodging through the park in a bound-and-cover move. "Runt," she commed.

"Go ahead."

She watched the man lift a weapon. "Unfriendly, two—"

The man pitched forward, stumbled. Collapsed. Someone cursed.

Peyton scanned the bloody body, the area, the preternatural silence gaping as she sorted the scene. Leif hadn't shot the guy. But . . . "Andrew." He was moving the body out of sight.

*Crack!*

"Down! Down!" Adam shouted, his hand on her head and shoving her face down. Her cheek rammed the rifle. She grunted. "Taking fire! Coriolis is taking fire!"

Peyton's face stung, and she knew something had sizzled her skin. She dragged her weapon and low-crawled to another position.

"You okay?" Adam shouted, his tone wild with fury and concern.

"Coriolis, talk to me!" Leif barked.

"I'm fine," she gritted out. "Ticked. The shot came from the west," she said, mind pinging. Another sniper sniping at the sniper. "Find him."

"Coriolis, this is Overwatch," Command said a moment later. "Shooter to your three, nearly fourteen hundred yards."

Peyton widened her eyes at Adam. "Three-quarters of a mile." Resting her face on the stock, she ran through options. There weren't many. "If we leave this nest, we leave Reaper vulnerable. And the Neiothen."

"If you don't, you could get killed." His hand crept to her elbow. "We can move. Relocate."

"It'd take too long. The attack's happening now. The team needs me."

"You *don't* have to." He only said that because he was afraid she'd get hurt.

*She* was afraid she'd get hurt. Or killed. "Yes. I do."

"All right." Anger chewed his expression and lit his blue eyes until all that was left was fierce determination. "What d'you want to do?"

Her resolve hardened. "We have to eliminate that sniper." Amazed he didn't argue, that he chose to stuff what she saw in his face—desire to protect her, urge to insist she leave now—she knew she'd marry him if he asked. "Fourteen hundred yards—that's . . . that's luck."

Adam nodded, lying flat with her. "Slightest variation in wind or aim and you miss—by inches."

She nodded, her thoughts rapid-firing. That was why *she* was still alive. Variance altered the trajectory of his shot.

"And he'll return fire." Grief tangled up his features, tweaking his beard, fear that he'd lose her.

She slid her left hand to his beard. "I'll just have to trust I'm the better sniper."

"You are."

Her breast swelled from his unwavering confidence in her. His belief. Though she tried to smile, her body wouldn't let her.

Peyton keyed her comms. "Overwatch," she said, holding Adam's gaze. "I need your eyes. Tell me what you can on this sniper."

"Understood. Analyzing SATINT now," came a controlled voice on the other side of the world. They provided GPS coordinates.

Adam pulled them up on his device. "Far corner. Atop an industrial unit on the roof." He showed her the screen, and she familiarized herself with the building.

Peyton took a deep breath. Snugged the rifle into her shoulder. Still beneath the ledge that protected them, she lined up the trajectory, imagining the building out there. Readied her-self—low enough not to lose her head—so she could simply push upward. The other sniper would have the advantage, not having to move. Would probably anticipate her revenge.

"You got this, Pete—sorry, I know you hate that."

"No," she said softly. "I don't." She drew in a breath. "Ready?"

He gave a sharp nod. "Three . . . two . . ."

Peyton thought through what she'd do. Push

up. Rest the barrel bipod on the roof. Sight the building. All in a second.

"One."

In fluid motion, she rose with her cheek pressed to the stock, staring through the scope. Waiting for the reticle to cross the target. Saw it. Felt the bipod settle.

*Crack! Snap!*

She heard the sonic boom almost simultaneously with the concrete shards spitting at her. Wind variance had probably saved her life yet again. The sniper had missed. Would she?

Though she heard Adam curse, Peyton focused on her task. Find the sniper. Kill the sniper. She located a black lump atop the AC unit. Breathed out. And fired. The weapon bucked into her shoulder. Staring through the scope, she slid the bolt back to expel the spent round, then forward again to chamber the next round, ready to—

Air punched from her lungs. She felt herself falling. Found herself staring up at the sky.

"Pete! Pete!" Adam leapt over her, hand crushing her shoulder.

She cried out, only then sensing an explosion of pain. Felt warmth sliding down her chest and back.

"Peyton! Oh God—please, no!"

*What happened?*

Her hearing hollowed.

"Coriolis is down! Repeat, Coriolis is down! I need immediate evac!"

Vision graying, Peyton could only think that she'd never see Adam again. "Ask me."

Amid a flurry of curses, he scowled at her. "Pey—"

"Ask," she breathed. Coughed.

Tears ran down his cheeks and into his beard. "Pete, c'mon. Hold on!"

She blinked, but her eyes wouldn't open.

*"Pete!"*

# CHAPTER 35

## TAIPEI, TAIWAN

Stunned, Leif stared at the roof of the science center. "Badge? Badge, talk to us."

"Coriolis is down! She's—" Lawe's curses seared the line, mangled with tears and growls.

"Air evac en route," came the controlled voice of Overwatch. "Coriolis eliminated the sniper."

Leif expelled a thick breath, mind warring between Devine and the ongoing mission.

"Veratti will be ticked," Andreas said.

"He's got nothing on me," Leif growled. It took everything in him to stay down here, stay engaged in the fight, not sprint to the other building to help Devine. There was nothing he could do for her. Instinct pushed his gaze back toward the front of the park, toward Mercy, who was walking away from the park security detail that had questioned her and Baddar. "Kitty, you okay?"

Mercy looked stricken. "I . . . y-yeah. Pey—"

"She's getting help. Head in the game." He spotted Iskra with a bottle of water moving along the outer perimeter toward the main gate. Had she noticed something? "We still have a Neiothen loose. You have eyes on the president?"

"Distantly," Mercy responded.

"Move in. Watch for your newcomers."

"Copy," Baddar said.

And they still hadn't found Huber. "Reaper, anyone have eyes on the target?"

Mercy and Baddar reported negative. Saito—negative, but additional detail were now clearing part of the park. The only good thing happening at the moment.

"People, I want this guy," Leif growled. "End this. And them."

"Got him," Cell said. "Well, not at this moment, but surveillance shows two minutes ago he bought something at the souvenir shop, then headed out."

"To where?" Leif demanded, glancing up at the purple cars gliding along the rail over the park.

"He exited the shop. Stepped into sunlight."

That wasn't helpful. No, wait—it was! "Sunlight means south of the bumper cars." He moved in that direction.

"Chopper's going to make them nervous," Andreas noted.

"Foursome is at the same ride as the presidential party," Mercy muttered. "Nothing out of the ordinary, but I can't see their faces."

"Stay with them," Leif said. "If they—"

"Holy Madame Hydra!" Mercy gasped. "It's *her*—Sienna Gilliam! That's Sienna with the three men."

Leif stilled, confused. "Move in. If she—" A

familiar blue-gray blur snagged his focus. "Got Huber! Heading to the Wave Swinger. Cor—" He gritted his teeth, realizing he was about to ask for Devine's help.

Speakers crackled through the park. "Bushi. Bushi. Two. One—"

"No! No, shut it down!" Leif shouted. "Shut the freakin' thing—"

A razor-sharp pain sliced the back of his head. "Augh!" It drove him to a knee. He staggered beneath the blinding, debilitating pain. He squinted toward Huber but saw someone he wasn't sure was real. Couldn't be . . .

With blurry vision and ringing ears that left him disoriented, he barked at Andreas, who spun after Huber.

". . . Zero. Initiate rise. Rise. Rise."

"Take Huber down," Leif ground out through the comms as he found his bearings and broke into an all-out sprint. It felt like there was an ice pick in his skull. "He's going for the monorail. Do *not* let him get on."

Seeing the kids, seeing all the people lined up for that ride . . . This was going to be a slaughter. No way they could resolve this quietly.

Leif tugged out his weapon and fired three shots into the air.

Parents and children froze, then screamed. They gathered to each other, eyes wild with fright, then made for the exits.

"What in the blazes was that?" Iliescu asked. "Who fired?"

"Clear the park," Leif ordered. "Whatever it takes."

"But you said—"

"Runt," Cell said, his tone ominous. "He bought a bubble blower."

"What?" How did that make sense? Leif peered across the monorail platform and over the park, tracing the route of the rail. His gut clenched—it went right around the Drop Tower and would sail over the crowds still scurrying from the gunshots.

Huber could use the bubble blower to spew out the poison. Their attempt to save the civilians could very well kill every one of them. He started running.

"Monorail's . . . not . . . his exfil," he pushed out as he ran. "It's his means to disperse the poison. Get them out!"

More shots were fired, and people started running past him, shoving. Pushing. Mayhem ensued as Leif threw himself into the lower level of the monorail building.

"He's got a kid!" Culver choked out. "He boarded the third car and has a kid as hostage."

Andreas was already at the top of the platform, ordering the ride operator to shut it down.

"Can you lock the doors?" Leif asked as he reached them.

"Presidential party is heading to the Drop

Tower," Saito said. "We're clearing areas as we go."

It was all hitting too fast. Too many things. They weren't going to pull this off. "Send them back. Shut it down! Shut it down!" Leif shouted, hurrying back to the operator, who scowled at them, clearly not understanding English.

The rail was still in motion. The cars sat on a concrete beam, and the lower sides hung two feet over the beam. There was no way to dislodge the cabins.

Leif pivoted in time to see Andreas hook the neck of the attendant and put him into a sleeper choke hold, which left the operator to Leif. He waved his weapon at her and motioned her out of the booth. He cut the power, initiating an emergency stop.

"Rail is stopped. Eyes out!"

Now to prevent Huber from exiting the car, but even as he had the thought, he could see the purple cabin door buck, throwing shards of sunlight outward. "If he gets it open, he can disperse the poison."

"He's far from his target," Culver said.

"No, he is not." Iskra sounded panicked. "Sienna's leading the president's group to the bumper cars. They're letting the kids play as if shots haven't been fired. What is wrong with them?"

"Detail was told the loud noises were faulty

fireworks," Saito said. "That there was nothing to worry about. They aren't listening to me anymore."

"If he freakin' believed that, he doesn't deserve to be president," Culver said.

"But he also doesn't deserve to die an excruciating death," Mercy countered.

The distant *thwump* of rotors pushed Leif's thoughts to Devine. He couldn't help but glance at the chopper as it lifted off.

And . . .

Something wasn't sitting right. It tugged at his brain. He eyed the purple cabins of the monorail sitting quietly. Like a rat in a trap, Huber was just sitting there. For a trained Neiothen, he wasn't fighting very hard to finish his mission.

No. This was wrong. Why? Why was it wrong? *What am I missing?* His gaze hit the bumper cars on the third level. "What if there's someone else?"

"Someone else how?" Culver asked.

Leif studied the multistoried building. "Where's the president now?"

"Still in the bumper cars," Baddar reported.

Leif recalled what he knew of the bumper cars. They weren't in the open like some places. It was a vented, covered, upper-level section. Something in that mental snapshot punched his gut. His attention skipped to Hermanns' protégé, tall and sandy haired. "Kolya."

Slowly, ominously, Andreas turned to him.

Leif stilled but had no mental energy to waste on sorting out why he kept calling Andreas by that name. "Air ducts in the bumper cars. He's going to gas them there."

"I would've seen that—the maintenance closet is right here," Saito countered. "Huber wasn't near it."

Leif eyed the monorail, then again the building. Third level. Enclosed. "There's someone else."

Andreas scowled. "Who?"

"Go after him," Leif said, indicating the monorail. "I'm going out there." He started jogging down the stairs to the ground level of the monorail building, hoping and praying he wasn't making a mistake. "Cell."

"Yeah, Boss?"

"I think Huber's a decoy. Culver—on him. Stop Huber." Leif sprinted around the spinning teacups toward the doors to the bumper cars, where he saw a swath of dark suits. He slowed. Hand on the door, he stopped. In a flash, he had his answer. "Cell."

"I have no idea who—"

"Carsen."

"Um, did you hit your head again? He's dead."

"His dossier. Pull it up." Leif shifted to the side and eased his weapon out. Why? Why hadn't he thought of it before? "You got it?"

"Loading—yes. And yep, lookee there. Dead."

"Gilliam's sister was listed as his insurance beneficiary."

"Right."

"Look at that again. Read her name."

"C. Sienna Gilliam."

"Her file—quick. What's the C stand for?"

"Uh . . . oh, fire and brimstone, we are so screwed." Cell took a deep breath. "Listed as emergency medical contact: Carlyn Sienna Gilliam."

Leif felt the impact of that name against his chest. The spot behind his ear seemed to swell and push against his skull. "It wasn't Car*sen*. It was Car*lyn*."

The steady thumping of rotors preceded a shadow that spirited over them, like a ghost come to call.

Carsen had been trying to protect his sister, not himself.

"We got it wrong. Carsen wasn't the Neiothen. His sister is—Sienna."

# CHAPTER 36

## TAIPEI, TAIWAN

"Ossi. Ossi. Two. One. Nine. Initiate rise. Rise. Rise."

Iskra froze at the mechanized voice. A familiar one that had called out each Neiothen in their time. But Huber's initiation had already come through. So what was this? She looked at Sienna, who had a phone to her ear.

"Reaper," Leif announced. "Sienna Gilliam is the second sleeper. Stop at all costs."

"Annnd," Culver said, "sounds like she just got initiated."

Disbelief spiraled through Iskra as she turned, her attention landing on the woman in the dark green pantsuit with a contingent of men. But she wasn't working for the men, she was leading them. Straight to the president.

Glad the children and president were in the railed-off area for bumper cars, climbing into their vehicles and lowering the bars, Iskra drew her weapon and took aim.

Across the way, a hairy guard spotted her. Shouldered Sienna aside as Iskra fired. The bullet struck a column.

Someone lunged at Iskra.

She stepped back with her right foot and swung around, effectively forcing him to roll away, bringing her sights back up to—

A weight plowed into her back. Pitched Iskra into the wall, her cheek colliding with concrete. Just in time to lock gazes with Sienna. Sunlight glinted off the glass doors, blinding Sienna and bouncing around the bumper car arena. Iskra looked in that direction.

Leif slipped into the enclosure, SIG cradled confidently in his hands as he glided forward. "Don't do it, Sienna," he called.

Relief hit Iskra at the sight of him, at the presence and confidence roiling off him. He knew his business, and it was good to be safe again. Gave her the courage to buck off her attacker, but he wrangled her back against the wall, pressing the barrel of a gun to her temple. She stilled.

Leif jerked, spine arching toward the doors in pain. Eyes squeezed tight. He gripped his knees. Then he was straightening, the gun wavering. What had happened? Had he been shot?

Crushed beneath her attacker's bulk, Iskra could only watch as Sienna produced a thick-barreled weapon and aimed at the black ventilation system hanging over the bumper cars. "No!"

Shouts rang out from the presidential detail, who snapped their weapons toward Leif.

Iskra's heart pitched into her throat at the

standoff. At Sienna hesitating, then realizing the security detail hadn't seen her. They were protecting the president and his daughter from Leif. That left Sienna clear.

Oh no.

Saito skirted the edges of the bumper cars, hands lifted. "Whoa, whoa, whoa! Friendly, friendly."

Another shape blocked the light behind Leif— Mitre.

"Put it down, put it down," the security detail yelled at Leif, advancing on him.

Leif lined up his sights.

Fingers digging into her arm, the man with the gun to her temple shifted. "Metcalfe!"

Leif's gaze swam the room and saw her. Surely he knew—*knew* he had to take the shot. Stop Sienna.

"Do it," Iskra ground out.

Leif refocused on the Neiothen.

The crack of a weapon echoed in the enclosed space. For a split second, Iskra thought it was the one pressed to her head. But when she didn't feel pain, she snapped up her hands, flipped the grip on the stunned man, and aimed the gun at him, forcing him back.

Children screamed, and adults took cover.

Her attacker looked toward Sienna, saw her down, then met Iskra's gaze. He panicked. Shoved into the crowd of children fleeing.

Blood pooled around Sienna Gilliam's head. A guard knelt next to her, trying to save her life, but the profusion of crimson told Iskra it was a lost cause. With that much blood this fast, Leif had hit an artery.

"Hands! Hands!" Guards were shouting, rushing Mitre. Only then did Iskra realize Leif hadn't taken the shot. Mitre had.

Saito hurried over and assured the guards they were not the enemy. Security for the president rushed him to safety, while others swarmed Reaper.

"Target is down," Culver announced as he strode in. "Runt got her. It's clear."

Mercy joined them, wincing as she met Iskra's gaze. "Did Madame Hydra do that to you?"

Iskra blinked. Felt the bruise on her cheek. "One of her goons. Excuse me." She threaded through the queue rails to reach Leif, but he looked up, saw her, then turned and walked out of the building.

# CHAPTER 37

## SAFE HOUSE, TAIPEI, TAIWAN

"Peyton is in surgery and critical. We're being updated hourly and will keep you apprised as well," Dru said into the camera, eyeing the team, who had holed up until the jet arrived. The fewer Americans seen on the ground in the aftermath, the better. "We've confirmed that before she took that bullet, she did indeed kill the ArC sniper."

"Hooah!" Culver shouted.

"News agencies are calling this a terrorist attack against the people of Taiwan and its president and his daughter, who were unharmed in the incident. As you can imagine, we're in the middle of a media storm," Dru explained. "It is purported to be an attack by Americans, but we have produced credible sources who are countering that dialogue. The former story, we believe, is being perpetrated by ArC. Still, we're sorting details for you to be safely retrieved and delivered to an airstrip friendly to us."

"So this whole time we were hunting down Carsen Gilliam, visiting his friends, his psychiatrist, his superiors," Mercy said, an edge to her voice, "we should've been hunting

Sienna." She folded her arms over her chest. "Peyton said that woman was a mess."

The mention of their sniper draped the room in a moment of quiet.

"I'm ashamed at how easily that got missed," Cell admitted. "The majority of her documents and files were under Sienna, which technically is part of her legal name, but how the military allowed her to use her middle name instead of her first is a legit question." He heaved a sigh. "The biggest takeaway from all this is that interpreting prophecy is a lot harder than one might think."

"What we learned," Saito said, a sting in his words, "is how *little* power a president has when enough people want him out of office."

"Obviously this was the work of ArC and shows what they are willing to do and who they are willing to sacrifice to attain their goals." Mercy's nostrils flared. "The final count on kids in that park when the president arrived? Four hundred seventy-one." She grunted. "That disgusts me. Rather than let him—her," she corrected herself, "kill the president in a safe, quiet area, they were going to risk hundreds of innocent lives."

"This wasn't about the president." Leif finally spoke up, his tone . . . different. His gaze hard. "This was a statement. Even though the president survived the attack, ArC has established a majority hold in the sway of politics and trade across more than half the world. Reaper failed.

A lot. And while there are countries we've protected against his control, it's a bitter pill to swallow. Especially when you realize that Ciro Veratti is now not only prime minister of Italy, but his man is in charge of NATO."

"So what are they planning?" Culver asked.

Grateful for the information Leif had deposited and that he was still in the game, Dru nodded. "I think we have but to look at the Book of the Wars for that answer."

Cell cleared his throat. "Isn't there something we should discuss?"

"What?" Leif said, challenge in his tone. Fire in his eyes.

Dru willed Cell to leave it alone. It was too soon. Too dangerous. "Right now, rest up, prep for transport, and watch for word from Lawe about Devine."

When Cell glanced at the camera, Iliescu knew they needed to call it. But he couldn't. Not yet. Calling it meant Dru had failed. He wasn't ready to concede, and he'd never give up.

He shifted his gaze to the side where, off camera, Canyon Metcalfe stood talking with a cluster of brass.

"Sir," Cell said. That kid had more gut instinct than most people had guts.

Leif wouldn't know how close he'd come— many, many times—to being killed because he got too close to the truth, which seemed like he had a motion-sensitive device implanted in his life. He'd asked Dru right off the bat why he wanted him to lead the team. It had been a dangerous tango of wits, pitting him against the very enemy who had altered his brain.

Well. That was the way it seemed. He still didn't have definitive proof, but all indicators pointed to ArC like flaming arrows.

"We're good," Dru said firmly, shutting Cell down. "We'll debrief fully back here. As soon as Devine is out of surgery and cleared for travel, we'll bring her back as well."

"Director," a Marine said. "Jet's forty mikes out."

He nodded, then looked back at the team. "Jet will be on the ground within the hour. See you in two days."

Son of a batch of cookies. No. The director would not get away with that. Sometimes Cell had gut instincts about something that said $X$ was right, but then some expert balked at being shown up and said no, $Y$ was right. And that just left them one off and one dead, playing alphabet soup.

No, Cell would not sit by. He stood and pivoted toward Leif. But he was gone.

"He is not himself right now," Iskra said, stepping in front of Cell. "I would give him time."

Cell hesitated, glancing at the shutting door at

the far end of the warehouse they'd overtaken. "Do you know?" It'd make sense for Miss Russian Mafia to have it figured out, especially considering who her brother turned out to be.

"There are many things I know here." Iskra smiled and touched her temple. "But I know better things here." She laid a hand over her heart. "He needs room."

Cell squinted at her. "Lady, I have no idea what you're talking about, but Leif doesn't need room. Room to him is space to split. Leif needs to be called—"

"Cell." There was something strangely psychotic and threatening about her when she pulled up to her full height, eyes darkening. Lips thinning. It reminded him that she had skills to snap necks and kill people in more ways than he probably even knew existed. "Rest," she insisted. "He needs rest."

*Rest* of the day to figure out how to escape? "Right."

His incredible desire to stay alive told Cell to sit down. Shut up. Wait till she was distracted or talking. Or sleeping. He planted himself on a crate near the hall. Tugged out his phone. Reminded himself why he had to do this. Why confrontation was the only way to save the usurper.

"You okay?" Mercy joined him, sitting cross-legged on the concrete floor with a bottled water.

"Not in the least." He skated a glance at Iskra, who had a line of sight on the hall—and him.

"You looked ready to kill her a second ago."

"Me? She's the assassin."

"So what gives?"

Telling her what he'd learned, what he'd largely guessed about Leif, felt like a massive heaping pile of dung-like betrayal. "You ever find out something about someone that you didn't want to believe?"

"You mean like when I thought Ram turned on us all?"

He snorted. Nodded. And yet he still wasn't going to be the schmuck to out Leif. Not like this. Not till he talked to him. He wasn't ready for the one guy he considered a hero to go down in flames.

Well, not in flames. But maybe down in shame.

Why shame? Leif Metcalfe hailed from a long line of heroes. He had served in the military, protected his brothers in arms. Saved Iskra. Saved the little girl in the village.

So maybe he was wrong. Had to be wrong.

"Cell?"

His gaze bounced back to Mercy. "I need to talk to Leif," he said quietly.

"And she won't let you."

A flick of his eyebrows was his answer.

"I got this." Mercy tousled his hair, then stood and walked over to the makeshift kitchen that had a fridge, sink, and island. She poured herself a drink.

How exactly was that helping?

He glanced at Iskra, who still had him in her sights. Should he just try it? Sprint back to the room?

Right. And have his life severed for crossing Viorica?

Ha, no thanks. He liked his blood warm and pumping in his veins, not cold and spilling across the concrete.

Without warning, Mercy was there, talking to Iskra. Cell considered heading down the hall now, but Iskra shifted, narrowing her gaze at him. Okay, so he'd wait it out.

That went on for a long while, then Baddar got into the conversation—which was about Iskra's brother. How did they lose contact? Did she know he worked for Hermanns?

And the opening presented itself.

Cell hurried to the back room, gave a soft rap, and let himself in.

Leif spun from a spring mattress, his weapon coming up as he did. Aimed right between Cell's eyes.

"Wait," Cell hissed as he closed the door. "I just want to talk."

"Not in the mood." Leif hadn't lowered the gun.

"Dude." Cell lifted his hands. "Seriously? Going to shoot me?"

"Thinking about it."

Cell's heart shuddered.

"You started digging, Barclay."

Swallowing was harder with a pound of guilt in his throat.

"Just couldn't leave things alone."

"Then it's—" Cell finally noticed the pack on the bed. Leif was going to leave. "No no no." He grunted and moved to the other side of the room. "This isn't how this was supposed to go."

Leif glowered.

"I was supposed to come in here and say, 'Don't do this. It's not who you are. You have friends.'" He patted his chest for emphasis, then motioned to Leif. "And you were supposed to say that you didn't have any other options, that you were maybe scared and—"

"Scared."

Cell faltered, realizing he'd *never* seen Leif scared. "Right." He rubbed his hands together. "So not scared, but you didn't know what to do. There was something inside you that you couldn't control."

"So I'm a robot."

Cell cringed. "Okay, I suck at this. But you *can't* do this—" He indicated the ruck.

"What am I doing?"

"Leaving!"

"We're all leaving. Dru said there's a jet inbound."

Was Leif serious? Did he really plan to just return to the States? Or was Leif playing him?

*He's calm. Way too freakin' calm.*

"I know," Cell finally admitted. "I got enough intel from the system before Mei's Trojan killed it. And I . . . I accidentally saw the video Carsen sent you." Did Leif's chest just heave? Maybe best not to say more about that tell-all video. "And I know that last activation at the amusement park wasn't for Sienna. Huber's came through, but Ossi?" He drew in a staggering breath. "That's you. You're Ossi."

Nothing changed in Leif's expression. It was like he'd been carved from stone.

"You didn't take the shot that killed Sienna. Andreas Krestyanov did."

Still no response. Was he programmed not to respond or something?

"Please, Leif." Cell swung a hand toward the wall, indicating where the others were waiting. "We're a team. We're brothers"—he shrugged, knowing Mercy and Peyton wouldn't appreciate the gender reference—"and sisters. Er, siblings." Okay, that just made it worse. "A family. We go out on a limb for each other. Cover each other's sixes, just as you've done for every one of us." He pressed his palms together as if praying. "Please. Stay. Let us help you."

"I have no idea what you're talking about."

"Augh!" Cell growled, spinning around and

facing the windows. Grabbing his head. How did he convince him? What would it take—

An arm hooked his throat.

"No!" he choked out.

Pressure was applied to his head as Leif drew his forearm into Cell's throat. Cell thrashed, unable to call out, but Leif held him fast. *Please please please. No.* A tear slipped free. *I just wanted to help.*

The edges went gray.

His hearing hollowed.

*We were friends. . . .*

**Ronie Kendig** is the bestselling, award-winning author of over twenty novels. She grew up an Army brat, and now she and her hunky hero are adventuring on the East Coast with their twin sons, a retired military working dog, VVolt N629, and Benning the Stealth Golden. Ronie's degree in psychology has helped her pen novels with intense, raw characters. Visit Ronie online at www.roniekendig.com.

**Center Point Large Print**
600 Brooks Road / PO Box 1
Thorndike, ME 04986-0001 USA

**(207) 568-3717**

**US & Canada:**
**1 800 929-9108**
**www.centerpointlargeprint.com**